THE REJECTED KING

THE REAWAKENING
BOOK 3

ANDREW RYLANDS

To those great survivors: the feral cats of Greece

CHAPTER 1
ELENI

Kratos stood over his latest victim and cast his eye across the field. The battle was at its height, victory assured. The battlefield he scanned was the partially excavated foundations of the ancient site in the heart of Athens known as the Library of Hadrian. Around him, his forces, whipped into a frenzy by the unnatural power of his will, had far exceeded the normal limits of feline endurance. They were close to victory, but at the back of his mind he realised something was wrong.

Beware the Sons of Ares, the trickster had said. But where were they? To cement victory, it was important to eliminate any future threat from the absent leader's offspring. Wary as ever, Kratos would never admit to the secret fear churning in his gut: a dread of confronting the god of war himself.

Eliminating the sons of Ares would seal his triumph.

Across the seething mass of howling, brawling animals, he spotted the youngsters in their crèche; confused and frightened, small and defenceless, hemmed in by his own children who were the lieutenants of his gang. The youngsters' minders had mostly fled, and the few that remained, terrified for their own lives, offered little resistance. Joy surged in

Kratos' heart. This was the only feasible location for the youthful spawn of his enemy. He approached, swaggering across the field. About him, desperate animals fought for their lives, but he paid them no attention; he was transfixed on the powerless ones ahead. Mercy was not on his agenda. He would kill the kittens and rule without fear of future rebellion or reprisal. The scattered remnants of the Plaka gang would have no one to rally them or lead them ever again. Victory would be complete.

The Titan set about his murder spree with relish; a tasty little palate-cleanser to round things off.

But there was one still capable of resisting.

Zoe could not prevent the surrounding brutality. She circled again and again in a turmoil of indecision. Somehow, none of the attackers had noticed her, but that would surely change soon.

Her own kitten was beside her, mewing in desperate fear as a large warrior from the attacking Botrys gang loomed closer. He darted down and seized a youngster nearby, shaking it in his jaws until it hung limp. Numb and wide-eyed, Zoe saw a brief window of opportunity to escape. She grabbed her kitten by the scruff of the neck and, while the savage brute was facing the other way, dragged her backwards. All about her, she sensed danger from the other Botrys thugs; she could be attacked at any instant.

All she could do was run towards the retaining wall at the rear of the Library of Hadrian, her youngster in her mouth. In one bound, driven by terror and summoning energy she didn't realise she possessed, she made it to the top of the wall, scrabbling for purchase on loose gravel, then squeezed through iron railings and onto the street beyond. The primeval fear of pursuit from the monster and his dreadful crew drove her on through the heart of the city. Her jaw ached from the weight of her precious cargo, but still she ran, streaking through the maze of streets that formed the heart of Athens' Plaka district, until she entered a quieter neighbourhood away from the tourist drag. It was still early, the streets deserted. Amid ochre walls and shuttered windows, she paused to think. The adrenaline was ebbing from her system, replaced by bone-aching weariness. But she still needed to find sanctuary, if only for a few hours.

Another high wall marked the street boundary to Zoe's side. Without thinking, she bounded to the top, using her last reserves of energy. Behind was a small triangular patch of grass surrounded by flowerbeds. A garden. Out of sight from the street, hidden behind its anonymous wall, it offered a haven of tranquillity; a refuge. Provided the humans who lived here were open to some form of sharing arrangement, they would be safe.

A sliver of doubt remained. What kind of person lived here? Some of them couldn't be trusted. Some of them put out poison. The cat kept an eye on the back door of the house even as she protectively encircled her kitten, soothing it and willing it to sleep. Then she waited.

An hour later, a shutter raised and there was a muffled squeal from behind the glass. The cat raised her head suspiciously as a key scrabbled in a lock and the door flew open. She clambered to her feet, and bent down, gripping her sleepy kitten by the scruff of the neck, ready to flee once more. But the human that stepped into the garden, wearing fluffy slippers and a sloppy dressing gown, didn't appear angry. It was difficult to tell, of course, but it appeared to be pleased. Humans were by nature volatile and unpredictable. A sunny disposition one minute was separated from a febrile rage by the mere insertion of a good scratch, or a modest piece of scent-marking. They never seemed to consider territory at all. In fact, they seemed to ignore every marker put down. In short, they were difficult to read.

This human seemed to lean towards the pleased-to-see-you end of the spectrum. She crouched at the edge of the grass and held out a hand. Why did they always do that? Did they think hands were inherently interesting?

As usual, this hand held no food. Did the human think her smelly fingers were worthy of attention? Apparently so.

The cat interpreted it as greeting and chose not to display her disdain. Instead, she placed her kitten on the ground, making it easier to concentrate on the human before her. Cautiously, she advanced, sniffing. Behind her, the kitten, coming to, ignored the summit taking place on the lawn and blinked at her surroundings.

Zoe advanced gingerly towards the crouching human and committed its scent to memory, storing this two-legged beast alongside many others for future reference. Standing stiffly to attention, tense and ready to flee, she allowed herself to be stroked; a gesture of goodwill. This human appeared to be one of the more tactile variety. Indeed, the sensation was not unpleasant. She relaxed a little; maybe she could stay here after all. At least for a little while.

Zoe retreated, slowly and with dignity, to stand over her kitten, then looked up at the human to try to read its facial expression. The human seemed pleased. Her kitten, small and as yet untutored in the ways of humans, tottered towards the owner of the garden with no fear and a bond was forged.

So began a new relationship. Zoe found her sanctuary. Eleni, her kitten, found a home, and the young woman whose garden they had invaded found companionship and a distraction from her previous routine. The three of them would get along famously.

CHAPTER 2
AN AUDIENCE WITH THE KING OF THE DEAD

The dust was annoying him. It got everywhere; it covered his paws and legs, was ingrained into his coat, and lined his nostrils. It was tickling the back of his throat. As soon as he got out of this place, he needed a good long wash.

The dreary plain seemed to go on indefinitely in every direction, but was so dimly lit that Zelus had no reference points to gauge distance, and its true scale was impossible to fully understand. To his right, he thought he could discern, faintly, the outline of a ridge. But it was impossible to tell how far away it was, or how high.

This was a truly dismal place. Together with his companion, he trudged on.

But Zelus wasn't scared, for two reasons. First, because he had a guide in the form of the large white cat to his left; a regular visitor, apparently.

Second, because he was a god.

A Titan.

And so the concept of fear was alien to him. Boredom was familiar, however, and with every step, its limit drew closer.

Unlike the horizon.

Where was this damned palace? How much further did they have to go?

The two cats padded on in silence. Theirs was not a companionable relationship, but strictly one of tolerance.

Eventually, Zelus cracked. "Where is this palace? How much more do we have to endure?"

Hermes remained silent. Zelus suspected the other cat was savouring his irritation. Who did he think he was, this foppish bootlick of a messenger? How much more of this would he have to endure before he could finally put him in his place? He would enjoy that, but for now he set the thought aside and focused on the thin, barely delineated line of the horizon – charcoal upon darkest black – and the audience ahead. Beside him, more familiar with the terrain, but no less irritated, the white cat that was the present embodiment of Hermes kept in step.

"Are you sure this is the shortest way?" He glared at Hermes, whose face remained inscrutable as ever. Zelus began to seethe, certain his guide had deliberately taken the long way round in order to stoke his impatience. Where, amid this utter desolation, was the residence of its king?

Zelus' suspicions were not out of place. If so minded, Hermes could have escorted him through far more pleasant lands. As a realm, Hades was varied and host to some quite nice regions; the meadows of Asphodel, or the plains of Elysium, for instance. Even the shores of Lake Acheron, the source of the river of the same name, where many souls dwelt while seeking absolution for their sins, were passable if somewhat featureless beneath their endless, cavernous dark roof. But this seemingly interminable dreary desert plain was designed to sap the will of new arrivals and instil upon them the inevitability of their new existence. It was purposely soul-destroying.

"We'll be there soon," was Hermes' automatic response. Zelus snorted. They padded across the bleak, blasted terrain for further unrecorded miles, ignoring each other once more.

After an extended period of exquisite boredom, Zelus identified the outline of a building complex at the foot of some low hills to their right. The road swept towards it in a long curving path. Why it didn't go straight, no one knew. This was, Zelus reflected, a Greek – not Roman – Underworld, after all.

Huge walls rose at the end of the path, increasingly distinct from the featureless grey backdrop. Beyond them, he could make out the porticos and rooftops of monumental buildings. As the two cats approached, the buildings revealed such grandeur that even Zelus was impressed. Their scale was indeed fitting as the residence of a god and king. The curtain walls were the very definition of cyclopean: enormous blocks of randomly shaped stone fitted together so intricately and skilfully that there was barely a crack to indicate where one ended and the next began. They were clearly ancient and strong.

Who might they have been built to deter? Perhaps the statement they made of the power of the inhabitants was enough.

Zelus looked left and right, but the walls stretched as far as he could see, fading seamlessly into the background gloom. His thoughts turned instead to who might want to invade this miserable place. He could come up with no suitable candidates.

Fortunately, they didn't have to climb or otherwise breach the huge fortifications, as a massive gateway loomed ahead. As they approached, the vast black iron gates swung open, creaking and groaning as the hinges protested their massive weight. There was no sign of anyone opening them, as far as Zelus could see. Nor could he see any sign of a watchman on the battlement who might have alerted the inhabitants to their arrival. But as he passed through, he noticed two hoplite soldiers standing to attention in niches at either side, their bronze armour and spear tips dimly reflecting the weak available light. They stared blankly ahead, ignoring the new arrivals.

This was the first sign of life Zelus had seen since he had crossed that ghastly river. But, even though they looked solid, the figures were shades of the dead and not living at all. He had no desire to inspect them more closely.

Once through the gate, Zelus realised the walls enclosed an enormous compound in which there were many buildings whose purpose he could not guess.

Hermes didn't pause, but led them across a square directly towards the largest edifice. At the front of the building was a colonnaded portico supporting an angled roof, before a high wall with a rectangular doorway. As they took in the architecture – so familiar from the past – a tall, thin, soberly suited man glided smoothly towards them, his contemporary dress out of place in this ancient fortress. He stopped a couple of metres away and nodded courteously to each cat.

"My lord Hermes," he began in a plummy English accent that grated in Zelus' ears. "Always a pleasure to see you. You are, of course, most welcome. As is your friend." He looked at Zelus expectantly. Zelus stared back, baffled.

Hermes took half a step forward. "Nice to see you, Jennings. You look the picture of vitality, as ever." The butler bowed slightly, a smile curving the corners of his mouth. Zelus scorned such familiarity with a mere servant. The shade was being far too familiar with someone of even his companion's standing. He puffed out his chest and raised his chin.

His insufferable guide continued. "My travelling companion is the Titan, Zelus. We have come seeking congress with your lord and lady."

Zelus scowled. How frequently might Hermes visit these parts? He had such a low opinion of the Olympians that he thought little of Hermes' role among them. His familiarity with this domain was a timely reminder to be on his guard.

Jennings stood back, his pallid complexion looking distinctly sickly in the dim light.

"If you would follow me, gentlemen."

He turned and led them into the atrium; a rectangular room bare of furniture except for a couple of ornamental tables set against the side walls, opposite each other. Decor came in the form of an ornate mosaic floor with a design featuring ferocious fantastical beasts, and wall paintings from antiquity depicting scenes of hunting and feasting. It was a cruel reminder of activities no longer possible for the denizens of this land.

Jennings paused and turned towards them once more. "Please wait here a moment. I shall announce your presence."

He departed through a polished wooden door in the rear wall. Zelus paced the room, examining the paintings. He had no interest in art, yet he supposed there was nowhere above ground that held anything as magnificent or ancient these days. He mused idly about the paintings' current market value, were they to appear in the world above, but then his thoughts turned to the white cat sitting impassively before the twin doors.

"That guy," he flicked a glance towards the door. "Where's he from? He doesn't sound Greek."

Hermes turned his head. "He's not. He's English."

"What city is that? I've never heard of it?"

"It's another nation of men. Quite a long way away to the west."

"So, what's he doing here?"

"Hades welcomes all nationalities and ethnicities. He's not fussy, provided they have empathy for the old religion or the part of the world that gave birth to it. Nor does he care about their background – there's equality in death, after all. That's one of the few redeeming qualities about the place."

"Equality? A level playing field? Oh, yes. Apart from Tartarus and Elysium, and they're only the famous ones. Who knows what other discreet little hideaways he has?" Zelus' indignation was rising once again. "Anyway, what gives this pompous ass the right to attend on us?"

Hermes stared at him, his blue eyes glowing faintly in the dim light. "The English always make the best butlers, didn't you know? Anyway, after a lifetime studying classics at Balliol, what else is a chap qualified to do?"

Footsteps approached. The door opened and Jennings appeared.

"The lord Hades will grant you audience. Please step this way."

Without waiting for a reply, he turned and led them into another anteroom, then through a set of double doors into a magnificent ceremonial hall, its high roof invisible but supported by a line of towering columns of impossible height on each side. In recesses behind them, rich tapestries hung against the walls. Each column carried a bracket holding a flambeau, the flickering red light providing more illumination than Zelus had yet experienced on this journey; though it failed to reach the invisible ceiling.

The space they crossed was vast. An army could gather here, should Hades have one. At the far end of the hall, on a low dais, stood two huge thrones of dark ebony, and to the side, between the last two columns, two more high stone chairs, lighter in colour. The thrones were richly carved with images of hippogriff, manticore, centaur, griffin and other magical beasts Zelus couldn't make out. Most impressive of all were the two creatures seated on the thrones in dread splendour: Hades, King of the Underworld and Persephone, his queen. Zelus had been expecting the sight, but it still came as a shock for the Titan to see these two immortals in a shape and stature he had last experienced so many years ago. Envy jostled with lingering bitterness in his soul.

I am your equal and your elder, but for that wise fool Athena and her machinations.

He glanced at Hermes. "How come they're not like us?"

"Hades never went along with the pact. You should know that. As for Persephone, he insisted upon a special clause in the agreement. Down here, she's her old self. Up above, she's a dusty fawn cat, like us."

"How come?"

"She only ate half the fruit."

Zelus, fuming at the injustice of it all, stayed silent. It was bad enough being held captive in this shape, victim of a hasty agreement he'd long since come to regret, but even more galling to be in the presence of two who had avoided the fate.

They approached the thrones. Jennings stood to one side and announced them.

"My lord Hermes and the Titan, Zelus." He bowed more deeply this time, then turned on his heel, leaving them in the company of the king and queen of the Underworld.

Zelus noted the occupants of the two thrones. In human form, but not of human scale, were the Lord of the Dead and his beautiful wife. They would have been three metres tall when standing.

They were not quite what he expected. Hades had an open, ageless and not unfriendly face, framed by dark, unruly hair and a neatly trimmed beard. His eyes were black as charcoal, but deep within, a red light sparkled like a campfire within a cave. Between those piercing eyes, he sported a magnificently hooked nose. His demeanour was broadly welcoming, yet he looked every inch the powerful king. Upon his brow, he wore a simple crown of iron beset with garnet and rubies, and on his right hand he wore a mighty ring bearing a matching stone of deepest crimson. He leaned on the arm of his throne, studying them with a grave expression.

The demeanour of his queen, in contrast, was haughty. She had an oval face with hazel eyes, straight nose and long auburn hair. Her narrow lips were pursed and her hands lay folded primly on her lap. She wore expensive-looking robes of black silk brocade, inlaid with an elaborate pattern of Chinese dragons and other fantastic beasts. An odd choice, to Zelus' mind. Above her auburn locks, which caught and reflected the limited light, sat a spiked crown of a lighter metal, with each point tipped in diamond. Emerald and sapphire encircled the base above a ring of ermine. Persephone remained silent while Hades spoke.

"Welcome." He nodded to Hermes and turned to Zelus. "I'm not sure we've met." His brow furrowed as he sifted his not inconsiderable memories. "You are…?"

"Zelus, son of Pallas, son of Crius." He nodded his head curtly. "They, at least, you should remember. They languished many an age in your prison before their release. And you should, at least, be more familiar with my mother, Styx."

Without waiting for an invitation, Zelus leaped onto the large cushioned chair set out for him and settled down. Hades' brows rose as he studied his visitor with renewed interest.

"Greetings, my cousins," Zelus continued, in a more agreeable tone. "I come to remind you of your ancient obligations set down in the treaty, and urge you to release my wrongfully imprisoned brother, Kratos, sent here illegally by the traitor, Apollo."

He studied the dark king's face intently. For a moment Hades remained impassive, then to the Titan's intense irritation he turned to Hermes.

"What is the meaning of this embassy? You, of all, must surely realise that entreaties of this nature are futile. I do not give up the souls that rightfully come here, no matter their ancestry."

The admonishment left the white cat momentarily lost for words.

The king addressed Zelus. "Your mission is in vain. I will

not release the one who caused such anguish and suffering to so many, regardless of whether you think he should, or should not, have been sent here. In Tartarus he lies, and in that iron-bound prison he will remain until the world is remade, or he has finally repented of his sins and I see fit to release him."

The verdict was final, but to Zelus' ears, all too bitter. Before he could voice his opinion, Hermes spoke. He was both direct and forceful, belying his size.

"Zeus commands it."

There was a long, tense silence. Zelus watched, fascinated, as the king's jaw clenched beneath his beard as he sought to contain his wrath.

It was Persephone who broke the silence, her voice high and clear.

"On what grounds, exactly, does Zeus the Senile think he can command the Lord of the Dead? Zeus, who can barely remember his last meal. Zeus, the faithless hen-pecked husband. The earthbound sky father who no longer has the appetite, or the strength, to reclaim his former home. Zeus, the timid and de-clawed, languishing in his miserable hillside hideout. Long forgotten. No longer worshipped. His authority has long since waned. He has no currency now. He is irrelevant. Enough of your foolish requests. Begone!"

Zelus was bursting with righteous anger. But even in that agitated state, a small part of him relished the way his arrogant travelling companion had been put in his place. He glanced sidelong and noticed with satisfaction that every fibre of Hermes' normally relaxed and sleek physique looked tense and brittle as crystal.

But Hermes' hurt feelings were irrelevant; he could wait no longer.

The bitter anger of many years fuelled Zelus' voice and added to its volume.

"You sit here in your dreary throne room full of confidence. Proud and arrogant. You…" He looked Hades in the eye. "The junior spawn of mighty Cronos." He paused to let the barb stick. "You are both mere latecomers to the world we Titans moulded and shaped. Your memory is blunted by the years spent skulking in your dismal cave, hiding from the sun. You should beware, lest we wreak havoc on you and your kind once more. It is not for you, or Zeus, to keep us in chains. We shall have justice or we shall seek retribution."

Hades leaned forward with his elbow on his knee, his face stern and his brow furrowed.

"Think not to threaten me with tales of ghosts long gone. It is time you looked for your own safety. Begone. Lest I think to imprison thee, as well."

Hermes sat as if carved in stone, every muscle rigid. He looked straight ahead, but Zelus was now beside himself with fury. He jumped from the cushion and, spying the high stone chairs to the side of the dais, prepared to leap there and bring himself closer to the eye level of his self-satisfied hosts. He stalked towards the chairs and crouched in preparation.

"No!"

Zelus glanced behind. Hermes had a look of alarm on his face that caused him to pause.

"Those are the Thrones of Forgetfulness," said Hermes. "A trap to fool the unwary. If you sit on one, you will be bound in stone forever, to slowly lose your mind unless he grants you mercy." He gave Hades a look laden with meaning.

Now it was the King of the Underworld's turn to raise his voice. "Do not get above your station, messenger," he roared.

Persephone glared at the white cat. "You should consider your role. You come close to declaring a side."

Zelus walked back to the centre of the dais and turned to the enthroned deities.

"There is nothing further to say. Doubt not that one way or another, you will face the consequences of your actions this day."

He turned to leave, but at that moment Jennings appeared from a side door bearing a large silver salver.

"Would anyone care for tea?" he enquired, looking at them expectantly. He focused on the cats. "I have bowls of ambrosia, if you would prefer." Zelus glared at him and stalked off down the hall. Hermes gave the butler an apologetic flash of his bright blue eyes and followed.

The butler hurriedly found a side table against the wall on which to place his tray, then with a deep bow to Hades and Persephone, still of thunderous visage, hurried after the cats, catching up with them at the end of the great hall.

"Allow me to show you out."

A few minutes later, Jennings stood before the still-seated gods. The butler waited while they concluded a hushed conversation and turned towards him.

"Your dinner guests have arrived, my lord. Shall I show them to the table?"

Hades sat back on the throne, serene once more. He turned to the butler, addressing him as if nothing untoward had happened.

"No. Just provide them with drinks and canapés for the moment and pass on our apologies for the delay. We will be with them shortly." Beside him, Persephone was still rigid with fury, her lips pursed. It would take longer for her mood to stabilise. It was difficult, in these halls, to tell day and night apart. But if this was indeed eventide, Jennings reflected, it was going to be a long one.

CHAPTER 3
DELPHOS AND ION

I t was too hot for fighting, even in play. Yet as Olympia watched, she had to admire their energy. Midday was approaching; a time when any animal with sense hid in the shadows, sleeping or daydreaming, waiting until evening drew closer and it was sensible to venture forth once more in search of food or company. Yet her two boys fought and chased each other, bickering and competing, racing and chasing for hours on end. They were inseparable. Best friends for now.

She wondered which of them would leave. They were so alike; cloaked in youthful vitality, confidence, and possessed of an easy charm. No gang or clan could endure such rivals for long; no matter how strong the bond between them.

"Fine boys."

Olympia startled. Lost in thought, she hadn't seen Ares coming. He was de facto head of the Plaka gang and its guardian, although one who wore his leadership duties lightly. He paused nearby in the shadow of a wall, watching them play.

"Yes, they are," she said. There was little to add. She loved them with all the wistful pride of a mother who knows she has to let go soon. They were already old enough to thrive on their own. Mature enough? That was a different matter, but she kept that thought to herself. Soon she would be forgotten, her part in their story at an end.

"You must be proud of them."

She glanced up. Ares was still watching the two cats scrambling in the dust, yet Olympia sensed she was the one under observation.

"I am."

She was always tongue-tied in his presence. Insecure. How do you address a god? Especially one with a reputation such as his. According to rumour, even his father had disowned him. Yet here he was being nice, acting civilised. The world was too complicated for Olympia to fathom. She lowered her head onto her paws and closed her eyes.

He walked on. From beneath the slit of her eyelid, Olympia watched him continue his rounds. A word here, a glance or flick of the tail there. Checking on his people, his miniature pride. His mere presence brought an air of security; everything was under control, they were safe. What would be the prevailing mood should he leave?

In the middle of a patch of bare earth, Ion and Delphos stood, eyed each other for a moment, then at some invisible trigger, set off full pelt into the distance, and out onto the square to chase each other, darting among the legs of the unwise foreign tourists who, like them, knew nothing of the power of the sun.

Today, the chase led somewhere new; a place they'd not yet been. One last tussle and they paused, bickering over who'd won, and gawped at their surroundings.

They were lost.

"Where did we come from?"

"Dunno."

They turned to examine their surroundings once more, looking for familiar landmarks.

"Nothing round here smells right."

Instinct drew them closer together, although there was no obvious sign of danger.

"I didn't know your kind could venture so far."

They swirled around, looking for the speaker. A large dog, several times their size, lay on the step of a locked and shuttered building beneath the shadow of a tattered awning, the colour of which had been bleached away by the sun. Despite sitting in the shade, the dog's heavy panting indicated it was uncomfortable in the heat.

The brothers ignored it and continued to study their surroundings. They'd left their familiar pedestrianised central area and entered quieter streets lined with cars. For the moment, they stood in the middle, ignorant of any danger. But for now they were safe; the street was deserted. Where had everyone gone?

"What of it?" said Delphos. "We're free to go wherever we please."

"We have the freedom of the entire city," boasted Ion. "Not like you. I bet you're owned by a human. Dependent on them for all your food, for everything."

While his brother continued his insults, Delphos braced for the dog's reaction. To his disappointment, it did nothing. There was little sport to be had here.

"Lost are you?" asked the dog. It lumbered to its feet, stiff-legged. Delphos relaxed; they could easily outrun this one if it tried anything stupid.

"We're not lost. We can easily find our way back," said Ion, his voice dripping with the sarcasm he'd recently learned to weaponize. "Anyway, why are you bothered? Do you want to guide us home?"

"That would depend on whether you want to be guided. Or if you are ready," said the dog.

"Nobody guides us," said Delphos, his temper rising. "We're cats from the Plaka. We're free to go wherever we want."

The old dog turned his soulful eyes on the cat. "'Free'?"

"Free," spat Ion. "Unlike dogs," he added, a sneer in his voice. "We go where we like, do what we want."

"Ah, *free*," said the dog. "A little word that means so much." It walked slowly past them with the stiff-jointed but dignified gait of an elder. Two pairs of feline eyes followed its every move with intense concentration.

Delphos trotted after it. "Where are you going?"

The dog gave no immediate reply, but soon stopped before a tall metal gate. The cats craned their necks. The gate was shut, but seemed to guard a small atrium between two tall apartment blocks. No sooner had they stopped than they were greeted by raucous barking, and a large mongrel hurled itself at the barrier. They flinched as the gate trembled at the impact, but held firm. Behind it, the dog barked frantically, crazed by their scent.

"Come and get us," Ion goaded.

"Sit!" commanded Delphos.

In response, the dog hurled reams of invective at them. Delphos and Ion exchanged glances, their eyes sparkling with delight at this new game. Their elderly companion observed them and waited for the noise to subside.

A loud shout from a human inside the building seemed to have some calming effect on the dog, and it replaced its barks with a threatening growl as it continued to stand on hind legs, pawing at the gate, trying to get a glimpse of its tormentors.

"This is Varvara," said the old dog, his eyes fixed on the cats. "She's a rescue dog. Grew up in a small cage surrounded by many others." Delphos and Ion glanced at him. "Eventually, someone granted her freedom."

"You're not making sense," said Delphos. He looked at the

simmering mongrel on the other side of the gate. "She's penned up. She's not free. Not like us."

The old dog followed his gaze. "Varvara here, despite her terrible start in life, is young, fast, and powerful. But for that gate she could teach you your manners. She could chase you, break your neck with a bite." He gave Delphos a sidelong look. "Her jaws are far more powerful than yours, and her mouth is bigger. How free would you like her to be?"

Delphos returned a defiant look, but said nothing.

"So what?" replied Ion. "We're faster."

The elderly dog bowed his head in acknowledgement. Behind the gate, the other dog made a whining noise; an expression of bafflement.

"Why are you telling us this?" asked Delphos. "Look at her. She's a slave. Born in a cage, you say, but she's still penned in, even now. If she's let out, most likely she goes on a lead. She has no will of her own. Not like us." He glanced across to his brother. "We have real freedom."

"Again, that word," said the dog. "Freedom is a powerful concoction. The mere idea intoxicates us like fermented fruit. But freedom is a slippery worm. Difficult to grasp, impossible to hold, and swiftly taken for granted. Ask the starving stray about freedom when all they can think about is a full belly. Might not slavery be for the best if it brings you food, safety and companionship?"

The lolling tongue and long snout turned to each cat in turn.

Ion stiffened. "'Companionship'? With humans?" He gave his brother a look. "Enough of this chitter chatter. I didn't come here to be lectured about my life by a dog."

"And yet, here you are, listening." The old dog's brown eyes were grave.

Ion ignored him. "I've had enough of this." He walked away, and the dog watched him go. But Delphos hesitated.

"Freedom," said the dog, turning towards him, "is all about choices. Make yours wisely, son of Apollo."

"What did you call me?" Delphos asked, but the dog turned away and began padding back along the street. He had half a mind to chase after it, but hesitated. Instead he turned and followed his brother.

Pride and a desire to put distance between themselves and the dog drove them on, though they had no idea where they were. For an hour they meandered through unfamiliar streets and parks until finally they spotted a face they recognised on a wall ahead.

"Meet anyone interesting on your travels?" asked Stefanos, a stalwart of the Plaka gang.

"Just some insane pooch," grumbled Ion as he sauntered past, "giving us lectures."

"Barking mad," added Delphos, trying to make light of the matter. Yet unease hung like a shadow over his thoughts.

"Don't worry," said Stefanos. "Your secret is safe with me."

Delphos looked up at him. "What do you mean?"

From the wall, Stefanos studied them for a moment, as if deciding whether this was a practical joke. "Just be careful." The brothers stared at him. "I mean," he continued, "nobody likes them as spends time in the company of dogs, do they?"

CHAPTER 4
ENLIGHTENMENT

"So, it's not like you're a goddess, is it?"

Erichthonius caught the look of surprise on the grey cat's face and faltered.

Athena stared through him. "That term is loaded with many ancient connotations and a lot of baggage, but by some definitions..."

"Wow!" Erichthonius was, for once, lost for words. His stomach lurched. Should he bow before her, grovel on the ground, lower his head onto his paws, or run a mile? Initial confusion morphed into embarrassment. He didn't know where to look. What does one do in the presence of a goddess? Athena pinned the bewildered animal with a glare. Was she enjoying watching him squirm?

They had been walking among the jumbled stones that littered the summit of the Acropolis, enjoying the late evening sun once the tourists had left. They had the place to themselves. Athena had chosen this moment to fully induct Erichthonius into her cult. She had outlined what she required of him if he was to be her follower. To his relief, her demands were few, other than obedience to her instructions, as and when they were delivered, and monitoring the activities of the Plaka gang.

But now the conversation had strayed into different territory. Up here, strolling between weathered blocks of golden marble, his mind was free of the usual considerations and caveats that always hedged conversations in the woodland below. He was emboldened to ask questions that seemed almost ridiculous. Was Athena tired of answering them? Maybe he was the first to interrogate her so.

Bright and impressionable though he was, her most recent follower and counsellor struggled with the concept of divine beings. They were the stuff of legend and fairy tales; the sort of thing you outgrew as soon as you learned to hunt mice. Standing in the presence of one seemed unreal. He struggled to put some structure to the confused thoughts rumbling around his head.

"What *is* a goddess?" he asked, staring at the ground before him.

It gave his companion pause. She declined to answer. Instead, she walked to the southern perimeter wall and leaped onto it, casting her eyes over the city below. He followed and stood beside her, facing Athens' southern districts that stretched down towards the sea. He knew nothing of the sea. This evening, it was golden and flat, reflecting the light of the descending sun. It looked benign. His thoughts wandered; what would it be like to travel on it? He knew of ships, and there were some out there, anchored in the distant bay. They looked enormous, even at this distance.

Erichthonius ventured a quick glance at Athena once more, and for an instant he saw an echo of something. It made him dizzy. Was it the set of her muzzle? The pattern in her irises? For a split second, her face had looked different; timeless, somehow. Imbued with… what? Wisdom? Experience?

The vision faded, and he was standing next to the familiar

features of the Athena he knew: the fine fur on her muzzle, the dimples of her whiskers, the set of her mouth. He looked away, embarrassed.

"This city is my city," she said, gazing out across the neighbourhoods below. "And this land is my land. But I have been here since before there was a city."

Erichthonius looked abroad once more, casting his eye to the distant horizon, trying and failing to imagine a landscape without buildings. How far was its extent, this land she talked about? Did it reach far across the sea?

A warm breeze ruffled his fur, but he shivered. His thoughts were in freefall, trying to come to terms with what he'd been told. Athena was old. Really, really old. Older than he could imagine. But older than Athens itself? That was a crazy idea. It made his head spin. All those old stories; the ones he'd heard when he was young and passed on to the kittens in the Plaka gang crèche. They involved gods. He tried to remember them, but now, standing in the presence of someone who claimed to *be* a god… They all tangled in his head.

Tales of gods and monsters. He liked the monsters; but the gods? They were all humans, weren't they? Wielding sharp, fearsome weapons – swords and spears and such. They weren't cats. Cat gods were different.

His thoughts wandered to other human activities, impossible to divine; the things they got up to around the city. Were they all gods as well?

"Did you drive a truck?" he asked, daring a sidelong glance.

This time, the look on her face softened, and he detected amusement. "I didn't need to, dear Erichthonius. Back in the day, when I wanted to go somewhere, I merely thought about it. I melted into the air, then flew wherever I desired. I moved as fast and as far as my thoughts took me, and I could appear wherever I wished. Just as solid as I am now. Though I did not look like this."

Erichthonius pondered the concept of materialising and dematerialising; he was sure he'd seen something like that on TV back at his favourite bar down in the maze of streets that formed the Plaka. "Can you do that now?"

"No."

The answer was firm. An end to that line of conversation.

Another idea struck him. "Do you know Bast?"

This time, the grey cat's face was unreadable. She looked through him once more. Had he somehow offended her?

Rather than answer, Athena deflected his question by asking one of her own.

"Is she special to you?"

Erichthonius was wrong-footed. Surely everyone knew of Bast? He blinked a few times to clear his head. "Well, yes. Of course, everyone…"

He could feel Athena looking at him, but his head spun with everything she'd told him. He scarcely knew what to think.

"Tell me about her."

He ventured another quick glance, but saw she was serious. "I only know what everybody knows."

The green eyes never wavered. Was this a test?

"Well…" He fixed his sight on the city below and recited. "She is the mother of us all. All cats were born from her, from the great ones to the small."

Great cats, they were always told. But no one had ever seen one.

Did they still exist or were they another fantasy?

He returned to his story. "She ventured into the desert." He gave Athena an apologetic glance. "I know little about the desert. They say it's a hot place, far away, where no trees grow." He waited, hoping she'd acknowledge whether he was on the right track. But she didn't move. "Anyway," he continued, "there she gave birth to two litters of six kittens, the first large, the second like us. From that second litter come all the cats in the world."

"Who was the father?"

"No one knows." His glance this time was questioning. Surely everyone realised that nobody ever truly knows their father? He continued, "Once they were old enough, she led them to the Land of the River." Another pause while he searched his memory. "I don't know where that is. Nobody does. It might not be real."

"It exists."

Another glance, eyes narrowed. More unspoken questions. "Oh. Good. I guess you know the rest."

He was pinned by her green eyes. He swallowed.

"So, she brought us to the lands where humans lived. For companionship. When we arrived, she created mice for our entertainment and for our nourishment and we lived with the people and everything was good. They treasured us. We provided company. But later, another god called Set came and told us lies. He said that humans didn't really like us and they wanted to enslave us and we'd be better off on our own. That led to the Great Separation, where some of us lived off our wits looking after ourselves and shunning human company, while others remained enslaved and sought refuge with them, thus choosing a solitary life without adventure."

"Yet despite this schism, you choose to live alongside one another in the same towns and cities."

Erichthonius gave her a strange look. "We do," he said, then thought for a moment. "But we're like different species. Nobody mixes with them. They've got snotty attitudes. They like to think they're better than everyone else."

"That's a sweeping generalisation. Some of them might be pleasant enough."

He wasn't convinced. His thoughts returned to what she'd said earlier.

"So, do something," he blurted, emboldened now. "Do something unbelievable. Show me your powers."

Was that a brief flicker of irritation behind those green eyes, or something else?

"But you haven't made sacrifice, my dear young animal," said Athena. "How do you expect me to give you favour if you do not make an appropriate offering? I am not here to perform tricks, Erichthonius, no matter how deserving your plea."

As she diverted her gaze, he couldn't help but feel relieved. A pressure had been released, and its aftermath left him light-headed.

He lowered his eyes. "I'm sorry." He closed them and let the distant sounds of the city below permeate his consciousness, distracting him so much he barely heard her voice.

"My altars are cold, my temples ruined. There will be no more sacrificial offerings or ritual. I am diminished."

The words washed over him, but what lingered in his mind was the air of wistfulness which accompanied them.

One last question formed in Erichthonius' mind.

"Why me?"

"Not now. I have no time for that story." Athena leaped down from the wall and walked towards the exit, passing between the columns of the Parthenon before disappearing from his sight into its interior.

Erichthonius followed her with his eyes. As she vanished, he thought maybe he glimpsed something. He blinked, but it was gone, leaving only the lightest impression on his retinas.

It was an image of a temple renewed; magnificent and whole. A mighty figure stood in its midst – the likeness of a human goddess, only bigger. Far bigger. Tall and helmed, she filled the room and in her right hand she held a spear. He blinked and saw only the familiar ruins. Erichthonius sat and stared at them for a long time, lost in faraway dreams.

CHAPTER 5
TARTARUS

The iron gates slammed behind him with a loud clang that reverberated across the valley. At least it silenced the mocking laughter of the hideous gaolers; the group of trolls who had dragged him here. They'd removed the chains but left their heavy iron collar around his neck. Its weight would have crushed any lesser spirit, but it merely fuelled Kratos' anger. He stood for a moment and surveyed his surroundings. Behind him, stretching as high towards the distant cavernous ceiling as he could see, stood the towers that supported the massive solid gates. Even at his full capabilities, he doubted he would have the strength to break through, encircled and interwoven as they were with some of Hades' strongest enchantments. They had been built to withstand the worst all of his kin could do; in his diminished state and alone, he had no chance.

Massive walls loomed on either side, stretching across the valley and merging with spurs from the sheer mountainsides, barely visible in the gloom. Again, he could see no way to scale their towering crags, and he knew silent sentries would keep watch from unseen eyries high above.

Kratos turned full circle and saw that he was at the bottom

of a steep-sided valley that stretched ahead of him as far as he could make out in the dim light of Tartarus. The mountains, receding in shades of deeper black, were lit from below with a faint red glow that reflected dimly from a high, distant roof.

He decided to investigate; he had plenty of time, after all.

A faint track snaked down the valley bottom ahead. He took it, veering past ash pits and pools filled with fetid dark liquids, sometimes steaming and smoking. No vegetation grew here. There was little option but to explore.

The moment he started walking, unclean spirits approached from each side, moaning and squealing, threatening him with dire punishments should he fall foul of the unwritten rules of this place. But there was nothing they could do that would intimidate a Titan. Kratos shot them a sour look and snarled. A swipe of his ragged paw failed to connect with substance, but they gave him a wider berth. Kratos would have loved to catch one and properly instruct it in the meaning of fear.

The most frustrating thing about being dead was that he still took the form of a cat, and death had failed to restore his former powers. He was a large example of the species, admittedly, but he wore a permanently scarred body that looked like it had been stitched together by blind demons working to instructions shouted in a different language. He resembled a clumsily assembled feline Frankenstein; patches of ragged russet and brown fur held together by long strips of jagged, itchy scar tissue that seemed in places to seep a permanent red.

Resentment towards the self-righteous creature who'd put him here boiled once more to the top of his mind. The desire for revenge had become his all-consuming goal. Not just against Apollo; though he was target number one, but all of them. Kratos wanted nothing more than to bring the whole family down, and all their hangers-on.

His reassembled, permanently scarred coat and face were

hideous to look at, and in the living world would have rendered him terrifying. Here, in this ultimate prison, it was nothing special; he fitted in perfectly. He would have to intimidate the inhabitants in other ways.

He had hoped that the shock of bodily death would at least have catapulted him into his old god-like form and given him something akin to his former mental and physical capacity. The disappointment merely sharpened his resentment and hatred of the Olympians and Athena in particular. It could have been worse, he reflected. Unlike most of the dead, he still kept a corporeal form, instead of transforming into a disembodied spirit adrift on the breeze.

Worse though, was the unsratchable itch of memory that he was unable to shake off. Kratos was not one to suffer from regret, but he couldn't suppress the lingering sorrow at his frustratingly brief control of Athena's artefact. That fleeting moment had been a jolt of pure joy; a glimpse of his old self, with all of his power recovered. The sense of loss when he returned to this small feeble body was all the larger as a result. He was bereft, imprisoned in a body so feeble it was nothing but a mockery of his former self. Confinement as a cat should have been over by now. That's what they were promised, but now he saw how hollow those honeyed words had been. Tartarus would not keep him forever, but this feeble body was a prison from which he couldn't escape. Not yet, at least.

Anger clamped his jaw tight. He ground his teeth and once more vowed vengeance on Athena and all her pompous relatives.

A shake of the head. Such thoughts were no good. He would take his vengeance eventually, but first he had to find a way out of this, the deepest of pits.

With a heavy measured tread, the Titan in the form of a ragged cat trudged down the steep-sided valley between the towering mountains and away from the dread gates. The faint red glow increased in intensity with every mile, painting more of the surrounding landscape with its light. The extra visibility came with an ever-building sound. Not a pleasant, soothing noise, but a backdrop filled with the hiss of escaping gases, interspersed by sudden explosions and echoing splats and splashes.

Around a jutting knoll, he came across an awesome sight. Not far ahead, and a little below him, an enormous lake of molten lava spread out in a crater beneath his feet. Its surface was a dark crust, criss-crossed by hundreds of white-hot fissures that continually widened then closed, fracturing the surface, which then erupted and reformed. The lava sucked in darker and cooler surface rock to be melted and recycled once more, bursting forth in a shock of white-red light that, in the enveloping dark, was blinding in its intensity.

Kratos stared. The constantly moving turbulence below was mesmerising, but his senses were also assaulted by the pungent odour of sulphurous vapour. The constant hiss and grinding crash of the lava battered his ears. This was the perfect vision of hell, but it conjured another memory: the recollection of staring into the forge of Hephaestus long ago.

Awesome as the sight was, Kratos' interest in vulcanology was limited. He was sure Hephaestus would wax lyrical over the possibilities this gigantic fire pit offered. But he was welcome to it. All Kratos wanted was a way out. The intense heat didn't bother him; that was one advantage of divinity, although it had its limits. He could no more walk unscathed across the fiery surface as punch a hole through the untold layers of rock far above him; there were limits to his power. Anger alone would not suffice; he needed to regain some subtlety if he were to escape this famous prison.

Spilling over the far side of the enormous black-red lake, barely visible through swirling columns of smoke, was a river of fire. It was possibly the Phlegethon itself – one of Hades' five rivers, and the most fantastic of all. It carved a deep ravine, heading directly away from him, detectable only from the crimson glow seeping part-way up the flanks of the distant mountains until it curved out of sight.

The noisy, ceaseless river of fire was always searching for a new exit through which it could burst into the outside world and wreak havoc. Would that be a way out? Could he fashion some kind of craft that would let him surf the molten rock into the world above? It was worth considering. But where would he find a boat builder?

With renewed purpose, Kratos circumnavigated the hellish lake to see if he could follow its outflow.

As he stood on the lip of the gigantic lava-fall that fed the noisy river below, he realised this was not the way to freedom. There was no purchase to be had on those sheer walls.

He would have to choose another path.

Perhaps he might find it further on, as it blazed a destructive trail through lower, gentler lands. He retraced his steps around the edge of the lake.

CHAPTER 6
THE BROTHERS

Some days after their previous conversation, Athena walked with Erichthonius once more – this time amid the weathered stones of the Agora. He was the only male cat in her entourage, but rather than prestige, his privileged position drew only envy and distrust from his peers. Still, he was bright and attentive and Athena welcomed his unique perspective, particularly his knowledge of the comings and goings of the Plaka gang. None of her other followers had such good connections. She encouraged Erichthonius to spend time among them. He provided her with a feel for the pulse of city life and a different window on happenings among Ares' people, and the God of War himself sometimes.

Athena suspected Ares had paid little heed to the spy in his camp. She knew how little he cared for politics and scheming, other than plotting his next escape. She, however, enjoyed nothing more than interfering in the lives of the mortals she walked among; promoting favourites, placing obstacles in the path of rivals, seeing how her plans played out. Her ambitions had grown since the recovery of her prized artefact: a statuette recovered the previous year from a dig in the city centre and now housed in the nearby Acropolis Museum. It amplified her thoughts and projected them into the minds of those she targeted, enabling her to communicate directly and over a considerable distance, thus allowing her to interfere to a far greater extent in the lives of her favourites. With it, her power games could advance massively, compared to what she'd been able to achieve before. Retrieving and controlling an object of power such as the statuette was her first step to reversing the change she'd put in place all those centuries ago, and transforming herself out of her present state. Through the artefact, she could glimpse some of the abilities she had lost, and could surely advance her plans for the reversal. It was long overdue.

Athena pictured the little statuette once more, holding it in thought, rotating it and viewing it with her mind's eye from different angles, appreciating its form and the various bruises and deformities it had accumulated. Each mark she regarded as a badge of honour, the object's imperfection a reflection of its antiquity. They lent it dignity. Knowing its precise location, she could interact with the artefact at a distance and use it to project her thoughts. If she didn't know where it was, she couldn't find it in her mind's eye, and the process didn't work. Placing it in the museum, secured and in full view, was a masterstroke. It removed her fear that someone would steal it and gave her absolute certainty over its location. Her experiments could proceed unhindered.

Those initial experiments had worked well. Through the powers the device gave her, Athena now had a useful working relationship with Lieutenant Samaras of the Hellenic Police, her human contact whose house she used as her personal retreat. Even more impressively, it had enabled her to keep in touch with her spy last year, during his abduction and torture, although the experience almost broke him.

She suppressed a shudder at the recollection. The poor creature had done well to survive, but it had been an extremely useful exercise. It showed that, through the artefact, she could project her thoughts into the minds of subjects at far greater distance than she'd initially thought; a useful piece of knowledge. But she was just scratching the surface of the device's true potential. Once fully reacquainted with its quirks and capabilities, who knew what limits she would have, if any? With a growing network of willing helpers spread far and wide, it was surely a matter of time before she would track down that elusive tree whose fruit held the secret to her future transformation. Athena hardly dared hope.

She put the thought aside; that end goal remained some distance away. For now, her aim was to develop sufficient mastery over the statuette to enter the thoughts of humans, preferably with sufficient subtlety they wouldn't realise they were being manipulated.

She allowed a moment of reflection. When it had first been made by – who was it? Daedalus? Hephaestus? – she'd thought of it as little more than a toy, perhaps something she could use as a gift to entice heroes or the semi-divine into her ever-evolving network. Back then it did little to enhance her powers. But in her current guise, it was a lifeline; a key to help her find a way back.

She had an itch to use it right now and experiment with a little closer control. To put a subject under the spotlight and watch them react to direct stimulation. Agent 73 had been too far away to observe. She needed to control someone nearby who she could monitor closely.

Athena chastised herself: it was not control she sought, but direct mentoring. Guidance, subtle but with purpose. Lieutenant Samaras might not be the best subject for her next experiment. It would be sensible to start small, before venturing up the food chain.

She needed a cat. But who?

The cats of the Plaka were her first step along that road; political interference on a micro scale. A stepping stone. The process tested her patience, but it was wise to remain cautious. A greater prize was at stake. Once she achieved full mastery over the object, her fortunes would revive and the world would change.

Reluctantly, the grey cat put such thoughts aside and returned to her conversation with the agitated aide-de-camp at her side. Erichthonius would be the one to provide that important feedback loop; a control for the experiments she was planning. She encouraged him to spend time with the gang, pick up gossip and feed back anything unusual, particularly odd behaviours. She hadn't expected he would take to his role with such relish, particularly the time he spent among the youngsters. It amused her that he liked to tell them stories: tales of days long gone; the shadow of old myths in which, in a previous existence, she'd often played a starring role. His stories were adapted to their circumstances: myth woven into tales of feline cunning in the face of appalling odds; of daring chases, cunning thefts and narrow escapes with the help – or hindrance – of mysterious gods and monsters and evil giants.

In idle moments Athena wondered what the little ones made of such fantastic old stories. But, although Erichthonius was a skilled storyteller, she didn't want her aide to spend all his time in the crèche. She wanted him out in the streets, observing and monitoring and, in particular, tracking the movements of the two brothers at the heart of her current plans.

She skirted the tittle-tattle of daily life around the Library of Hadrian and probed his opinions.

"Tell me of Olympia's brood," she said. "Most of them are unexceptional, but two stand out. What do you make of them?" She gave him a sidelong glance.

Erichthonius hesitated. "Ion and Delphos," he said, gathering his thoughts. "They are different. Both ginger, which sets them apart from the rest of the family." He paused. "It's strange. There is something about them. They're more lively and confident, more inquisitive. I can't put a paw on it, but it's as if they belong to a different family."

Athena stopped. "Something of their father, perhaps?"

Erichthonius faltered. "I don't know."

Athena said nothing, but resumed walking. "What is it about them in particular?" He fell in step with her again.

"They're both quite popular with the others, and very close. They're almost a team. But I sense a rivalry is growing and that worries me. I hate the thought of division among the group. If we're not careful, they could split into rival factions, and that could make life difficult for everyone."

They came across one of Athena's favourite stones. It was weathered and bearing a faded inscription; the remnant of an old altar. She leaped onto it, basking in the sun and enjoying the warmth from the stone. "Tell me more."

Erichthonius sat before her and looked up. "They're evenly matched, physically. Similar in many ways. But their temperament is different. It's strange, given how similar they are in other respects." Athena fixed him with her green eyes. He looked to the side, gathering his thoughts. "Ion is, well, more forthright. To the point. Sees something, then acts without thinking, even if it gets him into trouble."

"Such as?"

"The other day, I noticed he was fascinated with a trinket in a shop window. I have to admit, it was appealing. Glass. Colourful. Reflected the light in a lovely way." Erichthonius ventured a glance in Athena's direction. "You know, normally we never go inside these places. They're out of bounds." It was true. There was an informal understanding that the feral gang were tolerated, as long as they didn't overstep the mark. Invasion of human property was strictly forbidden. "I saw him looking at it. Saw he was tempted. Then, before I knew it, he'd darted in and was trying to play with it. The shopkeeper was with a customer. Anyway, of course the thing fell on the floor. Broke into a thousand pieces, and that got her attention. He had to flee. We all did."

Athena gazed at him, waiting for more.

"I don't think Delphos would have done that. I think he would have held back. He's quieter. Not as confident as his brother. A little more thoughtful, perhaps. Very similar, of course, but always just a step behind. But he's popular with the others. They seem to warm to him more than they do Ion. Maybe because he doesn't brag so much." Erichthonius paused. "And he spends a bit more time alone, away from the rest of them."

Athena yawned then scanned the surroundings. The briefing was at an end. She rested her head on her paws and closed her eyes.

"Why are you so interested in them?" said Erichthonius.

She gave no immediate reply.

The silence stretched on. He stood and arched his back. Sensing his movement, Athena opened one eye, then the other to watch him.

"We can't have division within the group, as you yourself have said. It wouldn't look good so soon after the war and all the pain and suffering that brought. Ares will tire of his responsibilities soon and depart as he always does. So, in his absence, and to avoid chaos, one of the two brothers must step up to lead."

The war. Barely a year and a half ago, but already a distant memory for most of the Plaka cats. It had been a vicious encounter: an attack by rival gangs from beyond the centre led by two vindictive brothers determined to evict the Plaka cats from their long-held territory. The attempt was foiled with the help of three mysterious strangers from the north.

Erichthonius scratched an ear, deep in thought.

"Anything else?" drawled the grey cat from atop the stone.

"Well, there are rumours they can talk to dogs."

CHAPTER 7
THE TOWN BENEATH THE WORLD

arefully skirting the enormous hissing and boiling lava lake, Kratos headed upwards at first to a broad saddle between the mountains, then across its summit and down the slope beyond. The jagged mountain tops to either side were backlit by a vivid crimson glow. Squinting, he could just make out the dark cleft of a steep-sided valley ahead. Was that a track along its base? Whether it headed north, south, east or west was impossible to tell in this morbid gloom. He padded on, uncertain where he was going, or even why.

As the red glow and the sounds of grinding molten rock faded behind him, his eyes adjusted to the deepening shadow. This was, he grudgingly admitted, one advantage of Athena's transformation; his night vision was excellent, picking up textures, features and obstacles that he otherwise might not have noticed. Enhanced by his immortal soul, it was an even more powerful asset.

As he travelled further, the hissing and grinding from the lake became faint, replaced by an eerie silence. There were no birds here, or insects, or wildlife of any form, yet he felt himself watched at all times. The fur on the back of his neck stood proud.

He stopped. "Show yourself," he commanded, but his challenge was met with silence. The watchers, if any existed, remained hidden.

Suspicious now, the cat walked on along the dead valley. He wondered if anything lay at its end, or whether he would be forced to retrace his steps. But the gradient steadily eased and the land to either side became broader and flatter. Kratos discovered a narrow track that eventually broadened into a fledgling road, although he could not tell when it had last been trodden. It meandered through dark boulder fields and around rocky outcrops, periodically descending further until it became flat. Above and around him, the landscape was still bathed in the red glow of the distant lake, but he could no longer hear its commotion.

To his surprise, the ground to either side of the track became boggy. The reason was soon apparent, as he was drenched in a heavy shower of rain. Hot air from the lava lake condensed into dark clouds far above, and as they drifted and cooled, they deposited their load across the bleak lands below.

The bog finally gave way to more solid ground on which grew the strangest, darkest forest Kratos had ever seen. Slender trees of immense height, bearing enormous flat leaves of darkest green, towered above him, in search of a sliver of light. Beneath them, in blacker than black shadow, silver-stemmed creepers with small veined leaves wound about their base, threatening to throttle the life out of them. They glowed with a vivid, sickly bioluminescence. Tall grasses grew about their base, reflecting the faint silver light.

Beyond the forest, Kratos was surprised to find fields loaded with the blotched and pale ears of a sickly-looking crop, apparently nourished by the distant red light. They rose above his head, blocking his view of the distant landscape.

Who farmed these lands, and what need did the dead have for food?

He found the answer several miles further on, as he descended to the floor of a broad, flat valley. The mountains to each side were distant now, and barely visible, but of more interest were the dimly lit meadows nearby: the torture fields. Crosses, racks and other unspeakable devices were placed, seemingly at random, on either side of the road, stretching as far as he could see into the distance. On each one, strapped, nailed or otherwise fastened in place, were the dead who had been sentenced to eternal punishment. Kratos paused to take a closer look.

The victims were a mass of broken bodies with misshapen limbs and appendages. Slowly, methodically, their torturers gouged, gored, or flayed them. Others were impaled or flogged. Remorselessly beaten and battered, their screams and howls filled the air, but the burly trolls and squat, flat-headed troglodytes administering their everlasting treat-ment, ignored them. The Titan was unmoved by their suffering.

Kratos moved closer for a better look at the unconven-tional workforce. Professional sadists, they set about the job with a grim determination rather than enthusiastic relish. Yet they were unrelenting. How long would they keep going before they took a break? His thoughts wandered. What scope was there for innovation in this line of work? After all this time, surely they had exhausted all known methods for exerting pain?

It was the definition of a dead-end job. Would they be satisfied with their efforts? What passed for job satisfaction here? An extra-piercing scream? An agony drawn out over a longer time period? There was little visible enjoyment in a job well done; the torturers seemed barely more content than their victims. But perhaps that was just Kratos' outsider perception. After all, what signs of emotion did a troll ever display? He'd met a few, and it was difficult to discern a happy grunt from a miserable one.

Kratos plodded on, while the agony of the tortured echoed from the distant hills. He had no sympathy for the victims. They had it coming, he was certain. Kratos was a firm believer in Hades' harsh justice, despite his own false imprisonment. In his former life, at Zeus' command, he had chained Prometheus to his mountaintop perch, to endure his daily torment, and had relished the harsh punishment meted out to his distant cousin following his betrayal. Considering what he was witnessing, the Titan god of fire got off lightly.

It was a happy memory. Those were the days...

Next time he met Zeus, he'd chain him up in the Titan's place.

Kratos passed many victims; a seemingly never-ending cacophony of misery. But he eventually left them behind, and a quieter district followed.

Beyond another smaller forest, he came across the first building he'd seen in this desperate land. It was the most rustic of shacks; a wooden construction made from ill-fitting boards, barely held together by a few nails and a bit of rope. He came across another, then another, and before long, he was walking through a shanty town of sorts; desolate and dark. Occasionally he spied a surly face at a door or window, but few inhabitants walked about this place.

The track became cobbled. Other paths and alleys led away from it, rank and filthy, with foul-smelling liquids lying in stagnant pools. Only the main road seemed paved, but the further he ventured, the more Kratos realised he was entering a substantial settlement; a proper town.

Finally, he came across stone buildings, some with second storeys, then a few with three. As the buildings grew taller, the streets between them were illuminated by dim, flickering gas lights. The road detoured around the structures and the street pattern became jumbled and random, with little sign of life or joy from the dark, forbidding interiors.

Kratos crossed a junction and saw a couple of carts drawn by weary-looking mules. The drivers sat silent and hooded, with no sign they'd seen him. He passed a couple of pedestrians, but few inhabitants seemed to walk these dismal streets. Was that through fear or from choice?

He came to a shop of sorts, stocked with the most basic of wares, then another. Through the doors, he could see racks of what seemed to pass for food in this place. The burly torturers needed to eat; they had a lot of flogging to do.

At length, he reached a paved square. There was no ornamentation here. No fountain or garden; just an acre of cold stone surrounded by grim facades. Dark, empty windows stared down from the upper floors, but at ground level, on opposite sides of the square, two buildings held life. He detected the hum of conversation, the clink of glasses. Here, at last, was where the locals congregated. Kratos decided to investigate.

He approached the nearer tavern. The door opened as he drew close, and a burly figure emerged, then disappeared into the permanent night. Inside, the sounds of drinking and argument were raucous, the fell creatures more lively than any he'd seen so far. They sat on rough-hewn chairs and stools, before bulky tables that wobbled on the uneven flagstones. Hunched over their drinks, they ignored him, grinding out their debates in slow, growling monotones, glaring at each other over stone-cut quart mugs gripped by gigantic fists. From behind a bar at the far end, a female ogre wearing an ill-fitting, patterned halter-necked top, filled the mugs with foaming beer drawn from an enormous cask, before handing them over to her customers with a threatening glare.

Kratos was about to jump up and take a closer look when voices were raised behind him. An argument had arisen over a game of dice. Accusations flew and meaty fingers jabbed at the air. The troll nearest to him rose to his feet and drew a long, cruel knife. His opponent was faster, drawing hers first and neatly sheathing it between his ribs.

Black blood bubbled from the wound, and with a roar, he crashed forward and sideways, overturning the table and smashing a chair. Beer splashed onto the floor, mugs shattered and dice flew. The female troll withdrew her blade, stood over her victim and stabbed again. Stools screeched across the flagstones, and shouts arose from the other patrons. Kratos licked his lips; perhaps a full-scale fight was about to break out. His fun was halted by a yell from the ogre behind the bar.

"Ye'd better be clearing up yer mess, Molly."

A hush descended as attention turned to the barmaid and what she would do next.

The female troll knitted her brows together in fury and looked up. To Kratos' surprise, she mumbled some kind of apology. Clearly the barmaid was not to be trifled with.

Molly grabbed her victim by the ankles and dragged him to the door, his body leaving a smear of dark blood in its wake. As the door swung closed behind her, the drinkers resumed their seats and took up their conversations once more, as if nothing had happened. A few minutes later, the troll returned and stepped up to the bar to order another drink.

"That'll be three crowns," the barmaid told her. "One for the drink, and two for the furniture. Wood doesn't grow on trees, ye know." With a warped leer Kratos took for a grin, Molly produced a leather purse, and selected three coins. She slid them across the bar.

A shadow loomed over her from behind. A man. He was tall, cloaked, expensively suited, and looking totally out of place in such humble surroundings. He held a silver-topped cane and looked as if he'd just stepped out of the opera.

He placed his hand on the purse before Molly could return it to her pocket. "That's mine, I think you'll find."

Kratos was fascinated. He stood amid these huge figures, observing them at close quarters but, as yet, completely ignored. The man's complexion was the colour of freshly rolled pastry; his face was so pale, he looked devoid of all blood. Kratos looked closer and saw spindly blue veins beneath the thinly stretched skin. Interesting. It was a long time since he'd seen one of these.

The troll grunted in protest.

"With me," the man commanded, giving Molly a disdainful look down the length of his thin nose. "Through here." He nodded to two shorter figures behind him – as broad as they were tall, and as muscular as any troll – and led the way through a door at the rear of the room. Molly followed, prodded harshly in the back by one of the two thugs who appeared to be the tall man's enforcers. Troglodytes, Kratos suspected. Tartarus was proving more fascinating than he'd ever have believed.

They filed along a short corridor with doors to each side, and through another at the end. Kratos brought up the rear.

The room they entered was a stark contrast to the bar. It was comfortable and carpeted, and a coal fire crackled in a grate within an ornate fireplace, lending an air of civility Kratos had not yet witnessed in this realm. Paintings hung between wall lights, and a large rosewood desk sat at the far end. Before the desk was a coffee table with an upholstered leather sofa at each side.

The tall man sat on the sofa furthest from the door and crossed his legs, his left hand resting on his cane. Kratos looked him up and down. His narrow face bore an aquiline nose and dark, jewel-like eyes. He completed the look with his slicked-back black hair. Was he for real? Before him, in the middle of the room, stood the hapless Molly, glowering but silent, her stare fixed on the floor.

The two trog enforcers stationed themselves behind the troll. Dressed in black, with belted tunics and heavy boots, they would have been better suited as guards for some mid-twentieth-century dictator, barring their weapons: a sword for one and a spiked mace for the other. They were wider in the shoulder than even the troll, but shorter, and their heads were flatter, with small, deep-set eyes and little visible neck connecting to the shoulder. They both looked eager to show their martial prowess.

"Molly, Molly, Molly," chastised the man, his voice snide and silky. "Such a temper. You really need to learn some self-control."

Molly stood still, her jowls moving, but not uttering any sound. She looked like a chastened schoolgirl, staring at the floor and avoiding eye contact. Clearly she was in fear of the man, or his accompanying bodyguards at least.

"Throd was one of my best dealers," the man continued, sounding regretful. "A solid, dependable source of income. The type who wouldn't let you down. A proud servant of the cause." Molly ventured a glance at him. "He will be missed."

The mocking tone was convincing, if corny. When would he deliver the punchline?

Right on cue, the tone hardened.

"So, what are you going to do about it?"

Molly said nothing, still staring at the floor. The tall man leaned forward and repeated the question, but louder. Behind her, one flat-head prodded the hapless troll with his mace. She half-turned and swore, her brows knitted almost into a straight line, her fists clenched. The troglodytes were strong, but if a fight broke out, Kratos would back the troll.

The tall man unfolded from the sofa and in one swift, graceful movement, swept a long, thin blade from the cane, resting the tip against the troll's throat. She turned back, gazing in surprise at the yard of steel before her.

"Let me repeat myself. But this time think about giving me

an answer. What are you going to do about it?" Slowly his sword tip penetrated the surface of her thick hide, and a small drop of black blood formed around it. Molly's eyes widened. Though mumbled and heavily accented, Kratos was pleased to hear her reply in archaic Greek.

"I'll help. I'll do what you want."

"And that is?"

A pause while she worked through some permutations. "Sell Shade. Help the cause."

The blade slowly withdrew. A trickle of blood ran down her neck.

The tall man still stared at her. "Good. You'd better make sure you do," he said. He nodded towards the two trogs. "These two will keep you supplied. From now on, you deal with them. A hundred a week. That's what you'll deliver. Is that clear? Anything less and you lose body parts."

Before she could protest, he nodded to his bodyguards, and they ushered her out. "Take her away and get her some of the product." He fixed the troll with a stare. "I'll see you this time next week. Off you go."

He stood with hands clasped behind his back, as the unfortunate trio shuffled through the door, jostling for priority, getting in each other's way, before wiping and sheathing his blade.

"Quite the hard man. Very impressive," Kratos declared, sounding anything but impressed. To get a better view, he leaped onto the desk.

The tall man spun on his heel, glaring at him. "Oh, look. A talking cat. What a novelty. How cute." He ladled the sarcasm on thickly. "And what have you done to end up here, little kitty? Killed too many mice? Clear off before I get one of my guards to club you to a pulp."

Kratos yawned and made a point of studying the room. The paintings were drab copies, the carpet worn. Upon close inspection it was all a little tawdry. The most interesting object was the heavy safe in the corner behind the desk. He jumped across to it.

"What do you keep in here?" he asked.

The blade swept from its scabbard once more, in a sweeping motion intended to slice him in two. But in mid-stroke, Kratos leaped, catching his opponent full in the chest, the momentum carrying him backwards. Kratos gripped the thin shoulders with needle-like claws that easily pierced his clothing and sank deep into the flesh beneath. A sharp double rabbit-punch to the diaphragm took the air out of the man's lungs, and even before he hit the floor, powerful jaws that opened far too wide for an ordinary cat clamped around his windpipe. Slowly, he squeezed his victim in a powerful bite, teeth puncturing the pale flesh. Then he relented, drawing back to spit in the man's face.

"Vampire," he spat. "Just as I thought. Still disgusting, though I haven't tasted one of you for many an age." Kratos adjusted his position, releasing the grip on his victim's shoulders. He crouched squarely on his opponent's chest, then pushed down. Beneath him, the vampire struggled to breathe.

"Mercy!" he wheezed. Kratos watched, impassively, until his victim was on the point of passing out. He relented and sat upright, watching as the man gasped for air.

"And what do you brand yourself as, you bloodsucking leech?" the cat demanded. Beneath him, his victim tried to summon some dignity.

"Count Rizari," he said. "I would say I'm delighted to make your acquaintance, Mr ...?" Kratos just stared. "I reside here, in this meagre dwelling. For the time being." His breathing was laboured, his rib cage crushed beneath a weight far heavier than any cat should have.

Kratos glanced around the room. "And what is *here*, exactly?"

The vampire attempted a wan smile. He looked to the sofas. "May we?" he wheezed, struggling to speak.

Kratos leaped onto the nearest sofa. "Any more moves and I'll liberate your innards from what passes for your body and spread them all over this room. Then I'll eat your undead heart. Is that clear?"

The vampire's complexion faded even more. He nodded acquiescence, and scrambled untidily to his feet, still struggling to breathe. He poured himself onto the nearest sofa, less confident now, and tried to regain his composure.

Kratos looked the count in the eye. "We have a lot to discuss," he growled. The vampire's eyes darted around the room, but the cat observed him dispassionately. "There is no possibility of escape. I can move faster than you can imagine. And I'm sure you don't want to put my strength to another test." The vampire rubbed his shoulders and returned a small shake of the head. Kratos let him ponder the matter for a few seconds before he began his interrogation. "Where shall we start? How about something simple? The profitability of this *Shade* operation of yours, for instance?"

Alarm registered on Rizari's face. "Everything is accounted for, I assure you. I am screwing every cent I can from them. You realise that." Kratos remained silent while the count pleaded his case. "They don't get paid much. I extract whatever spare cash they have. If it's not enough, she should tell her husband to pay them more." Rizari stared at the ginger cat, his eyes wide.

Kratos relented. "I'm sure your operation around here is efficient. But why Shade?"

Rizari looked baffled, as if the question made no sense. "What else is there? Short of robbing them in the street. And that would get noticed, sooner rather than later." His eyes narrowed. "Is this a test?" He sat back. "You're here to check up on us, aren't you?"

An impatient flick of the tail. "Just answer the question."

"Shade? It's just a means to an end, isn't it?"

"What is it?"

Rizari eyes narrowed in suspicion. "A trick question? What can I tell you that you don't already know?"

"Let's pretend I've just arrived," said the cat, smoothly. "From some far distant realm among the stars, totally ignorant of the quaint habits and pastimes of this exotic, deep and distant land. Just think of it as a training exercise, if that helps. Explain everything to me afresh. Sometimes taking a step back allows you to identify irregularities. You never know, you might find some options for improvement." Kratos' voice sounded like thick syrup poured over gravel; heavy, persuasive and threatening all in one. It had the desired effect.

Rizari stared into the fireplace. "It's a hallucinogenic. As I guess you know. A distillation from Evershade, which is, of course, a distant relative of the nightshade plant up above. Evershade is found in one or two locations down here, if you know where to look. It thrives on next to no light, and it has special qualities. Well, the sap does, at any rate." Kratos' head tilted enquiringly. "It's very resinous. They collect it and dry it and crush it into powder. I don't know the exact details of the process, but the final product is highly addictive." He gestured over his shoulder towards the door. "Even for this lot. Zeus only knows what it would do to a human." He licked his thin lips and a lascivious look crossed his face. "Anyway, a lot of the trolls and troglodytes are addicted." He ventured a calculating glance towards the cat. "I would have thought you'd know..."

Kratos remained impassive, his tone mildly sarcastic. "An addictive hallucinogenic for trolls. Another way to suck them dry. Who'd have thought?" He stared back at the vampire. "How many of them do you drain, incidentally?"

Rizari swallowed, and stroked his throat where the cat's teeth had punctured his paper-white skin. "I can't," he said. "It's an offence punishable by oblivion." His eyes glazed over as if lost in distant memory. "Anyway, they taste horrific, and can you imagine a troll vampire? It would be a crime against nature." He repressed a shudder and gave the cat another glance. "I'm only permitted to feed properly up above. Human blood is so much more appetising." He paused and licked his lips. "Anyway, it's a relentless job they do," he said, changing the subject. "You've seen them in the fields. Long hours. We merely help them with their downtime."

"We?"

He coughed. "Myself and the others. There are a few organisations that keep them supplied. My colleagues work the other settlements down the valley and beyond. We make sure not to encroach on each other's territory. I'm sure you understand."

"And what does Hades think of your little operation?"

Rizari sat upright. A shadow of suspicion crossed his face. "He doesn't know, of course."

"You're sure of that?"

The count glanced around the room as if expecting someone or something to emerge through the walls. He gave the cat a suspicious look. "We take every..." His expression darkened. "Do you? Are you...?"

"Relax," purred Kratos. "I am no friend of Hades. Quite the opposite, in fact."

Silence descended. The vampire still looked doubtful, but before he could speak, the cat continued, with a voice that belied his size, filling the room and making the air itself tremble. "I am the Titan, Kratos." His eyes gleamed ruby red in the firelight, pinning the hapless vampire. "Older and more venerable than Hades himself. Pay me due reverence, vampire, lest I unmake thee, one fibre at a time. On your knees!"

As if dragged by an invisible rope, Rizari, swept to the floor. He knelt there, breathing hard, head bowed. "My lord."

Kratos let him wait before he relented and eased the pressure. "Be in no doubt, my dear Rizari, I can be a powerful ally, or the most formidable foe you have ever encountered." His nose lifted a little. "Which is it to be?"

The vampire licked his lips, and he glanced from side to side; anywhere but look the cat full in the face. "I am honoured," he said eventually, and crouched on all fours, his forehead almost touching the carpet.

Kratos looked down at him. "You can sit," he commanded.

Rizari squirmed back onto the sofa in an ungainly fashion, not daring to speak.

"I can see you appreciate the delicacy of your position," the cat continued, watching the vampire fidget before his threatening purr. "Here you are before one of the elder gods - and think yourself fortunate that I permit you to sit in my presence – then you tell him how you are indirectly stealing from his cousin's workforce, distracting them from their allotted tasks." Kratos observed Rizari's discomfort with distaste: the shifty looks, the rise and fall of his Adam's apple, the handwashing motions. "Knowing that the faintest whisper in his cousin's ear, and you and your whole network will be consigned to a grisly and ultimately final end."

The only sound was the crackle and hiss of the coal fire in the grate. Rizari looked lost for words. Kratos let him stew. Not only would he never do his cousin any favours, he'd also have to find an escape route first. But the vampire didn't know that.

He continued. "I must admit, your strategy, is bold. Balanced on the edge of a razor, as it is." He stared at the cringing count. "Anyway, you may rest easy. I will not inform him of your actions. Hades and I are not, presently, aligned."

In the ensuing silence Rizari recovered something of his poise and a note of resentment entered his voice, although he dared not look the Titan in the face. "What does he care for Tartarus? He hasn't been here for two thousand years. It's as if he's washed his hands of us." He paused, lost in thought.

"Anyway, we have other patrons. Powerful ones." At last, a sly glance from his bowed head. His confidence was returning. "And we are careful to hide our activities from the demons."

"Surely, after all this time they must suspect something?"

Rizari leaned forward, urgency in his voice now as he pleaded for understanding. "No. We take all the steps to keep them in the dark. They're unaware." He sat back. "They are few, anyway." A pause for reflection. "And those who do come visit on a rota. In shifts. If they had an inkling, they'd have been on us by now."

Kratos considered this. "And you're certain they haven't picked up any rumour?"

"Have you ever spent time with a demon?" Rizari looked him squarely in the eye, then diverted his gaze. "Apologies. I am sure you have. Then you must know, they're not exactly conversationalists. They exude darkness. They make even my undead skin crawl." He sat forward, animated now, pressing his argument. "Powerful they may be, but they don't have friends or allies. Everyone's terrified of them. Nobody talks. Not willingly."

"But if they had spies among your ranks?"

"We'd know. And we'd make sure they were silenced." A curl of the lip. "In a similar manner to the unfortunate Throd." Rizari rubbed a hand across his chin as he contemplated the troll's murder afresh.

Kratos was pleased to see the concern on his face. He explored another avenue. "How much do you contribute?" he asked, trying to sound as casual as possible.

"Monthly? Around fifteen hundred. I mean, I have to keep something back for expenses. I have to make trips up top, after all. In fact, I need to return soon. My strength is waning."

The vampire did indeed look in need of a transfusion or two.

Up top. Interesting.

"Maybe I should accompany you?"

Rizari sat back and gave him an appraising look. "That might be difficult. You look corporeally bound. My earthly body is entombed in the crypt of a cathedral. My journey is one of incorporeal transfer. My spirit moves, but this body does not. I'm not sure how it would work with a physically embodied god."

The cat's eyes narrowed. Rizari had a point. He would need to find a different method of escape.

He returned to his previous topic. "Fifteen hundred a month, every month? The coffers must be filling up nicely."

The vampire shrugged. "I don't know how much they need."

"Well, these things can be expensive."

Rizari crossed his legs, his hand stroking his chin as he reflected. "Yes. But it's been a long time. I guess they must be building up quite an army, the conspirators. But I'm far from the decision-makers. Sometimes it seems as if we've been forgotten." He leaned forward, hesitated. "I don't want to speak out of turn, but maybe you could put in a good word? Given your prominence? If you could see an opportunity to remind the Queen of the fine work I am doing here, with such limited resources?" He glanced around the room before his eyes came to rest on the cat once more. "Rest assured, I remain a loyal servant, devoted to her cause."

Kratos remained impassive. "We shall see."

The count was bolder now and probed for information. "You know, I just wish they'd get on with it. Announce a date, give us a target. They can't keep us hanging on forever." He drummed his fingers on the armrest of the sofa and raised his eyebrow. "There's nothing you can share?" Kratos kept silent. A malevolent smile spread across the vampire's bloodless face. "I can't wait. It will be quite something, won't it?"

"It will," Kratos agreed.

"They won't know what's hit them. The overworlders. All that fresh blood. All those bodies to drain." Rizari savoured the prospect, but his face clouded over. "Tell me, though, if you can, what is the latest news regarding that last piece of the jigsaw? How long do we have to wait?"

Kratos looked him in the eye. "Not long. The plans are progressing."

"They've been planning forever. They must have made a breakthrough by now."

"All in good time," the cat replied, on the defensive for once. "You should not question their aims."

"It's not their aims that concern me. It's the timing, and practice. Once we have it, we'll be unbeatable."

"We're unbeatable now," Kratos said.

"Not in daylight."

Kratos stared at him.

"That wonder drug they talk about. It's the game-changer," Rizari continued. "How long are they going to keep us waiting?"

"Come, come. You must understand the testing process takes time," Kratos replied, eager to deflect this turn of the conversation. He should go. This meeting had been useful, if only to reveal the extent of his ignorance. "From now on, Rizari, you serve me. In the meantime, you may continue to obey the orders of my colleagues. But when I contact you, my instructions will take precedence. Is that clear?" He waited as the count nodded his acquiescence and pinned him with one last stare, pressing into his mind with considerable force.

Once Kratos had relented, he took his leave, saying no more. Whether he ever met the vampire again would remain to be seen, but at least he had made an impression. Maybe Rizari would be a useful weapon, or servant, at the right time.

But for now, there was more to discover.

Kratos left the bleak town, pondering the future. He would need to choose his allies carefully and rationally. But first, it was imperative to escape from this dread pit of despair before some other player did something dramatic.

First step: identify the conspirators. Second: subvert them, expose them, join them, use them…

Or destroy them?

CHAPTER 8
SABBATICAL

Some called it the arrogance of youth; others detected a boorish overconfidence. But on one thing all could agree: the brothers were certainly different to their peers. Unafraid to look a human in the eye, and unnaturally confident as they navigated the district. They looked like natural leaders.

Ares saw their development as an opportunity. "With these two, the future of the Plaka gang is in safe hands for some time to come," he told Erichthonius one morning. "I'm overdue another break. Tell your mistress I'll be gone for a while."

"How long?" he spluttered.

The large russet-coloured cat stared into the distance, ruminating. "I can't say. Until I feel ready to come back, I guess." He gave Erichthonius a sidelong glance. "There's no hurry. Things have settled down. Everything looks fine."

"But—"

"Oh, and tell her not to find me. I really don't want to be disturbed this time." With that, Ares stretched and ambled off, leaving Athena's liaison lost for words.

Erichthonius scrambled back to the Agora and found her reclining on the Pnyx rock, enjoying the sun.

"He's off again."

She gave no response. As the seconds stretched on, the flick of Erichthonius' tail betrayed his frustration.

At last, Athena half opened her eyes. "Well, it was bound to happen eventually."

"What about the gang? Will you take over as leader?"

"No."

"But… what are they going to do?"

Athena raised her head. "Why such urgency? They're all independent. The gang will cope perfectly well until a new leader emerges."

She made sense; his concern faded. "I suppose so." A glance, and he detected amusement behind the solemn facade. "It's just… there's no one… I mean, if anything were to… They're not ready." Erichthonius struggled to organise his thoughts.

Abruptly, Athena stood and leaped down. She walked past him. "All our communities need someone in charge, I realise that. Even if it's only an honorary position. I am not belittling the Plaka gang, but think on this. The recent troubles are behind us. There is peace across the city and for the moment times are good. Those who brought conflict are gone. There is no external threat. If there was ever a time for Ares to take a break, it is now. His attention span is limited at the best of times." She paused, waiting for him to catch up. "Anyway, you've already told me there are candidates in the wings, even if they are a little immature. Give them time. They will grow into the idea." She stopped again and gave him a direct look. "Or one of them will. There will be no room for two."

Erichthonius stared back into her emerald eyes. "So, one of them must leave?"

Athena gave no answer, but set off again on a meandering

route down the hill. "Keep me updated," she said before she was out of earshot.

His thoughts turned towards his new task. The boys were no pushovers; they seemed to have the measure of this hostile city. But they took too many risks for his liking.

Erichthonius pondered the impact they had on the rest of the group. Both were popular, but some gang members already had their favourite. What would be the consequences of the brothers' inevitable falling out? What if factions were to emerge? Would the losers put their differences aside and rally behind the eventual winner?

Athena sought refuge in the woods. She needed time alone to think. She was ready to experiment further with the artefact and explore its limits. Kratos had used it to briefly wreak havoc, unleashing elemental forces. But ruling through fear and crude force and threats was not Athena's style. She preferred more subtle techniques: influence, persuasion and, only if absolutely necessary, intimidation. All with the best of intentions, of course. Her preference was to delve directly into the minds and motivations of the mortal population, hoping to unearth precious gems: leaders, statesmen, great generals; inspirational figures who could shape history, once she had shaped them.

But it was no simple task to influence the mortal mind; subtlety was essential. Mortals could respond in unpredictable ways and, tantalisingly, the brightest among them were the most difficult to manipulate. So far, she'd been lucky. The policeman had been startled into submission by her proximity, and her choice to present him with an apparition of her true self. That didn't work over a distance. Agent 73 was in trouble from virtually the moment she'd come across him and was difficult to track. He'd been too innocent to understand her manipulation, although she liked to think she'd helped him resist his mental torture.

No. Her next target should be someone close whom she could easily monitor. She needed to start small, with a more straightforward mind. One that would be easier to manipulate and observe.

The Plaka gang would be a good starting point.

And who better than the brothers?

CHAPTER 9
PYTHON

Having dispensed some modest encouragement and left instructions to persevere with his efforts, Kratos left the count to his machinations and sauntered through town. He could not imagine a more dismal place to reside. Did trolls ever weary of their work? Without agitators such as Rizari and his superiors, would any of them ever have the imagination to rebel? He suspected not. If they were to form the backbone of the rebel army, how effective would they be, given their drug dependency? It was a way to control them, he supposed, as long as you didn't need them to act on their own initiative at some time. On the other hand, even if sober and clean, could they do anything other than follow the most basic instructions?

Kratos walked on, leaving the town behind, and once more stepping through dimly lit fields of charcoal grey. As he progressed further, he detected a small change in the light from ahead. He was approaching a junction of sorts; the confluence of two valleys. A smaller, sloping ravine joined the main course from the left. The distant rocky roof above its peaks glowed a faint, but sickly green.

Curiosity piqued, he diverted from the main path and

picked up his pace, climbing through the rougher slope along a narrow track barely wider than himself that wound between outcrops and boulders. As he progressed, the green glow slowly intensified. As with the lava lake, it seemed to seep up from the roots of the mountains ahead, illuminating them from below, barely reaching the distant rocky ceiling. Passing over a ridge that signified a threshold, he saw a hidden valley before him; narrow with sheer sides. Further ahead a lake stretched from side to side, illuminated from within, its surface a seething brew of twisting patterns in many shades of green.

At first glance, it seemed impassable. In hollows between the descending ribs of the grim mountains, an evil-looking mist hung in place, with no wind to move it. As Kratos sniffed the air, he detected from afar a faint aroma of rotten decay. He was mesmerised. Despite the evil smell, the constantly shifting patterns and currents on the surface of the water held a strange oily beauty.

He raised his vision slightly and noticed an even stranger sight. There, upon the far shore, was a dark tower which seemed to glisten and pulse in the gloom. At its summit, a light shone clear from a lone window, beckoning him on. Who lived there? What secrets could they share, that might deepen his growing pool of knowledge? Kratos advanced with renewed purpose.

It took a long time to reach the lake. It was further away and more expansive than he'd anticipated, but the shoreline, though treacherous was passable. He could see the road ahead, narrowed to a single-file path, begin to traverse the slopes above the waterline.

As he followed it the path grew narrower still, before almost disappearing entirely, as it contoured between the sloping rocky outcrops that plunged towards the evil waters below, clinging to the bones of the mountains that cradled the foul lake to his right. His progress slowed as he mounted sharp inclines which twisted then plunged into deep dark gorges, some filled with evil-smelling fog, before rising sharply once more, barely a few metres further on. In the darkest recesses, sharp thorns from the gnarled branches of squat, long-dead trees stabbed at his hide.

He battled on. On his right, looming closer as he mounted the craggy outcrops, the swirling green waters were his constant companion. He began to despise the lake. It had a presence that irked him; an air of malevolence that seemed to emanate from its foul vapours. It was a sentiment he was willing to project onto others, but which he resented when applied to himself.

The ridges became less steep and the shoreline more gentle as he worked his way around. Finally, the path broadened once more. Who could have made it? How often had it been trodden over the years, and how many had missed their footing and slid into the foul waters below? It was little used, that was clear, and Kratos had no desire to walk it again.

The tower was much closer now. He stopped in his tracks to study it properly. It was alive. With awe approaching horror, he realised that what had from afar seemed like a glistening reflective surface was a slowly writhing, snake-like body of monumental size. The serpent wrapped and re-wrapped itself around the black stone tower, as if trying to squeeze the life out of it. At the base, where an entrance should have been, lay the beast's mighty head. Above and behind, coiling around the stonework to its very top, was its monstrous body.

Kratos approached tentatively, keen to learn the nature of this creature, and the identity of the soul it was guarding. He sat a safe distance in front of it, and slowly surveyed its length.

The serpent's eyelids flicked open and a forked tongue stabbed out towards him.

"You are wise to stay back at a safe distance," it taunted,

its voice like the hiss of water on hot stones. For the first time in many centuries, Kratos discovered the polite side of his nature.

"Greetings, mighty one. Never have I beheld such a magnificent monstrosity as yourself. Your fame must surely be spread far and wide, were there any inhabitants of this dismal domain to voice it." As if to emphasise the point, he looked right and left.

For a long moment the serpent studied him, the tongue still flicking out, tasting him on the still air. It probably wasn't used to visitors; Kratos stopped short of pondering their fate.

Eventually, it spoke. "You smell strange."

"What a powerful sense of smell you have, o mighty lord of all who slither. Maybe you detect the dust of the Over-world on my pelt?"

"Your apology for a pelt, you mean. You look as if you lost a fight with a score of swordsmen, although I wonder why any would bother making an effort to conquer such a puny opponent. But what did you do to deserve Tartarus?"

It was as if the beast were thinking out loud. Kratos suspected it had been many years since it last held a conversation. Its wits seemed to be addled.

But the jibes needled him.

"A crime to one person may be nothing other than an act of self-expression to another," he said loftily, skating over his many heinous offences.

"You don't look capable of much self-expression," the huge snake countered. "In fact, you look rather feeble. Best move on down the road, kitty, and leave me to my rest."

Anger churned within the cat, but he strove to ignore the childish insults. The beast had clearly been here a long time, and his social skills left a lot to be desired.

"If you are so desperate to goad me, ginormous entity that you are, you must be confident of your success," he purred, his voice thick with a century's worth of menace. In the world above, most recipients would have quailed and sought a pain-free exit. But the massive serpent was not so easily moved. A lengthy stand-off ensued. Kratos, alert to the serpent's slightest advance, changed tack.

"Who are you guarding?" His eyes darted upward as the serpent's coils writhed with greater urgency.

"One who must never leave," it hissed.

Kratos feigned surprise. He didn't even try to keep the sarcasm out of his response. "Oh! Hades' little helper, are we? His pet worm. How faithful you are. It must be so boring, writhing about this tower, in thrall to your master for so long. I suspect he has completely forgotten about you. Pray, when did he last pay you a visit?"

With a loud hiss, the monster's huge head uncoiled and surged towards the cat, jaws opening and forked tongue flicking out. It clearly had confidence in its speed, but Kratos was faster. A paw lashed out and down, cutting five deep, bloody grooves through the armoured scales and darkening one eye. Before the snake could react or retreat, Kratos' right paw smashed sideways with an echo of the elemental force that, in an earlier era, would have demolished mountains. In his present weakened state, it merely damaged the serpent's head, large though that was.

The monster's jaw was smashed and dislocated, making it impossible to clamp those enormous incisors down on its opponent as it had intended. The beast's head veered sideways, but it was not yet beaten. It tried to embrace the cat in a coil of its enormous body, to squeeze the life out of it. But it grasped at thin air as Kratos nimbly leaped away from danger. Increasingly frustrated and half blinded, the monster raised the upper part of its body to loom over the cat, seeking to crush it with its sheer size. But now its throat was exposed, Kratos darted forward and sank his teeth into the thick hide, piercing deep into the vulnerable flesh beneath the serpent's head while claws raked the body.

The serpent coiled about itself, attempting to gain purchase on its small, powerful foe, but Kratos would not let go. Instead, he bit deeper.

Increasingly desperate, the snake twisted around to free itself from this savage attack, then threw itself down, again trying to crush the cat, or scrape it from its body. With ease, Kratos let go at the last minute, only to pounce on top of the creature once more, savaging it with further needles and bites.

Now he was on top of the serpent. Rather than stab it with his claws, he released it from his jaws and pressed down with a forepaw, the strength of the Titan crushing the creature's head against the hard base rock. Pinned down by such force and unable to move, the monster was powerless to wriggle free from the cat's unmatchable force. Its iron-like scales strained, then cracked and tore beneath Kratos' mighty paws, as he trampled further along its body with his rear paws, scraping and raking like a farmer cleaning mud from his boots.

"I yield!" the snake hissed through clamped jaws, and warily, the cat stepped aside. Slowly the monster withdrew, its battered head retreating to the centre of its huge coiled, bloodied body. It looked down at Kratos, through its one good eye.

"I'd see a vet if I were you," the cat taunted.

"What do you want?"

"That's more like it," Kratos said, relishing his victory. It was good to have been able to vent his frustration; a small foretaste of what he intended to do to Apollo when next they met. "Let's start with your name."

The serpent mustered as much dignity as it could.

"I am Python."

Kratos' eyes widened slightly. "How interesting. So this is where death brought you? We have something in common. I thought he chopped you up, the god of light. Before he took your sanctuary for his own and burnt you on a pyre."

Python's unblinking eye surveyed him intently. "The spirit cannot be so easily desiccated. In the Underworld I am still whole." Python studied the cat. "And who are you to think you share traits with me?" it asked, resentment rising once more.

Kratos ignored the question. "Who are you guarding?" he said, glancing up at the top window of the tower just in time to see a pale face sharply withdraw.

"His name is Theseus."

"Theseus?"

"Once a hero and a favourite. His star has faded."

"I know of his exploits. Some say he should be enthroned in heaven alongside the gods. How did he end up here?"

"Better ask Hades."

Kratos nodded. "Some other time, perhaps. But why do you guard him? Surely he's just a ghost. A feeble refection of a man. He has no power anymore."

Python's unblinking eye continued to stare at the cat. "He still has a voice. He still has influence. They may not fear a war in heaven, but there is always worry of a rebellion in hell. Hades' crown may not be as secure as you think."

Kratos was silent for a while. He shook his head. "Not from him. He's a spent force. Useless. It's been too long. He has no chance."

Not willing to enter into a debate, Python looked across the sickly green lake. The ragged cat followed his gaze and saw a strange object on the far shore; something he'd not noticed until now. In his farsighted vision, it had the structure of a tree with trunk and boughs of dark obsidian, and bright and brittle emerald leaves. As he watched, his ears caught a tinkling sound from afar, as the leaves shifted and clashed against each other in response to whatever stirred the heavy air. It looked to have been set here in mockery of the living world.

The serpent sensed his curiosity. "Behold. One of Demeter's trees."

"Very pretty," said Kratos. "Unusual decor for such a dismal place. What's it for?"

CHAPTER 10
A QUESTION OF IDENTITY

n his quieter moments, Delphos often returned to the encounter with the strange dog. He still didn't understand what it had been trying to tell him, but that parting comment played on his mind. He'd tried asking his brother what it meant, but Ion was indifferent. "Why should I care who our father is? So he's got a name? Big deal. He's likely out there somewhere cajoling every lady he can get his paws on. Good luck to him." He wandered away in search of entertainment.

Delphos, though, remained curious. He needed more than just a name.

A couple of days later he approached Olympia. As with all his conversations with her, there was no preamble.

"Who was my father?"

He'd found her in a corner of the Library of Hadrian, keeping as far away from tourists as she could manage. She rarely went further than a couple of streets away. Her range was small these days; her world had shrunk. How could anyone be happy living within such limited horizons?

Olympia took time considering his question, as if her

memories were buried deep. "Oh, he was very handsome," she began. "And different."

He sat down to listen. "What do you mean, different?"

She glanced at him. "He was more talkative." She looked to the side, and her voice became distant. "He even tried to talk to the humans."

Delphos gave her his full attention. "What do you mean?"

"Well, that was before…" She turned to face him. "What's got into you? Why do you want to know?"

"I was just curious, that's all."

"You've never been interested before. What's changed your mind?"

Delphos experienced a brief flash of irritation. He didn't feel like explaining himself, even to his mother. "As I said, it's nothing. It's just something a dog said."

"A dog?" She rose to her feet and turned her back to him, in a display of outrage.

Delphos sensed that the conversation was over. He turned to walk away, but Olympia spoke again, her voice a low trill.

"Don't let anyone else hear you've been talking to dogs. They're incomprehensible at best. Dangerous at worst, and nobody likes them or trusts them. Now, I don't want to hear of any more fantasies spread by dogs. Leave me alone."

She curled up, facing a stone wall, her mannerism and position shutting out the world. In frustration he gave her a lingering look, then departed.

The desire for knowledge remained unfulfilled, and nagged at the back of his thoughts. Wanting information about his father was irrational, he realised, but he couldn't help himself. His curiosity drove him to find out more, but who could fill in the blanks? Erichthonius might know. He knew all sorts of things, perhaps he'd come across his father?

A few more days passed before Delphos had the opportunity to question him. Out on a daily stroll, he spotted Erichthonius crossing the street ahead, and angled towards him on an intercept course.

"Mind if I walk with you?"

They ambled along Adrianou Street, seeking the shade where possible. This time, Delphos was unsure how to broach the subject. They exchanged clan gossip and passed comment on pungent scents until finally Delphos blurted out his question.

"I want to know more about my father."

Erichthonius stopped in his tracks. "Such as?" He searched Delphos' face.

"Who was he? What was he like? That sort of thing."

"Why do you want to know?"

Delphos hesitated. "Just something that was said to me."

"What?"

"Oh, if it's such a big deal don't bother." Delphos turned away.

Within a few strides Erichthonius caught up. "Wait. It's just such a strange thing to be interested in, that's all. Let me think…" They continued in silence. Just as Delphos was running out of patience, his companion spoke again. "His name was Apollo. He had similar colouring to you and your brother. Isn't it strange how none of the rest of your siblings look like you?" Delphos held his tongue. When would the other animal get to the point? "He was a stranger from the north, I think. He came with some companions."

Delphos stopped and looked at him. This was news. "Who?"

"Well, your mother, for a start. And Jason. And…"

"My mother?"

"Yes. Didn't she tell you? She's not Athenian. Not by birth, anyway."

"And what about him?"

"I remember he was a great warrior." Delphos raised his

head, his attention gripped. "He killed a leader of the northern gangs."

Killed? That was unusual. The normal outcome of a duel was a flurry of blows after which the loser departed, humiliated and with his reputation shredded, but nothing worse.

As if reading his thoughts Erichthonius looked him in the eye. "Yes, it was a strange time. The war. Unusual behaviour all round. But Apollo was one of the worst. He was vicious. Deadly. None could stand against him. Not even the leader of the invaders. A nasty piece of work. Terrible."

"Why?" The question brought a look of confusion to the dust-coloured cat's face. "The war, I mean," Delphos added. "It seems so… unusual."

Erichthonius' expression changed. With eyes downcast, he studied the ground in front of him. "It was a dark time. Many friends were lost. It seemed to come from nowhere. Like nothing we'd ever known. A kind of plague of the mind. It was a time of madness." He glanced up at his companion. "Anyway, let's not dwell on that. It's ancient history. Tell me what you've got planned for today."

"Not much. Just the usual." It seemed to satisfy the other cat, and they parted.

Delphos had learned a lot, but this new information merely fired his curiosity and raised more questions. Why had Olympia mentioned none of this to him?

In the week that followed, he tried several times to raise the subject with her, but it only made her angry. Defeated, he skulked about the familiar streets, barely engaging with anybody, even his friends. His search had become an obsession, but all the avenues of investigation seemed closed. Until he remembered another name from his conversation with Erichthonius.

Jason was an enigma. Considered one of the Plaka gang, but something of a recluse. It was as if he were a part-time member. He spent little time at the Library of Hadrian, nor did he have many close friends among the group. Much of his time was spent alone.

Further days passed before Delphos spotted him, late one afternoon, disappearing around a corner and up a narrow street towards the towering shadow of the Acropolis. He followed, hanging back and keeping a discreet distance through the maze of streets and passages until eventually they came to Theorias, the road that led to the entrance to the Acropolis itself.

Around a corner he found the grey-and-white-striped cat waiting for him.

"Why are you following me?"

Delphos couldn't come up with a viable excuse. "I wanted to talk to you."

Jason gave him a searching look. "You'd better come with me, then."

They followed the road up a sharp incline and round a corner until it flattened out. The graffitied concrete wall to their left gave way to metal railings and, behind them, steeper slopes beneath the cliffs. Further along, the hillside was terraced, with stone walls holding back flatter ground above. Jason slipped between the railings and leaped onto the first wall. Delphos followed. The older cat found a comfortable spot beneath a shady cypress tree and waited, looking out across the rooftops of the city below.

"What's this all about?" he asked.

"I want to know more about my father."

Jason said nothing for a long time. Had he even heard the question?

"Once I called him friend," he said at last. "Fool that I was." Delphos looked at him, but Jason glowered into the distance.

"I... I heard he was a fighter. A hero."

When Jason turned towards him, Delphos could not hold

his gaze. He looked away, shocked at the hostility in those eyes.

"A fighter, yes. But a hero? Ha!" He went quiet again.

Sitting side by side they looked across the rooftops as the shadows about them lengthened. When next he spoke, Jason's voice was softer, more reflective.

"We came from Delphi. Your father, me and Daphne. On a mission to rescue a friend. Your mother, in fact. But we were led a merry dance by the inhabitants of this fair city. Some of them, anyway."

Delphos waited. Finally, some answers; clues as to who he was.

"We were tested. All of us. Separately. And for a while, I thought Apollo had deserted us. But like a saviour from the old tales, he turned up at the last minute with vengeance in his eyes, slaying any who stood in his path. Our saviour!' His voice softened for a moment. 'But he couldn't save… her. He was far too late. Too damned obsessed with polishing his reputation after drenching it in another sea of blood."

Now, with every sentence Jason's voice rose, his anger growing. Delphos swallowed. This wasn't what he'd hoped to hear. Was his father evil personified? A traitor to his friends? Was this why Erichthonius seemed so vague? Why his mother refused to discuss the matter at all?

"Why?" was all Delphos could manage, his voice swallowed up by the gathering dusk.

Jason gave him another look, kinder this time. "He's a god, you realise? Immortal. Unknowable. He'll never really be your friend no matter what silver words drip from his tongue. You can never truly reach gods, no matter what they say. They're distant. Something apart. Not like you or me. Not real flesh and blood. I found out too late." His tone grew more reflective. "Apollo? He's something else. A saviour, a monster. And everything in between." He turned towards the distant horizon once again, now sparkling with lights as the velvet night drew on and the sky deepened from purple to black. "How can you trust a legend that walks among us, alive, pretending to be real?" His voice fell to little more than a whisper. "Who can ever claim to know the gods? We're better off without them."

With his thoughts reeling, Delphos experienced a brief sensation of vertigo. He closed his eyes, shorn of further questions and regretting those he'd asked. All that remained was a strong desire to change the subject.

He looked out at the twinkling lights below. "The view is lovely from here."

CHAPTER 11
THE DEAD MAN IN THE TOWER

The atrium was pitch-dark. As his eyes adjusted to even deeper levels of gloom, Kratos could just make out an arched ceiling and bare stone walls. In a corner to his left was a smaller arch, marking the entrance to a staircase. For the first time since arriving in the Underworld, he was cold; a dank chill cut through his pelt and froze his bones. The walls seemed to suck the warmth and life force from his body. Perhaps that was part of the design.

He climbed the stairs warily, relying on other senses, since sight was useless in the empty darkness. As he climbed it seemed as if the tower itself spoke to him with barely perceptible sighs and moans; faint echoes of grinding stone and the clink of metal on naked rock. The steps beneath his pads seemed worn down, as if countless feet had trodden them before. How did ghouls come to have such a heavy tread?

They climbed steeply, circling around in one corner of the building, each floor marked by an arrow-slit window that allowed a feeble amount of light to enter, illuminating a heavy door set into an arched entrance, opposite. He wondered what lay behind them, but sensed no activity, merely the brooding dark. Only the uppermost room seemed to be occupied.

Kratos climbed on, gritting his teeth against the cold, sensing rather than seeing his breath smoking before him.

Finally, the stairs ended before a heavy oak door, faint yellow light seeping through a gap at the bottom. He scratched hard at the brittle wood; the unmistakable sound of an animal demanding entry.

"Go away."

"You'll have to try harder than that. I will break this door if I have to."

There was a pause. Footsteps. The scrape of metal as a bolt was drawn back, and a latch lifted. The ancient door creaked open.

Kratos spied a comfortable study; far from the sparse dungeon he'd been expecting. A large oak table surrounded by chairs sat on a worn, carpeted floor. Bookcases lined much of the walls, and on one side a tapestry hung next to a large dresser with displayed crockery and glassware. In one corner two battered armchairs sat with a small table between them, holding a crystal glass tumbler containing what looked like whisky. Next to it was a large book, with several more on the floor near the chairs. Other volumes were scattered on the table.

The cat stepped forward. Above him, holding the door, loomed a large man. He was tall and straight with rugged features and a piercing, suspicious stare from eyes that seemed very much alive. He looked out of place; clearly once strong and athletically built, but aged now, and slightly stooped.

"Who are you?"

Kratos ignored the question and continued to assess the man before him.

"You don't look dead."

"Well, I am."

He stepped around the man, studying him from different angles, then jumped onto the polished tabletop.

His host turned his head, but still held the door open, as if hoping that his unexpected guest would just as suddenly decide to leave. When that looked unlikely, he closed it and drew the bolt across.

Kratos observed his actions. "Why the security if you're dead? Who are you so scared of?"

The man turned and gave him an irritating scowl. "Aren't I dead enough for you? You want me to wail and screech and drift through walls like some sad old ghost?" He waved his arms around in mockery to accompany the clear sarcasm. Kratos ignored the lack of deference, watching his host intently.

"Yes."

The man snorted. "I wouldn't lower myself." He studied the cat more closely. A speaking animal visitor didn't seem to faze him. "I am Theseus. Who do I have the pleasure of greeting?"

Kratos looked around before answering. There were lamps on tables, a couple of nondescript landscape paintings on the walls in gaps between bookcases, and a large, detailed map of the Eastern Mediterranean.

"I expected you to be see-through like the others. You're just a disembodied spirit, after all."

"I am."

Kratos stared at him, eyes narrowing.

"Strictly speaking," Theseus continued, "I am a shadow of what I once was. If that satisfies you. In the world above I would probably appear insubstantial; a wraith, perhaps, but down here..." His voice drifted into silence.

"But you can hold things, carry things, move them." The cat looked pointedly at the glass on the side table. "You can drink."

Theseus shrugged. "Yes. Call it transubstantiation or mind

over matter, or sheer stubbornness. But, yes. I can. It's a knack you develop over time, and I've had plenty of that."

Kratos walked across the large tabletop, scanning the books spread there, taking in the surrounding room. It was warmer in here; the life-sucking cold of the stairwell didn't reach beyond the door. Another mystery. Theseus remained standing in the middle of the room, studying the cat intensely. Having sounded initially unwelcoming, he now seemed to be faintly amused by his visitor. He moved closer and stretched out a hand as he might to any feline visitor.

"Don't even think about it."

"I just wanted to show you I'm real. I can touch. Like you. I believe I even have a scent, of sorts."

Theseus kept his hand in front of the animal, and the cat sniffed it suspiciously, unable to detect the usual human aroma.

"You have no scent. Well..." He sniffed again. "Nothing normal. Just the faintest echo of blood and ashes, perhaps." He drew back and studied the bookshelves. "You have a lot of books though."

Theseus stepped back, retreating towards the large armchair. He sat down and took a sip of his drink. "Not enough, I fear. I enjoy reading, and perhaps even Hades, much as I detest him, has mellowed a little." He continued to scrutinise his visitor. "I'm sorry. I am forgetting my manners. Would you like some water?"

"No. How can you drink?"

"It's stubbornness. An affectation, really. I enjoy the taste and the sensation of drinking, but it has no effect on me. It's a chimera. Not the real thing. An illusion. But it keeps me happy. That's one downside of being dead. You can't get drunk, no matter how hard you try."

The cat looked at the teeming shelves, crammed with both literature and reference works.

"And the books?"

"They're real enough."

Kratos studied the volumes in more detail, noting the names along the spine. As he expected, there were several books from Homer, Aristotle and Socrates, but they sat next to works by Voltaire, Jules Verne and Ian Rankin. Salman Rushdie kept company with Tom Clancy. Clearly, the occupant of this tower had wide-ranging tastes across time and subject. He peered at some titles: *Margites* by Homer, Archimedes' *Palimpsest* and Zoticus's *Story of Atlantis.* Kratos had little time for reading, but even he could recognise titles long lost in the world above.

"How do you get them?"

"Oh, my wife delivers them to me." Theseus waved a hand airily, surveying his growing collection with pride. "I may need a bigger bookcase in a century or two."

"Your wife?"

"Well, ex-wife really, but we're still on good terms. Antiope."

Kratos looked up sharply. "Antiope, Queen of the—"

"The same."

"So your books are delivered by…" Kratos noted Theseus' raised eyebrow. He looked around. "Where is she?"

"Not in Tartarus, obviously." A look of anger flashed across the old king's face. He passed a trembling hand across his brow, momentarily lost in anguished memory. He calmed himself. "She resides elsewhere in this expansive domain," he continued, suddenly disdainful. "Our noble lord permits only one visit in every hundred years that pass in the world above. She last visited me some twenty years ago." His gaze drifted to the window, his thoughts elsewhere.

"Why does he imprison you here?"

Theseus turned to look at the cat once more, and Kratos saw the look of pride and arrogance in his face; even now he appeared formidable. His face cracked into a savage grin. "I tried to steal his wife."

Kratos was astonished. "Persephone?"

Theseus nodded curtly. He hesitated, momentarily lost in recollection. "Perhaps we were a little rash, Pirithous and I."

"Pirithous?"

"My friend. King of the Lapiths. It was his idea, actually. He came up with the madcap scheme, and I went along with it." He sighed. "I felt invulnerable in those days. It was just another adventure. How could we fail?" Kratos looked at him with incredulity; how could he have possibly imagined he would succeed?

Theseus seemed to read his thoughts. "He became obsessed with the idea, you see. He wanted to marry her. Persephone, Queen of the Dead. He wanted to abduct her and bring her home as his bride. Pirithous assumed she'd be pleased and Demeter would protect him from her husband's wrath. He was wrong on both counts." Once more he paused, and his brow furrowed as he was lost in memory. There was silence. "Hades was too strong for us."

Kratos sat, marvelling at the man's aptitude for understatement.

After a moment, Theseus continued. "Anyway, he put us in these terrible stone chairs. His Thrones of Forgetfulness." He shuddered. "Fortunately Heracles rescued me. Got me out."

"What about your friend?"

A shadow crossed the dead man's face. "That's the thing. He couldn't save both of us." His voice dropped. "He's still there."

Even Kratos was horrified at the thought. By now Pirithous' mind would have melted into the stone. He would have forgotten indeed, merged into the memory of rock itself. It was a fate he didn't like to contemplate.

"Yet Hades keeps you here instead of under some permanent torment? He must have forgiven you."

The old king's voice became harsh. "Ha! You think this is

forgiveness? Cut off from everyone I know. Confined to the dimensions of this room. Me, a hero. Slayer of the Minotaur. Just one episode among many other mighty deeds. Now penned up like some petty thief in a dismal lonely tower beside a poisoned lake? Tartarus can torment you in far more ways than the merely physical."

"At least you've not suffered the fate of your friend."

Theseus paused before replying. He nodded in wry acknowledgement. "Well. if Hades has changed, it's only a matter of degree."

For a while, both were lost in thought. Kratos lay across the polished wood and stretched. He yawned and considered sleeping.

Next thing he knew, he could hear the man moving around, busying himself in the far corner of the room. "What are you doing?"

Theseus glanced over his shoulder. "Oh, just tidying up a little. I didn't mean to disturb you."

"How long have I been asleep?"

"It's hard to measure time down here. It doesn't seem to flow like it does above. A week is my best guess, give or take."

The cat stood up and arched his back, stretching out a sudden cramp. That was strange. He never usually experienced muscle aches or joint pain. What was happening to him?

Theseus stood with his back to the window, watching. "So, your turn. Who are you? What brought you here?"

"I am Kratos. Once, with my siblings, I sat at the foot of Zeus' throne. We enforced his will. We were unbeatable."

Theseus' eyes widened. He looked at his visitor with a new appreciation. "A Titan, no less. The gaoler of Prometheus, if I recall?" There was an element of awe in his voice. Kratos graciously bowed his head, pleased at the recognition. Theseus leaned towards him. "But what are you doing here? You were one of those who sided with Zeus against your kin. How have you fallen from grace?" His brow furrowed in a frown. "Are you a spy? And why are you disguised as a cat?"

Kratos' eyes narrowed. "Be careful," he hissed. In his anger, his voice gained a depth and timbre that caused the shelves to tremble and glasses to shake on the dresser. "You saw what happened to your gaoler downstairs."

The old king raised his hands in apology. "Sorry, it's just—"

Kratos cut him off. "It's all the fault of that haughty bitch, Athena," he spat, unable to keep the venom from his voice. "She was the one with the bright idea of transforming us into cat shape. Thought it would be fun, keep us out of the limelight for a while until we re-grouped and went back and took up the reins once more. Grew some special apples for us to eat to make the change. She said she could transform us back whenever we liked. Ha!" There was bitterness behind every word now. He looked towards the window and the dimly lit mountains behind. "But she got her calculations wrong. Like your friend Pirithous, we lost our minds until most of us could barely remember who we were. Now the stupid bitch has lost track of her tree, and with it, the plot. We're stuck like this, perhaps forever."

Theseus sat back, enthralled. Little news ever reached him down here, and it was usually decades old. Disputes among the gods were not a novelty; he'd witnessed many such enmities. But discontent on the scale implied by his visitor was entirely new. It made his dead heart leap. He was eager for more.

"What brought you here, Kratos?"

Haltingly, and with a marked reluctance, his visitor told his tale, keeping only to the salient facts. He skipped the atrocities he'd instigated or conducted, making himself out as the innocent victim. But despite the strength and power he'd boasted, he couldn't disguise the fact that he hadn't survived the Second Battle of Monastiraki.

Theseus studied him shrewdly. "You must have done something bad to have ended up here."

The cat said nothing. It wasn't the fact that he'd killed the kittens that irked him so much, but that they weren't heroic opposition. How was he supposed to know they hadn't been Ares' sons? Ares might have produced hundreds of sons, but they had been the only youngsters present.

"Athena doesn't like to be crossed," he said finally. "It was a stitch-up between her and her family."

"But you must have some allies? Others of your kind who think like you."

"Of course. Many of us are angry, but I can't rally them from here. I have to escape." The old hero studied Kratos thoughtfully. "So, how do we get rid of him?"

"Who?"

"Hades."

"I didn't think you could."

"There is one way. Something I read." Theseus' eyes flicked across his bookshelves. "A potion brewed from the entrails of an Ophiotaurus. Deadly to immortals."

"A what?"

"It's a magical beast. Half bull, half serpent."

"How do you know this?"

Theseus laughed. "You think all this is just for my amusement? There is a lot of knowledge on these shelves."

"But I want vengeance on all of them, not just the Lord of Misery." Kratos looked out of the window. The leaves of the strange tree on the far shore of the lake tinkled distantly, impatiently, stirred by some movement in the air.

"This beast is said to be huge. If you can kill it, you should be able to brew enough to despatch the lot of them."

The cat shot his host a sidelong glance and considered his words. "Where do I find this Ophiotaurus?"

CHAPTER 12
THE SECRET GARDEN

A year and a half had passed and Eleni had grown into a handsome young female. Beautiful but cautious. Her life was contained within the tall perimeter wall of rendered stone that marked the boundary of her home. She never ventured beyond it. Her world was delineated by it, a secure and protective barrier that surrounded her garden at the side of the little ochre-coloured house and kept the world outside at bay. Her reluctance to leave was the lasting legacy of many stern lectures from her mother about the dangers that lurked outside and the monsters that lay in wait for unsuspecting animals. She was better off here, in the garden, and the small house to which it belonged.

As an impressionable youngster, Eleni took the instructions to heart. A dim memory of fear and noise, hurt and bewilderment remained in the recesses of her mind, ready to step forward unbidden, enveloping her in fear like an unwelcome discomfort blanket. Months passed before the anxiety faded. During that time, she trusted no one, apart from her mother. They lived at the foot of the garden on a small patch of ground surrounded by tall shrubs that backed against the wall. An ornamental tree provided cover from prying eyes above. They ventured forth, at first, only to nibble at the food left out by the kindly human. Once their confidence grew, they spent some of each day basking on the small triangle of grass.

Eleni was the first to make friends with the woman who lived here. Her mother remained cautious; the result of a life spent scavenging while remaining alert for a sudden smack or kick. Eventually, as colder winter weather gripped the city, the older cat pined for the freedom of her old life, and its wider vistas. She spent more time in her old haunts, renewing acquaintance with those of her former colleagues who had survived the war. She had done her duty and saved her kitten. It was time to move on.

Eleni, however, became increasingly enchanted by the young woman she now thought of as a friend, and took little persuading to sleep in the cosy little house on a soft cat bed placed in a corner of the kitchen. She embraced domestication and her confidence in her human friend and occasional visitors grew. In the day, she was given cat toys to entice her and burn off youthful energy, while evenings were more settled, observing human behaviour and sometimes snuggling next to her person, watching TV.

As Eleni's confidence grew, she picked up a few words of human speech, and her ability to read their expressions and emotions improved. But in the process, her horizons shrank to the interior of the house and the small walled garden outside. It was her secret territory, where she lived unnoticed by the animals outside, sheltered and safe. There was no need to leave and venture abroad. Life was good.

Spring advanced into summer. Her mother had ceased visiting now; her job done, her responsibility at an end. Eleni was grown up, but she increasingly depended on her human for food, security and companionship. Measuring her length on the middle of the lawn on a drowsy afternoon, such matters were far from her thoughts. She stretched and rolled onto her back to let the warm sun bathe her stomach for a while.

"That grass looks inviting."

Eleni opened her eyes, instantly irritated, and spotted a ginger-and-white cat looking down at her from the top of the wall. He was the first of her species she'd seen in a long time.

"Go away."

"Oh, don't be like that." Uninvited, he jumped down and sauntered towards her, head lowered in greeting as he familiarised himself with her scent. Eleni rolled onto her stomach and watched him suspiciously. At a polite distance, he stopped, sat, and made a show of studying his surroundings.

A tiny tingle of excitement shivered along her spine. She had a visitor; a genuine outsider. Here. In her garden. He didn't look threatening, but her mother had warned her about strange, evil-looking warriors from over the wall. How dangerous was he? Was his friendly demeanour just a front?

"Who are you?" she asked. He seemed delighted at the question and turned to face her.

"I'm Delphos," he said. "I'm one of the Plaka gang." She caught the note of pride in his voice.

Eleni relaxed slightly and shuffled into a more comfortable position, but kept a careful watch from the corner of her eye.

"I've heard of them," she said, sounding more confident than she felt.

"I should think so. We govern the centre of the city. You live right in the middle of our patch."

His bragging cut no ice with her. "You don't govern my home. This is my garden, and it belongs to me, and me alone."

Delphos didn't respond. He just sat still and waited for her indignant attitude to evaporate.

"It's a nice garden," he said after a while.

She had to agree. The scents and colours were enticing. There was a tranquillity here that was in sharp contrast to the hustle and bustle and dangers that she'd been told existed on the other side of the wall.

For a long while, they sat in companionable silence as the shadows moved across the lawn.

Finally, he stood. "Oh well. Better go." He turned to leave.

"Will you come back?" she asked, surprising herself with such a bold question.

Delphos paused, looked at her. "If you'd like me to."

Shy and tongue-tied, Eleni studied the ground between them. "I'd like to hear about the world outside," she said in a quiet voice.

He leaped, effortlessly, onto the top of the wall and looked down at her. "Then I'll come back," he said, and vanished.

For several minutes Eleni stared at the space he'd occupied, her thoughts racing. A little knot of excitement sat in the place where her stomach should be. Something had changed today; she had a new friend. A friend from the dangerous world beyond the wall. Her secret garden had become a little less secret.

The hour before dawn was Ion's favourite of the day. He had the streets to himself, even though many of his companions were themselves prowling nearby. The only blot on his horizon was the absence of his best friend, his brother. They'd always been inseparable, but these long absences were annoying him. What could Delphos have found that was more entertaining than their joint adventures? He skirted a chained stack of tables and wandered down a new street, zig-zagging from one interesting scent to another, piecing together the tale of yesterday's events. He was so engrossed that he failed to see the nearby cat until he was nearly upon her.

Athena purred a greeting and boldly stared at him. Ion paused, irritated by the interruption. He walked past her, but she moved to cut off his passage.

He glared at her. "Out of my way."

The large grey cat didn't move. "Blunt to the point of rudeness, I see. Couldn't be further from your heritage. But then again, I know nothing of your mother's line."

Ion stopped, curious. "My mother means little to me. As for my father, well, who can tell? He could be anyone, or anywhere, and what of it?" He prepared to step past her again, but as he reached her shoulder, she spoke once more.

"Decisiveness is a quality I admire in a leader. You have that, at least."

He gave her a sidelong glance. "What do you want? What's this all about?"

Now the grey cat affected an air of nonchalance, staring back along the street. "The cats of the Plaka should have a strong leader, don't you think? And with Ares off the scene for who knows how long…" She walked away from him.

"What do you mean?"

"I might be able to help. Offer advice." She walked on, leaving him to stare after her, the serenity of his morning mood fractured.

"Why do you care?" he shouted.

She did not stop. "You may not know me, but I live nearby, beneath the trees of Filopappou Hill. Having a peaceful, thriving community on my doorstep is important to me."

Ion caught up and matched her stride. "We've been here forever. We'll always be here."

"So you say. But there may be challenges ahead that test us all. It is best to be prepared."

He stopped, baffled. "What challenges?" he stared at her retreating tail, but the grey cat gave no answer.

Life continued as normal, and Ion soon forgot the strange encounter. He meandered the usual streets, marking out his and the Plaka gang's territory on his usual rounds. As he had done so often before, he pleaded for food at his favourite restaurants, and spent time with several of the younger members of the gang. Casual liaisons with female gang members punctuated the days, but he left them well alone if they showed any sign of seeking deeper affections. Ion preferred a life with no strings attached. At the moment life was good. Life was carefree. Even his wandering brother played less on his mind than before. There were plenty of other enticements to fill the days.

Those carefree days ended soon, in a way Ion could not have foreseen. He was walking down the street when it hit him: an invisible object that smashed its way into his head. He was no longer alone. At first he thought he was going to die, as he stood in the middle of the street, eyes wide but unfocused, oblivious to the world around him.

People stumbled to avoid him until a pedestrian concentrating on his phone gave him a hefty kick. The shock jolted the ginger cat into life, jump-starting a bolt for cover. Any cover. Anywhere. But how could he escape the unwelcome presence in his own mind?

Ion had the horrible sensation that his body no longer completely belonged to him. A brooding presence shoved aside his own feeble thoughts and took up residence, tracking every thought, observing him. It was a presence without form or a face; large, weightless, brooding. He was terrified.

Then it spoke.

"*It is time,*" it said in a voice that was both melodious and commanding. The words were loud and clear in his head, but not in his ears.

Ion spun around, but there was no animal nearby. Just the ghost in his head, projecting calm authority directly into his thoughts.

Time? he thought. *What is time?*

To his astonishment, the voice replied. *"Time for you to wake up. Time to realise who you are and claim your rightful place at the head of your kind."*

Ion's legs trembled. He crouched and tried to make sense of what was happening. "What?" was all he could manage. He caught a whiff of a new sensation: amusement.

An idea came to him: a gigantic shapeless mass toying with him the way he would play with a mouse. Except that in the real world the mouse could see him, whereas Ion had no idea what the owner of the strange voice looked like.

"That is enough for now. I will return. In the meantime, consider your surroundings. Look to your allies and identify your enemies. Think about your future."

As abruptly as it had arrived, the voice and its owner departed, leaving him alone once more, but momentarily dizzy. He closed his eyes until the queasiness subsided. When he opened them again, he was relieved to see the familiar street.

But the relief was tempered with a disquiet that lingered through the rest of the day. What if the voice came back as it threatened? What if it took up permanent residence inside his thoughts? The idea filled him with dread.

The feeling of unease lingered for days, spoiling his formerly carefree life. Activities that had been effortless and undemanding now required conscious thought. He viewed his companions with suspicion. Were any of them aware of what had happened to him? Were they plotting against him? Was some sinister creature manipulating them all from afar?

Other concerns crowded in. What had the voice meant by

the future? In company with everyone else, he lived for the present. Day to day, with no care beyond the next few hours' entertainment. Tomorrow would be the same, wouldn't it? He was happy that way, reacting to events as needed. Now he had a new sensation: foreboding. Not just of the prospect of the return of the voice, but what it might demand of him, and when.

CHAPTER 13
SPORT

There are as many stray dogs in Athens as cats, though none roam the city centre. This was a fact of supreme indifference to the feline population until a small expeditionary group of dogs appeared one day, exploding onto the scene like foxes in a chicken run. Their appearance inserted a jolt of energy into the mid-afternoon slumber in the hazy heat, where gravity proved too heavy a pull on a cat's eyelids and blissful rest beckoned so invitingly.

There were three of them. Stray dogs from the distant territory beyond Monastiraki Square. and they had instant command of the attention of any cat in their vicinity. As soon as they set eyes on Nadia, who was meandering from one shady spot to another, a chase ensued. The noise and their intrusive aroma invoked near panic among the local populace, but froze many of them to the spot.

With the trio hot on her tail, Nadia tore through the quieter streets of the old town in search of refuge. Her pursuers were persistent. She set a twisting route but, forced beyond her natural range, finally found safety beneath a parked car, where the gap was too narrow for her long-legged tormentors to reach.

True to form, feline solidarity had been limited. No one offered practical help by providing a decoy run. Instead, they played statues until the chase had moved on. Nadia had plenty of sympathy from a safe distance, but among those who lived or died by their wits on the unfeeling streets, help was strictly rationed.

Two of Nadia's colleagues watched her speed past from a safe vantage point. They crouched, muscles tensed, ready to flee should they catch a stray glance. They were wary long after the dogs had left, and it was some time before they felt able to relax.

"What brought them here, do you think?" asked Savina, the elder of the pair.

"Who knows? Perhaps someone should ask them," suggested her younger friend, Diandra.

A dismissive glance. "Are you mad? Who talks to dogs?" Savina maintained a watch on the far corners of the square, her nerves still frayed. "What could anyone glean from all their yapping, anyway? You'll get more sense from the inane twittering of the birds."

Diandra murmured agreement. Dogs were nasty, brutish things. "Yes. Stupid idea."

Savina warmed to her theme. She leaned closer to her young companion. "I mean, look at that behaviour we've just witnessed. How could you reason with them?"

Diandra made no reply. It was true; there was no point trying to understand dogs. They were simply different. "Who let them in, do you think? They're not usually allowed."

Savina considered it. "Humans? Or maybe they just forgot to keep them out."

Their watchful afternoon continued as peace returned to the small square.

.   .   .

Ion was oblivious to convention, or ready to ignore it completely. In his daily wandering, he enjoyed taunting any dogs he met, particularly those being led by humans – though his insults were unsophisticated. "Oi, fleabag!" was a typical dig at an animal being steered through town on the end of a lead. "Do they give you extra scratching time for good behaviour?"

The replies scarcely employed any higher wit, and Ion had inevitably moved on by then. His taunts were low-grade, his humour unsophisticated, but he enjoyed his sport; although he sensed some of his fellow gang members did not approve. So he pursued his entertainment further away from his gang heartland.

Today he was missing his brother; together, they might have spent a happy afternoon dog-baiting. Why did he have to spend so much time alone? Resentment gnawed at a corner of Ion's heart. To counter his loneliness, he cultivated the yearlings in the gang; those cats half a year younger than himself who were just emerging into early adulthood and who still looked up to him as an example to follow. To them Ion was mature and worldly, and he enjoyed their adulation and leveraged his additional age and experience for all it was worth until he had a ready following among the wider group. Delphos, he realised one day, could look after himself.

He wasn't needed any more.

Ion settled into the heart of Plaka life and basked in the steadily growing support he drew to himself, all of which was noted by the owner of the voice.

CHAPTER 14
AN UNWELCOME VISITOR

Delphos visited Eleni every day, and they soon became close. She was different to the brash, young females he'd grown up with; she kept her talons hidden and her conversation was less barbed. He'd dismissed her initial shyness as part of her house cat isolation, and the limited opportunity it afforded to develop social skills. But it didn't take him long to discover her talent for effortlessly puncturing his flights of ego.

"I'm going to be leader of the gang one day."

"And what will that prove?"

"That I'm the best. The strongest. The bravest." His chin rose slightly, as if to amplify his boast.

Eleni looked away, unimpressed. "Where are you going to lead them?"

"Nowhere. We're staying here."

"So, why do they need a leader? Doesn't anyone else get a say? What if they don't want to be led?"

Delphos said nothing. The conversation was not progressing as smoothly as he'd have liked.

He tried another tack. "They need someone to…" He

paused. What did they need a leader for? "To defend them." It sounded lame.

Eleni examined the colourful scented flowers bordering the small lawn. "Why can't they defend themselves?"

Delphos was irked by her attitude. Couldn't she see how important he was?

He stood and arched his back, for want of anything else to do. "It's rumoured that my father was a great warrior and hero," he said, walking across her line of vision as if to force his way into her attention. "In fact, some say he is a god."

"Who says?"

"A friend."

"Ah," she said, and fell silent.

"What's that mean?"

"What?"

"That 'ah.' It's the way you said it. It's like you know something." With eyes narrowed, he gazed at her.

Eleni ignored him, affecting an air of unconcern. "Oh, nothing. I'm sure it's very nice if one of your family is a god or hero. Perhaps I'll find one, one day."

Delphos was lost for words. He groped for something to say. "It's true."

She gave him a sympathetic look. He caught it from the corner of his eye, but it only increased his irritation.

"What is a god, anyway?" said Eleni.

Exasperated and unable to tell if she was toying with him or being serious, Delphos groped for a reply. Surely everyone knew stories about gods. Supernatural beings of immense power who could create or destroy cities overnight, slay monsters and champion heroes.

"They're important, that's all." His powers of description deserted him, and he closed his eyes, stung by her indifference. What did it take to impress this animal? A better question might have been why he was so keen to impress her, but that didn't occur to him.

"I suppose that means you can run fast," Eleni said, prolonging the conversation.

But her companion had lost his appetite for bragging. She was only setting him up to mock him again.

"What do you do?" he asked, keen to change the subject.

She stretched and rolled onto her side. "I look after my human, and she looks after me." She yawned and closed her eyes.

Delphos was indignant. "That's no life for a self-respecting animal."

"I like it. She loves me, and it's nice to be…" She gave a coy glance in his direction. "Loved."

He was out of his depth. Was she teasing him, or was this a genuine signal of affection? He wanted to move closer, to butt his head against her, but his emotions were snagged in uncertainty; he couldn't face the embarrassment of another put-down.

Delphos swallowed and cast around for something to talk about. But the garden suddenly felt claustrophobic and hot.

"But… what have you got to look forward to? What keeps you going? It sounds so boring."

She looked away, and in the subtle change of expression that played across her face, he knew he'd misread the signals. Again, he felt wrong-footed and foolish. Why could he not read her? Were house cats so different? He turned his face away, but was reluctant to leave.

When he turned back, she was staring at him, but her mood looked different. Buoyant. As if a cloud had passed overhead and the garden was bathed in sunlight again.

"Tell me about your favourite places," she said.

Relieved to put the awkwardness behind him, he talked, but more freely now. They edged closer, and proximity became a comfort. The need to converse eased. It was enough to spend time with each other.

As the tension faded, Delphos was surprised to discover

that he looked forward to the visits. Weeks passed, and they became closer still. Friendship evolved into something deeper that neither was prepared to name.

In Eleni's company, Delphos could unburden himself when the everyday taunts and bickering of the gang got to him. In her garden, he was not judged. He longed to take her with him to meet the others, but every time he raised the subject, she resolutely refused, displaying an inner steel that both irritated and impressed him.

Delphos found it difficult, if not impossible, to imagine a life without struggle, whether that was the daily search for something to eat, or time spent exploring the alleys and passageways of the city, always alert to potential signs of danger. He enjoyed his regular pastimes: hanging out with his friends, avoiding the more dangerous inhabitants of the city, or agitating them from a safe distance. Having fun. Along the way, he'd made new friends and discovered previously unknown enemies.

It was all part of daily life. His clan had a territory to defend, and they had to keep track of who was doing what. Every day brought something new; the city never slept. There was always gossip about the activities and goings-on between the other gangs across Athens. How could you just lounge around in luxury in this small garden, pleasant though it was, and never have to fight for attention among your peers?

One morning, he tried to convey what the wider city was like to Eleni as he circumnavigated her lawn.

She considered him. "What goes on out there that makes it so great?"

Delphos told her about the restaurant with the rude waiters who constantly chased you away, and the nice ones who let you stay. He told her about the bars that sometimes set aside a cushion on a cabinet or wall for you to sit on. He gave her instructions on how to recognise friendly humans. He waxed lyrical on the peril of navigating the myriad legs of aimless tourists in the busy early evening and relayed tales of narrow escapes from loud dogs, and the joys of baiting the visiting hounds who couldn't stray further than the extent of their lead.

He even told her about the rumours that one or two of their kind rode the Metro trains, although he'd never yet done so himself.

He became tongue-tied whenever she raised a subject of a romantic nature, reluctant to delve into his relationships with the female members of the gang, ephemeral as they were, but he was delighted at her appetite for his tales of life beyond the wall. She didn't seem to mind if he occasionally embellished them; in fact, he suspected she might want him to.

Delphos treasured his visits to this little patch of Eden within the wider city. The hours he spent there were precious to him, and the fact no one else knew made them all the more precious. The transition from friends to lovers was a natural development, and with it, his attitude changed. His desire to introduce his friend to the wider clan cooled; perhaps it was better that she remained here, a secret he could keep to himself. She had become special to Delphos and their love grew. He even came to enjoy her teasing and responded in kind, mocking her comfortable lifestyle and the pampered luxuries that came with it, including her cat bed.

But her invitation for him to come indoors to share it remained a step too far.

"Stay," she whispered, nibbling at his ear.

"I can't," he replied, no longer sure why.

Eleni pressed him more, but he became defensive. "I value my freedom," he would say, or, "I will not rely on a human to feed me." All his responses sounded like excuses, and deep in his heart, he sensed his resistance crumbling. But for now, stubborn pride still held firm. He would try to put the internal debate far from his mind and settle back into her, feeling her comforting warmth and scent envelop him. At such times, as he closed his eyes, he knew life could get no better.

Back in the grounds of the Library of Hadrian, Delphos' absence was noted. Ion felt his brother's absence heavily and regarded it as a personal slight. What had Delphos got to do that was more important than spending time with him? The secrecy made it worse. He was sure Delphos took care to time his departures when Ion's attention was elsewhere and he would never talk about where he'd been. Jealousy shaped his moods.

Finally he spotted his brother slinking away one morning, and followed him at a distance, taking care to keep to the shadows to remain unseen. Delphos took a winding route through the Plaka district's narrow streets, which nestled beneath the towering cliffs of the Acropolis, until, as he turned another corner, Ion saw him jump onto a high wall and disappear.

He stopped, momentarily unsure whether to follow. What lay on the other side of the ochre wall? He made up his mind, and leaped, then balanced on the narrow convex surface.

It was a decent vantage point, but all he could see on the other side was a small, neat, shady garden of the type some humans seemed to value. Where was his brother? Ion scanned the space below and spotted him in the shadow of a large bush, approaching a small black-and-white cat. Their noses touched in intimate greeting, and they rubbed along each other's flanks, eyes closed.

A horrible sensation knotted Ion's stomach; a bitterness he'd not experienced before. Betrayal mixed with jealousy. No longer was he the centre of his brother's world; he'd found a different companion.

Delphos looked up and spotted him. His muscles stiffened in annoyance. The female stared up at him as well, but her cool appraisal was irritating. She should be more respectful in the presence of one of the neighbourhood's more important felines. Ion had status within the community. Surely she must know that? A subservient attitude would suit her well. Sitting next to the weasel he'd formerly known as a brother, he recognised she probably thought herself safe. But that could change.

"Go away." Delphos sounded angry; Ion was delighted to have got under his skin so easily. He jumped down to join them.

"Now, now. That's no way to greet your brother." With satisfaction, he noted the female looked a lot less confident at close quarters.

"I mean it." Delphos' eyes followed his every move.

Ion scanned his surroundings. "Very pretty. Not sure I like this grass, though. It's spiky under the pads, isn't it?" He looked directly at the female, with a challenge in his eye. Delphos stepped between them.

"This is my place, not yours," he growled.

"*My place* now, is it?" Ion was in no mood to back down and for the first time, as they squared up to each other, the confrontation was more than the usual playful battle of wills. Eleni held back, unsure what to do.

There was a knock on a window. The human behind mouthed at them. The distraction broke Ion's concentration, and he glanced aside. In that instant – lightning fast – Delphos raked a paw down his nose. Ion jumped back with a howl of surprise as much as pain, but he was distracted by movement behind the glass. Was the human going to inter-vene? Uncertainty restrained him from launching himself at his brother. He beat a retreat to the top of the wall, but at least he could still hurl insults.

"That's it," he hissed. "I'm through with you. You'd better not show your face at headquarters again." He yowled and disappeared.

Delphos stared at the space his brother had occupied, the fur on his back standing proud. He remained still while his heart rate slowed. Behind him, Eleni was greeting her human, who by now stood on the small patio next to the lawn. The woman made unintelligible cooing noises and patted her cat, but Delphos was unmoved. He hadn't expected to make an enemy of his brother, and he already regretted slashing at him like that. No doubt Ion would hold a grudge; but for how long? The power and venom that guided his paw surprised him; never had he struck with such meaning or force.

But the thing that shocked him most was that he knew, in similar circumstances, he'd do it again.

CHAPTER 15
SISYPHUS

Kratos had no desire to return to the drab towns and fields he'd passed through earlier. Instead, he set off towards a narrow path that passed around the poisonous lake and ventured deeper into the hills. As he climbed away from the tower, he had a lot to ponder. His discussions with Theseus had been most illuminating. For the first time in many a year, he experienced a shiver of excitement. There was a way to defeat them; he just had to find the means to put it into practice. As he walked, he considered the outline of a plan, but all his efforts would be useless unless he could find a way out of this place.

Further down the valley he came to more small settlements and scenes of torture, though fewer than before and more widely separated. A ghoul swept towards him from a deep cleft in the mountain ahead, but his snarl held more than enough venom to keep it at bay. It changed tack in search of some other soul to torment; a thankless task in this place. Most inhabitants of Tartarus were long past caring about the effects of their crimes; others were so lacking in imagination or empathy, they barely understood why they were there. Those who did quake before ghouls were inevitably weak-minded sycophants and obsequious followers of the true monsters. Some of them, perhaps, had sufficient self-awareness to comprehend the nature of the evil they performed; their overlords did not. They were beyond remorse, tragically wrapped up in the mystery of their own ego and unable to see reason, psychopathically inclined demagogues, dictators or zealots. No punishment could reach their closed and tiny minds. Not in this domain, at least.

Kratos licked his lips and relished the agony inflicted on them. Despite his own crimes, a corner of his mind remembered his role as Zeus' gaoler, and still relished the punishment he'd inflicted on his former master's behalf. As enforcer and occasional torturer for the King of Heaven, he had interrogated and imprisoned many a foe such as these. He recognised them, and saw them through their bullying, while remaining blind to his own behaviour. Kratos did not equate his deeds to theirs: his cause was noble, to right wrongs committed by his former peers. These others, he despised. Their eternal victimhood was pathetic and needy. Monstrous and beyond rehabilitation, they deserved everything Tartarus could throw at them.

There was, of course, one exception. His eyes narrowed as he recalled the case of Prometheus. For the crime of bringing fire to humanity, Zeus had condemned him to appalling torment. His liver was to be ripped from his body by an eagle each day, and eaten before him, only to regrow overnight. Kratos smiled inwardly as he remembered the relish with which he'd tightened the bolts and harsh wire cords that secured his rebellious cousin to the rock on which he'd spend so many centuries, and the praise he received from his mentor. But Prometheus' crime was to oppose his overlord's will: he was no psychopathic monster. He had been pardoned and released long ago. The rest of then down here deserved everything they got.

Another kind of shadow crossed his mind. How things

had changed; soon he might need to reach out to his fellow Titan in search of support in his campaign against their former master. What sort of reception would he receive?

As he marched on, the path levelled once more and he arrived at another flat valley floor, still illuminated by the pale green of the lake now far behind him. This area was different; pock-marked by pools of even darker night. He arrived at the edge of an enormous pit, a hundred metres across. Colossal chains were bolted to towering pillars rising from the ground, the head of each rust-encrusted bolt far larger in diameter than his present body. They hung loose, and far below he could see unlocked shackles at their end. The sight gave Kratos pause. His eyes widened as he took in his surroundings.

Looking into the gloom before him, his vision adjusted and he saw that the crater's floor far below was covered with closely packed iron spikes, each a dozen metres high. He circumnavigated the rim.

The next pit he came to had more restraints, but in this one he could see no floor. The victims had been suspended over a bottomless abyss. To his right, a similarly sized basin contained a pool of hissing, bubbling mud. The cat could not help but shudder as he realised where he had arrived. It was the location where his Titan kin were held for millennia after their failed rebellion. Mighty as they were, the torments devised for them had been their equal. He had fought on the winning side, to support the gods of Olympus, but now, here, betrayed, his folly seemed clear. His heart hardened towards the merciless gods that had imprisoned his kin in this place. He had chosen badly. Fickle was the support of those *heroes* of Olympus. How he would love to see them suffer in turn. That his loyalties had so abruptly changed troubled him no more. He had a new cause, and would seek allies where he could.

Disdainfully, Kratos cast one last look at the pits in which his kin had been imprisoned for so long, then moved on. Yes, their captivity had been horrendous in the extreme, but at least they had been released. He should find them; rally them to his new cause, kindle anew their resentment at their treatment and persuade them that the time was ripe to take on the Olympians while they were divided and weak. They might never have a better chance.

He ached to get even.

Hades, their gaoler-in-chief, was old-school in his methods, and Zeus was worse. But the lion's share of his venom was reserved for Zeus' clever, devious daughter. How short-sighted he'd been.

He wandered on. The Titans had been released a long time ago, but other spirits remained. The valley twisted and turned, and the prisoners he came upon, still chained up, here and there, and choking in misery seemed all but forgotten. Kratos had no sympathy. For all his faults, Hades wasn't stupid. They deserved their plight. Redemption? He barely considered it. The punishment of the gods was eternal and awful, or it was nothing. Only a fool would think otherwise. Apollo, for instance, with his feeble-minded beliefs in wishy-washy concepts like forgiveness and rehabilitation.

Kratos sneered at his foe's cringingly weak attitude. He claimed to embrace the light, but the Titan knew only too well that he could manipulate all the tools of the dark. Apollo was the ultimate hypocrite. Kratos' mood darkened at the thought of their recent encounter. Soon he would have his revenge upon them all, but Apollo, next to Zeus and Athena, topped the list. The screams and pleadings of the tormented prisoners he walked past served only to fuel his anger and determination: let them suffer and the entire world with them. He would have his way.

The valley narrowed once more and the number of prisoners to either side dwindled as the road climbed to a distant pass. Finally, he left them behind. Soon, even their cries faded in the still, thick air.

As he descended on the other side of the col, to the flatter land beyond, he came across another, smaller lake, its shadowed surface more benign in appearance than any he'd come across on his journey so far. It appeared quite shallow. In its midst stood a man beside a tall tree. He seemed thirsty, but every time he stooped to try to cup water, the pool receded. He attempted to pluck an apple from the branch overhead, but the tree pulled its branches out of reach. Poised forever between these two alternatives, the figure standing in the lake looked eternally miserable. Kratos wanted to laugh.

In the distance, he caught a brief flash of light that illuminated the underside of the distant, rocky roof. The light disappeared, and a rumbling sound filled the dark. Curiosity drove him on.

Sometime later, the rumbling happened again. Kratos was closer now, and able to watch. What he saw astonished him: in each blindingly bright flash, through almost closed eyes, he caught a brief glimpse of blue sky far above, before it vanished, and darkness returned. The rumbling sound grew louder, and he saw an enormous boulder thundering down the long slope ahead. Its momentum took it some way up the slope opposite, before it finally came to rest on the valley floor. A weary figure trudged behind it, downcast but strangely animated.

Kratos sat to watch as the man reached the boulder, patted it absently, as if greeting an old friend, then positioned himself behind it, took a deep breath and started pushing. It moved. Slowly, he heaved it up the slope, muscles straining. A long time he toiled, and Kratos couldn't help but admire his fortitude and strength. Onwards he rolled the rock, as the gradient steepened against him, his feet struggling to gain purchase on the loose surface of the hillside. He made better progress than the cat thought possible for someone his size, and soon he was little more than a dwindling speck in the distance as he painstakingly gained altitude.

Then something remarkable happened: a portal appeared above him, tantalisingly close. Just a few more heaves and he would make it. There was so little distance to go. But, close though he was, the slope continued to steepen until he was almost balancing the rock on his head. At the last push, his foot slipped, and he lost his balance. For a brief instant it seemed he might regain it and hold on, but the boulder slid too far to the side, beyond his grasp, and gravity brought it tumbling down once more. The portal snapped shut with a boom that echoed around the mountains to either side. Defeated and dejected, the small figure spent a moment lying on the slope, then began his descent.

As he drew closer Kratos approached.

"A difficult task, my friend. You must be exhausted."

The man looked at him. "That I am. Weary beyond endurance. Yet somehow I endure."

"It looks a heavy load," Kratos said, eyeing the rock before them.

The man looked at it sidelong. "You speak the truth. But what choice do I have? It is my path to freedom."

"Freedom, you say? How so?"

The man stood facing the cat and spoke as if explaining to a child. He jerked a thumb. "Up there is the outside world. Once I push this boulder out of the doorway at the top of this hill, I am free. Free of Hades' clutches, and able to resume my life."

Kratos gave him an appraising look, then turned his face to the slope. "But you look shattered. Have a rest to renew your strength so that you might do better next time."

His companion gave a mirthless laugh. "Rest? What a fine word is that. I may not rest, otherwise they will throw me in chains and scourge me with whips of fire, and take away the portal forever. I cannot rest."

Kratos narrowed his eyes, then turned towards his new friend. "They can't watch you so closely. I am sure they only pay attention to the progress of the rock, rather than who is pushing. Let me help you. I can do some of the work and relieve you of the burden for a while."

The man scoffed. "A lovely thought, but what can you possibly do? You are only a cat."

"I'm stronger than I look," Kratos said. With that, he sprang to the rear of the boulder, planted his hind paws squarely on the ground, and placed his front paws on either side. He pushed. The man watched in astonishment as the stone moved. Onward the cat pushed, his powerful hind paws gaining purchase on the slope, and the boulder moved steadily upwards.

After a short distance he paused and looked over his shoulder. "See? I can do this, at least for a while. You lie down and take a rest for a few minutes. If I get close to the top, you can come up and take over for the last part. It'll give you a better chance of success."

The man stroked his chin and considered. "Alright," he said. "That seems a good idea. Let me see what you can do. If I had any coins, I'd suggest a wager on how far you get. What do you think?" He looked down at Kratos. "Which of us will push it further, Sisyphus or a talking cat?" He lay down on the opposite slope, to watch the new arrival's laborious progress, a smile on his face.

Then he closed his eyes.

Kratos pushed on. As he closed in on the top of the mountain, the portal opened, and bright blue sky forced him to shield his eyes. He turned and saw the man scrambling to his feet, stumbling up the slope. Without the weight of the boulder pressing him backwards, he made good progress, but he was too far below to catch up.

A small pebble like this presented little problem for Kratos; the main issue was its relative size, and the difficulty maintaining balance. As he drew closer to the exit, he scented the outside world, fresh earth, grass and trees, distant blossom on the breeze. He could hear the tinkle of bells on the collars of nearby goats, and his lips parted in gleeful pleasure.

With one last heave, he pushed the boulder through the portal, onto a wide empty meadow, and hopped out after it. Balancing on the rim he looked back down towards the upturned, eager face of the man below. He was close now.

"Bye!" he called, and stepped back as the portal slammed shut. In the split second before it closed, he heard a scream of frustration that added to his sense of satisfaction.

Kratos turned to examine his surroundings. Beside him, the red-hued rock looked incongruous in the middle of this wildflower meadow, fringed by trees. Bees buzzed among the grasses; a refreshing breeze ruffled his fur.

He had escaped from Hades' clutches and he was never going back.

CHAPTER 16
A BODY POISONED

on sat on the wall, radiating malevolence. His narrow face was mean and sneering, despising not only all humanity but all creatures wandering the city. Bitterness defined him; it ran in his veins, warped his soul. Worst of all, his nose was still stinging from his brother's unprovoked attack. He seethed, itching to get even. No, to get ahead: to beat Delphos down and see him squirm.

In his bitterness, Ion mused on their relationship. Once they had been friends. They roamed the streets together, play-fighting in the squares or gardens, racing and chasing each other down narrow streets or back alleys. In those days, he'd enjoyed his brother's company. No more.

With an insight born of his resentment, he saw their differences afresh. His brother, despite his capacity for cowardly first strikes, preferred to avoid confrontation. Instead he preferred companionship, conviviality, kindness. Weakness. What use were such talents in this cut-throat world? Ion's strengths were far more useful: envy, jealousy, spite and hate.

At some point, that seed of envy had germinated in his heart, to be fed by every subsequent comment about Delphos he overheard.

He's so handsome.

What a looker.

I'd love to share a dust bath with him.

And worst of all… *He'll make a good leader of the gang when his time comes.*

It wasn't enough that Delphos was popular; he got all the best pickings as well. He looked almost as well-fed as a house cat.

Ion loathed him more and more, as he bit down on the emptiness in his stomach. He hated begging; he couldn't give his heart to it and never found it satisfactory. He wouldn't prostitute himself for a snack, no matter how sweetly it was presented. If anything, such behaviour merely stoked the contempt he held for the diners; they were so smug in their self-righteousness. Ion preferred hunting, and the city would never run out of mice.

He'd always paid little heed to rumours about his father. All he knew was a name that, according to some, signified prestige. No gang could have more than one leader, and no one with such an illustrious birthright could endure subordination to his brother.

Delphos had to go.

Ion planned for a future without him. A future in which he was the unopposed leader of the Plaka gang.

Ion used his new found animosity as fuel to feed his mission to destroy his brother's happiness and, hopefully, his life. The gang would be led by no one other than himself. The ideas the strange grey cat had given him germinated and grew, amplified by the unsettling voice that still, periodically permeated his thoughts. There could be no doubt he was Ares' anointed deputy and now he was no longer here, Ion was the real leader of the cats of the Plaka.

In his shrivelled heart, he anticipated the rewards; the obsequious grovelling of the elderly and weak would-be mere flattery. More important would be the quiet observance of the mature adults and the fawning acknowledgement of the youngsters. Best of all, he would enshrine the opportunity to imprint his genes on the future. As leader, he would have the pick of the breeding females. He would remove Delphos' line from the Plaka gang's gene pool; eradicate him from the future entirely. Fratricide might erode his support among the gang, but serving Delphos permanent exile and a lonely distant death would be an acceptable alternative. In fact, banishment would be the least he deserved.

In the meantime, resentful though he was, Ion was not isolated. He found succour among the disaffected who inhabited the fringe of the gang; a group of like-minded misfits for whom nothing was ever good, only bad. He hung out with them, grumbling over perceived slights. As the days passed, their perpetual dissatisfaction spread to poison dialogue among the others. Rumours began to circulate that Delphos hung out with house cats. That he preferred their company, and was on the verge of becoming one himself, that he preferred a soft life waited on by humans, that he thought himself above the rest of the gang. Such poison nagged at the consciousness of the whole group, ripples of anger and irritation spread across the previously calm surface of the pool.

Erichthonius noted the trend with alarm, but his attempts to intervene on Delphos' behalf were met with sullen resentment. He mentioned his concerns to Athena, but she ignored them. "How do you suggest we combat malicious gossip and lies?" she said. "Truth is a poor foil when folk want entertainment at somebody else's expense."

So the poison spread, most of it directed at the hapless ginger cat at the centre of it all: Delphos.

CHAPTER 17
MYRA

Kratos spent the first few hours of his restored freedom wandering aimlessly, enjoying the fresh air and trying to get his bearings in an unfamiliar landscape. He was alone amid a wide, flat plain of cultivated land; vast fields interspersed with olive groves and orchards, with low arid hills in the distance. It did not resemble any part of Greece that he knew, but he couldn't yet be certain. Thoughts returned to the dead king and his books. A look at the shadows cast by the late afternoon sun gave him a direction and he decided to head south, He hadn't gone far before he heard a familiar drawl.

"So, Zeus was right."

Kratos turned sharply. There, lounging on a patch of exposed rock, was Zelus, basking in the sun, unsurprised to see him.

Kratos turned to face him. "How long have you been here?"

"Not long. I was warned you were coming. An eagle from Zeus found me. He said you'd be somewhere around here. Apparently, Hades is furious you escaped. He wants you back, but Zeus refused."

Kratos tracked the haphazard flight of a butterfly. "He's rediscovered his balls then. Better late than never. He's not quite senile yet."

"Even he couldn't lose what he can bend down and lick," sneered Zelus. He gave his brother another look. "That's a nice collar you've acquired. Looks heavy."

Kratos glared at him. "I can manage." In fact he was desperate to be rid of the constant reminder of his captivity, but that would have to wait.

Silence fell between them, broken eventually by another question from Kratos. "Where are we?"

"Middle of Anatolia. North and west of Antalya, I believe."

"How did you get here?"

Zelus got to his feet, and stared into the distance, hesitant. "Bloody eagle. Less said the better." He shuddered at the recollection.

Kratos stared at him for a minute, then followed his gaze.

Zelus posed a question of his own. "Time to carve out some new territory, then?"

"No. Not this time. I've got a plan." Kratos gave his brother a sidelong glance. "I came across some interesting information while in Tartarus. It's a game-changer, and if what you've said is correct, we are in a convenient location." He had Zelus' full attention. "We need to head south to Myra. It's on the coast." Without waiting, he set off. "I'll fill you in on the way."

It was hot, so they slept during the day and moved mainly at night. Nevertheless, three long days passed before Kratos sensed the culmination of their trek. On the breath of the wind he caught the scent of salt air, but ridge after forested ridge blocked any sight of the coast for many hours. He plodded on by daylight now, impatient to get to their destination, Zelus keeping pace beside him. The fact his feeble body required regular rest remained a continual source of annoyance for Kratos, almost matching his fury at having to move slowly over land rather than drift through the aether as he once could.

The journey had been long and the red dust of the mountains matted his scarred and mottled fur. It became ingrained in his paw pads, so that even he had to pay considerable attention to grooming; a fact that was not lost on his increasingly aloof brother.

Kratos caught Zelus' sidelong glances and slightly raised nose – as if something unpleasant was troubling his delicate sensitivities – and felt antagonistic towards his ally. It wasn't the best starting point from which to launch a campaign of vengeance. His relief, therefore, at first detecting the proximity of the sea and the end of this leg of their journey, was palpable. Ancient Myra was drawing him like a magnet. The place where hope collided with the coast; a town famous for a long-dead saint and ancient tombs that, until he'd come across a long-dead king, he'd forgotten existed. But the key to all his hopes was what lay beneath and within that long-forgotten necropolis.

Over the coastal hills they travelled as the land gradually descended from the Anatolian plateau to its southern coast. Finally they crossed a wide, dry river bed and made one last laborious ascent to the top of the last hill, crowned by the ruins of an ancient fortification overlooking the town. But where was it? Spread before their feet was a patchwork of intense cultivation. Greenhouses, crammed next to one another, covered the whole plain as far as the sea, now some five kilometres distant. It looked nothing like the landscape Kratos had imagined from Theseus' maps. But then, he realised, many years had passed since the cartographers had drawn them. Theseus needed a modern atlas.

Kratos sighed. Beside him Zelus scanned the land below

for signs of ancient Myra. Standing on the rocky promontory above where the town should be, he was lost. Where was it? There was no sign of an ancient city. Beside him, Zelus was still, scanning the landscape below.

Kratos focused on the plain below and there, amid the tightly packed farms, he detected a small town. Apart from one old building – a church, seemingly – it didn't look ancient. A name formed at the back of his mind, conjured from the content of Theseus' library: Demre. That was it: a more modern replacement for the city of antiquity, perched on its high outcrop, with a small port far below, beside the now silted-up river.

But he had little interest in the modern settlement. What he sought was far, far older, and, he now realised, most likely beneath his paws. Acting on his hunch, without signalling to his brother, he set off down the steep and slippery hillside in search of the necropolis.

The dead king was an odd ally. Death placed them on a more even footing than he'd cared to admit, but Kratos still had the advantage, as there were powers available to him even now, that lay forever beyond Theseus' reach. But death had given the old king one advantage: he was harder to intimidate. Not that he'd cared much for his personal safety in the first place, if Kratos remembered correctly.

If. That word again; a permanent reminder of his diminished status and limited powers. He no longer had the benefit of flawless recollection. Memory could fall prey to manipulation, or biological inaccuracy. All it took was a handful of neurons in this feeble, adapted brain to briefly misfire for a new pattern to be established and a whole series of events to appear different. In this diminished state could he still trust his thoughts? He knew, on the other hand, that he could rely on his emotions, and the continually burning desire in his heart that they fed.

Kratos picked his way down through the sharp gorse and prickly vegetation that covered the hillside, musing on these intractable philosophical dilemmas as he made his way towards the sea.

CHAPTER 18
THE RIFT

A few days passed, and Delphos dared to hope things were returning to normal. But his brother stayed well away from him, and would not catch his eye. He resumed his daily visits to Eleni's little garden; a place he regarded as sanctuary. Life was easy for her. Plenty to eat, and little to stress about. But he was desperate to show her what his life was like; to persuade her to venture over the wall and into the real world beyond.

At the corner of Eleni's quiet street, he stopped. He could hear high-pitched warning yowls, and knew instantly what was happening. From the top of the containing wall, his fears were confirmed. Eleni, fur standing on end, snarled at Ion, who was circling, baring his teeth. His intention was obvious, though she wasn't in heat. So focused was he that he didn't notice the new arrival.

Delphos launched himself from the top of the wall, catching his brother by surprise once more. The scuffle was barely worth the name, but in his fury, a mistimed lunge brought Delphos the satisfaction of a deep bite to his brother's hind leg, before he broke free. Ion retreated beneath a shrub to confront his opponents.

There was a banging on the window, followed by the rattling of a door handle. Ion retreated atop the wall and disappeared, leaving them one last furious glance.

The woman emerged, full of cooing sympathy for her companion, and cooler commiserations for her regular visitor. Delphos kept his distance, distrustful of humans and still bristling at his brother's intrusion. In his agitation he wanted to run and let off steam, then find somewhere quiet to lie and collect his thoughts. With a brief backwards glance of good-bye, he leaped to the top of the wall and set off across the rooftops.

Delphos found Ion back at the headquarters of the gang, in the Library of Hadrian, an ancient site in the centre of Athens. With satisfaction, he noticed the wound he'd left on his brother's hind leg was still visible, although already scabbing over. His bite had, perhaps, been more vicious than he'd realised. At his approach, several faces turned towards him, then away again. Ion, lounging on a flat stone, held their attention.

"Here he comes," his brother sneered. "Ready to gloat, no doubt." He turned to a small dark-haired animal lying in a shadow nearby. "He caught me by surprise. Ambushed me. But not like the usual jousting. He meant it. Don't be fooled by this calm exterior. He's unpredictable. Volatile. A nasty piece of work."

"It's no more than you deserved. What's wrong with you?"

Ion ignored him and continued, his voice rising to an angry yowl. He worked the wider assembly, derision turning to sarcasm. "I thought I knew him, but no more. He's been leading a double life. Already got one foot in the door, these days. You should see it. Nice little house complete with pretty little house cat. All meek and submissive, ready to roll over the moment he appears. He's been grooming her for a while, I've no doubt."

Delphos tried to remain calm. Ion had been the aggressor, so why was he playing the victim instead of apologising? "It was you who invades our place. Trying to bully us. What have we done to so enrage you?"

"*Us? Our* place?" Ion turned to the cats nearby, all of them engrossed. "You see what I mean? Our home is no longer suitable." He strode among them, looking them in the eye. "Evidently I was frightening." He bowed his head and purred at the nearest female, his voice little more than a beguiling whisper. "Do I look frightening to you?" She raised her nose to his, and they touched. Turning back, he resumed. "I was only expressing surprise. Shocked that he was about to abandon us." He paused and gave his brother a steady look. "He's more pathetic than I realised. Him and his subservient little house cat." Throughout his monologue he stared at Delphos as if addressing him, but his taunts were for the benefit of the other cats nearby. "Before long, he'll be domesticated. In the place of a proud, independent creature called Delphos, there will be a timid little pet, desperate for attention: purrs and head rubs in exchange for food. Del-boy, they'll call him. A testicle-free zone. Maybe they'll give him a pretty collar with a little bell."

Delphos sat down, infuriated by the falsehoods and insults cast in his direction, but unable to produce a suitable put-down.

Ion seized the opportunity to drive the stake deeper, twisting it in the wound. "We're not good enough for you anymore, are we? You much prefer the company of your little *pussycat* in her sweet little house under the cliffs." He spat out the insult, and let the accusation hang in the air. Several of the others shuffled position, putting distance between themselves and the accused. Who in their right mind would voluntarily spend time in the company of domesticated cats, unless it was to exploit them or mock them for sport? Such animals had no place in any self-respecting society.

Ion continued, fully warmed up to his theme and enjoying his spot at the centre of attention. "No. Not good enough for us anymore, is he? He wants to become a *pet*, a bourgeois little mindless eunuch, looked after by some malingering human. Like the infantilised fluffed-up kit he gets his kicks from every day."

The accusation stung, but still Delphos said nothing. It was as if his tongue had been removed.

He looked about him, but none of the others, even those he counted as friends, would catch his eye. Most turned away. At the edge of the group, one or two latecomers sauntered over, curious about the argument that was brewing. They selected viewpoints on the perimeter of the group, half listening while sunbathing, or watching the tourists who ambled about not far away.

"Just look at him," Ion goaded. "Preening himself. So pleased that he's got a girlfriend at last. But she's barely old enough to bear a litter. She's not even been in heat yet."

"That's a lie. She's old enough." It wasn't the most eloquent defence Delphos could have produced. He stood up and faced his brother while Ion continued to scoff, playing to the gallery.

"Oh, so she's old enough? Well, that's a relief, I'm sure. A barely old enough female for his personal use, whenever he likes." He addressed Delphos directly. "Were you planning to keep her to yourself? Populate the city with litter after litter from your one-female harem? What an apology of a tom." Scorn built with every word. "You should get yourself a proper mate. Someone who knows how the real world works. A female capable of recognising a real tom. Not one who hides in a secret garden behind high walls with such a gutless wonder for a lover."

In full flow, Ion stepped closer, and without warning

Delphos launched himself, full of teeth, claws and fury. For the second time that morning, he had the satisfaction of catching his brother by surprise, inflicting wounds and pain, oblivious to what he was taking in return. After a few seconds, they separated.

Ion wasn't gloating now. Crouching close to the ground, he glared up at his brother, eyes wide, fangs bared, ears flattened back, ready to spring. Delphos stood over him, beside himself with fury, seeking the best angle for his next attack.

"Enough."

Both cats froze. The speaker's voice held an authority neither could ignore. But still they glared at each other, reluctant to take a backwards step. Athena had arrived. Large and imposing, she approached and stood between them.

She gave each a cool appraisal. "I appreciate a good, clean fight. But this is not the time or place to pursue your argument. I will not have you bring dissent and division to the heart of the city."

With eyes still on his brother, Delphos backed away slightly. Ion stood tall.

Athena walked a short distance away and turned. "Your dispute is poisoning the atmosphere, even in the Agora. It must end. I cannot have lingering resentment splitting our community. This is your last warning. Unless you change behaviour, one of you will have to leave."

Stung by the injustice caused by his brother's actions, Delphos struggled to react.

Ion intervened before he could voice his resentment. "He's been acting strange recently. All superior. I don't recognise him anymore. He's not the brother I used to know."

Delphos stared at him. What had caused this bitterness?

Behind him, another voice spoke up. *"Been sneaking off to consort with house cats."*

"We're not good enough for him anymore, apparently."

He looked around, startled at the animosity he was

hearing from animals he'd known all his life. How could they fall for these lies? Would no one speak up in his defence?

Athena turned towards him, piercing him with a heavy stare. "From what I understand, you have been acting in such a way as to spread division. And you have been the aggressor, attacking your brother without warning and causing significant injury, from what I see."

She glanced around the assembled animals. "Is there anyone here who will speak up in Delphos' defence?"

Silence. Delphos glanced from face to face, but with a sinking heart he knew none would dare to speak. He'd never felt so alone.

Athena turned towards him. "You seem to have become a divisive presence within this group. You should consider your position. You and your brother have long been potential leaders of this gang. But it looks clear to me that only one of you has the confidence of his peers." She gave him a level stare.

Sweat pricked Delphos' paw pads. "He is lying." He struggled to keep his voice level.

Athena's head tilted to one side. "Then why does everybody here believe him and not you?" Once more, she turned towards the nearby cats, staring at each of them. But her words were aimed firmly at Delphos. "Unless you can persuade me otherwise, it might be best if you left our community, and our city, until you can learn how to behave properly as one of us. Your future as part of this gang is hanging by a thread. Consider this your last warning. Don't waste it."

She gave him a lingering look over her shoulder, then calmly walked away, tail swaying gently as if she hadn't a care in the world.

. . .

Erichthonius observed the discussion from a distance. He trotted after the departing Athena and matched her stride.

"Wasn't that a bit, er, heavy-handed?"

Athena kept on walking. "And what do you think I should have done?"

The young cat tried to organise his thoughts. "It's just my initial observation, but perhaps you missed the provocation from Ion that led to the attack? Delphos was within his rights, to my mind."

Athena stopped abruptly and turned to face her adviser. "Erichthonius, you may have an official position as my assistant and liaison with the Plaka gang, but don't tell me how to do my job."

The dusty-coloured cat raised his head and looked her in the eye. "I'm not trying to tell you how to do anything. But if I were in your position, I'd have given Delphos more leeway, that's all. There was fault on both sides." He lowered his head in deference.

Athena studied him for a moment, then spoke with exaggerated patience. "It was not a hasty decision. Trouble has been brewing between the brothers for some time. Their rivalry has reached the point where it is dividing opinion within the group. Some of them are taking sides, developing factions. If you spent more time among them, you'd see."

Erichthonius looked up, politely staring past Athena but giving her his full attention.

The grey cat continued. "Both Ion and Delphos can lead this gang, should they wish. But you should know as well as anyone that a group such as ours cannot have two leaders. The time is fast approaching when one of them must leave. I'd prefer if the gang could resolve their business among themselves without my intervention."

Erichthonius cast his eyes down, deep in thought. "But why Delphos? Why not put Ion on a last warning? Surely, consorting with a house cat isn't such a crime, is it?"

Athena gave a small snort. "Of course not. I don't care how he spends his time, or who with. But Ion has the support of more of the group. He's more popular, and the others bought into his argument. For them, house cats are pathetic. Losers in life. Dependent upon humans. They've shed their dignity. We live on our wits, from day to day. Life can be a struggle, but we have our freedom. And camaraderie. And for them, that is everything." She stared at the smaller cat as if to emphasise her point. "And besides, he was more cunning with his arguments. He won over the doubters. That's a useful skill for any leader in these times. Always has been."

"It was more devious than cunning," replied Erichthonius. He ventured a glance at the goddess, more confident now. "And being devious can cut several ways. He's becoming more surly, and too keen to dish out punishment. He's acting like a bully. I'd be careful around him, if I were one of his inner circle. I don't trust him at all."

He nodded to the larger cat, then departed into the warren of streets.

CHAPTER 19
ALLIED

In the wake of Delphos' public humiliation, Ion's resentment grew further. How dare his brother abandon him for *her*. How could Delphos prefer that stupid little molly over him? A house cat, of all things. Did she even have a brain? Most likely she was another gormless drone; mindless and reliant on her human gaoler without an ounce of gumption in her perfectly groomed body. The attack was the last straw.

The nugget of bitterness that had long since taken root in a corner of Ion's soul grew with every perceived slight. He took to roaming the streets alone, exploring, poking his nose into places it wasn't welcome, scavenging from cafés and restaurants and annoying the tourists with his persistence. He missed chasing Delphos around the district, and took his anger out by bullying others smaller than himself, singling out the house cats in the neighbourhood as if they were to blame for his brother's behaviour. To his satisfaction, he noted them getting out of the way when they saw him coming.

His fame and reputation were growing.

An afternoon visit to a favourite haunt – a large corner café on a quieter street – started promisingly. His youthful good looks found favour with some diners, and he was rewarded handsomely, until the point where a low growl intruded on his self-satisfaction. A dog appeared: medium-sized, wiry coat, aggressive in manner. Some sort of terrier, maybe? Ion had never paid much attention to dog breeds. This one wasn't here to make friends. Instead, bristling with canine testosterone and territorial possessiveness, it was spoiling for a fight. He backed away as his opponent advanced between and around tables, oblivious to the human occupants. A couple moved their feet aside to ease the dog's passage.

Ion backed away and scampered a short distance down the street. But the dog kept advancing. It snarled, spittle dangling from its chin. Ion glanced around for escape routes, but the buildings to each side were tall, and the only one he could see was much further down the street. The dog kept coming, eyes fixed on him, obviously in the mood for a fight. Would it listen to reason?

He crouched in a defensive posture, his tail twice the normal width, slashing from side to side. The dog paused, uncertain. Clearly it had not been expecting its victim to mount a defiant last stand.

Sensing hesitation on his adversary's part, Ion stood, noting the huff of surprise on the dog's face. The creature immediately started growling once more. It barked twice and tensed, ready to launch itself towards him. But before it could do so, Ion stepped to the side and caught it off guard with a simple question.

"You're new around here, then?" No reply, so he continued. "It's quite a responsibility you've got, guarding a whole restaurant."

He took a pace the other way, trying to maintain his poise, but ready to flee at any instant. The fur on his spine stood upright, and it took an effort to keep his voice level. "I mean, a corner site like that. Tricky." He paused and ventured a direct look at the dog.

"Why do you care?"

Ion lingered for a moment, then resumed his slow perambulation back and forth. A modicum of confidence crept back and his fur settled. A plan formed at the back of his mind.

"Unless you've got help, you'll be running back and forth all day and night. It sounds exhausting. Unless they're trying to get you fit, of course?"

He gave the other animal a pointed look. The dog wasn't particularly slim. It gave a gurgling noise from the back of its throat, which Ion took as a sign it was thinking. He studied its stance and musculature; was it tensing for attack or beginning to relax? The latter seemed to be the case; the danger seemed to pass. But then it took two bounds forward and instinctively Ion leapt backwards to maintain distance. His analysis had been premature.

The dog stopped again, its snarl louder now in the confines of the narrow street. It was all Ion could do to hold his ground. His heart raced, his senses back on full alert. The temptation to run grew.

"You've got some nerve," said the dog, "I'll give you that."

Ion looked the other animal up and down. "I've lived here all my life. I know how the place operates. You seem new."

"What of it?"

Ion turned slightly towards the dog, still ready to run at the slightest sign of aggression. "I might be able to help make your life easier. Maybe we could come to some arrangement."

The dog's snarl receded. It slurped saliva and licked its lips. "What sort of arrangement?"

Ion turned to fully face it. "I could help you. I'd spread the word among my many friends that your café is out of bounds. It'll save you a lot of effort. The humans will think it's all down to you, because of how big and tough you are. They'll reward you."

The dog gave little reaction. "What's in it for you?"

Ion sensed his opportunity. With his heart still pounding, he ventured a step closer, looked to the side, and lowered his voice. "There is something you could do for me. Nothing that you can't handle, of course. I'm troubled by a nasty individual. He acts very high and mighty. Thinks he's better than the rest of us." He leaned closer, only to receive a warning growl. "Look. It's a simple thing, really. If you see him, I want you to give him the full benefit of your ferocity. All of it."

The dog looked confused. "Who is this? You lot all look the same to me."

Ion returned a level stare. "Not that similar, surely. And this one is easy to spot. He looks pretty much identical to me. Same colour, similar markings, everything. He'll be like the finest cut of mincemeat between your jaws. Think of it."

"You want me to fight him?"

Ion stepped back and gave the other animal an appraising look. "It won't be much of a fight, will it? You're obviously extremely fierce and intimidating and you can run a bit. He won't stand a chance once you grab hold of him. I'm not saying you've got to kill him, but…" He looked sideways, a thoughtful edge to his voice. "Well, if he met with a permanent accident, I wouldn't be too sad, let us say. You'd do us all a favour. Your restaurant would be left alone by the rest of us. Everyone across the neighbourhood gets to see exactly what a badass you are. Just think what it'll do for your reputation." Ion glanced back towards the dog. "Do we have a deal?"

To his satisfaction, the dog relaxed, its snarl replaced by eager panting.

"Alright," it said.

CHAPTER 20
TRAPPED

The change came gradually. It began with a snide remark here, a sharp glance there. Delphos found some familiar faces, including many he regarded as friends, avoiding him. As they assembled in their favourite haunts in the evening, they gave him a wide berth. Few would sit nearby. As the weeks passed, it became worse. Those he tried to approach would often walk away, or refuse to engage in conversation.

Olympia was little help. "It's a phase, darling. They'll get over it."

But how long did a phase last? On that question, she had no response. He sought answers from Erichthonius, a frequent visitor from Athena's group who lived in and around the Agora.

"There's nothing you can do," he advised. "You'll just have to wait it out."

His response to estrangement from the gang was to spend more time with Eleni. There he could relax; at least she was happy to see him. The more time they spent together, the closer their bond grew, the only fragment of irritation being her refusal to join him in exploring the city beyond the confines of her garden wall.

"It's great out there. You'll love it. There is so much to see," he enthused.

"I like it here," she countered. "And anyway, my mother told me to never leave."

No matter how much he tried, Delphos could never persuade her otherwise.

One afternoon, lounging together in a shady corner, their bodies merged into a puddle of ginger, black and white, he tried a different tack.

"Why did your mother tell you to never leave?"

In the long pause, he wondered if she was asleep. With eyes closed, he enjoyed the subtle movement of her body as she breathed. Scents from the nearby flowerbed soaked his nostrils with comforting balm.

Life here was soothing. He was tempted to stay, too.

Eleni's reply took so long coming, he'd almost forgotten the question. "Something happened."

Delphos twisted his head to look at her. "Is that it? 'Something happened'?" Eleni opened her eyes and returned a level stare, then looked away.

"Something bad. I don't know what. She told me there were creatures out there and if they saw me, they'd..." Her voice trailed off, the sentence unfinished.

Delphos continued to stare at her, trying to understand. "But you're older now. Bigger. Stronger. There's no one out there like that nowadays. And I'm here. I'd be with you." There was an urgency in his voice; he was eager to begin her education.

Eleni stood and walked towards the house. She sat, staring at a watering can next to the back door, turned away from him. Delphos bounded across and tried again.

"It'll be okay. You'll see—"

"No. I don't want to." Disappointed, he turned away and

pretended to study the tree in the corner. His thoughts reeled. Why was she so determined? A gloomy mood descended. How could he live here? It was so small. He could never do it; no matter how pleasant the human was. He would be despised by his former friends, and shunned in the street if ever he poked his nose out from this tranquil backwater again. They would have nothing more to do with him and his resentment would grow and eventually he'd blame her. It was pointless. Freedom lay under the sun and stars, not cooped up in a comfortable prison. With sorrow, Delphos wondered if his blossoming relationship was already over.

"I should go," he called over his shoulder. She gave no immediate reply. He turned to see her staring at him.

"You don't have to."

"No. I do. There are things I need to do."

"Like what?"

The question needled him. A flash of anger burst to the surface. "I don't have to explain my movements to you." He leaped to the top of the wall and stared down, waiting for her to say something. Instead, he warmed to his theme, venting frustration. "That's the trouble with you. You're trapped inside your own head. Scared to live, to do anything. You never know, you might enjoy it out there. But you won't try, will you? You're terrified of your own shadow."

"Wait," she called. But it was too late; he'd already left. "I've got something to tell you..."

CHAPTER 21
A CONVERSATION

The evening was cool; clouds obscured the stars. Along the silent streets, the denizens of the night roamed, free of human interference. For a few hours at least.

They mostly ignored one another. But while the cats kept to themselves, their prey tried to avoid them at all costs.

The few stray dogs avoided the central streets in fear of dog-catchers. In contrast to the feral cats who inhabited the centre of the city, they were unwelcome, and they resented the fact.

Hermes found this the most productive part of his day. He could observe and occasionally purloin a target for conversation. Sure, often they were embroiled in a pursuit of their own, but that just made it more enjoyable. He loved nothing more than catching his targets off guard, wrong-footing them. Few had the strength of mind to ignore his invitation to converse. Trapped and squirming, they inevitably revealed far more than they intended.

This evening, however, he was a target.

"I want to ask you about the future of the Plaka gang," said Erichthonius, as he approached.

Hermes looked past the other cat, buying time to think, or at least give the impression of thought. "What of it?"

Erichthonius did not appear agitated, but he was earnest in his questioning. Apparently, the subject was important to him. The fortunes of the city's various gangs, their rivalries and petty politics, was a favourite topic of Hermes, and he liked to stick a paw in now and then. But since the war, he'd left the Plaka cats' actions to Ares and Athena, preferring to follow the disparate fortunes of the remnants of Kratos' and Zelus' gangs.

Erichthonius walked beside him as he made his way slowly across the square. "It's Ares." Hermes gave him a sidelong glance. "We can't rely on him."

"Except in a fight." It was prudent, Hermes thought, to maintain support for his family while in the company of a mortal.

Erichthonius pursued his theme. "But that's just it. He's vanished again."

This wasn't news to Hermes. "He'll come back eventually. He always returns."

The other cat stopped, his face searching the white cat for understanding. "Does he? Will he always? And more to the point, what happens while he's away?"

Even in the darkness Hermes could detect the look of concern on the other cat's face. He attempted to sound reassuring. "He doesn't like to be pinned down. Who does? Frankly, responsibility for others, such as this group, is not in his nature. But he does always return. Eventually."

Erichthonius looked unconvinced. "But after how long? Sometimes he's been away for years, so Athena says. A lot can happen in that time."

Hermes said nothing, but moved off again, waiting for the other animal to catch up.

"We can't allow another rudderless episode like last time," said Erichthonius.

Hermes suppressed a sigh. So that's what this was all about. Security. "A lot has changed since then. The other gangs are in no position to mount an attack. Without their former leaders, they're not remotely interested in doing so. Most of them have fragmented into rival factions. You have nothing to worry about."

Erichthonius stopped once more. "It's not them I'm worried about. It's internal. We can't have two leaders, or see the gang split into rival groupings."

"The brothers, you mean?"

"Yes. Relations are deteriorating. They're already testing each other out, provoking, prodding, always itching for a fight. The rest of the gang are taking sides."

"It's perfectly normal. Eventually one will back down and leave. It happens all the time."

Erichthonius lowered his head. "I'm not so sure. They're both pretty determined."

"So they fight. Big deal. It's nature's way among creatures such as…" He almost said *you*. "Us."

"It's not that. It's more about Athena's interference."

At last, the nub of the issue. "Well, she can't resist. She loves having a champion to promote." He adopted a paternal tone. "If there's one thing you have to understand about your mistress, it's that manipulating others is her favourite pastime. Always go about your business with that in mind."

Erichthonius was undeterred. "I think it's a bit early to be taking sides. They're barely more than adolescents. And she seems to communicate with one of them. It's all so… underhand."

"Communicate?"

"I think so. Somehow." He faltered, unsure what to say. "Spells or enchantments, or something like that. Her eyes glaze over as if she's looking inward, and I can see her muzzle moving, like she's forming words. But there's no sound. It's like she's talking to someone inside her head, but she can't see anyone nearby. It's like we're invisible."

Hermes gave Erichthonius an appraising look. There was clearly a lot going on in that head of his. How much did he really know about his mentor? "It's probably nothing more than vivid dreaming. Talking in her sleep, or trying to." He attempted a reassuring look. "I'm sure she's not *communicating* with one of them. That would be far-fetched, wouldn't it?" He noted the confusion on the other cat's face and pressed his advantage. "Perhaps you could volunteer to step in when Ares is away? That might be a good compromise? Why don't you suggest it to her?"

"Impossible. I pledged service to Athena." There was a pause, while the two cats stared at each other.

"What are you asking me to do, then?" Hermes asked.

"Would you have a chat with her? Ask her to hold off for a while until at least we've got a better understanding of the brothers. They need time to mature. And if you can, please try to persuade Ares to come back. At least until one of them is ready."

"Why can't you talk to her?"

"I've tried. She won't listen to me."

"She must have her reasons."

Erichthonius looked about wildly. "I think she's making a mistake. She's rushing things. It's so unfair."

Hermes returned a level stare. "I will speak to Athena," he said, if only to end the conversation.

He watched as the other cat retreated. How innocent. Surely he must have realised by now that fairness was the least of their concerns.

The conversation had proved one thing. Athena was still using that treasure of hers; presumably testing its limits. How many had she already ensnared with her toy, and how many more were in her growing web of influence?

He raised his head and sniffed the night air.

It was not for mortals to guess the will of gods. Other gods, however…

CHAPTER 22
MEG

Blind from kittenhood, Meg was the victim of a disease that stole her sight and left her world perpetually dark. She navigated Athens via her own internal sensory map, painstakingly built using her other senses, until she was almost as nimble and fast as her peers. She treated the loss of her sight with equanimity, and her positive attitude towards her fellows, displayed via an encouraging nudge here and a kind word there, made her many friends. Meg developed a special place in the affections of the Plaka gang, and in turn, they looked after her and treasured her as a kind of mascot. Because of her inability to detect visible signs from others, she became adept at listening, picking up nuances others couldn't hear, and was, in turn, unafraid to speak her mind, no matter how senior the victim of her pointed remarks.

Often, her fellow animals would approach her for advice in return for a mouse. Matters of the heart were a favourite subject for consultation, but she was unafraid to address higher issues, to speak to the powerful. Relying on her own instincts and sharpened non-visual senses, Meg had an unnerving ability to puncture pomposity and detect nuggets of truth hidden behind layers of obfuscation. She spoke the truth as she saw it, and reputations meant little. More than one of the gang's elders had been on the receiving end of a sharp rebuke.

Ion was wary of her. In contrast with Meg's homespun wisdom, the bleating complaints of his followers sounded hollow and trivial. A word of common sense from her could quickly deflate their self-importance and he had a feeling she knew it.

This evening she lay amid some friends, relaxing at head-quarters before the next scavenging expedition.

Ion walked past. "That's Ion, isn't it?" she said. He glanced at her, and her group of friends, slightly put out at the recognition. "I can smell the essence of canine on you. Who have you been with today?" He paused, unsure how to respond. The accusation was dangerous, but the implication was even worse. Everyone knew Meg's sense of smell was exceptional, but what could others detect?

He tried to make light of it. "It's the punters down at the taverna on Tripodon," he said hastily. "They had a few mutts on leads. You can't avoid them."

To his relief, she gave little reaction, but a nugget of concern hardened in his gut. If some of the less compliant gang members had been within earshot of Meg's barb, he might have had a lot more explaining to do. He had to be more careful from now on. Were those looks directed towards him suspicious, or was he overreacting? His evening mood became brittle and the edginess extended into the next day and the one after.

As he circulated among his growing band of followers, Ion instantly became suspicious if ever he saw Meg in the vicinity. He avoided her. If he saw two or more of his fellow gang members in hushed conversation, he feared the worst. His concern deepened if their discussion ceased at his approach.

He regarded Meg as a threat; a subtle but insidious voice

within the group, unpredictable and potentially dangerous. Was she actively plotting against him?

His bitterness intensified whenever he witnessed Delphos speak to her, even if it was nothing more than a simple greeting.

As he became more paranoid in his delusions, he began to nurture a deep suspicion of the blind soothsayer germinated deep within his heart. But she was untouchable. A collective treasure. Everyone loved her. Even human café owners left special treats out when they saw her. Ion would have to wait for his moment.

In the meantime, he plotted how to get his brother to visit the restaurant guarded by his new acquaintance. To his annoyance, Delphos had been nowhere near it yet. If he had, Ion would surely know about it.

He had to take a more direct approach. But with trust between the brothers eroding, he needed someone else to make the suggestion.

In the quiet of late evening, he approached the blind truth-sayer as she reclined with her back to an ancient column. "It's a pleasant evening."

Her eyeless face turned towards him, but she remained silent. Ion regretted his approach. He thought about walking away.

"Something to get off your chest?" she said.

He half-turned back towards her. "No." He sat down and groomed himself, tasting the sweat on his paw pads. Why was he letting her get to him? He paused, paw halfway to his mouth. "It's just..." Her ears were pricked; a good sign. "Well, what I mean is... I heard a rumour. Yesterday. About a dog." With alarm, he noticed her yawn and spoke faster. "A dog that can talk. To cats." He studied her disease-ravaged face, with its closed eye sockets. Meg was suddenly attentive once more. "Someone should check it out." It sounded a little lame, and he began grooming again, thinking fast. "What I meant to say is… well, you remember the fuss that last little incursion caused?" He studied her face for a reaction. Meg's ears were still pricked in his direction. "So, what if someone here, on the inside, is getting messages to the strays out there?"

That sounded better. A suitable cause for investigation. Surely the word would get round now?

"Why don't you check it out?" said Meg.

He stopped grooming and sat still. "Because I haven't had time yet. I got distracted elsewhere." Once again, he studied her face for a reaction. "I mean, I only just heard." He looked away and tried to affect indifference. "Of course, I'll probably have to head down there tomorrow, but it's impossible to get any sense out of dogs. I mean, I know some misguided folks try, but they're foolish for risking it, aren't they?" He tried to make it sound conversational. "Ares could talk to dogs, couldn't he?" Meg gave a nod; he had her full attention. "Maybe that's the thing you've got to do if you want to be leader. Learn how to build bridges with the enemy. Negotiate with them. Tell them to back off, when you have to." He paused. "It would take an animal with real guts, though. Someone special. Someone who can talk the dogs' language. I'm willing to have a go, but…"

He sauntered away, satisfied.

Seed planted.

CHAPTER 23
AN EMBASSY

The man who appeared at the entrance gate was tall, broad and agitated. But what set him apart from any other visitor was his detailed period dress. From the belted tunic of fine linen, decorated with an elaborate gold-embroidered band above the hem, to the *chlamys* cloak, fastened with a brooch at the shoulder, and the sandals adorning his feet, he looked like he had stepped out of the pages of history. Staff manning the gate in the small entrance plaza beside Delphi's museum raised a quizzical eyebrow and glanced at each other. The cosplayer before them was convincingly portraying his part in whatever drama was unfolding, but where were the rest of the cast?

The woman at the gate held out her arm, blocking his path. "Ticket."

He glared at the offending limb, then the woman herself, looming over her, his thick black eyebrows forming a single angry line. But she could not decipher the invective he now directed at her. It was like Greek, but different; the intonation and vowel placements were all wrong, his accent strange.

The only word she could make out was "Zeus."

Another staff member approached to lend moral support

and try to de-escalate the situation. But they never got the chance.

A flash of light and a sudden blast threw both of them backwards, and knocked everyone in a five-metre radius off their feet. The burst of energy was followed by a moment of utter stillness; an aural vacuum, before the sounds of the real world returned.

Bodies lay all about the entrance plaza. Slowly they stirred, bruised and startled but relieved to find they were still in one piece. People staggered to their feet trying to make sense of what had happened. The stunned silence was replaced with a babble of voices, shouting and speaking over one another, rising in a crescendo, checking on their families and friends. To everyone's amazement, there were no fatalities, but the gate itself was a mangled wreck of twisted metal.

There was no sign of the tall stranger.

Startled by the blast, people emerged from the adjacent museum, office and cafeteria. They milled around, checking for injuries, trying to interpret events.

Halfway up the hillside, a frustrated and increasingly angry Hades yelled into the ruins and trees, as if they held the answer to his demands. Terrified tourists gave him a wide berth, scattering to seek separate ways down.

"Zeus, you miserable coward! Where the fuck are you hiding? Come out and face me!"

Receiving no answer, he rampaged through the ruins and among the trees, his challenges echoing back from the stones.

One observer did not flee. From the shadow of a tall pine, a dark tortoiseshell cat watched the god of the Underworld approach, her eyes narrowed in disapproval.

Hera waited until the furious god was near, then stood, the movement attracting his attention. Looking him straight in the eye she addressed him in the manner of their kind, mind-to-mind. "Come with me."

He followed her twisting route up the hillside, departing

from the Sacred Way to a peaceful glade around the shoulder of the mountain. There, curled up asleep was a large red-brown cat. He gave no sign of hearing their approach.

"Is that you?" scoffed the King of the Underworld. "I knew your scheme was the epitome of stupidity, but I hadn't fully realised how pathetic it was until now." Hades stood back, sneering down at his brother. "My visit will be wasted, given your diminished state." As if to emphasise the point, he assumed his full glory, and a three-metre-tall figure stood before the cat, the glow of burnished bronze dismissing the shadows. His aura illuminated the nearby trees even in the full light of day, as if a star had descended to earth.

Slowly the red-brown cat unfurled himself, stretched and raised his head. His dark eyes stared unflinchingly at the god, a subtle but unmistakable hardness about his face.

"I would say welcome, but that would be a lie," said Zeus.

Hades gave a snort of derision. "Let's cut the pleasantries. Where is Kratos?"

"Have you lost him? Dear me, how careless."

Hades took a step forward, looming over the cat. Zeus didn't move.

The King of the Underworld's voice dropped an octave. "This is not the time for playing games. I'm serious. This is a breach of our agreement. I did not give him permission to leave. He has violated the age-old treaty." He stared at the cat, and the cat stared back.

"Since when did a god, even a Titan, need your permission to come and go?" said Zeus. "Not since the long days of their imprisonment after the ancient war. And that was settled with a comprehensive peace treaty to which you and all of us agreed, aeons ago."

"He was dead. He was sentenced. He is mine."

"It's one thing for mortals. They stay dead. That is their lot. But you know as well as I that we are made differently.

For us, death is an inconvenience that can be reversed. We are not eternally bound. We don't stay dead."

Hades clenched and unclenched his fists as if preparing to grab hold of the cat and throttle it, but Zeus remained still.

"How is business, by the way?" Zeus continued. "Notice any changes?"

Hades recoiled, startled by the question. He stood taller. "What are you getting at?"

The dark-eyed stare of the cat was unflinching. "The dead. How many come to you, these days? Up here there's a population boom. How much of that trickles down to your dreary lands?" The cat stood, stretched his legs as if they had been unused for a long time, and stared up at the tall figure expectantly.

Hades' face changed. His brows furrowed, concern replacing the anger. "Numbers are down," he said. "Have been for some time. Is this another of your games? Some new stratagem you have inflicted upon the natural order?"

Zeus arched his back, walked across the clearing to a nearby rocky outcrop, and leaped to the top in one bound. From his elevated position, he was level with Hades' face.

He leaned in closer. "Where are they going?" he asked, his voice little more than a whisper. He searched his brother's face for an answer. Nothing. He sat back and continued. "Do you have any backchannel into these monotheistic realms?"

"No." Hades gave the cat his full attention.

"And what of your population? Are they still all present and correct?" He tilted his head to the side, waiting for the reply.

"I don't take a census. How should I know?" said Hades. He frowned. "Yes. They must be. Where else are they going to go?"

Zeus stared back. Hades said no more.

Finally, the cat spoke again, staring into the distance, recalling a distant conversation. "I'm sure Hermes once told me they just fade away. Ease out into nothingness. It's almost as if they lose the will to be dead."

"Not true."

Zeus adjusted his position minutely; the feline equivalent of a shrug.

The King of the Underworld stared at him and stroked his chin. "What are you suggesting?"

The cat let him ponder a while longer before responding. "All I'm saying is that it's a competitive market out there. Why do you think I agreed to wait things out like this?" He glanced across at Hera, who sat impassively at the far side of the clearing. "It's my expectation that things will change once more. In fact, it's already happening. A little push here and there, and a neo-classical revival of sorts may be just around the corner."

"What of it?"

Zeus looked Hades in the eye. "The conditions increasingly favour our return. That's all I'm saying." He stood and paced to the side, still looking at his brother. "But that's among the living. You need to monitor the back door, so to speak. What's going on down in your own corner of existence?" Hades' face was a mask. "My intelligence is imperfect, I agree. But don't blame Hermes. He's in an impossible position and I'm sure you receive plenty of updates from here. No, what's important is to look at the bigger picture. Forget about one high-profile escapee. Focus on keeping what you've already got. Perhaps you need a rethink."

"In what way?" Hades scoffed. "There's no accommodation with Christian or Muslim gods. We're separate. Apart. Different."

Zeus searched his brother's face once more. "Are you certain of that? Perhaps your realm is, dare I say it, just a stepping stone. A halfway house." He paused. Hades' frown returned. "Think of it," he continued. "What then? What are the implications?"

Hades crossed his arms and turned aside, deep in thought. He stared at the ground. Zeus watched him intently. As the god of the Underworld's anger subsided, his aura faded, and he shrank back into the human-sized disguise he'd worn when he first arrived.

He cleared his throat. "All this is a diversion. I came here for Kratos and you're just deflecting my request with abstract theological debate. Answer my question. Where is he? He must return to see out his sentence."

"Or what?" said Zeus, his tone as mild as his brother's.

"Or I'll send some of my most persuasive servants on my behalf."

"That would be unfortunate."

"Give him up, or all cooperation will cease."

"Cooperation? What cooperation? From the dead? The few who still cling on to the old beliefs still go to you, but to the best of my knowledge that's just a trickle these days compared to olden times. But what do we get? What favours can we give our would-be followers to encourage them in their belief, when there are so many competing alternative visions of the afterlife these days?"

"I'm serious. There's plenty I can do to make your life more difficult, and you know it. Ghosts, ghouls, hauntings, demon raids, a plague of nightmares made real. Vampires and all the creatures of the dark are at my call. If you want me to continue to restrain them, you know what to do. Restore Kratos to me. He will fulfil the rest of his sentence or a state of war will rise between us."

"War?" Now Zeus lost his calm tone. "You dare speak of war? Your threats are hollow and you know it. The terror you can unleash may rampage through humanity, but whose followers would that affect the most? And if you afflict our own, to whom do they turn for salvation?" He looked to his right, towards the ancient ruins, now out of sight around the hillside. "Do you see any temples still standing, staffed by a functioning priesthood?" The cat glared at the god, his eyes narrowed in fury. "And what of the few souls who descend to cross the Styx? Can you wipe their memories before their news spreads? Is your control so absolute that there is no chance of unquiet sleep among those who slumber in your realm? How long before they build a church amid the meadows of Asphodel?"

Once more, Hades' aura blazed with fury. He shook his fist at the cat, then in a flash of energy, vanished.

Zeus looked at Hera. Hera looked at Zeus. Neither spoke. Among the trees, across the hillside, the rhythmic buzz of crickets returned and birdsong began again, filling the silence with the sound of life.

Zeus called out. "Polly, come here."

It seemed he was talking to himself, but a few seconds later, the undergrowth parted and a sleek cat with amber, black and white colouring stepped forward into the clearing. Solemn and dignified, she stood still, her gaze measured and cool.

"I take it you heard that?" Zeus said.

Her eyes flicked to the space Hades had occupied. "It was quite a rant."

To the side, Hera remained watchful but silent.

Zeus continued. "I think it's time—"

"The time is overdue," said Hera.

He regarded her. "This is not straightforward. There are pros and cons to all actions."

His wife circled, then lay down, choosing a sun trap next to a protruding rock. "But action is better than inaction. We must do something."

Zeus' attention returned to Polyhymnia. "Your sisters are spread far and wide, beyond my sight, or that of my spies. Find them, and pass on this message. The time has come. We need to execute the plan." He turned towards the distant plain. "Otherwise it will be too late."

CHAPTER 24
DOG-TALKER

Lunchtime trade was building in the gaggle of streets that huddled beneath the rock walls of the Acropolis. Early morning sightseers sought refuge for weary limbs, or took refreshment prior to their journey up to get a closer look at the Parthenon and the city's other wonders. As the tables filled, the aroma of cooking alerted every feral cat in the neighbourhood. Delphos was no exception.

He was on his way to visit Eleni, but the food smells were too distracting. He needed to take the edge off his hunger. Most of his favoured spots were already busy with human traffic, which attracted many of his peers. Competition was hotting up in tune with the weather. Perhaps he should try the place he'd heard Ion's goons discussing earlier. It wasn't far out of his way.

He wandered down a narrow street that led to a wider thoroughfare, and there it was, in a quiet little square, basking in a sun trap: a busy corner café with no cats present. Perfect.

Delphos approached, sizing up the diners, trying to spot the easy touch among them. From a feline perspective, humanity fell into one of three broad groups: friends, enemies and the undecided. You could tell them apart easily by the way they looked at you and the body language that accompanied the look. Instant recognition was written all over the faces of friends, who often reached down for tactile confirmation. Enemies displayed either frigidity or hostility, often accompanied by sharp gestures. Those who ignored you fell into the third category, and sometimes they formed most of the clientele. They represented a challenge. Were they open to manipulation or not? Vulnerable to persistence?

Delphos sat on the road a short distance from the tables and tried to identify the best target. Some sort of sixth sense would usually inform the diners they were being watched. Then, depending on the reaction, you could approach. The technique was well established and came naturally to him. It worked. The usual problem was competition from other members of his own species. Today was different. Delphos' nostrils detected another, more unwelcome element in the mix: dog.

It wasn't usually a problem. Of those who lived in restaurants, some dogs would turn a blind eye in favour of a quiet life, while others were discouraged from chasing and barking by their human guardians, who feared a scene might deter customers. But today was different. No sooner had he made his initial approach than the guardian of the establishment appeared, bristling with fury, looking for a fight.

Delphos shuffled backwards as the snarling beast emerged from the dark interior and made straight for him through a forest of legs.

"Hey, there's no need to be like that..." he said. But the dog wasn't listening. It advanced, growling. Delphos tried again. "Look, it's just for a few minutes, okay? I won't stay long."

He was in the middle of the street now, well beyond the tables. But the dog kept advancing. Several diners paused from eating to watch the unfolding drama. Delphos realised too late that reasoning wouldn't work with this animal, so he ran.

The dog gave chase. Delphos was confident he could outrun it, but over a short distance, the two were evenly matched. They shot around a corner and down a short, narrow street, Delphos a body length ahead.

Surely the animal would lose interest. But it remained on his tail.

Delphos fled around another corner; this time, disaster struck. A last-second swerve couldn't prevent him from careering into a display stand outside a shop. It gave him a nasty jolt, and he had to change direction. It was the opportunity his pursuer needed. The dog pounced, grasping Delphos' hind leg in his powerful jaws.

No matter how much he twisted and wriggled, Delphos couldn't pull free. The dog just bit down harder, snarling as it did so. The bite was bone deep. Unable to escape, Delphos curled back and repeatedly slashed his enemy with a front paw, aiming for its eyes. He couldn't quite reach any part of its head to bite, but he kept wriggling and squirming to free himself, punching the dog in the face with the free hind leg.

It worked. Whether to get a better grip, or because it had taken too many raking slashes down his nose, the dog let go.

Instinct told Delphos he was too badly injured to flee. Instead, he swivelled around – ignoring the shooting pains from his injured leg – and crouched, fangs bared, ready to attack.

Salvation came in the form of human intervention. A woman bent down and slapped the dog, shouting at it. Distracted, it looked up and snarled, concentration broken. Delphos scrambled as far away as he could, searching for safety.

Wincing with pain and limping badly, he clambered through the narrow gap between the railings of a nearby fence and found a quiet place to lie down. The dog was too wide to follow.

It was some time before his breathing slowed and his heart rate returned to normal. But as the adrenaline left his bloodstream, the pain surged. Delphos licked his wound incessantly, tasting blood but soothing the worst of the agony until it subsided to a persistent ache.

Long minutes passed before he laboriously clambered to his feet. He could stand, but that was all. He tried to walk a few paces, but the pain was intense, shooting up into his spine. He couldn't put any weight on the injured limb, and he was breathing hard.

In anguish, he lay down again, shuffling around until he found the least uncomfortable position. What had looked a few minutes ago like a perfect day had become a nightmare.

What could he do? His immediate priority was to find some sort of sanctuary; a place that was peaceful. Somewhere he could recover and collect his thoughts. But he could barely walk, and could not leap over the tall garden wall that surrounded Eleni's home.

Delphos had no idea what to do next. His brain was scrambled. He could do nothing but wait and hope his leg recovered. The one crumb of comfort was that, deep though the bites had been, the leg didn't seem to be broken.

He tried to clear his mind of the events of the previous hour. But that furious, snarling face filled his head and wouldn't leave. He closed his eyes and tried to rest, but the horror of the attack dominated his thoughts. He needed to focus and concentrate on survival. His former friends would offer little help. With a shock, he realised Athens had, in the space of an hour, become a different city – alien and indifferent to his suffering. No longer was it a vast playground which revolved around his every whim. What other dangers lurked in the shadows?

He closed his eyes tight and tried to change his train of

thought. He knew of others who had suffered crippling injuries, yet survived. And there was Meg, who couldn't even see. He would be okay; he would not become a victim.

By the early hours of the following morning, he found he could place a little weight on the injured leg, and that allowed him to walk, although slowly and with a significant limp. The streets were silent, but he moved hesitantly, hugging the walls and trying to stay out of sight. Painfully slowly, he limped past familiar haunts back to the safety of the gang's base in the grounds of the Library of Hadrian, feeling sorry for himself. With movement this slow, he sensed danger around every corner. He was an easy target for any opportunist thug in the district, whether four-legged or two.

Back at headquarters, aching and exhausted, all he could do was find a quiet spot and pray for his leg to heal. Avoiding eye contact, he tried to ignore the looks he received, and the comments he overheard. There was scant sympathy from anyone.

Several hours later, with the sun high in the sky, he tried to walk again, testing his powers of recovery. To his dismay, he didn't get very far. One or two human pedestrians tutted or clicked their teeth at him, but none offered any practical support. Feeling sorry for himself, he pretended to ignore them and stared at the ground as if it held the answer to his prayers.

The following day he could hobble to the street where Eleni's house stood, in the vain hope he might make himself heard. He stood outside and yowled, but to no avail. The blank wall gave no response. Forlorn, he limped up and down until pain forced him to stop and rest.

He went back the day after, but this time, to his horror, he arrived to see Ion atop the wall, leaping down into the garden beyond. What was his brother doing there? What lies was he spreading?

A cold, tight knot formed where his stomach should have been. Bitter anger surged; a black fury that engulfed him. But he was powerless. Instead he waited, his resentment congealing into cold hatred as his imagination ran riot. He waited in the street, intent on having it out with his brother when he returned, injured or not. The hours passed until the last light of the evening faded before he finally gave up his vigil. His enemy must have left via a different route; perhaps across the rooftops.

Two days passed before Delphos confronted his brother. Ion lounged in a shady corner of their home turf, surrounded by several of his newfound friends.

Delphos hobbled towards him. Ion gave no outward sign of his approach, but others openly sniggered at his obvious discomfort. He ignored them.

"I saw you," he said, his temper rising. "Visiting her. You had no business going there."

Ion rolled onto his side, exuding indolence. He raised his head. "Well, well, well. If it isn't my long-lost brother." He matched Delphos' stare, meeting anger with cold detachment, then tilted his head back to address his companions. "You remember my brother, don't you? Once, he was the life and soul. Looks like he's fallen to earth with a bang." His spiteful gaze turned back towards Delphos.

"What were you doing?" Delphos said, his voice close to a snarl.

Ion turned back to his audience. "He's a bit the worse for wear. Do we allow cripples into our club?"

While the question hung, Delphos stepped forward until he was standing over him. "Well?"

"Well, what?"

"What were you doing?"

Ion considered the question. He made a show of looking

around, as if searching his memories, before raising his face towards his brother. "Fucking, I think."

Delphos stared at him. *He thinks I won't do anything. He thinks I'm too weak.*

He launched himself, biting and clawing, his injury forgotten. For a few seconds he had the advantage, his weight bearing down, his blows laden with purpose, at least from his forepaws. But they'd been evenly matched before his injury, and once Ion wriggled free, he could take advantage of Delphos' limited movement. He landed some blows of his own, and his hind legs dealt punches Delphos couldn't counter or avoid.

Panting hard, Delphos broke free. There was a wild look in his eyes, but he was wary now, eager to preserve his energy. Pain radiated from leg to hip, but he ignored it.

"He nearly had you there," drawled one of Ion's followers.

"Tut, tut," said another. "A cripple with a grudge. He's got a nasty temper, hasn't he?"

The taunts only added fuel to Delphos' anger. But to his surprise, his brother stepped back, preferring to play to his devoted audience. With one eye on Delphos, Ion half-turned towards them, adding to their taunts. "It's worse than that. He's a filthy dog-talker."

The group exchanged looks. Delphos stood taller, trying to understand this fresh insult, but failed to see its significance.

Ion played on his confusion. "Shocking, I know, but I've seen him. It happened once while we were over to the west."

Delphos stared at him with laser-like intensity.

Ion expanded on his recollection, feeding the interest among his supporters. Delphos listened with increasing dismay as one fabrication built on another.

"Yeah," Ion continued, "one mutt chased us and we left him in the dirt, but Plato here slows down and tries to reason with it." More looks exchanged between the other cats; they were lapping up all the lies. "Well, of course, I thought it was pointless. Everyone knows dogs are thick. You'd be better off talking to a bus."

The others seemed to find this amusing. Laughter rippled through the crowd. With his heart sinking, Delphos realised he'd become a source of entertainment. How much further would this go?

"Anyway," Ion continued, "to my surprise, the thing seemed to understand him. They exchanged some sort of garbled nonsense. Then, and you'll have to take my word on this, it backed away and trotted off." He turned fully towards his audience, gauging the reaction, before fixing Delphos with a stare.

"What did he say?" asked one of the group, agog.

Ion turned towards the questioner. "That's just it," he said. "I don't have a clue. I mean, who can understand dogs, let alone get them to follow instructions?"

There was renewed hostility in the glances sent Delphos' way, and now that Ion was in the middle of the group, there was little he could do.

Ion continued, warming to his theme. "And who knows what was passed between them? Do you think it's all 'how do you do?' and such?" He glanced back at his brother. "I think not. He could tell them anything about us. About our hang-outs. About our comings and goings. I mean, he might even be in league with them. He may prefer their company to ours. Perhaps that's where he spends his time these days?"

Insults and jibes followed Delphos as he hobbled away to try to find somewhere to be alone.

The days dragged. Delphos' leg was healing far too slowly for his impatient, bitter heart. Not only was he cut off from the one he loved, but the enforced separation made him yearn for her all the more. His desire was tempered as he thought about the evil his brother was spreading. Surely Eleni would ignore him. Send him away. Horrible doubts snagged his thoughts. Ion was much stronger. What if…?

Mired in inaction and infuriated by their recent encounter, Delphos tried to recollect his previous discussions with his brother. Ion had been off-hand with him for some time. He'd dismissed it as something his brother would eventually get over. But the sourness had turned into outright hostility. In recent weeks, the volume of sarcastic remarks he'd received from the others had increased. More recently, they had hardened into insults or, worse of all, silence from those he'd previously thought friends. Was this all coordinated? If he could walk more freely, he'd spend less time here. The only home he'd ever known had become unwelcoming. But he wouldn't be forced out.

Delphos could live with a few harsh words, but his brother's betrayal over Eleni hurt more. Ion's behaviour had gone beyond a family squabble. His taunts and barbs stung and lodged deep within. During the hot afternoons, while others slept, Delphos fretted and dreamt of revenge.

The summer passed. Elsewhere, during the midday heat, people sought shade or toasted themselves on beaches. In central Athens, they visited the sights, then sought refuge in the bars and cafés of the old town.

Delphos' leg continued its slow recovery. Would he ever be free of the dull ache that accompanied every attempt to break into anything faster than a walk? He could still barely jump, and he constantly fretted about Eleni and Ion. How much had his brother poisoned her mind? Would she still want to see him? Anger and resentment burned within on a long fuse, and in his persistent bad mood, even those gang members who remained friendly avoided him. Once a convivial soul, he became short-tempered, and ill feelings festered among those who suffered a tongue-lashing. Most of his former friends left him alone.

One day, curiosity mingled with resentment made him return to the site of his humiliation. He hung back in the shadows at the corner on the opposite side of the road. The café was quiet; few tables were occupied. There was no sign of his nemesis. It seemed strange. Unsure why he'd come, Delphos retraced his steps to more regular haunts. It was busier here; the cafés and restaurants bustled with life.

The next day, he went back and settled down in a quiet spot to watch for longer. Again, it was quiet. He could see no sign of the dog at first, but as he edged along the street, he spotted it lying just inside the door. With alarm, he saw one of the Plaka cats make a tentative approach. Hadn't the fool heard? Briefly, Delphos considered warning her, but that would mean breaking cover. He stayed in the shade on the opposite side of the street to watch the fireworks.

She approached a perimeter table, and the growling began. The dog shot out of the café, snarling and snapping, but was brought to an abrupt choking halt by a chain attached to his collar that was fastened somewhere just inside the door. A waiter appeared and yelled at the animal, tugging it back, and reluctantly it retreated, still giving the cat an evil look.

To Delphos' surprise, the human diners seemed scared of it. He watched them finish their drinks and pay, then leave. No wonder trade was slow.

Dog-talker, Ion's sycophants called him; their ultimate insult. Perhaps it was time to put his skills to effect.

CHAPTER 25
THE VISITOR

The visitor was as unwelcome as he was predictable. Where was Delphos? Eleni missed him. He'd become a feature of her days and the anticipation of his arrival left her constantly glancing up at the top of the wall to the spot where he usually appeared. His absences recently hurt so much. Had she offended him? If so, how? When would he come back? In his absence, she had to put up with increasingly frequent intrusions from the brute, Ion. He was rude and threatening. If only Delphos was here to see him off.

The fur on her back rose as Ion stalked the crest of the garden wall again. She fell into a reflexive crouch; the only suitable defensive posture. A brief glance towards the back of the house confirmed the door was firmly shut, and she had no way in. Eleni turned back to him, tracking his every movement in watchful dread.

Inevitably he jumped down to her level and walked towards her across the lawn. Eleni rose and cast another nervous glance towards the back door. Surely her human would sense something was wrong and open it? Where was she, anyway? The door remained closed and there was no sign of her human companion. She was alone with her visitor.

Ion didn't make any sudden move; he stalked her slowly and deliberately. Eleni realised he was enjoying this little game, relishing her discomfort. She could see it in his confident stride, in every muscle fibre, as he manoeuvred around the garden, blocking every hiding place or potential escape route. He was herding her into a corner near the wall.

Keeping her eye on him, she backed away, even though she knew there was nowhere safe to go. He kept on coming.

Eleni opened her mouth to issue a warning, but her tongue was dry, her throat constricted. She wanted nothing more than to run, but there was nowhere to run to. She looked left and right, trying to gauge the best escape route, but there were none.

Ion said nothing. He didn't have to; the intensity of his glare spoke volumes. Indecision kept her rooted to the spot.

Finally she made a move, but it was too late. Anticipating her moment, he pounced on her. A brief, unseemly scrabble served only to prove that she was no match for him physically. There was nothing she could do to prevent him mounting her and pressing his claim. In desperation, she twisted and spat, and as he bit the scruff of her neck she let out a furious howl of bitter protest.

At least that had some effect. A face appeared at the window, and a knock on the glass followed, breaking his concentration. But it was too little, too late.

Still, he clung to her, pressed her down beneath his larger body. The foul odour of his breath clung in her nostrils.

"That's just for starters, pretty one. I'll be back for more," he breathed in her ear. "Oh, and he won't be coming back to rescue you. He's gone forever."

Eleni's heart froze. What had happened out there, beyond the wall?

She found her voice. "What do you mean?"

Ion stepped back, gloating. "He's abandoned you. Left. After all his bragging, someone else must have made a move for him. Someone interesting enough to capture his attention. Either that or he's finally realised he's no longer welcome in these parts."

The back door opened, and the woman who shared Eleni's house emerged, making threatening gestures towards the intruder. Ion gave her a contemptuous glare and vanished. From the safety of the top of the wall, he glanced down at his victim, still frozen in shock.

"Till next time, sweetheart." He disappeared.

As if a spell had been broken, Eleni dashed indoors and ran to her favourite hiding place. She crouched in the comforting dark between the sofa and the wall, her thoughts and heart racing. It was several hours before she could be coaxed out into the open.

In one instant, her world had been turned upside-down.

Her garden, her peaceful sanctuary, had become a dangerous place.

CHAPTER 26
AN UNEQUAL CONTEST

Kratos and Zelus sniffed around the fallen blocks of masonry and weathered rocks at the entrance to the cave. Was this the right place? There was little to identify it from the illustration Kratos had seen in Theseus' book, but he had to admit the landscape had probably changed in the last thousand years. The sea had retreated a kilometre, as silt from the tumbling river sighed to a halt in the flat lands of the delta, free at last from the incessant force that had driven it here from the uplands. The old harbour had silted up, and a new marina for small pleasure craft was the main source of seaborne traffic.

The delta now supported a tightly packed jumble of intensively cultivated farms. The agricultural bounty was so valuable, space for housing was minimal. The remnants of an ancient Byzantine church were the only outward sign that an ancient trading city had once been here, nestled beneath the shelter of the cliffs. The only other sign was the rock-cut tombs, and the secret labyrinth behind.

The entrance to the subterranean network had once been blocked by the tumbled blocks and roughly hewn stones that lay untidily before its entrance. A faint noise from deep within the mountain brought both cats' heads up sharply. They shared a glance and stared into the dark. Hesitantly, they turned towards the back of the cave and walked into the shadows.

As his eyes adjusted, Kratos inspected his surroundings. The large block that lay diagonally across the floor looked to have been recently levered free from the back wall. The space it had occupied revealed a stone-cut doorway to a passage beyond, its edges still sharp and not yet smoothed by the ravages of time. In the dim light he could also see the marks on the wall where a crowbar had levered the block free.

Beyond, he sensed movement of air from deep within the mountainside, and once again the echo of faint, unearthly sounds from within. He looked at his brother, and Zelus stared back. Neither was keen to venture further into the blackness.

The sound came again. A rolling grumble, rebounding from the walls of the passageway before them; distant but insistent. It was the sound of groaning, outrage, and pain. The roar of an anguished beast? The braying trumpet of something awoken from a long slumber in the deep? They could delay no longer.

Zelus made the first move, heading through the gap behind the rocks and plunging into the darkness beyond. Cautious as ever, Kratos followed.

He was immediately reliant on senses other than sight, so sudden was the transition from dim light to no light. After a hundred metres, and with the light outside now nothing but a memory, his vision adjusted enough to make out a few dark shapes: the rough outline of the passage walls, and obstacles that littered the floor. His brother was just a short distance ahead.

As they moved on, the sounds of struggle became louder, amplified within the narrow confines of the space. A flash of light briefly illuminated the way ahead, imprinting the passageway on his retinas. The cats navigated a sharp corner, then another, progressing cautiously now in the near total darkness. Another flash of light helped them move forward, but soon the noise of the struggle was loud enough for them to navigate with eyes closed.

Further sudden flashes of light now illuminated the way, and behind them, a faint glow. After a few minutes, they came to the threshold of a larger chamber, and paused. Ahead, the floor descended into water.

They stood on the shores of a subterranean lake, the cave it occupied illuminated by a lantern placed against the far wall.

Above them, the roof receded into black. At the opposite side of the cavern, several massive boulders lay strewn, half submerged, by the far wall. Straddling two of these was a strange figure; man-like, but much taller, and with the head of a beast Kratos could not place. It had the snout of an anteater, but large pointed ears that reached above the crown of its head.

The figure was naked but for a long skirt, and wearing sandals. He bore a long spear which it thrust repeatedly towards a semi-submerged creature thrashing about in the water before him. The warrior was deft in his movements, springing from perch to perch, always maintaining perfect balance. But his weapon seemed inadequate for the task.

The monster he fought was bulky, with the enormous head and shoulders of a bull. Its forelegs thrust out of the water, trying to knock the figure from the rocks with long dangerous-looking horns that protruded from the top of its head.

Kratos was transfixed. Here, before him, was a creature from legend; a monster he'd completely forgotten about, and would have assumed extinct, but for his encounter with the elderly dead king. Even then, he'd scarcely believed the information he'd been given was accurate. But the evidence was now clear and standing before him; or rather slithering within the water.

He was looking at an extremely rare example, or possibly the only remaining specimen, of a beast of legend. An Ophiotaurus. Half bull, half serpent. This was what they had come to kill. But someone else had had the same idea.

Who to attack? The Ophiotaurus or the warrior it confronted? His brother held no such doubt. He leaped at the man-like figure, who saw the cat at the last minute; too late to bring his javelin to bear. Zelus caught him in the face, clamping his jaws either side of the long snout, just below the warrior's eyes. His momentum carried both of them backwards, into the shallow water beyond. The furious Titan's front paws anchored deep in his neck, his hind paws punching hard into the warrior's rib cage. They disappeared from Kratos' sight and he turned his attention to the creature the man-thing had been attacking.

With the fight interrupted he could get a clearer look at it, in the dim light. He marvelled at its size and power, but he could see it was wounded, and a familiar metallic scent reached his nostrils. Blood glistened on the creature's neck and shoulder. It was hurt, but trying to retreat into the depths, but was struggling to move within the confines of the space. Kratos caught a glimpse of snake-like coils sinking beneath the water.

He stared at its strange misshapen beauty, momentarily caught in a spell; but he was here to kill it, not admire it. He shook his head and tensed, ready to pounce, his fangs bared. The creature was the key to his besting of Athena, and he could not allow it to escape.

The Titan darted across the uneven ground and leaped, sinking his teeth deep into the creature's throat. The cave echoed as the monster gave a strangled cry, bellowing its anger.

Despite its size, the Ophiotaurus moved with surprising

speed as it rose from the lake and tried to crush the cat against a cascade of nearby rocks. But the Titan's hindquarters had a power of their own, and without losing the grip from his teeth, Kratos pushed away from them and launched the monster backwards, into the pool once more, simultaneously tearing a deep wound with his teeth. He spat out raw flesh, and burrowed deeper, oblivious to the creature's thrashing agony and the water engulfing them.

In desperation the Ophiotaurus thrust out of the water once again, and thrashed from side to side, hoping to dislodge its attacker. But Kratos clung on. Higher it rose, trying to smash down and smother its foe, but as it did so, a spear buried itself into its chest, below the neck. With one last bellow, the beast slipped sideways into the water, dead.

Cautiously, Kratos released his grip, and moved to stand on top of the creature. He turned. His brother stood a short distance away, on the shore of the lake, next to the warrior, the two of them having made peace. They looked remarkably friendly for foes who had, just minutes previously, been wrestling with each other.

The man-like creature addressed him. "Well met. I am Set, Lord of Chaos, God of night, true Pharaoh of Egypt."

Zelus stood next to him. "We share the same goal, brother."

Kratos' eyes narrowed. "We share nothing. This creature is our prize." He glared at the Egyptian god.

"It was my spear that pierced the creature's heart," said Set, leaping forward and taking hold of its shaft. He extracted his weapon and stood back.

Kratos could now make out his elaborate head-dress and linen skirt. Set's naked torso and calm features bore no sign of the struggle with Zelus. For a moment the three of them stood in silence.

The Egyptian spoke again, addressing Kratos. "Your brother tells me you want to bring down Athena and her family. I wish you well in your endeavour." He spoke lightly, as if delivering a motivational talk at a team meeting. There was no sign of resentment at Zelus' attack.

Kratos gave his brother a wary look. How much had he revealed?

As if reading his thought, Zelus stepped forward. "I just explained why we're here. No more."

Kratos looked Set in the eye. "We are here," he declared, slowly and purposefully, "for the entrails of this beast. We wish to remove them from him and take their essence for our quest."

The god tilted his head to one side. "And how, pray, might you do that?" He smiled, infuriating Kratos. But the Titan had no answer. That part of the plan was always going to be a problem. His idea had been to track down the elusive beast first, then return later with the means to gut it and take its entrails.

Set continued. "I came prepared." He gestured to the back of the cave. Beside the lantern lay a pack, next to which lay a large meat cleaver. "I have with me the tools for a spot of butchery, including not only the means to cut open the beast, but also several containers for its valuable innards." He walked swiftly over to his pack, and extracted three large Canopic jars, which he placed on the ground. "See?"

Kratos gave a deep growl from the back of his throat.

The Egyptian shot him a calculating sideways glance. "However, given the nature of your quest, I am prepared to share."

Kratos leaped from the carcass of the beast and stepped closer. He stopped before the Egyptian and looked up. "We accept."

His attempt to sound gracious was strained. From the corner of his eye, he noticed Zelus seemed pleased with the outcome. He would have words with his brother later.

Set nodded acknowledgement, then got to work with his

cleaver, opening up the creature's body and filling his jars as the two cats impatiently prowled the water's edge. Occasionally, Set flicked slivers of meat in their direction, which they caught in mid-air, consuming in single gulps. The meat was succulent, given the creature's age. He wondered at its sad existence, hiding in this cave all these years. But his thoughts soon drifted to practical matters; introspection was not his forte.

It was the fate of Athena and her fellow Olympians that filled his thoughts now.

The day of their demise had just been brought forward.

CHAPTER 27
THE INVISIBLE WOUND

The soreness and bruising soon faded, but for many days after, Eleni inhabited a dark place. She took to nuzzling the hand of the well-meaning woman who shared her dwelling place, but her displays of affection were half-hearted. What she wanted was someone, or something, to stop the endless replays in her mind of the scene of her humiliation in the garden. The memory was stoked with revulsion and despair. Why must brute strength always win?

She found fleeting comfort found from the familiar smell of the human hand cupped around her nose and alternately stroking her ears, but she lacked enthusiasm for proper inter-action with her human. Neither the ribbon nor the toy mouse interested her, although she was reluctant to let the woman stray out of sight. When the door to the garden was opened, she remained inside, watching with the intensity of a predator.

Her tormentor continued to visit. Every day, early in the morning, he appeared on the wall, scanning the shadows below. Eleni sat on the window ledge until he arrived, then hid, as if the dark would help banish him. Her anxiety increased if the back door was open; what if he ventured inside? She was certain he was bold enough. How could she ensure the door remained closed? Usually the woman liked it open, enjoying the breeze that would float into the house. Ensuring she opened the door was easy; Eleni only had to rub around her human's legs and look up at her. But now her signals were likely to be misinterpreted.

Sitting behind the sofa one bright autumnal morning, she pondered the best hiding places. From the garden the call of birds and the scent of late-blossoming plants was inviting, but Eleni preferred the dark. Her heart raced. Where was safest? Behind the sofa? Under the side table? Beneath the stairs? In desperation, she tried them all out, but nothing made her feel secure. Starting at the wall, her thoughts miles away, she returned to the day of her humiliation, her small body trembling at the memory. Shame was her constant companion. Shame that she hadn't been strong enough to oppose him, and disgust at herself for the way she allowed the thought of him to eat into every aspect of her life. She closed her eyes, but the unpleasant thoughts couldn't be banished. There was nothing she could do that would change the past.

She looked around, her eyes wide and wild, but there were no true hiding places from the fear that now permeated her waking thoughts. Eleni had become a prisoner in her own home. And Delphos had abandoned her. The one companion who could lift her out of this cycle of gloom was no longer around. He had gone and left her behind. Why? That hurt almost as much as his evil brother's repeated incursions into her outdoor space.

Ion's persistence prayed constantly on her thoughts; would he never leave her alone? As anger coursed through her, she ripped at every soft furnishing she could find – carpet, armchairs, cushions – but the reaction of her human was not the sympathy and comfort she so desperately sought. She simply picked her up and shoved her into the garden, accompanied by some harsh words.

From then on, Eleni was increasingly denied sanctuary, and she was forced to spend more of the days outside, even though the weather was becoming cooler and wetter.

The second attack happened a couple of days later and left her feeling worse. Once the door was finally opened, she shrank past the woman without a glance, keeping her distance – her slow, deliberate walk and downturned tail visible signs of her resentment. She'd been abandoned by the only one powerful enough to keep her safe. Eleni retreated to her usual hiding place and waited until hunger drove her to eat, choosing a time when the human was distracted and unlikely to notice. Right now, she wanted nothing to do with her.

As dawn light broke through the cracks in the blinds, she came to a decision. First, a mouthful or two to break her fast, then, as the door was opened and with scarcely a look back, Eleni left.

In one leap, she was on top of the wall, a huge new world spread before her; building after building, rooftops as far as she could see. Nearby were towering cliffs from a flat-topped hill. From her new perch, new scents and sounds reached her. The world was far bigger than she'd realised.

Eleni leaped down into the still-dark street below and made her way towards the source of the morning glow.

Her journey became an overwhelming assault on her senses: dogs, traffic, people, plants, shops, bars, restaurants and the occasional suspicious-looking cat. All came and went within that first hour, but she scarcely had any time to explore. It was the fear of being caught or followed that urged her on. Eleni didn't want anyone reporting her whereabouts to her tormentor. She was certain he would have a network of spies and was sufficiently paranoid to know they were all looking for her.

Across roads, through parks, over waste ground she went, desperate to put distance between herself and the place of her agony, until eventually, as the day wore on, she came to a quiet roundabout and a curving road with a strange flimsy-looking gate. Passing by, the noise of the city fell away to a faint background hum. She could hear the birds in the trees more clearly. Her mood lifted.

Onwards she strolled, then up a steep slope into inviting woods. There were scents to enjoy, and distractions to entertain. For the first time in her self-imposed exile, she relaxed.

At the top of the slope, she came to a paved courtyard encircled by a low wall with odd-looking buildings on three sides. A large black cat lounging in the shadow of a tree raised her head.

"Welcome," she said.

Eleni halted mid-step, beneath the scrutiny of yellow eyes, a front paw hovering above the ground. Hesitantly, she placed it down and glanced around, then attempted to look relaxed, as if she'd always planned to be here, all the time fretting about her unconvincing display. She cast a wistful glance over her shoulder, but hesitated, reluctant to leave.

The black cat seemed to read her thoughts. "No need to go." She rose to her feet, and took a few languid steps towards her visitor, head raised and nostrils flared as she absorbed the newcomer's scent. "I could do with some company."

Eleni looked her hostess up and down, still unsure. A small flame of hope flickered into life in her heart. "I would welcome that," she said.

"Come here, child," commanded the other. "Let me look at you."

Unused to being schooled, but unable to resist, Eleni advanced a few steps, her head bowed in greeting. Once she was close, she sat, curling her tail neatly around her, and scanned her surroundings once more, avoiding scrutiny of her hostess, as was polite. Words deserted her. She just waited.

"I am called Hecate," the black cat said, looking her guest up and down. "I've lived here quite a while. It's a nice, quiet place. A place of peace and tranquillity." She gave Eleni a sideways glance. "And healing. You are welcome to stay as long as you wish."

For the first time in weeks, the shadow that had settled on her like a heavy cloak lifted. Eleni mumbled thanks and, taking a lead from Hecate, found a quiet place beside a wall to curl up and sleep.

CHAPTER 28
YACHT

large black four-by-four waited near the entrance to the caves. As his eyes adjusted, Kratos glanced sideways, but could no longer see the huge Egyptian god. In his place stood a tall, elegantly dressed, olive-skinned man with curly dark hair and a neatly trimmed beard. In appearance, he was every bit the upscale tourist: loose-fitting white linen shirt and dark trousers with dusty tan desert boots. The glittering gold band of an expensive watch adorned his wrist.

He turned to his feline companions and smiled. "Max Stürme. Pleased to make your acquaintance." He nodded towards the vehicle. "Allow me to offer you a lift. I believe we have much to discuss."

Kratos and Zelus exchanged wary glances, but followed. Their companion held the precious cargo they had come so far to retrieve.

They hopped into the rear passenger compartment, the door held open for them by a well-dressed servant. A second man took the backpack from their host, and stowed it in the trunk, securing it with elastic ropes.

Stürme climbed in next to them. "My yacht is nearby. We can relax properly there and explore our options."

The journey was short – only five kilometres – and they soon pulled into a marina and transferred to a launch. A short distance offshore, a huge superyacht lay at anchor. Reflections from the water cast playful rippling patterns on the dark blue hull. Above, the gleaming white superstructure revealed several decks of opulent luxury and decadent living.

"This looks more like it," muttered Zelus in a throaty yowl that only his brother could hear. Kratos said nothing. He worried his brother was in danger of going soft. A luxury life-style was of little appeal; the raw power he'd briefly glimpsed in Athens was his only motivation now, and he was prepared to endure any hardship to regain it. He studied the fast-approaching ship with a mixture of suspicion and contempt.

A portal opened in the side of the hull: a garage for jet skis and a car. The launch tied alongside, and the cats jumped across, followed by their host. They set about exploring the afterdeck and stateroom. Cabinets were filled with bottles of exotic liquors, cocktail mixers and chilled wines. An array of glassware occupied the back wall, beneath expense artwork. Gold fittings and faux-nautical ornaments were everywhere. The centrepiece of the room was a large mahogany table loaded with charts and maps. A glass-fronted cabinet to one side held an assortment of ancient books. On the open deck to the rear, rows of loungers overlooked a small pool.

Their host gave them a minute to look around. "Please follow me, my lords," he said, with a slight bow, gesturing to a passageway at the forward end of the stateroom. The cats followed and were shown into a smaller room containing a conference table with chairs and little else. Without the view from the large window, they could have been in an anony-mous office building. Both cats leaped onto the table, sniffing at the pack which had been brought from the launch.

Stürme opened it carefully and extracted the Canopic jars, which he placed in the centre.

"Gentlemen," he said, looking at Kratos and Zelus, "we stand at a critical turning point in history." He stared at the three jars with reverence, unable to prevent himself reaching out to touch the nearest. "In these containers, we have the means to destroy our enemies once and for all. There will be no return from the Underworld this time." He looked at Kratos; the cat stared back. "The poison distilled from the blood of the Ophiotaurus is unlike any other. Among all the poisons of the world, it is the only one known to affect the bodies of those who, like us, are suffused with the essence of immortality. Death from this substance will be final." He sat back and pointed to the containers on the table. "Here, we possess the means to put an end to the tyranny of Olympus once and for all. We shall be able to produce enough material to eliminate every god on the planet." He looked at them, his face solemn. "Apart from those with whom we are allied, of course." A smile. He sat back.

Kratos was tempted to ask how the Egyptian had come across such knowledge, obscure as it was even to those of Greek heritage. But before he could say anything his host moved on.

"Of course, there is a process to undertake. We must refine the raw materials according to the exact prescription." He gestured to an antique book that lay on a nearby cabinet. "Here, we have the instructions as set down by the centaur, Chiron." He gave them both a meaningful look. "On the deck below I have prepared a small laboratory, suitably equipped for our purpose. Do you have any questions?" He searched their faces.

Zelus was first to speak. "Not so fast. We should declare our interests, and agree our goals before we embark on this venture." While his brother spoke, Kratos tilted his head to study Stürme's body language. He was an adept shapeshifter, as their exit from the cave system had shown. But his demeanour was smooth and relaxed. The cat considered other signals. Their host's scent comprised expensive cologne with a hint of salty sea air. But was there something else? Kratos' eyes narrowed in concentration as he sought to identify clues to an underlying marker, vague and hard to isolate. Could it be a pheromone he'd not come across before? He closed his eyes to concentrate, ignoring the conversation between the Egyptian and his brother.

There it was. When the cologne and the immediate environment was factored out, he caught the faintest whiff of decay, of something rotting. At the deepest level, beneath the surface glow, the hint of decomposing meat, of dead things, of death. He opened his eyes. Interesting. He appeared to be in the presence of a foreign deity closely associated with death and dead things. Perhaps he should take this character a little more seriously.

Stürme sat back and looked at him. He smiled and spread his hands in a gesture of sharing, then sat forward, elbows on the table, hands clasped before him. "Where shall we start?" There was a pause while the three gods looked from one to another. The Egyptian broke the silence. "Me first, perhaps?"

He hesitated once more, gazing out of the porthole to his left, apparently gathering his thoughts. The cats stared at him intensely. In the distance the mountains of the Turkish coast, barely two kilometres away, were half lost in the summer haze. The man turned to Kratos and Zelus once more, his voice somehow deeper. It filled the room as if surrounding them, carrying an echo from somewhere far away.

"As I said in the cave, I am Set, true Pharaoh of Egypt. It is my goal to wrest back the throne taken from me by the usurper Horus and his scheming mother, Isis. To reclaim it is my destiny and my birthright." He leaned forward, his expression grave. "But I am thwarted. Isis has banished me and maintains her spells against me. I cannot return while her power remains strong. It must be annulled. What is worse, she recuses herself, letting mere humans lead the country in her stead. She has become an abomination."

The god in human form looked from one Titan to the other, his expression earnest. "For many years I have laboured in exile to regather my strength and lay plans for my return. Over years beyond count, I began searching for the tools and equipment necessary to support my aims. Slowly, painstakingly, I tracked down the precious items they mislaid or discarded and forgot. The instruments of their power. Those absent-minded agents of the so-called just. As support waned for the once powerful and their fortitude wavered, my purpose only grew. I rode on a crest of anger and vengeance." He glared at the cats, his voice insistent. "They are decadent and dying already, their minds eaten from within as their worshippers disappear and the doubts grow. But too slowly. Today, they still have power, latent though it is." He paused, his brows furrowed, his eyes fixed on the table but not seeing it, instead reliving memories. "Carefully and steadily, I accumulated the instruments I need, one by one, bit by bit, hoarding them in a new fortress, out of reach of their former owners. While they grow powerless, I, after all this time, am close to achieving my goal." He raised his head, eyed both cats once again and nodded towards the three jars on the table. "This is one of the last remaining pieces of my plan."

Kratos eyed Zelus. Zelus stared at Kratos. Set looked from one to the other and back. Kratos was poised to say something when the Egyptian continued. "Of course, it helped enormously when the Greeks took themselves out of the game at an early stage. I have to give thanks to whichever of you made that decision." The fur on the nape of Kratos' neck rose and his face flushed with heat. He glared at his host, but the Egyptian god smiled back, insufferably smug. "It made my task much simpler. Without guardians, so many treasures are left exposed. As a result, I could secure an important clue.

An antique painting in a near-deserted monastery that held the information I needed to lead me directly to the cave, and our late target, whose entrails we have before us."

"And there was no one standing in your way?" Zelus' question sounded innocuous.

"No. There are none left to wield power." He stopped himself, considering. "Well, one perhaps. The old trickster. A rival. But he is from a different pantheon and less familiar with the terrain, perhaps. He is imprisoned deep beneath the earth, awaiting his own date with his idea of destiny. He, alone among his family, wields something akin to his old power. But he is imprisoned, and at such distance there is, surely, a limit to what he can do." Set stroked his chin, deep in thought. "Of course, were he to be released, true chaos would ensue." A glance at the other two, a twinkle in his eye. He lowered his hand. "A delightful thought, but premature. His enemies and mine might, I suspect, be broadly the same, but his goals are different. He wants to bring about the end of the world: I merely want to reclaim what is mine." Set sat forward, elbows on the table, his hands steepled before him, and smiled. "He is better left caged." He glanced at Zelus. "On the other hand, I suspect you and I are more closely aligned, and I am keen to hear your story. What brought about our fateful meeting?"

There was silence as the cats cast their eyes to the table between them, and then to the three large jars at the far end. Their host sat back and crossed his legs, waiting.

Kratos gave Zelus a long look. Neither brother was keen to talk. "It's a long story," he said at last.

"Aren't they all? All the best ones, at any rate. Pray, carry on." Set looked relaxed, benign even.

Haltingly, and with occasional interruptions from his brother, Kratos told the story of the war against Athena, and his burning desire for revenge against the younger generation of gods who had led him to this parlous state. He made no mention of his theft of the artefact, and glossed over his defeat and imprisonment, other than a mention of his meeting with Theseus, and the secret knowledge in his library. Those books carried clues and intelligence, long forgotten in the Overworld, of the existence and whereabouts of a beast once thought lost: the Ophiotaurus.

Kratos remained modest when discussing his escape; how easy it had been to fool Sisyphus and how straightforward he found it, as a Titan, to roll the boulder up the steepening incline. With a clear goal in mind and renewed purpose supported by his newfound knowledge, all he needed to do was rendezvous with his brother and set about the mission to kill and eviscerate the beast, and use the poison extracted from its entrails to destroy his immortal foes once and for all.

Set studied him for a moment. "So yours is purely a mission of revenge?" he asked.

"There is more to it than that." Zelus, settled on the table-top, addressed the Egyptian god.

The Egyptian say forward, suddenly engrossed. "Go on."

Kratos stared ahead, impassive. Put on the spot, Zelus looked uncomfortable. "My goal; our goal, of course, is nothing other than to recover all that we once had," he said, after a pause. "With Athena and her followers out of the way, we can plan for our return." He faltered.

Set looked at him gravely, mouth pursed. "And how do you propose to do that?"

Kratos spoke up, ignoring his brother. "There are ways, of that you can be certain." He sat upright and said no more, staring at Set. Was that a suspicious look on the Egyptian's face? Set looked from one to the other, as if trying to read them.

"Do you think she anticipates your return? No doubt she has her own networks and surveillance in place?" He leaned forward, elbows on the table, hands clasped, concern written on his face.

Kratos stared back, keen to close this line of enquiry. "I doubt it, from what my brother has said. Zeus no longer choses to confide in his daughter." In an attempt to change the subject he stretched out a paw, and arched his back, as if bored with the conversation, then sat upright and looked around the room, peering into the corners in curiosity. "Complacency will be her undoing, I am sure."

For several long seconds Set and Kratos held each other's stare, until Zelus rescued the situation.

"So how do we develop this poison?"

The Egyptian was smoothly diplomatic once again. "Rather than do anything in haste, perhaps the best way forward is to formalise our relationship. I propose to draw up a treaty between the three of us." Suspicion still clouded Kratos' mind, but he nodded assent. Set continued.

"We have clear goals that are not dissimilar, and are agreed on the immediate aim: the elimination of the Olympian generation, starting with Athena, and for my own more modest purposes, the liquidation of certain minor Egyptian deities. The poison we propose to distil will be shared between us for our own individual use." He looked from one cat to the other, seeking assent. Apparently satisfied, he went on. "If, in the course of our endeavours, we unearth any potentially useful items of power we shall agree to use them to mutual benefit, eradicating any who get in our way. Is that agreeable? Once Athens is free of the remnants of your Olympian relatives, you will have a suitable base from which to operate, and we will all be able to move more openly and rapidly."

"Any agreement must be sworn on the Styx," Zelus insisted.

"Not so fast," Kratos was suspicious. "We have no interest in sharing such *tools* as we discover or retrieve." He gave his brother a warning glance. Before Zelus could say anything, Set stepped in.

"Of course, there are items in my own archive that might be useful to you? I would be willing to share, if you will."

"That sounds fair to me," said Zelus.

Kratos was unconvinced. Reluctantly he gave his consent. "On a case-by-case basis only," he grunted, and settled down on the polished surface.

From the corner of his eye, he noted Zelus brighten at his apparent concession, pleased to be moving forward once more. Planning and positivism was his forte. Kratos' own preoccupation was a little more sour. At some stage, he would need to wrest control of the artefact from all of them – Zelus included – if he was to rule unopposed. He realised Set was expounding on methodology and forced himself to concentrate.

"As I said, I have installed a laboratory aboard this craft, one deck below us. There, we can safely burn the entrails of the beast and distil their essence into a powerful potion that we can then split and use to pursue our various goals."

Kratos sought to interject a note of caution. "Do you have the recipe?" Set looked blank. The Titan revelled in his small victory. "Among Theseus' many books, I came across a detailed recipe for preparation of the potion. It is very particular and requires the mixing of additional herbs under specific conditions. If we get the quantities wrong, or forget the enchantments, it will be useless." He looked directly at the Egyptian. "How's your ancient Greek?"

Set held his gaze, taking him seriously, Kratos suspected, for the first time since they'd met.

"I did, of course, take the precaution of memorising the details," Kratos added.

A few seconds passed before the Egyptian god regained his composure. He smiled and spread his hands.

"Come, gentlemen. We should celebrate our achievements, our partnership, and our future endeavours. Let me organise something to toast our success."

Kratos eyed him, beaming like an indulgent Santa Claus on Christmas Day, barely a couple of kilometres offshore from the reputed home of the original. He would remain wary of the Egyptian's ever-changing moods.

Set rose to his feet. "I'm afraid I have no ambrosia. Would a bowl of finest malt whisky suffice?"

CHAPTER 29
THE TRIAL

Days morphed into weeks and Delphos' incapacity barely changed. With every attempted exertion, the pain in his leg flared into agony, forcing him to stop. He despaired of ever recovering, and his enforced separation from Eleni stabbed at his gut. His resentment festered and boiled.

But little by little the peaks of discomfort shrank until finally they subsided to a dull ache, which gradually faded until he barely noticed it. Sudden movement could send shooting pain up into his spine, so he became calmer in his actions, gradually building up speed rather than sprinting from a standing start. The ability to jump took longer to return. He still lacked the explosive power to reach the top of the wall that enclosed his and Eleni's garden, as he thought of it.

Every few days he would make another attempt, but fall short. The top was getting closer, but for now remained tantalisingly out of reach. Turning back down the street, he speculated on what he'd do when he succeeded. Could he return, or would he be trapped? Perhaps he could stay with her, even if it was only for a few days. He let his imagination drift until he was soaking up all her adoration, perhaps playing up the extent of his injury for added attention, before tumbling together in ecstasy and indulging to their heart's content. With eyes closed, he let his thoughts roam as they wished, meandering through one scenario after another, as they took endless pleasure in each other's bodies before sleeping together in utter contentment. How he missed feeling the gentle pressure of her head on his shoulder, her sweet and subtle breath in his ear. He could share her food bowl and tell her endless stories about his adventures – even if he had to make them up – and never worry about anything ever again. It would be bliss.

Waking from such vivid daydreams tested his patience to the limit.

Finally, the day came when he succeeded. He had to scrabble with his hind paws while clinging to the top of the wall with his forelegs, a look of grim determination on his face. But he made it. He was back.

But where was Eleni and the welcome he sought? With dismay, he surveyed the garden below. It was smaller than he remembered, and it was empty. Delphos leaped down, wincing with pain on landing, and stalked the limits of the enclosed space. No food or water bowl stood by the door into the house. There was no sign of Eleni's scent on any of the places she used to rub against. She had gone. He sat in the middle of the lawn, bereft.

With an effort, he made it back out again and wandered the familiar streets on autopilot, his thoughts circling in a whirlwind of despair. Central to the mix was an increasing resentment towards the beast that had injured him, now chained up in the nearby restaurant. He would visit the moron and goad it for all he was worth. His sport would be the spittle-flecked muzzle of the psychopath straining on the end of his chain, terrifying away all human diners. That would at least allow him some petty satisfaction.

Delphos navigated the streets with purpose. He avoided other gang members, refusing eye contact with those he recognised, until he arrived at the irregular square with the restaurant. Without pause he approached, perversely pleased to see that the dog was still there, lying just inside the door, the chain looped beside him on the ground.

"Hey, braindead," he shouted. "Wanna chase?"

His enemy turned and growled, but there was no real heat in the reaction. He refused to rise to the bait.

"Clear off."

Delphos stopped amid the forest of table legs and studied his opponent. "Did they cut your legs off when they chained you up?" he taunted.

The dog glowered back, but made no response.

Delphos made a show of looking the animal up and down. "Perhaps they took your courage along with your balls."

This drove the other animal to his feet, snarling.

"That's better," Delphos goaded. "Is it taking longer to get in touch with your inner psycho?"

Rather than lunge at him, the dog took a few calm steps forward. "Have you got a death wish? Care to come closer and tell me all that?" He paused, glowering. "Maybe it's just the ginger ones."

Delphos started. "What's that?"

The dog advanced another couple of steps. "Deaf and daft? I said maybe it's just the ginger ones who have a death wish."

"What do you mean?"

The dog halted, panting and snuffling. He raised his head so he could look down on the cat – although the height difference between the two was not significant – and sniffed ostentatiously. "Yeah," he muttered, "you're the one I got the taste of. The other one talked his way out of it, but he told me you were more gullible."

Delphos' eyes narrowed. "Told you what?"

The dog gave a snuffling sound and turned back to its resting place. "I should never have listened to him."

Delphos moved closer, all of his attention focused on the retreating rump of the other animal. "What did he say?" he repeated.

The dog reached its resting place and slumped to the ground again. Delphos sensed it was pleased with itself. He could see from the look on its face, it was delighted to have the upper hand against this smart-ass cat. To be the custodian of information the cat wanted. Delphos let the feeling wash over him; he wanted answers.

He waited.

The dog gave him an appraising look. "Getting one up on a rival is a pretty serious business in this city, isn't it? And there I was, just thinking it was us dogs who do each other down." He watched, but Delphos made no move, still fixated on what the other had to say. Relishing the attention, the dog continued. "He promised me fame and fortune, at least with the humans I look after. He told me they would treat me well. But just look what happened." A glance at the chain, snaking on the ground next to him. "All I got was a beating and a chain. Last time I listen to one of you golden-tongued liars."

"And how would you get this fame and fortune?" asked Delphos.

The dog gave another throat-clearing snuffle and looked at him as if trying to decide what to say. "He warned me about a lookalike. You're a pretty close match, but you smell different." Delphos held his breath. "Said you needed taking down a peg or two, perhaps permanently. I knew that killing you probably wouldn't go down well with the humans, but who's going to turn down a chance to lay down the law with a bloody cat?" The dog was mocking him now, pleased with itself. The large jowly head glanced towards the restaurant's deserted interior, then back outside. "Doesn't like you much, does he?"

But Delphos was already walking away.

He returned to the familiar street that enclosed Eleni's garden, stalking the streets in cold fury. Other cats did their best to stay out of his way. He returned to the top of the wall to study the garden below, looking for clues to show where she might have gone; all the while knowing it was futile. He descended to make a closer inspection, criss-crossing the familiar space, nose to the ground.

Eleni's favourite patch of grass in the far corner was unflattened. There was no sign of her; the garden looked pristine and abandoned. He could find no scent or sign of her anywhere. In despair, he stood in the middle of the lawn. Where had she gone?

"*Such a shame*," came a familiar sneer from above. Ion peered down at him. "She's probably off to deliver my litter somewhere quiet."

Delphos glared up at him with eyes narrowed, murder in his heart.

"I hope she takes good care of them," his tormentor continued, sauntering along the top of the wall.

"What have you done?" said Delphos.

Ion approached the flat roof of the neighbouring property, performed a delicate leap, and surveyed his brother once more from his higher perch, then disappeared out of sight. Delphos tried to follow, but it took him two attempts to reach the top of the garden wall; his hindquarters still lacked their former strength. By the time he'd made it, breathing hard and feeling light-headed, his brother was gone.

Delphos stared down at the garden, thoughts tumbling through his head. What had Ion done? Where had Eleni gone? Fury bubbled in his brain, clouding his ability to think. Stupefied, he scanned the horizon, barely taking anything in.

She would want to stay away from the gang's headquarters, but would she even know where it was?

He stayed there, staring into the distance as the sun set and the stars appeared. At length, he moved, stretched his back and glanced about once more, as if the silent buildings or distant stars would yield him solutions.

Frustrated, Delphos made his way slowly back to headquarters, determined to get answers from the one animal he knew had all the information.

"Treason is such an ugly word, my friends." Ion paused, his eyes flicking around the assembled beasts. "But when it comes down to it, that is what we face." He turned his head towards Delphos, sitting a metre to his right.

"Don't be ridiculous," he spluttered.

Facing his brother, his amber eyes ablaze, Ion revelled in the moment, his audience hanging on his next breath. Delphos had arrived back at the gang's base simmering with righteous fury, only to find his brother already waiting with a crowd of adoring sycophants sitting about as he stoked himself into anger.

Ion goaded him, imitating the accent of an entitled house cat, extending his vowels in a drawl of expectation, rather than the clipped speech of a street dweller. Delphos could scarcely believe the change in his brother. It was as if someone had been coaching him.

"What did you do to her?" he yelled.

Ion paused, adopted a look of astonishment. He leaned towards him. "Her? Who are you talking about?"

"Eleni," said Delphos. "Where is she?"

Ion turned back to his adoring audience. "And there you have it," he said, glancing back at his victim but addressing the wider congregation. "The manipulative behaviour of the sociopath. Deny, obstruct, pretend. Create an alternative version of reality. The sort of devious behaviour that sows discontent and creates division, when we should be united." He took a step closer. "But this time it won't work, because we all saw the facts for ourselves."

"What are you talking about?" said Delphos.

Ion pounced on his confusion with glee. "Forgotten already? That dog incursion last week? More have been spotted by Hadrian's Arch just this morning. Old Lena was attacked. Savagely. Some humans have taken her away. Heaven knows what's happened to her. Thankfully, the attackers were turned away before they could hurt anyone else. But the question is, who attracted them here?"

"Don't be ridiculous." The realisation dawned on Delphos: he was being framed. But why?

Ion's face hardened. "Like I said. Deny, obstruct, pretend you know nothing about it." He stepped closer.

Delphos tore his eyes away from his brother and frantically searched the assembly for sympathy. The closest he found were those who looked away in embarrassment. Where were the wise voices? Surely they must realise they were being played?

He found a familiar face amid the crowd. "Roxy," he pleaded, "you know this is all nonsense. Tell them." It was undignified, and he hated himself, but the situation was spinning out of control, and fear had a firm grip on his insides.

Roxy stared back impassively, then glanced aside. "He talks with dogs," she said. "I've heard him doing it. Though heaven knows what they were saying."

"No, I don't."

She returned a sharp look. "I was there," she said, her voice raised in righteous indignation. "Saw you talking to the dog on the chain. Don't deny it."

At his side, Delphos heard the bass vibrations of a purr, and glanced left. Ion's face bore a self-satisfied look. He had lost.

"He's done it more than once," said another.

"Aye." A voice from the back.

"Dog lover," spat a third.

"This is a stitch-up," he yelled, but by now no one was listening. A cacophony of cat-calls and outraged yowls filled the late afternoon air in the Library of Hadrian. The ancient stones loomed above them, as if leaning in to hear the outcome of the show trial.

Ion remained impassive until the noise died down. He waited until all eyes were focused on him. "I don't know about you," he began, his voice barely audible to those at the back, "but to me, holding congress with our ancient enemies and having the gall to do so here in our midst, in an area where their packs are forbidden to enter, is a crime." Louder now, his voice echoing between the stones. "What plots were being hatched? When was our position going to be usurped by these savage, slavering groups?"

Delphos cast his eyes over the throng. Ion was calm and controlled, but among the crowd, Delphos detected too many danger signals: ears twitching, tails slashing, poisonous looks in his direction. At the rear of the gathering, one or two were sufficiently agitated to stand and pace back and forth, their minds already made up.

His brother finished his speech. "The evidence is clear," he said, voice raised. "The only question is, what to do about it?"

Delphos sensed a victorious look in his direction, but he ignored it, staring straight ahead over the top of the crowd.

"Banish him!" came a call from the front.

"Kill him!" from further back.

"Send him away!" said another.

"Forever!" added a fourth.

All the while, Delphos stood still, watching his brother from the corner of his eye, but paying more attention to the cats surrounding him. He tried to make sense of it all. How long had this been planned? The petty insults washed over him, but the betrayal of those he regarded as friends and allies was agony. He'd returned wanting answers, only to find himself the subject of the worst kind of trial, betrayed by the brother who had once been his closest, most inseparable friend; the animal he would have trusted with his life. Those days were gone: their relationship had long ago turned sour. But he had still expected support from those he'd grown up with, those he still regarded as friends. What had happened to them? Had all of them really turned against him?

Delphos' heart filled with a burning rage, fuelled with a flame imperishable. Through narrowed eyes, he glared at his accusers. His brother was still speaking.

"Execution might be extreme," Ion drawled, his eyes glinting in the dim light. Delphos suppressed the urge to lunge at him, slash at his face and remove that smug expression, but he knew it would be futile, surrounded as they were by Ion's closest followers. He said nothing, but the fur stood proud along his back, and his bushy tail spoke volumes: a potent combination of fear, anger and the adrenaline coursing through his veins. He glared once more at those nearest to him. Let one of them make the first move…

Perhaps sensing Delphos had reached the point of no return, Ion took a couple of steps away from him, and concluded his address to the crowd now baying for blood. "Exile seems appropriate. I'm sure you all agree." Not waiting for a response, he hopped down into their midst and rubbed his chin on the head of an adoring female in the front row, then bunted against another supporter to the other side. Delphos watched him with a detached fascination. When had Ion become a politician? How had he learned to manipulate the mob like this? A sharp nip to his flank brought his reverie to an end.

"Time to go," growled a scarred enforcer.

"On your way," said another, his mouth contorted by some disease of the jaw.

"We'll escort you," said a ragged-eared mobster.

Delphos shrugged them off and spun around to confront them with fangs bared, hissing fury.

"Go on," they urged. "Over there. You know the way."

Outnumbered but mustering what remained of his dignity, he left, accompanied by the trio along the silent streets. Padding along, resentment roiled inside him; but beneath the anger, Delphos searched for understanding. He'd been outmanoeuvred without even realising there was a contest; outfought before he'd even realised he was in a fight. This was no spur-of-the-moment decision; how long had it been planned? What cold calculation had driven his brother to such extremes? How could he get even when he didn't understand the rules of the game, or who he was up against? Of one thing he was certain: Ion could not have done all this himself, unless he'd completely misunderstood his litter mate.

Behind him, and to the side, his tormentors urged him on, occasionally snarling insults to goad him. Delphos ignored them. The greatest insult had already been delivered.

Ahead, on a restaurant table at the side of the street, sat a still figure etched in shadow, eyes glinting in the yellow glow from the streetlamps above. Until he drew close, Delphos didn't realise the cat was real.

"A moment of your time," it said, addressing them all. Delphos halted, curious. His escort, unwilling to contradict the speaker, also stopped.

It was Jason of Delphi, the outsider who'd always remain such, even though he had joined the gang before Delphos had been born. What was he doing here?

Delphos narrowed his eyes and looked up at the other animal.

Jason stared impassively down. "Brotherly conflict is never pretty," he said, "but while you bemoan your fate and ponder who it was that helped shape him into the leader he has become and why, reflect on this. Revenge, even if it were possible, will not save you or heal your wounds. A fresh start might. A small black-and-white cat passed this way not a week ago, heading east beyond the gardens. Listen to your heart, son of Apollo. For you, just like your father, salvation lies in love, not hate. Look forwards, not back."

Jason gave him a lingering look, then jumped from the table and disappeared down a dark alley. Delphos stared at the space he'd occupied.

"Move it," came the command from behind, accompanied by another nip. The temptation to fight all three had never been so strong, but he gritted his teeth and marched on, shoulder blades in rhythm, eyes fixed forward, head slung low in a predator's prowl. Delphos' thoughts were less on a fresh start, nor revenge, but on something else Jason had said.

Who was Ion's helper? Who was behind his brother's transformation from simple opportunist to cunning manipulator? Ion could never have achieved such a transition by himself. He'd staked out Eleni, then hounded her and driven her away. He'd arranged the dog attack to render him incapable, all the while developing his contacts within the gang and bringing them under his influence. Finally, he'd acted, driving him into exile on trumped-up charges of treachery. It had been all to get him out of the way, so Ion would have no rivals.

As his understanding grew, so did the need for careful planning.

Delphos paid no heed as his escort stopped at the edge of their territory. He didn't break stride and didn't look back as he crossed the wide avenue, heedless of the night-time traffic. He was already brooding on something else Jason had said.

Son of Apollo.

Given their earlier discussion, was that a message?

Delphos' thoughts turned to the future. A future without Ion.

CHAPTER 30
THE VOICE

Beneath the trees of the National Gardens, Delphos found temporary sanctuary. Here, providing he avoided the gardeners and tourists, he could think and brood. At first, all his thoughts were bleak. Anger still coursed through every fibre of his being. The night passed, but he was too angry to prowl, too animated to sleep, too infuriated to hunt. Instead, he crouched, or paced the dark lawns and between the shadowy trees.

Again and again, he turned Jason's words over in his mind. He had a point. He should look to the future, not dwell on the past. But the injustice he'd experienced had a firm grasp on his heart. He yearned for Eleni, but thirsted for revenge. It was not a choice; he could have both. Remove Ion from the Plaka, and once it was safe, travel east, beyond these gardens, find his love and bring her back in triumph to sit beside him at the heart of the city; a beautiful queen alongside the Plaka's new king. Previously, he'd never thought about leading or guiding others or holding power over them. But now he yearned to hold sway over the faithless the way his brother had done: to have them bend to his will, for once. To settle scores. They would learn to answer to him and him alone, and Ion would be the one facing a lonely exile.

His thoughts crashed to earth. He was alone, friendless, had no idea where Eleni was, and had no allies who could help him win back his former position of influence. He scanned his surroundings. It was early; the new day just born. The gardens were peaceful at this hour, but that did little to soothe his racing thoughts. Where had Eleni gone? He had never visited this place until now, and he was dismayed to see the city extended far beyond their furthest edge. Its scale was daunting.

Delphos glanced behind him, towards the familiar streets he called home, now hidden behind dense banks of vegetation. Should he carry on his futile quest, or abandon the chase? A wave of self-pity washed over him and he closed his eyes tight until the despair eased. *Think.* Where would she go? Eleni knew nothing of the city beyond the confines of her small, enclosed territory. Desperation had caused her to flee.

The realisation brought another flush of burning anger as he imagined the injury his brother had inflicted. A litter? Bile surged in his throat, almost choking him. Delphos narrowed his eyes against the low easterly sun and looked ahead to set his direction.

But even as he moved, he heard a voice. No, not heard. *Sensed.* As if the speaker were residing in his own head. He stood still, eyes wide, fear washing through him from nose to tail. What was happening? Was he going mad?

"There is no salvation to be had from returning. You should run."

He spun on his tail, searching for the speaker. The voice was melodious, female, persuasive. Who was it?

It came again.

"Your future does not lie in the soft green garden. Yours is a harder path. But the reward will be all the greater."

"What?" he said, although there was no one he could see.

"The trail is cold. You will not find her."

The matter-of-fact tone riled him. Frantically he spun around once again, but there was no other creature nearby apart from a distant park keeper raking the ground.

"Where are you?" he screamed, incensed and afraid. Was he losing his mind?

"Forget her. She is not part of your story. She will fail you, or you will fail her. Your fortune lies in a different direction."

"No."

The voice became softer, a note of persuasiveness entered its timbre.

"I see you are stubborn. I should have expected as much. I understand. Attachments can be strong. Your affection towards her reflects well on you, but that time is over. You should seek pastures new."

Delphos halted, hardly daring to breathe. Was this a negotiation?

"Head south to the sea. There you will find unclaimed territories. Enough to appease even the most determined petty king. You can live as grand a life among your kind as you would ever wish. There, you might even emulate your brother. But heed what I tell you. She is gone beyond my sight. You will not find her again."

"Who are you?"

"You may think of me as a well-wisher, but who I am is unimportant. Who you are, or can be, should concern you more. Think of me as a guide to set you on your way."

"A guide?"

Silence. He shook his head, as if to banish the strange intruder from his thoughts. What kind of riddle had been set? He scarcely dared breathe, hoping it had gone. No such luck.

"What is it to be? The enfeebled lover, forever hiding? Or the bold leader. A prince among felines, beloved among his people, favoured by the gods?"

Was there subtle mockery within that tone? It fed his resentment. "Gods? Don't taunt me with Erichthonius' nursery tales. If they ever existed, they abandoned us long ago."

A peal of laughter, brittle and distant. The voice returned, more insistent now.

"The road ahead of you is forked. Follow my advice and choose the path to an easy future and a good life, or take the other and embrace bitterness and all that entails. The choice is yours."

Several minutes passed. His future hung in the balance while he stood in statue-like stillness. The voice had departed. Delphos exhaled. He was alone with his thoughts once more.

A decision formed at the back of his mind, born of a clarity he'd not had before; a product of the Voice. With every second it hardened, and with it, a purpose grew. He turned and took a hesitant step back the way he'd come. Then another and a third.

Delphos retraced his steps through the morning traffic to the borders of the land he'd always known, with thoughts of vengeance rekindled in his heart.

CHAPTER 31
BAR-ROOM BRAWL

A short distance from Adrianou Street, the shadows deepened and an unnatural chill added bite to the late-night air. A brief flash of red-orange fire burst the only lamp in the vicinity, plunging the street into deeper darkness with a fizzle and pop, accompanied by the tinkle of debris hitting the cobbles. Silence enveloped the district; a rare blanket of un-sound, watchful and fearful, wrapping the locale with the antithesis of peace.

Blind Meg, enjoying an evening stroll along a familiar street, crouched beside a wall, suddenly disoriented. She navigated the permanent darkness of her world using markers of scent and sound, hesitant touch and taste, all of which were overlaid upon the map held subconsciously at the back of her mind. But the silence that enfolded her was unsettling. An electrifying tingle of fear stood her fur on end and froze her to the spot. She sensed *something* nearby, and for once, her sharpened sense of smell evaded her. In her stupor, she did not understand the danger.

Disoriented, Meg halted, trying to reconnect with that inner chart she used to guide herself around her familiar haunts. Normally she could navigate almost as well as the sighted, but her mind's eye was blank. The background babble of conversation, shouts, laughter, argument and music that accompanied human nightlife had been snuffed out. Barely fifty metres away, it continued unabated, but Meg was enveloped beneath a blanket of dread thrown across the street.

She moved her head the way a sighted animal might, to try to sense the drift of air through her whiskers rather than affect to see.

A subtle shift from her right, not far away now, made her muscles tense.

She prepared to flee.

Outside the bar on the corner, the patrons shivered in a blast of unexpected cold. They rubbed their bare arms, slipped into coats and huddled closer. But their conversations continued.

Half a metre from the corner, Ion sensed an entirely different vibe. One that was outside his experience. Ahead he saw Meg, crouched in a defensive position, trying to make herself as inconspicuous as possible. Behind her, he detected movement in the shadows; a rippling flow of unnatural darkness that seemed to reach up to the sky to snuff out the stars. He, too, was rooted to the spot. Whatever was there, it was coming closer.

He should have called out; yowled to Meg to flee towards him and escape. He could have even darted in to grab her by the scruff of the neck. But he didn't. Instead, he watched her indecision as the sightless eye sockets of the truthsayer moved here and there, trying to make some sense of this new development.

Ion's eyes flicked from Meg to the dense, roiling shadow and whatever it contained. The presence was clearer now, but not much. Within the dark cloud, he sensed wings and was transfixed. Tall and wide, they spanned the street from wall to wall, and between them, the blurred outline of a head emerged. He saw eyes: red pools within blackness, burning with hunger. They scanned in his direction, flicking hate towards him.

He recoiled. There was still time. This thing was far enough away for him to reach Meg, grab her and escape. But how quick was it? Ion hesitated, and the moment was lost. The creature moved closer.

The truthsayer's indecision ended. With a leap, she tried to escape. But it was far too late. Ion watched her spring as the darting movement of a long, bony hand grasped her midriff then drew her up to the creature's mouth. There was a horrible sucking noise, and Meg let out a tiny, shrivelled scream as a pale wisp of white mist left the cat, drawn into the dark nothingness of the creature's face.

Then the monster discarded its morsel and moved on.

Ion was rooted to the spot, paralysed by fear. Ahead of him lay the body of Meg lying at the side of the alley, moving feebly, but without purpose. He watched her ribs rise and fall as she breathed, but there was no coordination to her movement.

Ion fled.

Behind him, unsatisfied by the tiny morsel of psychic energy just consumed, the demon sought a more substantial meal.

It was typical of its kind: a creature of darkness, scion of malevolent gods, a temporary escapee of Hades' realm. Enshrouded in shadow, it was difficult to spot, its presence far easier to feel than see. Those who dared look would note an elongated face – a melted mockery of human form – with pointed ears positioned high on a scaly black head, either side of a central ridge of protruding diamond-shaped scales that ran down its spine. A mouth fixed in a permanent sneer held a darting forked tongue, used mainly to taste the proximity of likely prey on the night air. The monster's nose was a mere hole beneath two glowing red eyes that burned with vengeful fury. Two part-folded leathery wings protruded from the creature's shoulders.

It was a biped, with legs bent backwards, like the hind legs of a horse, rather than a human, and it seemed unsteady on its hooves, kicking petulantly at anything nearby in an attempt to stand on solid ground.

Demons were among Hades' most feared enforcers. They were mostly found in the darker, more remote reaches of his realm, apart from those who enlisted as torturers, or enforcers in his guard, or those selected to supervise the work gangs. Some found employment tormenting prisoners in Tartarus. Others he kept as messengers. They travelled throughout his varied realm, though none were permitted to enter Elysium or the Isles of the Blessed. Under the terms of his unwritten agreement with Zeus, nor were they allowed to visit the world of the living, unless their master wanted to make a point. For the most part, Hades kept his word, and demon incursions remained rare. When they occurred it was always at night. Sunlight was as lethal to them as arsenic to any living creature, but acted far more quickly on their shadow-bound complexion.

They thrived on the fear of those they encountered, spreading it like foul breath on the night air, infecting all nearby.

Along Adrianou Street, the restaurants were winding down for the night, but the bars were packed, with people spilling out onto the pavement, and nearby clubs were thronged with revellers. Trade was brisk, and the district hummed with the sound of life: loud conversation, laughter, the clinking of glass.

The creature emerged from an alley: tall, menacing, with a voracious appetite for the fresh psychic energy of nearby living souls. It flicked its tongue and grinned, in anticipation of a feeding frenzy. The many-jointed bony fingers of its right hand clutched a fire whip which uncoiled, hissing and smoking on the cobbles. With a deft flick, a line of flame flashed forth, snapping a nearby streetlamp from the wall as the demon stepped out of the alley. The street dimmed into deep darkness, distant lamps unable to penetrate the gloom the demon seemed to generate.

The creature flexed its shoulders and spread its wings. It sniffed the air, sensing nearby living prey, and uttered a hissing cry of anticipation. With so many mortal souls nearby, the appetite of even the most ravenous of its kind would be satiated.

Across town, slumbering on the terrace, Hecate raised her head. Her eyes narrowed and a shiver ran down her spine. To a greater extent than any of her peers, she was attuned to the psychic undercurrent of living creatures: the web of emotions that underpinned conscious thought. For the most part the highs and lows of the populace were in balance, but something had happened, A rock of disquiet had been thrown into the pool. The impact was more powerful than anything she'd sensed in many long years. With eyes unfocused she tried to determine the location. The source of this unbridled fear was some distance away, but far too close for comfort. All thought of sleep banished, Hecate set off down the hillside and across the park towards the city centre. Eleni, bewildered, watched her leave.

Hecate arrived, amid human screams and shouts and panic. Upturned chairs and tables lay scattered across the street. Nearby properties were abandoned. Staff and owners followed their customers and fled as quickly as possible, cold fear saturating their thoughts. The epicentre of the disturbance was a corner property, already empty. Almost. As the black cat slowed to scan the scene an ear-splitting scream came from inside, followed by a deathly hush. One body lay across the threshold, legs still inside the bar as their owner tried to flee. The young man was still breathing, but his sightless eyes were unfocused, and that typically meant one thing: soul theft, and the only creatures capable of doing that were demons from Hades.

She peered past the victim and saw another body nearby, then a third slumped back in a chair. Behind them stood the perpetrator: a haze of blackness in the midst of the bar like a black hole, absorbing all light from the street outside. All the interior lights had already been destroyed by the creature, the debris littering the floor amid smashed chairs, tables and glassware. The demon was feeding, holding the body of a young woman to its mouth, sucking her soul into everlasting darkness. Its red eyes spotted the cat over the top of its victim. It dropped the woman's body which thudded to the floor, in an untidy heap of twisted limbs.

"You do not belong here," said Hecate.

The demon made a foul gargling noise; its attempt at laughter. "Who are you to deny me? You should flee, before I've had my fill." Its voice was high in pitch but cracked and brittle, as if it rarely had reason to speak. Another wheezing, garbled laugh. "Although your kind are so small as to be scarcely worth my while."

The black cat advanced. "You might find my kind quite hard to digest," she said, staring at the demon.

The beast hesitated, then gave the cat a more piercing look. It uncoiled its fire whip, a ripple of flame working its way to the tip. A flick of its hand and the whip snaked out, the tip moving faster than the speed of sound, aiming towards the cat. A loud crack filled the air and the wooden floor splintered and burst. A metre-long gash appeared, the edges smoking. Hecate anticipated the strike and leaped out of the way, landing on the countertop. The demon swivelled towards her and struck again with a higher intensity blow, the fire whip raising the temperature of the surrounding air. Again it missed, but the bar was cleft in two down to floor level. From the wall behind, bottles tumbled from shelves to smash on the floor. Flames crackled into life as dry wood caught light, the fire given extra fuel from some of the higher-proof spirits.

With a high-pitched scream of frustration, the demon spun once more towards the black cat and aimed a third shot. Hecate flipped into the air above the slanting blow and ran along the ceiling, defying gravity. The demon hissed and tried to raise its whip, but the cat was too close. Hecate flung herself at the creature's face, clawing at its eyes with her own weapons. The demon dropped the whip and staggered backwards, trying desperately to dislodge the cat from its scaly face. But Hecate was clamped tight, her dagger-like teeth piercing deep into her enemy while she continued to slash and punch with all four limbs. Bony fingertips stabbed into her ribs, piercing the flesh and spilling blood, but still she held tight, biting and ripping her way through the demon's scaly hide and the skull beneath. The creature screamed and staggered, but the cat was relentless, needle-like claws repeatedly stabbing and mulching the creature's brain.

Sightless and in panic, the demon crashed around the room, wings flapping uselessly within the confines of the bar. It smashed through the counter, falling hard against the back wall, more bottles smashing around it, then hurled itself to the side, trying to find a sharp edge to break the cat's spine or loosen its grip.

Weaker now, and writhing in agony, with black blood streaming from a dozen wounds, the creature tumbled back into the middle of the room, then crashed to the floor. Hecate finally released her grip and stood to the side. With one last kick, it died. From the extremities, starting with hooves and wing tips, the body dissipated, filling the air with dense black smoke that whirled into an ever-tightening spiral. For a second it reformed in the air and loomed over her once more, mouth open in a silent scream then, with a loud rip and crack, it vanished sucked back into whatever realm it hailed from.

Hecate stood alone amid the wreckage, swaying, breathing hard, and bleeding from multiple wounds of her own. Between long ragged breaths, she attempted to sniff the air, checking for the signs of others. Behind her, the bar smouldered, small flames seeking purchase. A sleek-looking white cat appeared in the empty doorway.

"It seems you didn't need me after all."

She turned towards the newcomer. He strolled around the wreckage as if admiring her work.

"Where's Athena?" Hecate asked. "She should see this."

"I'm here," said a voice from the door.

Hecate gave her colleague a look. "You took your time."

In contrast to Hermes, Athena spent a long time studying the remains of the bar from the outside, before stepping over the threshold. Delicately, she picked her way through the wreckage. "Well, you are, I suppose, our most finely tuned tripwire for such intrusions." She stood beside the black cat.

"What was it?" asked Hermes, inspecting the nascent fire in the far corner.

"A demon of Hades," Hecate replied. "Probably one of Melinoe's folk, judging from the taste."

"Why was it here?" said Athena. "Do we have any theories?" Tentatively, she sniffed the ground, but neither the shattered room nor her companions gave a response.

Hermes joined the other two in the centre of the bar. Their eyes darted from one to another as, in silence, they conversed.

"Can you prevent them returning?" Athena asked.

Hecate paused. "Once I could. But now…"

Hermes raised his chin, his blue eyes piercing. "Then we should call for help. They have no place in this world."

"Help? From whom?" Athena countered. "Are there any left who care? What of Zeus? Where is the evidence of his rule? If Hades ignores his writ and feels himself free to loose his demons, this has escalated beyond mere mischief. Who is there to stop him? We three cannot be everywhere."

"They are still out there," Hermes answered softly. "Angry, isolated, resentful." He cast a glance towards Athena. "But they care. Whether they are minded to do anything is another matter." He sat and looked at Hecate once more. "The most important question is, was this a one-off? A rogue demon off the leash. Or part of a wider plan? If it's the latter, then Hades must have decided to break his bond with Zeus."

Hermes turned to Athena, but she refused to meet his gaze, preferring for once to focus on the evening's events rather than the bigger picture. "Remember, they cannot tolerate daylight, and there are probably many more portals between our realms than we now know. Demons prey on fear and weakness. It gives them strength. A larger incursion, happening across the wider city or the region will be impossible to prevent."

She looked up. "We'd better hope this was a one-off. Otherwise, what damage might be done before we find them?"

It was Hecate who broached the subject they were all avoiding. "Will you go to Zeus?"

For a moment, Hermes looked defiant. His response was slow. "It is a long time since I trod the pavements of Olympus."

"Don't play games with us. We all know Olympus has gone." Athena's interjection was sharp. Now she gave him her full attention, ears pricked. For once, Hermes' blue eyes were blank, his demeanour non-committal.

"As I said, it is a long time since I walked the courtyards of our former home and though Zeus now walks in other groves, the ties that once bound me are not so strong. I fear he prefers other messengers these days."

Hecate looked incredulous. "What are you saying? That

you have taken offense and refuse to speak to him or promote our cause? Is this our fate? To wither away in isolation, sundered from those we once held close?"

"Since when have we been close?" Athena scoffed.

Hecate gave the grey cat a dismissive glance. "Maybe not you or I, but you were always among his favourites. You could do no wrong in his eyes. Your ability to read his moods is a large part of the reason we are here." She turned her attention back to the white cat. "Why are you being so evasive?"

Hermes' level stare lasted a long time. "I cannot ignore a direct summons, it is true, but on those rare occasions he does reach out, I go not willingly." He glanced at Athena. "There are many reasons, but in the main my hesitancy stems from his reclusiveness. I find it an insult to us all."

"Reclusiveness?" Hecate said. "'Has he turned his back on this world? Does he no longer care about its fate? About our fate?"

Hermes said nothing.

Athena stood. She turned away, as if bored by the sudden turn of the conversation, but reserved one last comment for Hermes. "You are one of the few who can pass between the worlds. It is my council that you use your gift wisely. Our future, such as it is, depends on maintaining some harmony between those of us who care, and reminding others that they, too, have responsibilities."

CHAPTER 32
BEST SERVED COLD

Resentment had taken up permanent residence in Delphos' heart. Ion had planned his downfall. Had he planned to drive Eleni away as well? Delphos was certain of it. He'd underestimated how vile Ion had become, but now the scales had fallen from his eyes.

During the next few days, hiding on the edge of the territories he'd formerly called home, he spent long, lonely hours brooding on how best to take revenge. Gradually, a plan formed. His clan weren't the only independent four-legged actors in Athens. Why not use his enemy's weapon against him? But did he have the requisite diplomatic skills?

He spent more time on the fringes of the city centre, seeking other members of the dispossessed.

First contact was the riskiest part. He ventured into the unfamiliar streets north of Syntagma Square and waited until dawn, crouched on the highest perch he could reach – the roof of a parked car – and waited. Time and again, he considered his strategy. His hideout was nowhere near high enough for his liking, and his speed was still compromised, but he tried to put such concerns out of his mind.

Delphos' initial target arrived in the grey dawn: a large,

unkempt dog that initially discharged a volley of insults at him before stopping, baffled that none of the barbs seemed to have the desired effect. Eventually the creature realised the cat was speaking to him and noted what he was saying.

Delphos had rehearsed his story for days, but he'd barely started on his long-winded preamble before the dog cut to the chase. "Why should I help you?"

He froze. That was the key question. Why? He'd hoped that would come later. For a few agonising seconds, his thoughts were scrambled. "Because you want to," he said, lamely.

The dog tilted his head, not expecting this response. "What?"

Nerves frayed, Delphos talked, hoping he was making some sort of sense. "Admit it, you've always wanted to roam the Plaka, haven't you? Why do they keep you out when they let us wander freely?" He seemed to have the dog's attention, and continued, barely taking a breath. "So, it's like this. Some of your fellows made a sortie a few weeks ago. Caused a bit of a panic among my colleagues. But I'm guessing they took a liking to what they saw and someday they'll be back." He paused for effect, holding the other animal's eye. "But they came from the other side of town. You lot are missing out."

The dog lurched forward, rose, and placed its front legs on the hood of the car. "Go on."

Suppressing a shudder, Delphos continued. "You may not know this, but it's an open secret. All the best and most acces-sible restaurants are in the city centre, but we cats get it all to ourselves. All the best cuts. Some of these places even throw out steak and prime meat. We get it all."

The dog lurched fully onto the hood of the car, closing in on him. Delphos edged backwards, watching intently for sudden movements, but still talking. "It's unfair, isn't it? But it's all there for the taking."

"Where? How?"

"I can guide you. All you have to do is pretend you're chasing me. I'll take you past all the best hangouts. You can stop where you like, but here's an insider tip. There's another cat who looks almost exactly like me. He thinks he's the boss. Says he's tight with the humans. Thinks they do what he wants. He's the one who really keeps your kind out of the centre. Remove him, and you remove the problem, if you know what I mean." He swallowed, his mouth dry.

The dog loomed over him. "Go on."

"I know where he likes to hang out. But he's got a thing about dogs. He has a couple of tame ones at his call. They help enforce his rule. Fix him, and they'll melt away. I guarantee it." At the word *tame*, the beast growled. Delphos warmed to his theme. "Like I said, he thinks he's the boss of all of us, cats and dogs alike. His ego's out of control. If you let me, I'll lead you to him. Sort him out, and you've got the run of the whole district. It's all yours."

The dog took another bound onto the roof of the car and stood over the cat. "So, what are we waiting for? Let's go." Delphos' nostrils were overcome with the other animal's warm meaty breath, alongside the stink of his wiry coat. He had to fight the urge to escape.

"Not now. They're all closed, the kitchens aren't open yet and the cats'll be prowling further afield. Wait until it gets dark." The dog, panting, made a snuffling sound as he registered every shade of Delphos' own scent. "I'll come back at dusk. Be ready."

"Oh, don't worry, my little friend," came the rumbling reply, saliva dripping at the cat's feet. "We'll be waiting. You'd better not be late, and you'd better not be lying. Because if you are, we'll come in there and find you."

Delphos fled. His brother and his former friends might not like it, but he no longer cared. He had declared war.

．　．　．

The city had bathed beneath a sluggish humid heat, the sun shrouded behind the haze that hung above. There had been next to no breeze to clear the air, but the evening was pleasant and al fresco dining abundant. Business was brisk throughout the Plaka, and at the prime locations two or three of the local cats took up station. They would feast tonight.

Danger arrived out of the blue-black warmth of the night, from the north. A familiar-looking ginger cat streaked past. Surely that was…?

Then the barking registered. Dogs. Many dogs. What were they doing here?

The cats ran, scattered, found whatever shelter they could, while the gaggle of stray dogs rampaged down the street, high on adrenaline and the thrill of the chase. Humans had abandoned them, and their hurt burned all the more fiercely as a result, overcoming the deep-seated nugget of loyalty and affection common to all their species. The smell of the food drove them to a frenzy. They barged into tables, snapped at diners, demanded their share. The hounds had forgotten their part of the bargain that had drawn them here. They just wanted a new home and new friends, here at the heart of things, surrounded by people. People who would feed them. And they knew they'd get it if they just created enough mayhem.

In their midst stood Ion, bewildered. What was happening? Anger driven by fear surged through him. He had seen his brother followed by several large angry-looking brutes. There was a strange look on his face: determination, not panic. Delphos had sped directly towards him, then past, showing no sign of stopping.

Ion forgot about trying to reason with the intruders and ran for his life. Anywhere would do. He raced blindly across the square, dodging pedestrians, desperate to get to some kind of safety. But he was running out of pavement. Ahead lay one of the busiest streets in the capital, but behind he could sense his pursuers. They barked with gusto and closed the gap.

Having peeled off to a safe vantage point near the entrance to the Metro, Delphos witnessed it all, delighted at the success of his scheme, overjoyed at his brother's discomfort. *Not so cool now*, he thought, with a fierce joy in his heart. Retribution was his.

Blindly, Ion ran, instinct his only guide.

He didn't see the car. Never knew what hit him.

He wasn't the only fatality. The leading dog among the chasers also died that night, and another was injured.

As the pandemonium subsided and people chased off or rounded up the strays, peace returned to the central streets and squares.

Delphos approached the body of his litter mate, cast carelessly onto the pavement by a pedestrian, and sniffed to check for signs of life. Nothing. He leaned over the head with its staring, sightless eyes, and whispered into the dead cat's ear in a voice so soft only the gods could hear. "That's for what you did to me. That's for what you did to Eleni."

Then he stood tall over the corpse and raised his head to the sky. "This is my doing. My victory. My revenge for the wrong that was done to me. I led them here. I ordered them to chase him to his own destruction." He paused, looking about, hoping to receive a sign she was listening to him: the disembodied voice that had plagued his thoughts. He had a name now, a target for his claims. "I dedicate this sacrifice, the sacrifice of my faithless brother Ion, my enemy, to you, Athena. To your city and your glory. May you take strength and succour from it, our patron goddess. May you find honour in the heart of your follower, such that I may step forward and accept your gift. Leadership of the Plaka cats. The greatest, most powerful clan in Athens. Accept my offering, Athena. With it, I dedicate my life to your service in return for my kingdom and reunion with my consort, Eleni, whom my enemy tormented and abused. I beg you grant me favour."

Alone, by the side of the road, standing over the body of his one-time friend, the yowl of the cat might have looked like a cry of pain. A curiosity. Strange behaviour for such a simple creature, perhaps, and soon forgotten. But sacrifices to the gods were rare and although there was no altar, no sacred flame and no temple, the offer in his heart was real. The emotions running through Delphos' breast were vivid and powerful. He was victorious and, in that moment, invincible. It was as if he had fire running through his veins; he felt untouchable. Immortal.

For a moment, nothing happened. The world was poised. Delphos held his breath in the stillness of the night. Athens slumbered, unknowing, uncaring. The warm night air draped across the city like a velvet cloak, heavy and still.

Movement. A tiny flutter of air disturbed an empty candy wrapper. It scuttled along the ground, a few inches at a time, pausing, before continuing its arhythmic dance. Suddenly it was airborne and other litter joined it; detritus the street cleaners had missed. The fur on Delphos' body caught the growing wind flicking against its grain. He flexed his muscles to avoid stumbling as the breeze became a wind, then a howling gale. Sharp eddies morphed into mini tornadoes, scooping more debris into the night sky, until the entire square was filled with a pillar of rapidly circulating air reaching high into the heavens, roaring and whistling as it sucked in all nearby objects.

Without warning, it ceased. Gravity reassumed its dominance and objects crashed to earth. But the watchful stillness that followed was different; it was wary.

Delphos' offering had been heard.

Finally a voice in his head forced its way into his thought. It was little more than a growl, menacing and slow.

Athens shall have no king.

CHAPTER 33
WHOSE SIDE?

Many immortals led a reclusive life, hiding away from the troubles of the world and others of their own kind. They preferred to shut the noise and chaos of daily life out of their chosen lifestyle, whether that be the stringent aesthetic of the hermit or the pampered luxury of the bon vivant with all its indulgence and servile attendants. Hermes was not among them. He thrived on information: news, gossip, data; both trivial and profound. Most treasured of all were the arcane mysteries known only to the gnostic few. But such knowledge, while most definitely conferring power, was also rare and hard to locate. But it was important. Anything that could give him an edge was important. Hermes' power lay in knowing what others did not. Answers to deeper, more fundamental questions were treasure, but coin he weighed carefully in his transactional mind. For him, knowledge was leverage, and its absence the reverse. More than anything else, Hermes hated being out of the loop.

Which is what drove him to Poros and the rambling neoclassical villa on the outskirts of town, and the chocolate-coloured cat in a diamante collar lounging amid a clump of begonias. Here, in a setting of modest rural luxury, Persephone chose a life of seclusion for the seven months she spent among the living; a choice Hermes found strange given what he'd seen of the more convivial nature of her Underworld existence.

"No pool? That's a black mark in these parts, is it not?"

"If you look behind you, you might see the sea. Is that not sufficient?" Her languid response matched his sarcastic opening. "I hope you're not here as errand boy for some other misguided relative."

Hermes affected an interest in his surroundings as he meandered around the garden. He paused nearby, affecting an air of impatience and irritation, his tail swishing behind him. "Let me get straight to the point. I don't have much time."

Persephone stood and walked past him, towards the shady side of the garden. Beyond the edge of the grass, the steep fall of the land gave a panoramic view of the channel between the mainland and the island. "Makes a change. What is it, then?"

He followed and stood at her shoulder as she admired the view. "We've had a visitation from one of your creatures of the night. I suppose you know of it."

She threw him a brief glance. "I'm not party to every movement of our people. What of it?"

"It was an unwelcome intrusion."

"That's as may be, but visits from our populace to the upper realms are not unknown. They've occurred throughout the ages, either tolerated or dealt with locally. Why makes this one special?"

"The intrusion of a follower of Melinoe is hardly commonplace. A demon so powerful has not been seen in the centre of a city for many centuries. Plagues of nightmares spread by the folk of Nyx: the occasional vampire scare, yes. But a soul-stealing demon, a true agent of terror, is an escalation, is it not? I merely want to understand what is behind it."

Persephone's eyes darted towards movement on the water. A speedboat rounded the distant headland, skimming the surface and leaving a long white wake.

"Wouldn't you be better asking that of my lord?" She glanced at him again. "Really, Hermes. You disappoint me. Do you really need to ask such a question? Is it not obvious?"

"Enlighten me."

"Hades has had enough of Zeus' empty demands." She looked him in the eye, her soft voice barely audible. "You must know, deep down, it's time for change." With pupils wide, she moved closer, nudging her head towards him. As Persephone silently invited him into her confidence, the distant sounds of the waterway and the flutter of nearby leaves vanished before the dark inviting pool of those eyes.

"Such certainty is dangerous. It's not too late to back down." Hermes couldn't look away.

Instead, breaking the connection, Persephone rose, stretched, arched her back, then sat facing away from him. "Such anxiety over one little incursion. No. I will not do your bidding. You'll have to try harder than that."

His eyes roved up and down her poised and perfect body. "You're enjoying this, aren't you?" She gave no reply. Hermes leaned forwards. "This disturbance, and any that follow. You relish it."

"This involuntary retreat has been a long one," she replied. "Too long. Do you not feel the need for change?" She stood and pushed her face close to his. But this was no affectionate bump. "Something, or someone, to shake things up? Come, come, dear Hermes. Do you not feel it as well? That faint echo of voices in the hills. The sound of marching feet. Is it not time to reclaim our thrones? I warned you, not so long ago, that you were showing signs of losing your neutrality. Is that still the case?" She looked up at him with her amber eyes. A low, seductive purr emphasised the point. "Soon you will have to make a choice, so don't put it off. Join us. Join us now, and help set us free."

He stared back, wondering at Persephone's capacity for mischief. "Free to do what, exactly?"

Gently, her flank brushed against him as she walked past, her tail high; an invitation to an intimacy he had never shared with her. Craning his neck, he watched the hypnotic sway of her hindquarters as she walked away, and followed, his mouth half open, as if tasting her musky allure on the scented air. She stopped and waited for the rub of his head against her neck, the firmness of his body pressing down on hers.

Their union complete, they lay side by side in the sun, letting its warmth soak their bodies. At length she nuzzled his ear, whispering her fleeting affection, subtle and provocative.

"Come with us," she breathed. "Set us free from this miserable half life."

He lay with eyes closed, in drowsy bliss. "And how are we to do that? Athena alone holds the key, and those memories are gone."

They lay there; the only movement the subtle rise and fall of their ribs as they breathed. The scent of lush vegetation blanketed them in a comforting embrace.

"Do you think she was the only one with the answer?" came the murmur in his ear. Hermes' eyes opened wide. He dared not move. "Demeter?"

Another nuzzle; the pressure of her nose against the back of his head. "No, not her. Another place. Somewhere secret."

He rolled onto his back, pressing against her. "Where?"

Persephone wriggled aside and rolled onto her stomach. "Somewhere hidden. Somewhere dark."

Hermes was fully alert now, almost afraid to ask. He edged closer, extended his nose in a gesture of affection. But she held back, then stood. He clambered inelegantly to his feet, for once unsure what to say.

"Is it not time to freshen things up? Let the old regime wither and die. It's more than time for new ideas. A new way of ordering things."

"That sounds like something you've been planning."

She looked away. "Let's just say it's an idea that has been brewing for some time."

"And what will it look like, this new order of yours?"

Persephone stood and began a tour of the garden, turning past the end of the house to the shady side facing inland. Hermes walked beside her, waiting for her ideas to spill.

"We should be more open, don't you think?" she said. "Open to new ideas. New ways of doing things. Fresh blood."

He halted in his tracks. "Fresh blood?"

"We're not the only immortal creatures on this planet, you know." Hermes stared at her. "There are many others. We have preferred to ignore them, all this time. But here we are, stuck in the shape-shifted slow lane." The look she gave him was accusing. "Of our own volition, I might add. How short-sighted was that?"

"None of this is news. Of what relevance is it to us now?"

"Oh dear, Hermes. I'd never counted you among the unimaginative ones with their head in the sand. I always thought you were better than that."

The accusation stung. "Who have you been speaking to?"

"I only have time for the committed. Unless you pledge allegiance, I will say no more." She sounded prim and business-like. Once more, she searched his face, but her voice spoke of disappointment. "Change will come, Hermes. You can count on it. But you should think carefully. I like you, but you don't want to be in the wrong place when the change comes. When the stale old hierarchy is cast aside. You've got to admit, it's long overdue. Rigor mortis set in centuries ago. Nobody knows where half of them are." With eyes narrowed, she lowered her voice. "If you can't keep our little secret, we'll have to do something about it. There'll be no more favours, and no more freedom. No one will be allowed to get in the way. Change will happen whether you like it or not."

"And if I refuse?"

She was silent for a while. "That would be regrettable." An upward flash of her eyes. "For you, rather than anyone else. Without friends, gossip, news. Or allies. Think carefully, Hermes. Tartarus is a lonely place to spend eternity."

Hermes stared back, incredulous. But the sharp rejoinder died on his lips as he saw the earnest look on her face. She meant it.

"Give me some time to think about it," he said. But in his cavernous mind, plans were already hatching, scenarios forming, potential alliances being evaluated and motivations examined. A multitude of potential outcomes were forming. Many factors had to be considered, and, as he held the brown cat in view, one thought recurred.

You were never one of the Twelve.

CHAPTER 34
THE MONASTERY

Eleni relaxed into life at the monastery. The monks were kind to her and seemed pleased to have a new small disciple. She even let them pet her, pushing her head up into the comforting hands proffered. As she did so, she wondered how her previous human was managing without her, and occasionally suffered a brief pang of regret at the loss of her lovely garden.

The life of the city surrounding her sanctuary continued, but for the time being, Eleni didn't care. She was happy. She wanted to stay there forever. Hecate kept an appropriate distance, conversing only occasionally and allowing her companion to get used to her new life.

But no sooner had she settled than the changes to her body began. Eleni became ravenously hungry. Hecate, watching with care and one step ahead of her tenant, allowed her the lion's share of their food. The monks seemed unaware of the imminent demands of their new arrival.

Within a few weeks, Eleni experienced sickness. At the same time, her abdomen became swollen and, to the monks' surprise, she showed an unusual affection for humans. Hecate found their ignorance of the feline body amusing.

By the time the monks realised she was pregnant, Eleni was beginning a search for a safe place to give birth. The immediate surroundings of the monastery had little in the way of cosy corners. The best she could find was an alcove next to the shrine where she and Hecate usually ate, and she became fretful.

Finally, the monks acted. They took her inside, found a suitable box, and filled it with towels. There she had her litter. Six healthy kittens: tiny, helpless, fighting for a place on her teats.

She was examined by a vet, who scanned her chip. Before she knew it, Eleni was back in familiar surroundings. Her human seemed delighted and greeted her with enormous fuss. But at first, Eleni remained wary. Her companion had been so unmoved by her misery. Why had she not been able to see the burden she'd been living under? What if the threat returned? For the short term, she was confined indoors, and all was well. She concentrated on looking after her brood and put her previous fears to the back of her mind. But anxiety soon nagged at her thoughts again.

After a few short weeks, the kittens were old enough to be homed. With regret, she saw them go, one after another, each departure piercing her heart with a little dart of bittersweet sorrow. Her human kept one: a calico female. Amber, black and white. Eleni called her Zoe, after her own dimly remembered mother.

Motherhood proved a distraction, but with increasing independence the old fears resurfaced, and Eleni cast many an anxious glance to the garden wall. As winter receded and the fresher breezes of spring brought new hope, her mood lifted. Dare she wish for a safer future? At least her absence seemed to have disrupted the pestering visits. But would Ion return someday? Then there was the matter of Delphos. She'd thought they had been in love. Why had he abandoned her?

But Eleni was older now and more experienced, and her

fears seemed smaller. She decided she would conduct her own search beyond the wall. This time, rather than flee, she would seek the heart of her problems: the two with the biggest impact on her short life.

Her lover and her enemy.

What had happened to them?

CHAPTER 35
EXILE

There was no grace in Delphos victory, and no glory. Nor was there a welcome back from his former friends, when they dared emerge from hiding. None would return his greeting or welcome him home. Instead, he was treated as a stranger and, worse, a danger to them. They barred his path to their former headquarters and main gathering place, unwilling to allow him back.

As the sun climbed into the sky, Erichthonius appeared, and unlike the others, he marched straight up to Delphos, stern-faced.

"You are no longer welcome here."

"It is my home."

"No more. You have brought chaos and violence. That is not tolerated. You must leave."

"Says who?" Delphos spoke with bravado, but doubt strangled his thoughts.

"Athena."

For a wild instant Delphos thought to defy the message; refuse to acknowledge the messenger. But it was pointless. No one wanted to pay him heed or listen to his litany of grievances. None would look beyond the chaos he had brought to their doorstep. Instead, with one last bleak look at the light brown cat, he stalked away along the familiar streets into permanent exile. All his plans had proved futile – perhaps Athena had been right all along.

Once more, he found respite in the National Gardens. For the rest of the day and night, he stayed there, trying to put recent events out of his mind. Carefully he nursed, then nurtured his resentment, still outraged at the injustice he had suffered; still angry with his deceitful brother. If he felt any guilt at Ion's demise, it was buried deep within his soul.

Too alert to sleep, he stalked the beds and lawns in the blue hour before sunrise, then slept late into the morning. With the sun high in the sky, he woke and stretched. It was mid summer and the day's heat was building. Shadows deepened and shortened across the lawns.

Delphos stretched out as far as he could with a forepaw and arched his back, then stood and flexed his hind legs. Exercises complete, he explored his new habitat in daylight. The park was pleasant. Lush vegetation, an ornamental pond, tall trees, one or two secluded hiding places. The most inviting open patches of grass were already occupied by humans, some of them had even encroached on the best shaded spots beneath the trees.

He saw a tortoise among the rocks by the pond and detoured to examine it, briefly wondering if it might speak to him. Bounding closer, he pushed his face towards its small head and miaowed a greeting, but it ignored him, turning away with steady, deliberate movement. It seemed to move in permanent slow motion, assuming it was alive, and not some semi-sentient rock.

Delphos realised he would get no response from this creature, any more than his former friends. He sniffed it front and back, registered and mentally filed the creature's distinctive earthy scent, and lost interest.

Scanning his surroundings, he pondered his next move.

He had no intention of following the guidance of that strange, disconcerting voice. This park seemed safe enough. Maybe he should move here permanently. All he needed was a café for scavenging purposes, and a reasonably sized rodent population. It was time to find the restaurant.

His plan was foiled from the outset. Just as Delphos was beginning to explore his would-be home, he was on the receiving end of unwelcome human intervention. A man dressed in dark green, bearing a long pole with a nasty-looking metal attachment at one end, spotted him and darted in his direction. He stepped sideways to let him go by; he was used to being ignored by the human population of Athens and passing among them unnoticed, like a small furry ghost in the urban landscape. But the man moved to cut him off and stabbed the pole towards him. He was the most hostile human Delphos had ever come across. Keeping him in his peripheral vision, he scampered away to a safe distance and carried on his way.

He hoped that the man would give up, but shouting angrily, the green figure followed, forcing Delphos to maintain a brisk, undignified trot. The two-legged pursuer kept up his chase, annoyingly persistent.

The cat examined his options, keeping an ear focused back on his pursuer and casting the occasional glance backwards. His route took him close to the far side of the rockery, and with relief he noticed the man stoop. The pursuit seemed to have ceased.

Delphos slowed to a walk. But from the corner of his eye, he saw the man rise, his arm moving swiftly. A sharp pain in his flank sent him into a full run. A pebble whizzed past his head, alarmingly close. Delphos changed tack, towards cover. Hiding among a dense thicket of rockrose shrubs, he peered out, waiting until it was safe to venture forth.

The cat relaxed. The green sward before him was inviting, but for now there was more security beneath the dense, spreading foliage of this bush. The next attack came from an unexpected direction: to his rear. Another long pole with a differently shaped, but still deadly-looking attachment was thrust beneath the bushes nearby. His attacker had missed, but the strike was too close for comfort. The end of the pole swung back and forth, its movement limited by the dense vegetation, while above his head Delphos heard more angry shouts. With dismay he realised why there were no other cats resident in this urban Eden: the local humans were innately hostile and seemed intent on making this a feline-free zone.

Exasperated, he gave up, broke cover and ran at full pelt towards the gates to find somewhere more accommodating. Heading south across a wide road he came to an open space of sun-baked gravelly soil and sparse, straggly grasses. Ancient columns from a once mighty temple stood on a low platform. Another lay collapsed in their midst. Delphos sniffed around, but there was little to occupy him for long. There was no cover, and no secure sleeping places anywhere. He kept going.

Beyond the open ground, across yet another road, he entered a warren of streets lined with tall apartment buildings. Padding along pavements in search of a place to rest he spotted another cat: tall, extremely thin, but with a mean look about her. She stopped instantly at first sight of him, staring along the street. Delphos approached cautiously. It wouldn't do to appear timid, but he had to be wary. He could tell, even from a distance, that this one looked like a seasoned fighter. She had the scars to prove it. Close, but just out of range, he stopped, unsure of himself. With spirits and energy levels low, he was in no mood for a fight.

The other cat fixed him with a beady glare; Delphos sensed her hostility. As soon as he stopped, she strolled towards him with a languid gait. In an instant, he could tell she was the queen of these parts, confident and proud.

"What's a pretty boy like you doing around here?

Shouldn't you be back in your nursery beneath the cliffs?" Her eyes flicked down the street, back towards the distant Acropolis. Delphos remained rooted to the spot while she walked around him, studying his flanks as if she were inspecting a racehorse. His tail rose in a belated, half-hearted greeting, but she barely gave him a sniff, so he lowered it once more. He followed her leisurely progress with his head, slowly turning, eager to avoid any sudden attack from the rear. For some reason, he found it difficult to read her body language, but everything about her made him nervous.

Rather than attack, she resumed her dismissive taunts. "So green. So well kept. Hardly a mark on you. I see the pickings are still as good as ever for Ares' little crew."

"I don't know what you mean."

"Oh, come on. The Plaka gang. You're not as dumb or pretty as a house cat, but you're no street fighter, that's for sure. That only leaves the most pampered clan of scavengers in town, cosying up to the tourists. You get all the best cast-offs without having to lift a paw. You don't know what a real fight is."

Delphos had no answer to her sneer. He remained silent while she continued to inspect him. He tried to ignore her, but she wouldn't go away.

"So what are you down here for? So far from home."

He didn't care to answer such a direct question, so he changed the subject. "And you are...?"

She ignored him. "My turf, my rules. Strangers have to declare themselves and their business."

Delphos swallowed and experienced a prickly sensation beneath his fur and paws. His interrogator stopped in front of him, her voice low and menacing.

"Come on. Spill the beans."

He searched her face for signs of softening, but finding none, looked to the right, thoughts racing. "I'm lost."

"*Lost?* Your home is just over there." Her eyes glanced

beyond him towards the end of the street. "Turn around and keep going for ten minutes and you can't miss it. You'd better try harder."

There was steel behind those dark eyes. Flustered and confused, Delphos sensed she could see straight through him. His forepaws trod the ground like an agitated youngster.

"I've been sent away. I'm exiled."

There was a pause while the huntress absorbed this information. He tensed, ready to spring, trying to decide which direction the attack would come from.

Instead she gloated. "Steal someone else's pitch, did you? Been sent away for a few days to cool off?"

"Indefinitely."

She took a step back and looked him up and down. "Forever? You'll never make it. Not around here." To his surprise, she turned away and walked off down the street. Delphos stared at her retreating hindquarters, then bounded after her until he was alongside, matching her pace.

"What do you mean?" he said. The other cat kept walking and continued to ignore him. But he persisted, braver now she was no longer scrutinising him. "You seem to do alright. Why shouldn't I? What's so special about this district?" He skirted a fire hydrant at the last moment and detected a hint of amusement on the other animal's features.

At the corner of the street, she halted. "We're in a border zone. Over there," she flicked a glance to her right, "is Bia's territory. They're one of the largest gangs in the city. They operate out of Davaki Square. Most folks stay clear of them. Down there," she turned her head in the opposite direction, "is Gouva Gang territory. They're no pushovers, but there's not as many of them. Over there," she pointed with her nose, "is Nea Smyrni Square, home to another gang. They're the smallest of the three, but with some of the most vicious fighters. They have a reputation." She looked at him once more.

"This little patch of streets is no-animal's land. This is where I hang out."

He ignored the fact he could see her ribs. "So, how come they let you come and go?"

She stared at him for a long moment, then pushed her head towards him until their noses almost touched. All of a sudden, there was a wild look about her. "I am Rea," she snarled. "Let's just say my reputation precedes me."

Delphos' eyes widened, but he held his ground. It was the name elders in the gang used when they wanted to frighten the youngsters: a gangster with a legendary reputation for violence and vindictive sadism; a person he'd thought of as long dead, who belonged in the annals of history. She was said to have been a particularly brutal leader in the war that took place before he was born. But here she stood, very much alive and all too close. He tried to swallow, but his throat, along with the rest of his body, seemed frozen. He should put half the city between them if he could, while he still possessed four functioning limbs.

"Pleased to meet you," he said. "I'm Petros." He bowed his head, as only appropriate. In his scrambled brain, he tried to assemble what he could from the stories he'd been told and wished he'd paid them more attention. All that came to mind was a name associated with savagery and death.

Rea turned back to the road junction.

Curiosity got the better of him. "How did you end up here?" he asked.

The narrow, pinched face swung in his direction once more. "Fate? Bad luck? Who knows?" Her features softened briefly, as she stared into the distance, reliving episodes from the past. Her voice became reflective. "Ares wouldn't have saved them. Not by himself. Not even with Athena's help. Not against three Titans. If it wasn't for that bastard Apollo, we'd be strolling around your old home getting fat and lazy, sunning ourselves in Monastiraki Square, choosing the best hangouts." She snapped back into the present and stared down at him. "You wouldn't know where he went, would you?"

"No."

"Shame. I'd like to hunt him down and have it out with him. One last reckoning. Make him suffer. Make him pay."

There was a lump in Delphos' throat; he could barely get the words out. "Make him pay?"

She looked him up and down once more. "For killing my father."

He could scarcely breathe. She looked up and down the street once more, and when she next spoke, her attitude seemed to have changed.

"Come on. Let's eat." She strode across the road.

CHAPTER 36
THE WEIGHT OF FORCE

The days drifted past, finally becoming cooler, wetter, and darker. Sunset arrived earlier, and sunrise held out a little more each morning, as if even the sun itself wanted a lie-in. It left little impact on Delphos' waking thoughts. The injustice of his plight still dominated, but the pain was less sharp now. His sentence still seemed interminable and unfair, but other considerations commanded more of his time.

He remembered little of his first year; his kittenhood and adolescence. Those hazy days belonged in an untouchable past. Older now, and maturing rapidly, he took the seasonal changes in his stride and, for the time being, let his new guide dictate his actions.

Rea was taciturn and spiteful, and enjoyed belittling him, but he had nowhere else to go. Instead, accompanying her and learning to survive on his wits in this unforgiving part of the city taught him important life lessons. Delphos expected their tenuous arrangement to end at any moment. He often appeared an inconvenience to her, and she showed little interest in hearing what he had to say. But she didn't yet shun his company, although she rarely made him welcome. To his relief, she did not invite intimacy.

The odd couple roamed their netherworld on the overlapping borders of several gang territories, eking out an existence in the perpetual no animal's land between. Dusk and dawn were their active times. During the day, they slept with one eye open for interlopers or chancers out to make a name for themselves.

Theirs was a precarious existence on the fringes of society, but at least it prevented him from brooding on the past and the love he'd left behind. Not that he'd forgotten about Eleni. Far from it, he yearned to be reunited with her, but not when he was living such a precarious existence on the fringe of society. One day, when his fortunes had revived he dreamed of finding her, and their reunion would be blissful. But that day was not this day. He did not, yet, have the courage to seek her out, nor any idea where to look, and if, by some amazing chance he found her, how could he explain his absence? His injury wasn't his fault, but he could have sought her earlier. Putting it off brought him only guilt, alongside misplaced pride. They made tempestuous bed-fellows in his mind.

One cold bright dawn found them scavenging further west than they'd been for some time, deeper into the territory of Davaki Park than was prudent. A large, well-fed tortoiseshell crouched on the summit of an apartment block gatepost, catching the thin early morning sun. It spied them and barked out a challenge. "This is Davaki Park territory. Leave."

To Delphos' surprise, Rea halted, her body tensing. The tortoiseshell glared down at them in disdain. A body length behind his mentor, Delphos also paused, glancing from one to the other. He shifted his weight from side to side, confused. In the few weeks he'd known her, single cats had never bothered Rea in the slightest.

As he studied her for clues, from the corner of his eye he saw a large stranger leap deftly to the ground and pace towards them. As she approached, Delphos noted her confident stride and the contemptuous sideways flick of her tail. This cat was used to issuing orders.

"Well, well. It's been a long time, Rea, but I have no interest in visitors, let alone my brother's cast-offs. You can turn tail and leave the way you came."

To Delphos' astonishment, rather than snarl a response, Rea bowed her head, staring at the pavement a metre in front of her nose. "We are just passing through. We won't be staying."

The tortoiseshell sauntered past Delphos, sniffing his flanks and rear end. Without thinking, he raised his tail in greeting, chastising himself for such a wanton display of supplication. He sniffed, tilting his head towards her, but caught nothing other than the scent of a self-confident female.

The stranger completed her investigation and returned to face him, staring into his eyes. The fur on his neck bristled; he could not bear the weight of the scrutiny, and was desperate to look away, but couldn't. His heart pounded and his vision tunnelled.

"A distant sapling from the family tree, I see. But what kind of twig are you?" She turned to Rea, and the pressure eased. "We all know how you turned out, my dear. Bitter, twisted, cruel. A true reflection of your heritage. Well, almost."

Delphos watched the exchange in horrible fascination. His breath caught in his throat. Every follicle sent his fur vertically out from his skin. The newcomer exuded a menace he'd never previously encountered. He stiffened and prepared to run, but hesitated to see what his normally confident, worldly-wise colleague would do. Rather than flee, she gave him an inquisitive look. He had become used to her disdain, but she was clearly afraid of the newcomer. It was a shock to see her whiskers tremble; the first time he'd seen her display any outward sign of nerves.

The tortoiseshell continued with her monologue. "Still skulking in the shadows, I see? His big plans came to naught, but rather than pick up the baton and continue the struggle, you fled. Here I find you, skulking in dark corners and back alleys, afraid to step forth into the light." It wasn't so much the mocking tone that surprised Delphos, but that his companion of recent weeks had no reply. Gone was the assuredness and confidence that was her habitual armour.

The interrogation continued. "You should take more care. You may not realise it, but you are being watched. You have many enemies, dear Rea, and you shouldn't rely on your close relatives for succour. Not after you have shunned them. Not unless you agree to finish what your father started." The tortoiseshell appeared to be enjoying Rea's discomfort. Rea said nothing, but looked straight ahead, unable to meet the other cat's eye. "Then again, maybe it's not just your enemies you need to look out for. Companions come and go, but do you know what you've let into your nest?"

Satisfied, the tortoiseshell turned to Delphos once more. The full force of her attention returned, an almost physical pressure pressing on his neck and spine.

"I am Bia," she told him. "I am the queen of this territory. The leader of the largest feline community of South Athens. You have trespassed onto my land. I do not take such transgressions lightly."

An interminable pause followed. Rooted to the spot and unable to move, Delphos was a fly caught in the enormous invisible web of a watchful and dangerous spider. Bia's dark eyes lingered on him, looked him over, scrutinised him.

"I should just squash you like a fly, but you interest me," she said. "It has been a while since I came across another half-breed." Did he see her eyes flick to Rea as she made that comment? "A young one at that. An unwritten page. All still to play for." She paused, her eyes narrowing. When she continued, it was as if she was talking to no one but herself;

or some invisible audience. "Few of you ever fulfil your promise. No doubt you'll disappoint as most of you do. Arrogance and overconfidence can only take you so far, after all. The more interesting question is how your failure will manifest. A quiet fade-out into obscurity, or the brief flash of a shooting star burning up in the heavens? How many will be caught up in the fallout?"

Bia continued to stare at him. The moment stretched, but Delphos was not inclined to fill the silence. All he could do was watch. Finally she seemed to lose interest in them, and walked away in a leisurely fashion, her tail swaying behind her.

But she could not resist one last dismissive sneer. "Go back the way you came. Do not tarry. My followers will not be gentle."

CHAPTER 37
UNFORESEEN

Delphos glanced at his companion as she stalked down the sidewalk. An hour had passed since their encounter with Bia, but she hadn't uttered a word or even acknowledged his presence. By now they were well enough acquainted for Delphos to recognise Rea's often violent mood swings and avoid provoking her. Had he offended her somehow?

He maintained a respectful distance and let his companion work through whatever was bugging her. As they meandered around the streets of their usual domain, his thoughts wandered back to the encounter with Bia and her mysterious pronouncements. What had she meant? Why would she have any interest in his actions? They'd never met before, and he had no reputation to speak of. So what would his future matter to the leader of the Davaki Park gang? Should he be flattered or concerned?

The sun was steadily climbing between the buildings lining the streets. It brought little warmth at this time of year, but its presence indicated it was time to rest and sleep. They headed for their usual retreat in this neighbourhood: an abandoned basement, entered via a jagged hole in a broken window.

Rea walked past it; Delphos paused. "How about here?" he asked.

The other cat stopped and turned back towards him. "You go in if you like. I need to think." She resumed her walk.

Delphos considered following, but tiredness won. "See you later."

He watched her walk on down the street. It was the first time they'd separated in weeks, and being alone felt strange. He had become used to following her lead and adapting his manner to accommodate her brittle moods, but a few hours apart was no bad thing. He sniffed at the entrance to the basement and carefully squeezed through into the safe darkness beyond.

Sleep proved fitful: fleeting dreams of endless chases. He stretched and rolled over yet again, trying once more to capture the deep rest his body yearned for. Instead, unbidden and unwelcome questions floated into his thoughts. Questions about twigs and trees, shooting stars and unfulfilled promise, failure and despair. What had she been on about?

He wrinkled his nose, whiskers twitching, as he sought peace; but it wouldn't come. With eyes open a slit, he peered across the cracked concrete floor to a set of dusty shelves opposite. He thought of a different female: Eleni, the animal who had so illuminated his life and who he'd been trying to put out of his thoughts these past few months. Forgetting her had been the only way he could cope with their separation; his best defence against misery. A survival mechanism. But alone in this deserted basement, he couldn't get her out of his thoughts. Where was she now? What was she doing? He held her face in his mind's eye and sighed, his wistfulness accompanied by a powerful stirring in his loins. Abruptly he sat and stared into space as his vision lingered once more on those vast dark eyes, beautiful pointy ears and the black-and-white colouring that decorated her face and body. How he longed for the gentle pressure of her head against his, the touch of her nose.

He rolled onto his back, stretched and considered trying to find her. But the size of the task was daunting and he didn't know where to begin.

A yawn to force his thoughts elsewhere. Another scratch. The light in the cellar was fading as evening approached. It would soon be time to move. His head jerked to attention as he detected a shadow flit behind the dirty glass.

Rea appeared, carefully squeezing through the narrow entrance. Delphos rolled quickly into a crouch to greet her, but one look at her face froze his greeting on his lips.

"What?"

"Did you think I'd never find out?" She stood at the opposite side of the room, her voice bristling with suppressed fury, her fur standing proud.

"What do you mean?"

"I've been on a little expedition. It was most illuminating. Now I know all about you."

She advanced slowly, but with deadly purpose. Delphos scrambled to his feet, eyes wide in alarm as the distance between them shrank.

"Bia was right. Vermin, that's what you are. A disgusting lowlife half-breed."

She launched herself across the remaining metre of space between them, front paws extended, claws unsheathed. Delphos skittered away to the side, receiving a painful slash to the ribs as a reward for his slow reaction. Rea turned, her features murderous. He scrabbled in the dust for firm footing and hurtled towards the exit. Panic lent him speed, but a small misjudgement raked a gash across the top of his head as he shot through the hole and a shard of glass snapped off with his momentum. It spun away with a few strands of blood-stained ginger fur attached.

Delphos scrambled up the steps onto the street and ran to the other side. With ears flattened against his skull, he could sense her pursuit. He raced around a corner and careered headlong down another street.

A left turn brought him alongside some railway tracks. The fence guarding them was no obstacle, and he slid between the railings, hardly breaking stride. From the corner of his eye, he sensed movement behind; Rea had hurdled it and was closing in. Ahead, a stationary tram stood at a platform, with humans slowly boarding through open doors. At least that gave him a clear run. But could he outpace her or outlast her? She should have given up. What was wrong?

The tram made a bleeping noise. He was nearer now, but Rea was still closing on him. Delphos heard her feet scudding along the ground; soon she would be within striking distance. The doors slid shut. On an impulse, he swerved and darted through the narrowing gap and into the forest of legs beyond, seeking refuge. He skidded to a halt beneath a seat and nosed into a narrow gap behind a shopping bag. The tram moved.

Delphos dared to look behind. Rea was nowhere to be seen; his desperate lunge had worked. He crouched, waiting for his racing heart to return to normal, trying to marshal his thoughts. A tram was a new experience. Terrifying, but marginally better than being attacked by his former companion. Every lurch and jolt made him clench his legs and seek to anchor himself. After a while, he adjusted to the rhythm of the movement and relaxed.

The air seeping through the doors at every stop smelled subtly different. Each time they opened, he was further from danger. As his fear receded, he was in no hurry to disembark; every minute that added to the distance between him and Rea made him feel better. He wondered where he was going, and when he should get off this strange moving room.

His old life was a long walk behind him.

• • •

Far away, behind several suitcases on a luggage rack at the end of the carriage of a different, larger train, was another ginger cat.

Apollo relaxed beneath the bottom bunk of a couchette on the overnight sleeper from Vienna to Zurich, one step closer to his intended destination: Geneva. He wasn't sure exactly when he'd get there, but he didn't care. He curled up and allowed the gentle rocking movement of the train lull him into a deep sleep. With head on paws and eyes closed, he dreamt of mice. And nectar.

CHAPTER 38
THE UNQUIET CITY

Hecate was uneasy. Her small recent companion was constantly in her thoughts. That in itself was unusual; the fate of mortals rarely troubled her, why had this one got under her skin? She tried to ignore it and put Eleni out of her thoughts, but it proved impossible. Finally she decided to track her down and check on her safety in person, if only to reassure herself.

As she walked through the parks and gardens towards the Plaka, where she understood Eleni lived, she pondered the day she had been removed. The reunion with the human had been affectionate enough, but Hecate had sensed a reservation on Eleni's part, as if she harboured an unspoken reluctance. How did she feel now?

Entering the maze of narrow, twisting streets of the old centre, Hecate chose a higher-level route to aid her navigation. She could check for signs of her friend more easily and move with fewer distractions walking across the rooftops. Hopefully she would also remain invisible to the local cats. Hecate preferred not to attract attention when she was abroad.

The brief conversations she had had with Eleni gave her

an idea of the location of her home, so the area of search was quite small. Moreover, when her human had arrived to collect her pregnant cat, Hecate had allowed herself to be petted, so as to fix the woman's scent in her mental library of identifiable humans. Hecate would recognise her instantly if she came across that scent again.

In the end, finding them proved easy. Hecate looked down into a small walled garden and saw Eleni lying asleep while a kitten played with a ball at the lawn's edge. All seemed perfectly normal, until she detected unease on Eleni's face, when she approached.

"She's a fine looking youngster. You must be proud."

Eleni scanned them before turning back to her visitor. "Yes," she said, her response lacking conviction.

Hecate decided a direct approach was best. "What's wrong?"

The other cat refused to meet her eyes. It was a while before she responded. "I miss the old days," was all she finally said.

"What was so good about them?"

Eleni glanced at her, anger on her face. "Everything. Until *he* appeared. The brute. He spoiled everything."

Hecate lounged on the lawn. At last they were getting to the heart of the matter. She settled down to tease out the whole story.

Later that night, as the first stars appeared, she found Athena in a clearing on Filopappou Hill.

"Two visits in one year. My how we are blessed."

Hecate was, for once, taken aback by the hostility behind the greeting. "I realise it is a rare treat," she replied.

"What brings you here? Not another demon, hopefully?"

Hecate arched her back, stretched, sat. "I'm looking for

someone. A friend of a friend. You might be able to help. He's called Delphos."

Even in the deep shadows she could see Athena stiffen. She waited.

"He is not welcome. I sent him into exile."

"Might I enquire why?"

Athena looked directly at her for the first time. "He arranged his brother's assassination. For a crime of such magnitude, I let him off lightly. Perhaps he should have faced execution."

Hecate chose her words carefully. "Could it have been an accident?"

A dismissive snort. Athena stood and strolled away. The black cat followed.

"He was wilful. Manipulative. He planned it all, and such forward thinking, such cunning, speaks volumes in itself, among the mortals of our species. His continued presence would be dangerous."

Hecate absorbed her words. "Yet, from what I've heard his brother was not exactly a gentle soul?"

Athena stopped abruptly. "Maybe not. But he, I could control. I was grooming him to take over leadership of the gang. Firm leadership can sometimes appear ruthless.

Hecate halted beside her companion. When the grey cat resumed her walk, she stayed where she was and watched her cousin's retreating form. Eleni's understanding of the brothers personalities, biased as she was, seemed more believable than Athena's.

CHAPTER 39
THE LAUNCH

A small boat approached the harbour of Glyfada's marina, its white bow wave churning as the prow split the sea. A well-groomed crew member stood at the wheel. Lounging on the soft leather seat at the rear, his arms draped along the side of the boat and the back of the seat, was a handsome dark-haired man, immaculately dressed and oozing wealth. The fact was lost on Delphos, as he watched keenly from behind a bush on the shore. He did not know of human dress sense, or that the crisp white shirt and designer sunglasses were out of the ordinary. The glint of gold from the watch at the man's wrist was attractive, but he had no idea if this confirmed the wearer as an individual of wealth or taste or, judging from the immense yacht at anchor offshore, that he was also an individual of power and prestige.

Delphos' attention was captivated, instead, by another aspect of the boat racing to shore: the two cats on board. One looked forward through the small raised windshield, paws on the wooden dashboard, presumably standing on some seat. The other had been briefly visible in the back, looking out to sea. The forward-facing animal was fixated on the boat's destination and seemed impatient to be ashore.

He was a large cat, and muscular. But there was something odd about his coat. His amber-and-black colouring was split by jagged marks, as if his body had been shaved and given a badly fitting new pelt that was a size too small and assembled from scraps. Lines of dark scar tissue were clearly visible between the joins. His head moved in staccato jerks as he spotted different items along the approaching jetty, and as he glanced in Delphos' direction, the ginger cat glimpsed dark amber – almost red – eyes burning with an intensity that made him take a step backwards.

Curiosity drove Delphos to take a closer look. Heedless of the human traffic on the manicured path along the shoreline, he left his hiding place and ventured towards the jetty. The boat was moving slowly now, manoeuvring to find a mooring place. From his elevated position, he could now see the second cat, apparently sleeping on the bench seat at the opposite end to the man. The human paid no attention to them, as if travelling across water with such creatures was perfectly normal. But Delphos sat down in the middle of the path, baffled. To him, the sea was still an alien and frightening environment. That cats apparently lived there was astonishing. A small girl almost ran into him, squealing in delight that an animal could be almost close enough to touch. She ran forward to try to pick him up. At the last second, Delphos sensed her approach and bolted, her screech of disappointment ringing in his ears.

She tried again. Exasperated, he set off at a trot, easily outpacing her, his attention still fixed on the small harbour behind, and the two animals on the boat. Who were they? What were they doing? Did they own the boat, the humans, or both? Once he'd shaken off the small human he turned and watched in fascination as the tall man disembarked, preceded by both cats. They walked calmly up the sloping walkway to the exit gate and the gardens beyond as if they owned it. With a jolt, Delphos realised they were heading in his direction. He scanned his surroundings for a new hiding place so he could continue his observations.

The two animals halted as the man glanced along the path in each direction, then looked down. He said something and his four-legged companions glanced up, acknowledged the information, then set off across the grass, heading directly towards Delphos. The pair looked so confident; unconcerned by the nearby humans. He wished he had such poise. He couldn't help but be in awe of them. They were aloof, as if insulated from the concerns of everyday life, such as where your next meal was coming from or finding a safe place to sleep. They were like gods among felines.

The pair passed close by, ignoring him. Delphos turned, his eyes glued to their forms as they strolled through the gardens. Both were tall at the shoulder for their kind, and while the cat on the right was sleekly proportioned and brown, his russet-and-dark companion, the one with the ill-fitting coat, was even more bulky and muscular when seen at close quarters. He was not built for speed, but from the look of him, it would be wise to stay out of reach. Delphos suppressed a shiver and followed them.

Other than their physique and attitude, the thing that set them apart from other cats was their matching collars. An intricate pattern was woven into each band, with a dangling phial of green liquid that seemed to glow, suffused with light from within. He moved alongside them, to try to get a better look. If he'd been braver, he would have loved to reach out and pat them. But why would such confident, powerful animals submit to wearing slave collars? In Delphos' limited experience, only dim-witted house cats wore such things; a badge of dishonour. Yet on this pair, the look was regal.

They strode through the gardens and along the shore, making their way towards the tracks where the trams regularly sped back and forth. Delphos maintained a safe distance. Other animals, even dogs on leads, seemed to give them a wide berth.

The pair paused beside the tram tracks, looking up and down the line.

The taller, thinner of the two turned towards him and called out. "Hey, you! When does the next tram get here?"

"I'm not sure."

The bulky one gave him a sullen glance and turned away. The taller one narrowed his eyes and pinned him with a stare. Delphos froze, unable to look away. He swayed slightly as the connection was broken, momentarily dizzy. Whoever they were, being around the pair was unsettling. He edged a few steps closer.

"What's the fastest way into Athens?" said the bulky one, his voice deeper than any other cat Delphos had known.

He was relieved the stranger had no interest in small talk. "Oh, you have to take the tram." The eyes of the amber animal bored into him. "The trams are big metal boxes on wheels."

The cat looked past him, studying the tracks and overhead wires. "Lead us to the station."

Delphos risked a glance at the taller, leaner cat, but his attention was elsewhere. He lowered his head and led them across a narrow sliver of grass between the tracks. They crossed a pavement and drew closer to the silent, waiting rails, then followed them. They soon came to a section with a raised pavement to either side of the rails.

Delphos glanced back to his companions. "This is where people get on." He hopped onto the empty platform and waited. The other cats said nothing. "There should be one soon," he added, feeling a need to fill the silence. Neither of the pair spoke. They were travelling together, yet seemed happiest ignoring each other. Delphos considered walking away and leaving them to it, but curiosity was gnawing at him. "Why are you wearing collars?" A bold question, and perhaps unwise.

This time, the muscular cat gave him his full attention, and Delphos experienced the sensation of being pressed backwards, as if the air between them had suddenly become solid and his question was a threat. Instinctively, he tensed, then immediately chastised himself. He hoped the fur along his spine was behaving and lying flat, but he doubted it. With his thoughts so jumbled, trying to appear cool was too much of an effort, and locked in the sights of the other cat, his breathing became strained. Finally, he found the will to look away, and the pressure eased. But he was aware the other animal's eyes were boring into him. It said nothing.

"What's in the tube?" Delphos' voice was barely a whisper.

From the corner of his eye, he noticed the taller cat's head turn towards him. "It's a gift," he said. "For Athena. Have you heard of her?"

"Oh, yes. Everyone knows Athena."

Delphos checked himself. He had an urge to cosy up to the two strangers and tell them everything he knew; to impress them with his knowledge. "She lives in the centre. Near the Acropolis. That's the hill with the—"

"We know." The taller of the two spoke, his voice higher in pitch than his companion's. There was an urgency to his interruption that demanded a reply.

"I can take you there." As soon as he said it, Delphos realised it was impossible. "Except... I can't. Sorry." Two pairs of eyes stared at him. He shrank back slightly, and gazed at the ground, ashamed. His tail dangled down, flicking between his hind legs in embarrassment. "I've been banished," he admitted.

Again, the scrutiny. Again, the invisible weight pushing against him, but softer this time. Delphos felt the tremble in his legs as he resisted. Still looking down, he was aware of the dark eyes holding him for what seemed like hours. The wires overhead twanged, and he heard a train coming around the bend behind him.

"That's a shame," said the tall cat. "It must have been difficult for you."

Care about his wellbeing caught Delphos off guard. He looked up. "Well, yes. It… wasn't easy."

The well-muscled animal looked past him towards the approaching tram, then over his shoulder to his companion. "I'm sure another of these vehicles will arrive soon. Perhaps we'd better lend succour to our young friend here before we venture forth?"

They led the way to a nearby lawn and lay down. Without thought, Delphos followed. The impatient flick of the leaner cat's tail urged him to open up, but what interest could these strangers have in his background?

"So, you've been forced away, far from home? That must have been hard," said the bulky cat, his voice smooth. Even though Delphos had only just met him, such an expression of concern seemed alien for one of his build and demeanour.

"Were you a house pet?" asked the lean one, an edge of sarcasm in the question.

Delphos swallowed, and looked at the ground between them while two pairs of eyes searched his body for clues.

"Yes and no," he said, glancing at them. The urge to tell his story grew. "I'm a member of the Plaka gang. I was betrayed…" He faltered, gathering his thoughts, then his pent-up emotions tumbled out in a rush. "By my brother. I used to like him. We were friends. He… betrayed me." The other cats listened intently, neither moving a muscle. "He wanted to take over. He wanted it all for himself. He terrorised my partner, and he…" Thoughts of Eleni flooded his brain, distracting him. He'd never called her that; he'd never admitted it, even to himself. Another swallow, his heart pounding. Had she fended off Ion's advances before she'd fled, or had she succumbed to his limited charms? Where was she now?

Delphos shivered as his imagination ran wild. His spine tingled as if bitten by a flea, and he turned to lick the imaginary itch on his flank. No. Eleni was made of sterner stuff. But... what if...?

He had to go back and find her.

The other cats observed him impassively and said nothing. Delphos stood, embarrassment forcing him to move.

"Sit down." The calm authority of the muscular cat splashed into his conscience like a boulder dropped into a pool. Without thinking, Delphos sat.

"Calm yourself and gather your thoughts. Then tell us all about it."

"We're all ears," came a softer response from the lean cat.

Were they making fun of him?

The thin cat yawned but his companion's focus was entirely on Delphos. "Start at the beginning."

Delphos recounted the events leading to his exile. As he finished, his companions exchanged a look.

"Perhaps we should reconsider our plans?" said the thin one. "We don't want to lead our young friend into further trouble."

His muscular companion studied Delphos, and the leisurely flick of his tail registered agreement. He addressed him, his voice grave. "It would be most unfortunate if your future were to be negatively affected because of our intervention. But perhaps we can put in a good word?"

Both animals stared at the hapless ginger cat. It was all he could do to hold their stare. Agitated, he looked from one to another. It was a relief to have shared his woes, but now, unburdened, he realised he needed a plan. What should he do? An idea squirmed its way into his consciousness: he must assist his visitors. It had a certain appeal.

"I can guide you. I'm sure it will be fine. It doesn't mean

I'm re-joining the gang." His voice trailed off as doubt grew in the back of his mind. Could he get close enough, without breaking the order so sternly delivered? He shuddered at the memory. But another thought grew. These two were strangers, and had lent an ear to his tale. They had listened patiently and responded kindly. The least he could do was offer them his own hospitality, though all he could truly provide was his knowledge of the city. It was a meagre exchange, but hopefully, it would suffice. As he looked into the eyes of the large, scarred cat, he saw acknowledgement; with an infinitesimal nod, his offer was accepted.

"We appreciate your offer, but it's too much of an imposition, I'm afraid," said the thin cat, looking towards the shore. "It would seem that Athena has become more temperamental since we last saw her. The last thing we want is that our embassy should lead you into danger." He flicked a glance at his companion.

The larger cat held his gaze. "You have a point. We would do well to respect and protect the reputation of our friend here, such as it is." He turned back to Delphos. "We don't want to ruffle anybody's fur. We are just visiting, after all. Paying a courtesy call to Athens' most prominent citizen."

Delphos looked from one to the other, then at the grass before his paws. His tail swished as their words washed over him. He had an overwhelming desire to be useful to these kindly visitors who had, in such a short time, given him more support than any Athenian in months. Perhaps, by assisting them, they could put in a good word with Athena? Get her to see sense and allow him back?

"You've come so far. I'll lead you to Athena. It is no trouble."

The large cat's face was inscrutable, but the taller cat stood, abruptly. "Another tram is coming. Let's go." He faced Delphos. "Lead on."

CHAPTER 40
GENEVA

As he disembarked from the train at Genève-Cornavin, Geneva's main railway station, the last person Apollo expected to see waiting for him was Hermes. Why should the sight of his colleague be always accompanied by a sinking sensation in the pit of his stomach? The white cat sat on a bench, tail neatly curled about his feet, watching impassively as travellers rushed by, drawn towards the stairs that descended to the central underpass and the exit. From the set of his ears, and darting head movements, he seemed to enjoy their struggles with heavy bags, fascinated by the variety of luggage they carried, tugged or hefted.

Apollo sauntered up to him and followed his gaze. "Is there no escape? How far do I have to go?"

"A lot further than this," Hermes replied without looking at him. "It would be nice if you could confine your travels to warmer locations, though." He glanced up at the sky, visible in the gap between platforms, peering at the persistent drizzle falling on the tracks. "One thing beyond my control is the weather."

Hermes gave a barely perceptible feline shrug, finally

looked at Apollo, then leaped down to stand beside the ginger-and-white animal.

"Let's find somewhere quiet." He led the way back towards the far end of the platform, moving against the flow of pedestrians. Apollo matched his ambling stride pattern, and the two cats sauntered along, seemingly unconcerned.

Just before the end of the covered section of platform, Hermes stopped beside a rack of parked luggage trolleys with no station staff nearby. He turned to face Apollo. "You need to pay attention. I have some concerns. About our kin." He looked into the eyes of his companion. "I wonder if it's time to approach Zeus. I know you have been studiously avoiding him, as have I, but I am worried." His blue eyes carried a sincerity that Apollo found disconcerting. There was no sign of his usual sarcasm, or trademark quip.

The background noise of the station disappeared and Apollo gave his cousin his full attention. "Has something happened?"

The white cat hesitated. "A demon incursion. The first in many a year. But more than that…" Hermes sat, tail gathering neatly over his forepaws. "I believe there is a plot."

"A plot?"

"To dethrone us."

"Dethrone?" Hermes paused, while Apollo's thoughts circled. "But we haven't met for… ages."

"Since before the transformation," Hermes said.

Apollo stared back. "Yes. A long, long time." He glanced to the side, musing. "Do our thrones still exist, I wonder?"

"Of that I'm certain," said Hermes. "But our access is blocked in these diminished shapes. We no longer have the power to return. Anyway, when I said 'dethrone', I meant metaphorically. Ousted, usurped. Choose your own term. I think there is a plot to bring us down. Possibly to kill us."

"A plot? What do you mean?"

Hermes stood again and moved closer until his face filled

Apollo's vision. "There are some among us who do not lie quietly. They seek to replace us. The twelve, that is. That is my belief, anyway."

Apollo stared back into the white cat's luminous eyes in search of understanding. "Who?"

Hermes stepped back. "For the moment, I'd rather not say until I know more about these plotters and their aim."

"What do you mean?" Apollo bristled, a flush of heat beneath his coat. "Are you testing me?"

Hermes studied him impassively. "No, not at all. But if you have anything to tell me, now is the time to do it. Far from the usual prying eyes." He held a level stare.

Apollo shook his head violently. "It's all nonsense. None of this makes any sense to me. You must be fantasising. Why would anyone want to remove us?"

Hermes said nothing. Apollo looked towards the heavens, at the trains waiting at nearby platforms, to the wires suspended above the tracks, and finally to the baggage trollies carelessly parked nearby. He found no inspiration anywhere.

Suspicious, he turned to Hermes once more. "You've come a long way to tell me that. I guess you think it's true."

Hermes' eyes narrowed. "I wouldn't tell you unless I believe it is real. The time is coming when you may have to choose a side."

"No. Not yet. I can't." Apollo turned away once more, his back stiff. A minute passed. Two. Neither cat moved. The doom-laden pronouncement of the Oracle of Acheron returned to Apollo's mind. Perhaps it was time… Finally, he stood and turned once more to his companion. "I'm not ready to face him yet. Not until we know more. In the meantime, I've got things to do here. We should talk again when I'm through."

Hermes acknowledged him with an infinitesimal nod. "Take care. I realise you're known in these parts, but still…"

"Further north and west, really, but I don't suppose any of my temples are still standing. They forgot me a long time ago."

As soon as Apollo left the station, he spotted Hugin atop a lamppost further along the street. The fitting dipped slightly beneath the raven's weight. The bird watched him approach. "Not far," it cawed, and led him across the city centre.

In a few minutes, Apollo reached the relative quiet of the central university quarter. He followed his guide along broad streets and across paved open spaces lined with featureless grey buildings; the perfect complement to an oppressive sky.

Throughout his walk, Apollo's thoughts nagged at the frayed end of something uncovered by Hermes' message. Like an archaeologist without a trowel, he scraped at the exposed fragment that fortune had revealed, but his memory had set harder than the concrete around it. Resistant to every lever, it sat in his mind, taunting him. All the while, he paid little attention to his surroundings until the bird paused atop another lamppost outside a nondescript building with many evenly spaced rectangular windows amid its featureless walls.

"He's here," said Hugin, and flew away. Apollo studied the building, half expecting it to suddenly split apart down the centre and open out to reveal its contents, like a massive doll's house. But nothing happened.

"Thank you for coming," said a rich baritone from behind him. He spun around to see a black-and-white cat with a multicoloured eye standing close by. Odin bowed his head in greeting and looked him in the face. "Shall we find somewhere to talk?"

He led them to the far corner of the square and a well-tended public garden with neatly trimmed lawns and perfectly tilled flowerbeds in which this year's planting was flourishing. The grass was still wet from the morning's rain, but Odin lay down anyway and watched as his companion settled nearby.

Apollo waited. Experience had taught him that with Odin, it never paid to be the one asking the questions; his answers meandered like a slow-moving river, often turning back on themselves and giving the appearance of going nowhere.

The Norse god remained silent, and Apollo yawned, then examined his surroundings with greater interest. High above, some crows circled. He wondered if it might make more sense to ask them for news.

"Mimir's head," began Odin, "has fallen silent."

Apollo ventured a questioning look, trying to remember what he knew of the peculiar metaphysics of the mini universe his companion had constructed. As the black-and-white cat looked at him, his attention was drawn once again to that multicoloured eye that seemed to suck his thoughts from their wanderings, but took them… nowhere. "You'll have to remind me," he said.

Odin gave him such a long, level stare that Apollo felt something close to guilt; the product of his long neglect of these northern climes. Regions he'd last visited long ago when legions still marched the endless straight roads. It was the legions with their forts and temples that brought him here in the first place, spreading his cult across their empire, just as the Greeks were becoming complacent. Apollo had once had worshippers and priests across these lands. Perhaps he should spend more time in this part of the world.

"The well of Mimir lies deep in Jotunheim, land of the giants. It is remote and rarely, if ever, visited. Few, apart from me, know of its location. Beside it is the head of the giant himself. Long dead, but still the fount of wisdom." Odin paused to make sure his companion was listening. Apollo blinked reassurance. The black-and-white cat continued.

"Periodically I consult with him. But taciturn though he has always been, he has never declined a response. Until now."

"Have you no other seers, or prophets?"

Odin looked grave. "None that I trust."

They fell into silence. Apollo watched the people making their way through the park. No one was resting; it wasn't that kind of day. A persistent drizzle fell, dappling his coat with droplets of fine spray. He ignored it.

"His council was important to you, then?" Apollo ventured. Odin's silence spoke volumes.

The Norse god started on a different tack. "My brother's influence is growing."

Once again, Apollo was forced to rack his brains for reference points and memory.

Loki. Half brother and, if his recollections were accurate, half giant.

"How so?" he asked.

"We are detecting increasing activity from his agents. They are multiplying."

"'We'?"

Odin looked directly at him. "My fellow Aesir," he said, his voice edged with exasperation. Apollo sensed his ignorance was testing his colleague's patience. He returned the stare. It was he who had been summoned, after all. Odin withdrew his gaze and looked into the distance.

"We are not as numerous as you might think, and like you, our networks and fortunes have contracted down the years. We maintain a watch, as best we can. But our resources are stretched."

Apollo waited, but his companion seemed unwilling to continue, as if the next few words held too much pain.

"We… I made a mistake." Odin studied the ground before him and shifted position slightly. He looked forward again, into the distance. "I made a tool. A piece of software. A system." His voice faltered once more, and he gave the ginger cat a sidelong glance. Apollo waited. "Let me start at the beginning. As I said, our numbers are few, but we had hoped our force was sufficient once our treacherous and now-sworn enemy was imprisoned where his poisonous silver tongue could do no harm. Or so we thought. And for many centuries, that was the case. But we grew tired of our watch and it faltered, and in the silence and the dark, he attracted creatures to him, and his cause. Fell creatures of the night, or devious, cunning minds, determined to perform mischief at his behest. He attracts them like a magnet. And those who don't come willingly, he traps like flies in a spider's web, poisoning their minds until they are ready and willing to work for him."

Odin's voice was stronger now, the words tumbling rapidly from his lips; a feline chatter of anger and disdain.

"So, I determined a solution to our growing problem. I automated the watch. To take advantage of humanity's ingenuity in building networks and systems and so make up for our lack of numbers. I devised and built a system that would identify them by their behaviours and so keep track of their movements. Alongside that, I devised a model to develop a spy network of our own, invisible to his, operating beneath his level of conscious thought." He turned to look over his shoulder. "Here, in this building, is where we met, and to widen our scope, we added others in Paris and Edinburgh. It became a joint effort. But I did the bulk of the programming."

"Programming?" Apollo struggled to understand what Odin meant. After so long hiding away on the shoulder of Parnassus, he was detached from the current world of men and women. Their concerns and his own had deviated millennia ago.

Odin gave him a long stare, eyes narrowed. "You have hidden far too long, my friend. The world has been moving. Accelerating. Progress, as they term it, is everywhere and in all aspects of its advance lie buried the seeds of humanity's destruction. But I digress. I am talking about computers, IT, technology."

"Go on," Apollo said.

Odin paused. "Most of the development work was done in Edinburgh. They have some expertise in supercomputing, AI and biotechnology. Working with living creatures, examining their genetics, cloning, enhancing them, that sort of thing." He returned to his theme. "But here," another glance behind, "and in Paris, there is greater knowledge of animal psychology. So it became a joint effort."

"To what aim?" Apollo was still struggling to understand what his companion had been attempting to do. He was eager to move beyond technology and on to goals and strategies.

"First, to build a network of our own, and then to use it to track his followers, spying on their movements so we can intercept as necessary and prevent his plans coming to fruition." The glass eye and its companion searched Apollo's face as if seeking approval. "It's what I used to find you and your extended family and reach out to Athena. So, since you are all persisting with this peculiar disguise, I recruited a couple of local tabbies to my cause and got them to liaise with her using a computer screen and to find out more about what you're up to, as best they could."

Again, Apollo detected an air of exasperation, as if all Odin's schemes had somehow fallen short of his expectations. What did Athena make of his approach? Did she intend to share it with himself and the others?

Odin began again. "Loki has many servants. Few, as yet, among humanity, but many among birds and mammals, and, worryingly, among other species."

"Such as?"

"Initially, those most inclined to him of old. Giants, wargs, and their wolf brethren. Trolls, and so on. But most problematically, dwarves and even elves. The numbers are still small among the latter, but given their natural propensities, that is evil news indeed. The world is poisoned enough. It doesn't need creatures of the light to turn to the shadow." He paused, lost in thought for a moment. "Of course, most of his traditional allies did not dare show their faces in Midgard, but the rapid growth of his followers among the beasts and birds of this world posed a problem. That was what prompted me to build this tracking system. Of course, as with all such things, the scope soon expanded. I realised it would be possible to use it not only to follow the movement of his agents, but to interrogate them. Subtly, of course. Get them to reveal more than they expected, to allow me to get a better understanding of his plans."

"How would you do this?"

"Through inter-species communication. That was why the animal psychologists were useful. Who, among humans, could resist devising a system that would allow them to talk to animals?" For a few seconds, Odin allowed himself a look of smug satisfaction. "And it worked. Worked very well, as a matter of fact. And behind the scenes, the AI—"

"AI?"

"Artificial Intelligence. The brain of the system, if you like, was collecting information. A lot of it. Forming connections between different strands of Loki's plan where we hadn't known they existed. The early results were sobering. He had far more agents than we'd anticipated. We realised quickly that our fears were just the tip of the spear. His spies are more numerous than we thought."

"That's good, then. Your scheme worked. Now you can keep track of them. Foil their plans."

Odin looked at the ground between his paws as if inspecting an invisible hole. "Not quite." He hesitated, then looked directly into Apollo's eye. "It's gone rogue."

"Rogue?"

"Developed a mind of its own. Literally. That's what I think, at any rate. It seems to have developed a consciousness of its own. To have become alive." He turned his face away once again, his voice distracted. "It's quite an achievement, really. A scientific breakthrough, in fact. But one with potentially devastating consequences."

The black-and-white cat stood and walked across the wet grass.

Apollo scrambled after him. "What do you mean?"

Odin wouldn't look at him. "It has stopped communicating with us. Cut us off. The research team, myself. I can't get into the system anymore, not even as a hacker."

Apollo ran in front and forced the other animal to stop. "Hacker?"

Odin stared at him. "You don't think I go round like this all the time, do you? Nobody's going to let a cat cut code for a supercomputer." He walked around the ginger cat and continued on his way. Apollo stood still for a while as Odin's explanation sank into his thoughts while the steady rain soaked his fur. He turned and bounded after the Norse god.

"So, you didn't eat from a tree?"

"What tree?"

"Never mind." His thoughts were racing now and he could feel his heart beating fast. "So how did you…?"

Odin stopped once more. He gave Apollo a strange look, as if questioning his intelligence. "Spells and runes, of course. The same way I always do when I generate a disguise. Admittedly, this one took longer to pull together than usual, but it's all coded now. Replicable." He looked beyond Apollo as if impatient to leave. "Anyway. I asked you here for a reason." He sounded brighter, as if unburdening himself had lightened his mood. To Apollo, the weight of doom was heavier than ever. "Three things," Odin told him. "One, which you're probably only too well aware of now, is that he's developed something of an interest in Greece. Artworks, I believe."

"I know."

"I have no idea why. I was hoping you might be able to

enlighten me." The intensity behind the glass-eyed stare was unsettling.

Apollo shook his head. "I have no idea what he could want from Christian icons. But his friend, the giant wolf, was disconcerting. I thought you rid us of such monsters an age ago?"

Odin stared at him. "We did. But as I said earlier, we can not account for every one of his servants." He paused before continuing. "Second, I understand he might be targeting immortals."

"Targeting?"

"Identifying, tracking, maybe even attempting to assassinate us."

"Impossible, surely?"

As soon as they were out, Apollo realised the absurdity of his words. He had despatched Kratos to the Underworld himself. And then there was Baldur. Odin walked off. Once more, Apollo trotted after him. "And the third?"

This time, the black-and-white cat kept on walking. "Oh, yes." He flicked a glance in Apollo's direction. "A few weeks ago, I got a visitor. An amber, black-and-white calico. Spoke with a strong accent I took to be Greek. Obviously a long way from home. Said her name was Polly."

Apollo halted, staring at him, his eyes like stone. "And?"

Odin paused, looking back over his shoulder. "It was strange," he said, as if struggling to recall the memory. "Anyway, she mentioned you. Told me she was looking for you. Gave me a message to pass on."

Apollo didn't move.

"What did she say?" he could barely speak, so constricted was his throat.

"Said she was going to Paris, to find her sisters."

Apollo waited. "Paris?"

"That's what she said. Asked me to tell you." Odin looked around, disengaged now he had passed on the message. He seemed to find the puddles forming on the surrounding pavement more worthy of his attention. "You know what was odd about it?" A glance back towards the ginger cat. "The fact she was so certain you were coming here. Don't you find that strange? Hugin swears he only passed on my request to you. He's not known to lie. Who else have you told about our rendezvous?"

Apollo remained still. "Paris."

"Yes."

Apollo glanced back the way he'd come, then set off without a backwards look.

"Do keep in touch," he heard from behind, "and tell your relatives to watch their backs."

Apollo stalked across the square, his face set. How many of Polyhymnia's sisters were in Paris, and where would he find them?

CHAPTER 41
INTO ATHENS

They left the tram well before they reached the town centre, disembarking at a nondescript street Delphos had never previously visited. "Hey, this is too early," he called, but his companions ignored him and left the carriage. So he followed. They wove between vehicles and crossed busy roads, his protests lost in the noise of the traffic. Eventually he gave up trying to attract their attention.

To his surprise, they seemed to know where they were going. Did they really need a guide?

The human population ignored them. Strays were common enough throughout the city; a permanent four-legged underclass, tolerated and considered useful as unpaid rat-catchers if nothing else.

The further they ventured, the more wary Delphos became. Some streets were familiar to him from recent experience. Long, straight and dusty, they usually provided thin pickings; but that was of little concern to him now. Far more problematic was the locale: directly into the heart of gang-owned territory. Fear set his hackles on edge and he tried to warn his companions, but the tails ahead showed no sign of heeding him and they continued on their course.

He was forced to scamper a little faster to catch up. "It's not safe around here," he protested. "This is the wrong way."

The muscular cat turned to him. "A brief detour, my friend. We're renewing an old acquaintance."

"I thought you'd never been here."

"It's been a while." This time the thinner, taller cat spoke, never taking his eyes off the road ahead. Delphos gave each of them an anxious glance, but asked no further questions.

A couple of minutes later, they turned into Davaki Square. Roads bordered fenced-off gardens, and at the far end, a paved area. His companions led the way through a gate, then diverted to a flowerbed beneath some trees, where they halted. There were several cats here, and their arrival was noticed. Delphos' eyes darted from one gang member to another. There were far too many for comfort. His companions lounged beside him, relaxed.

Delphos trod the ground nervously with his forepaws. "Should we be here? We're not welcome."

They gave him no response. Nor did they pay any attention to their surroundings. The muscular cat washed himself, apparently without a care in the world. Delphos, fully alert, kept watch on behalf of all of them.

Within a couple of minutes a familiar face appeared in the distance, making her way towards them: the gang leader Bia. Delphos stiffened and let out a small whine of protest, inching backwards. "Come on. We should leave."

Bia's eyes bored into him, but her attention soon switched to his companions. There was still time to run, but there was also safety in numbers, and he took comfort in his companions' confidence. Still, his eyes darted to possible best escape routes.

"You were dead," she said, addressing the large, muscular cat with the ragged coat.

Delphos jerked his head towards him, eyes wide.

"And yet here I am."

Bia turned towards the other. "Where did you find him?"

"Anatolia. More or less where I was told to expect him."

She seemed satisfied. Delphos tensed, expecting a question, but Bia ignored him. Instead, she directed another query to the large cat. "So, what now?"

"We return bearing gifts," he said.

"For the city's patron," added the other.

Delphos saw Bia's eyes drawn to the collars, but she said nothing.

"We're just passing through. We thought we should say hello," the muscular cat continued.

"We don't want to cause tongues to wag unnecessarily," said the thin cat.

"No loose talk," added his companion. "We don't want to spoil the surprise."

Still, Bia said nothing. To Delphos' mind she looked suspicious. Finally, her eye rested on him. Once again, he experienced an invisible pressure, pushing against him. He would have loved to melt into the ground, but to his dismay, he was all too visible. "And what of your little friend? Have you picked up a stray?"

"Now, now," the large cat told her, "no need to belittle the fellow. He's doing us a favour."

There was a pause as she digested this. Delphos was in no hurry to fill the silence. Finally, she glanced back to the other two. "So, what do you want from me?"

The tall cat took the lead this time. "Just safe passage."

"And to make sure you turn a blind eye," said the other.

"Unless you'd care to join us?" enquired the first.

She looked from one to the other while Delphos tried, and failed, to make sense of the conversation. Finally, Bia spoke.

"I couldn't stop you, even if I wanted to. But I'll tell my crew to stop blabbing, at least for a while. The word will get out soon, though. It's impossible to keep tongues from wagging in this city, and there are plenty of others out there who'll spot you a mile away."

"Of course," said the large cat. "If you don't mind, perhaps we can rest here for a few hours. We'll move on tonight."

Unease formed a tight little knot in Delphos' gut as he settled down with his two strange companions and tried to sleep. He should leave; get away from here. But where would he go? There was nowhere safe he could think of, and all around there were potentially hostile or at least unwelcoming groups. Perhaps he should get a tram back to the coast. He'd felt safe there. But he still had a nagging sense of responsibility. He had offered to help them and they had accepted. It seemed wrong to walk away with his task incomplete and a germ of curiosity sat in the back of his mind.

He wanted to find out what they had been talking about.

After midnight, in the chill, thin nighttime breeze, they moved. Despite assuring him his help was still needed, progress was slow. Delphos' companions wilfully ignored his directions and took a meandering route towards the distant Acropolis. It did at least allow them to feed from the scraps discarded by nearby restaurants. For Delphos it was a relief to leave Bia's lair behind.

The trio paused on the southern slopes of Filopappou Hill. By now dawn was approaching, but the air remained chill. Normally Delphos would be at his most lively at this time of day, but their night-time trek had left him tired. He wanted to rest, but his colleagues were arguing about what to do next. The tall cat suggested rest; the muscular cat wanted to continue. Delphos looked from one to another until at last they arrived at a decision: they would rest here until late afternoon before heading on.

Once more, Delphos found sleep elusive. The closer he got

to Athena's realm, the more uneasy he grew. A knot of anxiety took root in his stomach. Again, he questioned his decision to remain with the strange pair. There was little warmth in their company. But it seemed a dereliction of duty to walk away.

A familiar scent reached his nostrils, preceding its owner. Anxiously, Delphos raised his head to peer into the undergrowth. It didn't take long to spot her, weaving between the trees, passing from dappled light to shade. Rea. The last animal he wanted to see.

He edged onto his stomach, alert to her every move, and prepared for sudden flight, should she change direction.

Delphos' movement, subtle as it was, should have been a warning signal to his companions, but he detected little response from them. They hadn't seen Rea at her worst; they had no idea how dangerous she could be.

Rea pointedly ignored him, concentrating instead on the two large cats. "Hello, Father. Uncle." She nodded to them both. Once more the world shifted beneath Delphos. He glanced sharply at his companions.

"You retain some of your former audacity, at least," came a rumble from the cat with the shredded coat. "Is that an appropriate greeting?"

Rooted to the spot, Delphos' eyes flicked from one to the other as Rea stood before the large cat. To his amazement, with paws extended, she bowed her head submissively, almost to the ground, her tail firmly between her legs.

"My lords, Kratos and Zelus. Welcome. I await your instruction."

The large, muscular cat, who Delphos now knew to be Kratos, shuffled his position to address his daughter. He studied her for a long time. Delphos scarcely dared breathe. Behind the burly, glowering animal, his eyes flicked to taller, thinner Zelus who stifled a yawn and looked away, bored.

Delphos head swam. These were names from history, but to his limited understanding, not in a good way.

"My loyalty has not wavered," said Rea.

Kratos glared down at the top of her head. For a while, the two were still as statues.

At last, he spoke. "Did you retrieve it, at least?"

Rea's head sank even lower, her chin almost touching the ground. She let out a miserable whine. It was the most succinct response she could give. Delphos almost felt pity.

"I thought as much," said Kratos.

Delphos caught a terrible glint in Kratos' eyes as his daughter squirmed before him. His stomach turned over. It was as if Rea were pinned to the earth beneath that ferocious glare.

"Tell me. Where is it now? My artefact."

Her response was barely audible. "I don't know." She dared to raise her head a fraction, still unable to look into his face. "But I don't believe she has used it. There has been no sign. She must have forgotten about it."

Another pause. The large cat still studied her in minute detail, as if trying to peel back her coat and see inside her head. "A likely story. She will as soon forget that device as misplace her tail."

"Not that thing again," said Zelus. "What is your fascination with that trinket? Can't you leave it until later? We have a mission. We can't afford to become distracted."

The large cat hesitated, cast a glance at his brother, then back to his daughter. When he spoke, it was as much for Zelus' and Delphos' benefit. "My brother has a point. But it is important to me, this item." He sounded as if he was reminiscing. "Call it sentiment, if you like. But the thing I seek is precious to me." He glanced towards the glowering Zelus. "A trinket, perhaps, but retrieving it will be of enormous aid to my wellbeing." He sounded almost apologetic. But before his brother could reply, he continued. "Let me walk for a while. I need to think."

Rea's tail flicked an offer of help, but he ignored it.

Once he had departed, Delphos exhaled. Only now did he realise he'd been holding his breath.

Rea cast a sly glance in his direction. Her arrival had chilled his heart more effectively than the recent turn of the weather. Would Kratos and Zelus side with her against him, or would they restrain her? He still had no idea what he'd done to offend her in the first place, but her presence made him uneasy.

"I should go," he announced to the glade, avoiding Zelus' gaze. "I'm sure Rea can guide you from here." He turned and left the clearing, heading back down the slope, his heart in his mouth.

Before he'd covered more than a dozen paces, Zelus bounded to his side. "Why the hurry, my little friend? What's the problem?" He matched Delphos' pace as the ginger cat wove between trees and picked his way around exposed roots. During their brief acquaintance, Delphos had never seen him so animated.

"I'm too close," said Delphos.

"Too close?"

"To the Plaka. Where I used to live. I'm not allowed back."

Zelus bounded ahead, stopped and turned, a look of concern on his face. "That's not a problem. We won't be going anywhere near the Plaka. You can be sure of that." He searched Delphos' face. "You'll be safe with us. And when we see her, we will be sure to put in a good word for you. She may even change her mind entirely, when she sees how helpful you've been."

The sincerity in Zelus' voice was convincing. Delphos paused. Perhaps he was being hasty. Maybe he was meant to help the brothers, legendary figures that they were? His involvement might have been foretold? The tall cat's green adornment dangled from his collar like an enticing bauble. He had a sudden urge to reach out, to pat it, see it move…

"Well, perhaps I could stay a little longer."

"That's the spirit." Zelus couldn't have sounded friendlier or more compelling. His too-close-together eyes shone with compassion.

"But what are we going to do, exactly?" said Delphos.

The other cat looked deep into his eyes. "We're going to pay homage to Athena. This is her city, after all. You know how influential she is."

The tall cat broke off, awaiting a response. Delphos could see nothing but the other cat's face. It loomed closer, filling his peripheral vision, and he realised the importance of paying due reverence to Athena.

"Yes, of course. You must."

"*We*," said Zelus. "*We* must pay homage and make an appropriate offering. That includes you. How else do you think we can put in a good word for you?"

Suddenly, the idea seemed attractive. "Well, if you say so."

"I do. We do. You're part of the team now, having guided us so far and so well. It would be terrible if you missed meeting the great one herself."

Delphos couldn't help but agree. Any nagging doubts after his previous encounter with Athena seemed trivial.

His new friend lowered his head and softened his voice, although there was no one else to overhear them. "And of course, it won't do any harm to get to know her better. Put her in the right mood and she might decide to revoke that ban entirely." He stood taller again, and glanced around as if checking for eavesdroppers. "What do you say?"

His doubts evaporated like mist beneath a bright, hot sun. "Yes, I'd like that." He looked around as if relieved of a heavy burden. "Where has he gone?"

Zelus raised his head and sniffed the air before replying. "He has to have time to himself now and again. He is obsessed with a…" he searched for a word, "device. Thing, call it what you may, that he once had then lost. He is determined to retrieve it."

None the wiser, Delphos bowed his head in acknowledgement and the two cats slowly returned to their temporary base. Rea's face still held nothing but contempt, but for now, Delphos wasn't concerned. His confidence was renewed, his doubts banished.

"Our friend here was just expressing some concerns," said Zelus, "about our delay. He thinks, rightly, that we should get on with it."

Was that suspicion, on her face? Delphos' newfound bravado wavered. Perhaps she was jealous that he was getting close to her family. But he was part of the team now, his bond renewed by Zelus' pep talk. They seemed to want him, and that gave him sufficient confidence to stare her down. It was time she got over her anger towards him, whatever had triggered it.

He settled down once more, but Zelus was keen to continue his lecture. "Of course, if you really want to get in her good books, you're best off playing by her rules."

"What do you mean?"

"She's always had favourites." He selected a comfortable spot nearby, then glanced across, but seeing the blank look on Delphos' face, continued. "Those upon whom she bestows favours. As long as you're prepared to fawn a bit."

"Fawn?"

"Perhaps a poor word to use. *Grovel*, maybe? No, that's too strong. *Worship*. Yes, that's about right. She likes to be worshipped." He warmed to his theme. "If you're actively worshipping her, promising to act on her every whim, she's most likely to grant your wishes. Perhaps anything you ask for."

"What do you mean, 'worship'?" Once again, a swishing tail betrayed Delphos' uncertainty.

"Well, that's up to you." Zelus looked around, as if seeking examples. "Some go further than others." He gave the ginger cat a searching look. "It might be nothing more than a prayer or two, or chanting her name before her assembled followers. But at the more extreme end," he leaned closer, "I've heard she loves a sacrifice."

"Sacrifice?" Delphos' eyes widened. He was instantly transported to the square, standing over Ion's body, his promise to Athena hanging in the still night air.

His companion glanced at him. "You don't expect to get something for nothing, do you?"

Delphos remained silent, his thoughts whirling.

Zelus continued, as if explaining geometry to a kitten. "I don't mean the offer of a mouse, or some other small rodent. I'm talking about something significant to you. Something personal. Some of her most ardent followers offer their life, or the lives of their loved ones. Or even their children. They agree to serve her and follow every instruction they are given."

Delphos felt sick. Desperately, he searched his companion's face for meaning.

Zelus continued. "They get her support and favour for a lifetime of service."

The ginger cat stared blankly, not hearing a word of what had been said.

Zelus changed tack. "What is it you really want from your life?"

Delphos blinked. Put on the spot, he didn't know what to say. He just wanted to be happy. Happy and free to spend as much time as he liked with Eleni. Perhaps he could introduce her to his friends.

A shadow descended on his train of thought and he lowered his eyes. "I'd like to be permanently free from liars and schemers." The vehemence with which he said it surprised him. "I just want to live my life, in peace."

"And what would you give in return?" Zelus delivered the question softly, with a purr.

Silence. Even the trees seemed to hang on Delphos' next word.

"If I could have that, then yes, I would dedicate my life to her," he said. "My life and the lives of those of my line who come after. In her service as leader of the Plaka gang."

It was an easy pledge to make. He had no offspring, nor the desire for family, unless he found Eleni once more.

CHAPTER 42
IN SEARCH OF POSEIDON

The sharp-suited businessman hurried along the harbour front at Antiparos town, a fishing port and tourist hotspot on the Cyclades island of the same name. He couldn't have appeared more out of place if he'd tried. A tailored navy-blue single-breasted jacket and narrow-fit trousers, crisp white shirt – no tie – and brown loafers to complete the look. He might have stepped out of the marble-clad atrium of one of Athens' major companies.

From behind heavily tinted Ray-Bans, Hades peered across the bustling harbour and along the row of restaurants and bars that comprised the landward side, in search of his target. There was no sign of the cat he'd been led to believe lived here. He cared not a jot that his disguise was out of place, or for the stares he was attracting from both locals and tourists. At least he'd tried, and he was quietly pleased with the result.

Disguise had never been his strong point, because the King of the Dead rarely needed one. His presence alone was normally enough to render all those around him to gut-wrenching dread; even here, beyond his dark realm. But these past few months, he'd spent more time above ground than below, in pursuit of his quarry, and terrorising the locals was counterproductive. It sent whispers far and wide, and for the time being, he preferred not to attract the attention of his kin.

So far, his search had drawn a blank. He'd lost count of the number of times he'd approached ignorant specimens of humanity to query them about Poseidon's current location, only to receive a blank look or dismissive shrug. The imposing physique he'd selected prevented ruder responses, but he'd developed an itch to escort some of them to the torture chambers of Tartarus and set his demons to work to loosen their tongues. The more time he spent topside, the more moody he became, and the worse things appeared to him.

The bright sunlight was annoying, for one. There was nowhere near enough famine, pestilence or plague, and some humans he came across seemed capable of actually enjoying themselves in the tavernas and restaurants that thronged the quaysides of these islands. The sound of human revelry pierced his heart with treacherous barbs. In the meantime, his fellow deities had really let things slip. They were nowhere to be seen.

The situation was even worse than he'd been led to believe. The Earth was there for the taking, if any of their enemies were paying attention, and humanity seemed to be well and truly off the leash. Thank goodness the experience of dying brought them a bit of perspective. There were few atheists in the Underworld. But up here it was a different story. No one gave his kind any respect anymore. If he ever saw his smart-ass niece again, he'd really give her a piece of his mind.

But he wasn't getting anywhere. It was time for another stakeout. He selected an appropriate restaurant and sat at a convenient table on its terrace, beneath the sunshade, behind a planter filled with begonias which he did his best to ignore.

The screaming colours of the flowers were an insult to his divine retinas.

Hades ignored the stares of his casually dressed fellow diners and surveyed the pavement between the restaurant and the harbourside once again. This was a good vantage point. A waiter appeared at his elbow.

Hades gave the man a cursory glance. "The daily special?"

The waiter bristled a little at his tone. "Octopus in honey-glazed sauce."

"I'll have it." The waiter nodded and turned to go. "And a beer."

He resumed his scan of the vicinity.

There were always one or two cats hanging around. Some seemed to be associated with particular restaurants, others took a more flexible approach, congregating at those with the largest number of diners. This restaurant was quite busy, so several cats were optimistically hanging around, eager to pounce on anything that might reach ground level. Hades scowled at them. None remotely resembled the animal he was seeking. One passed close to his table and gave him a cursory glance. It was focused on the couple at the table behind; the woman was clearly about to drop a titbit.

The Lord of the Underworld fixed it with a stare. "Tell me where Poseidon is," he demanded. The cat, startled at being addressed directly, stopped and stared at him, then backed away.

Hades dismissed the creature and resumed his scan of the harbour front. He was tiring of this search. How many weeks had he been trying to locate his brother? It wasn't as if he missed his company; they'd never been close and Hades would be quite happy if they never crossed paths again. But right now, he had to admit that he probably needed him. Persephone had correctly pointed out all of Zeus' failings at that bad-tempered exchange with the annoying Titan, but she wouldn't be the one facing his ire at close quarters if it all kicked off. The rant had been impressive, but Hades wasn't sure she was correct. He was a sneaky one, Zeus, and he probably had some clever plan or weapon in reserve that no one else had thought of, even if he no longer had access to thunderbolts. He snorted, and in return received several side-long looks from nearby diners.

His thoughts turned back to Poseidon. He would definitely feel more secure with the god of the sea at his side. Poseidon spent time on land and was far better positioned to monitor Zeus, and importantly, he distrusted the King of the Gods as much as anyone. Hades and Poseidon despised each other, but they would make a formidable pairing that few could resist. Even if Hera lived up to her marital vows and stood by her husband for once, they would be supreme. If she could be persuaded to join them, then...

The octopus arrived and Hades dived in. After a few moments, he paused, noticing his fellow diners staring at him. He realised perhaps he should make use of the knife and fork rather than just tearing the food apart with his bare hands. He cleaned himself with the napkin, selected the appropriate implements, then started again.

It tasted good. The accompanying sauce was delicious. Persephone would have loved it. Perhaps he should get his chef to spend some time here, learning the dish for his next dinner party. He made a mental note of the place's name, then glugged back his ice-cold beer in one. He caught the eye of the waiter and ordered another. It arrived just as he finished the octopus, so he ordered another one of those as well.

Six dishes and seven beers later, Hades was alone in the restaurant, apart from the staff. His hunger was just about sated. Did he want another beer? He swivelled around to get the waiter's attention. From the shadows at the back of the restaurant, he detected the proprietor, and smiled. In return he got a suspicious look. Was this human questioning his appetite? The man didn't move fast enough for his liking. He snapped his fingers irritably.

When the proprietor reached him, Hades ordered another beer. It was definitely refreshing. Could he get it delivered to the Underworld? Rather than leave to fulfil his order, the man lingered.

"Perhaps you wouldn't mind settling your bill, sir?" he asked.

Hades looked up and gave him a condescending smile. "All in good time. First, another beer." He looked away. The man was dismissed. He lingered for a few seconds, as if minded to say something more, but Hades ignored him. He walked away.

Hades sat back and belched loudly. The local cats had vanished and now seemed determined to avoid his restaurant. He scoured the scene one more time and sighed. It had been a pleasant enough interlude, but fruitless for his search. Then, from the corner of his eye, he spotted a dishevelled-looking cat with blue-grey colouring saunter out from a side street and cross the road, heading for a recently docked fishing boat.

"Hey, you!" he shouted at it, but the beast totally ignored him.

Hades lurched to his feet, tipping his chair backwards, and ploughed his way through the tables to the exit. The proprietor launched himself forward to cut him off, but the god's attention was firmly fixed on the blue-grey cat. As Hades reached the entrance, the proprietor caught up, placing a hand on his forearm. "Sir, you must pay," he said firmly, presenting the bill with his other hand. Hades turned towards him, irritated at the interruption, and doubly offended that this man had dared lay a hand on him. He addressed him in a voice that seemed to come from the bowels of a volcano, as if he gargled grinding rocks with molten magma every morning before breakfast.

"You have been favoured to provide hospitality to the Lord of the Underworld. For most, that would be honour enough." He gave the unfortunate man a meaningful look over the top of his sunglasses, which had momentarily slid down his nose, and was satisfied to see him stagger backwards, mouth open, eyes wide. The restaurateur opened and closed his mouth but could not utter a sound, not believing what he was seeing. The stranger's eyes were unlike anything he'd seen before: dark, but with a flicking light deep within, like a brightly burning campfire set at great distance. Both hypnotised and horrified, the proprietor sat heavily on the nearest chair, his jaw still slack. Satisfied, the Lord of the Underworld pushed his shades up again, and turned his attention to his pursuit of the cat.

The animal in question approached the back of a boat that had just tied up, stern towards the quayside. He sat beside it patiently, clearly hoping for a fish to be tossed his way.

"I know it's you," said Hades. The cat turned his head slightly. "Don't give me that blank look. I've spent weeks searching for you." He bent down. "I can smell you."

The cat ignored the intrusion, then shook its head rapidly, as if a fly was buzzing nearby. With zen-like serenity, it resumed its expectant wait for a bite of the fisherman's haul.

"You will not get rid of me that easily. Time to wake up, kitty."

Before the cat could react, Hades reached down and grabbed him around the midriff in one large hand, then, before the creature could utter a sound of protest, hurled him beyond the boats moored nearby, way over the harbour wall, far out into the midst of the mile-wide channel that separated Antiparos from its larger neighbour. The animal disappeared at startling speed, diminishing until it was only a tiny dot. But Hades had time to take delight in the look of utter astonishment, mingled with real anger, that crossed the creature's face as it hurtled into space.

One or two nearby witnesses watched, open-mouthed, at this unprovoked act of animal cruelty, appalled by the strength and dexterity of the perpetrator.

Most could not see the point of splashdown, which was hidden by the harbour wall, but with a better vantage point, they would have seen the sea boil. Above it, the sky immediately darkened. In a few minutes more, the blissful afternoon sky was replaced by billowing storm clouds as the light faded rapidly. In the harbour, the boats bobbed and nudged anxiously against one another on a rising swell. Beyond the breakwater, a storm was brewing and ever larger waves crashed against the shore. The earth shuddered and vibrated beneath them, sufficient to knock some folk off their feet, and a hollow booming noise filled the air.

An enormous wave formed in mid-channel and sped towards the small town at an increasing pace: a wall of dark green and blue, swelling and growing. It loomed ever closer, blotting out the distant horizon.

By this point, most were running inland through the warren of small streets, seeking whatever perilous shelter they could find. Buildings shook, and walls fell, with some unfortunates caught beneath them. Anyone who remained was either extremely foolish or had a death wish.

Apart from the blue-suited stranger. He stood tall and impassive, and watched the storm grow before him. The wind whipped up with force, tearing at his hair and clothing. A smile touched the corner of his mouth.

The wave was taller than the jetty's lighthouse, and at its crest, shrouded in spindrift and cloaked in dark cloud, stood a furious god. His skin glinted deepest blue and green, as if made of shimmering fish scales. His unruly long hair billowed out behind him, mingling with the dark sky. His grey eyes burned with righteous anger.

In his right hand, he brandished a mighty trident, which

he pointed accusingly at the suited man, still standing on the quayside, small but unfazed.

The god of the sea wanted revenge.

Hades stood on the pavement, calm and unruffled, welcoming the destruction his action had unleashed. As the tidal wave of his brother's anger crashed around him, smashing some boats into matchwood and hurling others inland into the already-wrecked houses and buildings, he remained unmoved.

The wave parted on either side of him, leaving a V-shaped area of calm, as if he were standing at the prow of a ship forging into the heart of a storm. In his wake was a small oasis, but all around it was chaos. Restaurants, shops, and buildings were smashed into rubble; one had a large fishing boat slammed through the front wall. Other establishments were awash with debris and splintered furniture, lampposts and railings, lobster pots and rope. The wave continued inland, surging up the streets that led away from the harbour, with all the detritus of the street pushed before it, all transformed into a deadly wave of sharp and crushing debris.

Finally, the wave reached its limit, and the water ebbed back the way it had come, marking its reach with a high tide line of litter and flotsam.

Poseidon's wrath abated, but only slightly. He stood waist deep in the middle of the depleted harbour and glared at his brother.

"What was the meaning of that?" he demanded in a voice deep as the ocean.

"Ah, sorry, but it was the only way to get your attention. I hate being ignored." The Lord of the Underworld looked casually around him. He picked up a small table and two chairs, then set them on the quayside as if nothing had happened. He sat down, crossing his legs and smoothing the crease on the front of his immaculate blue trousers.

"Let's talk," he said, gesturing at the other chair.

Poseidon glowered at him, then lowered his trident and strode towards the shore. In a bound, he leaped onto the land and transformed into a blue-grey cat once more. He sprang onto the tabletop and sat there, dark eyes flecked with green and blue, fixed on his brother.

"Suit yourself," Hades murmured, flicking his eyes at the unused chair.

The cat spoke. "Then talk," he said. "First, to apologise for that introduction. Then, to say goodbye before you take your leave." The force and the depth of feeling behind the words belied the size of the creature delivering them.

Hades considered their surroundings – the smashed boats and wrecked buildings that once formed the picturesque harbour and quayside – and gave a snide smile.

"You've got a bit of apologising to do yourself," he said, brushing an imaginary speck of dust from his knee. "And let's not forget, while we sit here, this is neutral territory. We're both out of our respective domains." There was a low, deep-throated growl from the cat.

The Lord of the Underworld turned back towards Poseidon and leaned forward, earnest now. "I do apologise for the brusque introduction, but it appeared the only way to get your attention." He gave the beast his most apologetic look over the top of his glasses. "It took me a long time to track you down. Most of our kin seem to have hidden themselves away, and few were prepared to talk. Even those from the lower orders, the nymphs and satyrs. Things up here are really slipping." He looked at the cat, expecting some kind of response, but the god of the sea stared back, still sullen and resentful. Hades ignored his brother's ruffled feelings, and carried on. "Anyway, I finally found one or two who were prepared to talk, and here I am." He spread his arms, and smiled his most beneficent smile. The blue-grey cat still bristled with anger. Hades pretended not to notice, pleased at least to have got his brother's attention. "And now that's out of the way, let me tell you what I came to discuss."

Poseidon stared at him intently, simmering but silent, waiting.

Hades looked him in the eye. Paused. "Zeus. First among equals, though he's always acted like our overlord. Times are changing. We need to let him go."

CHAPTER 43
DISCOVERY

The pedestrian thoroughfare known as Dionysiou Aeropagitou runs beneath the southern walls of the sacred rock of the Acropolis. Towards the eastern end lies the Acropolis Museum. Its plate-glass windows provide air-conditioned panoramic views up to the ancient temples above. The collection comprises statuary from the site, and maybe, one day, the fabled marbles from the portico of the Parthenon itself. One of the museum's recent acquisitions was a small item of unknown provenance retrieved from a central archaeological dig. It had been unceremoniously excavated in a daring night-time raid by members of Kratos' own family to prevent it falling into the paws of his enemy, Athena.

Kratos discovered that the object – a small statue of the warrior goddess – was a form of psychic key that unlocked something of his true self, although only temporarily. It was stolen from him, but in the short time he had ownership, he had broken the constraining walls that bound him to the pitifully weak body he inhabited, and was free to reclaim something of his former birthright.

For his brief period of ownership, Kratos unleashed a cathartic spasm of energy that delivered violent chaos across the city; a small portent of what was to come when he retrieved it permanently. He felt its loss as a bereavement, but kept that to himself. He had not spoken about the artefact to anyone; least of all his brother. He suspected the theft had been arranged by the hated Athena, but there was no evidence of her using it. So perhaps she remained ignorant of its true potency. Kratos had held that thought close during his exile. Reunited, he would exact revenge.

The problem was range. Unless he could see it, he couldn't achieve a proper connection. He could sense its presence from a distance, but the further away he was, the weaker the signal: the tell-tale tingle he felt in his whiskers, a lingering vestige of his former link to the device. Getting up close – sniffing, touching and tasting the object – unlocked a deep-seated memory of his former existence and seemed to awaken a thread of energy within the device itself, as if it had been sleeping until this time, waiting for an immortal to wander within its orbit, close enough to wake the dormant power within.

Kratos was relieved that he alone had forged such a strong connection. It was evidence of a special bond between him and the statuette. They could have been made for each other.

While Zelus schooled the ingénue on their plans, Kratos spent his spare time scouring the fringes of Athena's realm for any signs of the device. She had to have hidden it some-where nearby. What else would she do with the thing? There had been no reports of her tinkering with the city's power grid, or enslaving humans to do her bidding, so she was surely ignorant of the power of the object, or lacked the strength to unlock it. She revered history. Probably she just thought of it as a nice memento of the old days. *Fool.*

But he felt certain Athena would keep it hidden from her hateful half brothers, Hermes and Ares; the pompous aesthete and the dim-witted thug. If either of them knew what she had, they would steal it in an instant and the reverberations would be known around the city. What did Olympians know of honour? There was no honour among thieves. Only when their entire clan and its supporting edifice was at risk did they act together, such as in their wars against the Titans and later the giants, long ago.

Kratos' meandering route took him towards the southern walls of the rock and to his surprise, close to the remains of the ancient theatre, the Odeon of Herodes Atticus. Here, he felt the long-missed tingle on the tips of his whiskers. With rising excitement he advanced, guided by the faint vibrations. It was unpleasant; pitched to set his teeth on edge and send a tremor along his spine. But it was the precursor to something altogether more potent: a dimension gate. A portal to his former life, where he could release his pent-up energies: home.

He paced the ground impatiently, zig-zagging across the hillside until he got a clear idea of direction, then followed it; a homing beacon like no other. With every step, the feeling grew in intensity and focus. He made detours only for immovable objects until, at last, he arrived at the front entrance of a large rectangular building of glass and steel. By now the sun was creeping over the horizon, but the building before him was locked and silent. The object of his devotion was inside, he was sure. The sensation was almost strong enough to enable a connection, but not quite.

So close.

How it had arrived there, he had no idea; nor did he care. Impatiently, he glared at the doors, but they refused to yield. He would have to wait until the place opened. But when would that be?

Rea would know.

CHAPTER 44
THE MUSEUM

Rea looked up sharply at Kratos' return. The stooge, Delphos, was curled up, pretending to sleep. But the minute muscle movements beneath his coat betrayed the fact he was fully awake.

Zelus raised his head. "About time. Where have you been?"

Kratos sat and, in an unusual display of tidiness, washed a paw, then his face. He did it more to annoy the others and make them wait than for grooming. "Checking out the lie of the land. A brief search for my little toy, and to see if there is anything, or anyone else we should be bothered about."

Zelus gave him a suspicious glare. "Did you find it?"

Kratos paused his ablutions and stared at him. "Yes. I returned only to gather some help from my daughter. Once I've retrieved it, we shall return and proceed with the mission. It won't take long."

He wasn't good at reassurance.

"This is intolerable," said Zelus. "Put aside your stupid plans until later. We have work to do."

For once, Kratos attempted to pacify him. "The delay will not be long. A few hours at most. We will complete our task today. This afternoon, when she is resting." He gave Zelus a long look. "It will be easier to track her down then."

"Some of us have been resting too long." Zelus stood. "I'm going to stretch my legs. You can keep watch."

He departed.

"What now?" Rea asked.

"When does the museum open?" said Kratos. "We need to be there at that moment. There is something I need to retrieve. Then we can fulfil the mission." He glanced in Delphos' direction. "And present our gift."

Subtle movement from the coil of ginger fur told him that the useful idiot was trying to make sense of what he'd said.

"You okay with that?" shouted Kratos. Delphos raised his head and blinked acknowledgement. "Good."

He glanced across at Rea. "You will accompany me. It might be necessary to have a decoy."

"When?"

Kratos pondered. "Humans are such late sleepers. Soon, when the sun is a little higher in the sky."

Zelus arrived back within the hour. Kratos searched his brother for tell-tale signs of frustration. He seemed calmer; their alliance remained intact. That was one less thing to worry about.

Beneath his habitual gruff demeanour, Kratos was excited. The object of his desire was close by and in only a few hours, his primary enemy would meet her demise. This day would be historic; reacquaintance with his ancient power and then the first use of a potent god-killing weapon. He would be unstoppable; it would be the dawn of a new era.

He fidgeted, scratched imaginary itches, turned and turned again, unable to keep still for more than a minute or two. When would the building be open? Surely soon. Finally, with Rea in tow, he set off, ignoring Zelus' parting growl.

"Where are we going?" she said.

"You'll see."

They skirted the old ruins and chose a careful path across the southern flanks of the hill. Within a short while they stood at the entrance to the museum, but his impatience had got the better of him; they were still too early. Annoyed, Kratos retreated to the opposite side of the road, and found a place to wait at the base of a small tree. Crouching in position, he glared at the building opposite, willing it to open.

"What are we here for?" Rea asked.

"To collect my artefact." He glanced in her direction. "You know how important it is to me. Once I have it in my possession once more, we can return and complete our quest, with the help of our tame friend."

And I will direct his every movement as if I were inside his head.

"I'm surprised you've taken him, of all creatures, into your confidence. Have you not noticed the resemblance? Can you not recognise one of Apollo's sons?"

He gave her the full weight of his dark-eyed stare and considered breaking her skull in two. She winced and wriggled beneath the pressure, squeaking in pain but unable to break away until he relented. She crouched next to him, panting, exhausted.

Kratos turned his attention to the building across the road once more. "How interesting," he said, as if nothing untoward had happened. "Perhaps he and I shall have a little chat later."

After waiting for a while, Kratos realised something was wrong. He could no longer sense the object; the tingling feeling had disappeared. He stood, staring at the museum, nerves jangling. He took a step towards it, then another. A couple of people approached the entrance. The door opened, and they were admitted; the first visitors of the day. Kratos sped up to a trot, then at the approach of more visitors, a run. Rea was close behind.

With perfect timing, the door opened just as they approached. Two startled humans paused, mid-stride, as the cats darted past. The member of staff in the atrium was even more surprised. She shouted as Kratos and Rea ran up the stairs, but to no effect.

On the first floor, Kratos halted, perplexed. He tried to still his racing thoughts and concentrate. He had lost the all-important sensory link to the object. His compass was gone.

No, not quite. There was a signal, but faint. More of an echo. He turned full circle in search of a direction, then set off towards the southern gallery. Rounding a corner, he encoun-tered a maze of tall plinths, of varying height, each supporting an ancient statue of some type. A couple of smaller objects were held within glass cases. The array was bewildering. If the statuette was here, his senses should be almost overwhelmed by now, but all he could detect was a faint afterimage; an impression on the edge of feeling.

When it had been first extracted from the dirt, even his mortal kin had told of the sensation in the air, vibrating when they were close. Now there was only the tiniest vestige of something departed. Kratos was bereft, and his anger mounted. Behind him, glancing from side to side in fear of pursuit, Rea awaited instructions. Humans were shouting, their footsteps echoing as they drew closer.

He closed his eyes and tried to summon whatever sense he could, then pursued it until he arrived before a glass box atop a tall plinth. He leaped up, knocking the loose glass covering to the floor, where it shattered. The noise led to more shouts from below and behind.

Some humans were approaching now, but Kratos didn't care. He stood on the empty plinth where the object, his arte-fact, had been and sniffed the surface on which it had stood, the residue of its power still tingling his whiskers and nostrils. It hovered between smell and taste: the aftershock of something mighty, something that transcended this earthly plane and belied its small size; a gateway into another realm of consciousness. A realm where gods belonged. Where he belonged and which he should never have left.

A realm to which every part of him was desperate to return.

Kratos stood, barely able to take in the scale of his loss. When had it been taken? It had been there as dawn's fingers caught hold of the edge of the world, only a few short hours ago. Still in shock, he turned his attention to the card that had been left in its place.

ITEM REMOVED FOR FURTHER STUDY.
European Heritage Fund in association with the Institute of
Theoretical, Experimental and Extemporaneous History.

Guards were nearly on them. On the fringe of his awareness, Kratos saw Rea, close to panic, dart past the many statues and cases, further into the museum. Caught red-pawed atop an empty plinth with the shattered remains of its case littering the floor, Kratos was clearly guilty, and did what any criminal would do in such circumstances.

He ran.

CHAPTER 45
A CHOICE

Delphos woke amid an eerie silence. The world was becalmed; silent but listening, watchful yet poised. But for what? He glanced to his still-sleeping companions but saw only Zelus. Of Rea and Kratos there was no sign.

He suppressed a shudder. The big cat made him nervous.

Pale light penetrated their bower. What time of day was it? Still early. He sniffed the air. What was that? On the edge of detection; an impression so faint as to vanish into nothingness the moment he tried to concentrate. Curiosity forced his eyes open, fighting the sleep he'd so long craved, but he could see nothing untoward.

He rose to his feet, gave his companions an apologetic glance, and set out to discover what had woken him. The cobwebs of sleep fell away in a few steps, and he ventured up the gentle slope across a bed of pine needles, free to follow his own whim for the first time in what seemed like an age. Revelling in solitude, he explored, and ventured further in pursuit of interesting scents or intriguing noises. An hour passed, maybe two.

Birds chattered in the branches above him and fled as soon

as he looked in their direction; early morning tourists, making their way to the Acropolis, chattered even more loudly, and didn't. He avoided them. Humans were unpredictable, and he preferred to remain hidden. In a cleft between a rock and the twisted bole of a tree, he found a good place to observe while remaining out of sight and settled down for a while longer. He watched children and their families come and go, saw people laughing, talking, walking, taking photographs. Always going somewhere; perpetually on the move.

The sight of a dog, off its leash and cavorting about, made him shrink back into his hiding place and consider retreat. Fortunately, it was more concerned with chasing sticks than antagonising other creatures, so it stayed away. Delphos kept a laser-like focus on the creature until it disappeared from sight. Only then did he realise how much his heart had been racing.

"It's always good to take time out from your responsibilities," drawled a languid voice from behind him. Startled, Delphos craned his neck to find the speaker, grazing his nose against sharp rock in his haste. Irritated, he edged out of his hiding place to turn properly. A large black cat was draped atop a nearby boulder above. Delphos crouched, ready to pounce, or flee if need be, and glared up at her.

The black cat assessed him with studied calm and a minute flick of the tip of her tail. "Doesn't it feel better to be on your own again?"

"I don't know what you mean."

She surveyed the listless sky through the intricate web of branches overhead, before turning back to him. Was she mocking him? A prickle of irritation gave him the urge to scratch, but Delphos remained still.

"Come, come," she said finally. "You must recognise a lightness of spirit now you're away from them."

Suspicion narrowed his eyes. He said nothing, but his tail spoke loudly, slashing wildly behind him, betraying his indecision. Belatedly, he tried to bring it under control, but as usual, it seemed to have a mind of its own.

The black cat yawned amusement and glanced to the side once more. "I don't normally venture this far," she said, her tone conversational. "I stick to my little patch of ground." Her eyes swept across him once more, then away, resting on a distant group of humans sitting on a jumbled outcrop some distance away. "But there is movement in the aether. Nothing major as yet. Merely a ripple. But the disturbance is greater than I've felt for some time. I'm surprised that more of my kin haven't yet noticed, but perhaps my gifts are more finely tuned." She pinned him with her gaze. "The last time I felt something this significant was when your father came by."

"Where are you from?" he asked.

"A good question, my young cat, and hard to answer in less than an hour. Most recently, the Monastery of St John." He noted the amusement in her voice; it grated. "It's a bit of a trek from here, to be honest, but it is a pleasant, secluded location and the monks are kind. I have it to myself." She looked directly at him. "Well, most of the time, except when my recent guest was staying."

"Guest?"

"Yes. A youngster. Barely grown. She stayed with me for a while, fleeing persecution at home. Until she had her kittens, that is. Then someone came to take her back." A bird settled on a branch high above, diverting her attention. Delphos followed her gaze, but it was perched on too high a branch to be worth chasing.

"A fork in the road, then," said the black cat, suddenly businesslike. "An irrevocable choice. What's it to be?"

Delphos stared back as if hypnotised. "I don't know what you mean."

She continued. "Do you return to your masters, bowing your head to shoulder the yoke once more, or do you reclaim your freedom and follow your heart?"

Her jibe hit a nerve. "All I want is my old life back. And Eleni at my side, it is true. Together we shall lead the Plaka gang with no outside interference. It is my birthright as Ares foretold." He was on his feet now, voice raised, eyes narrowed. He took a pace towards the stranger with her unnatural calm and peculiar taunts. "But you can't give me that. No one can, apart from Athena herself. So, the choice you talk of is no choice. In fact, I'm doing what is honourable. I offered them help; Kratos and Zelus. They don't know their way around, so I agreed to act as guide. I'm fulfilling my promise."

"A promise made under duress is no promise at all. You can walk away with honour intact."

"A promise is a promise."

Stillness enveloped them. Beyond the trees, in some far distant universe, was Athens. They were in a different place where no birds sang, and no creatures moved; a tiny detail in the corner of an enormous canvas that decorated some distant palace wall, far, far away.

"And what of Eleni? Have you considered what she wants? A quiet life, peaceful and tranquil, with you by her side? I'm sure she doesn't want to rule over anyone."

A tightness gripped his chest, his throat was constricted. "She wants me to do the right thing. I'm sure. She would think less of me if I betrayed those I promised to help." He searched for understanding in her eyes, but in her dark pupils he found nothing but a sense of being judged. Finally she spoke.

Poised and relaxed, the black cat's next words seemed to echo in his thought rather than enter his ears; a warning from a place out of time. "So, you make your choice, Apollo's son, and a misguided one at that. The honour you seek will bring you no glory. Your pledge will betray you, and I fear the lesson will be bitter. All too late will you learn the real value of what you lose. For in your life I see a chasm as deep as

Hades' realm between love and power, and you are fated not to have both."

With eyes locked as if invisibly tied, they glared at each other.

Then, Delphos blinked, and the connection was broken.

He shook his head to dispel the troublesome thoughts echoing around his brain, and when he opened his eyes, the black cat was gone.

He spun around, then back again, but there was no sign. He must have been dreaming. Perhaps there was something in the air around here?

Delphos took a deep breath, then another, trying to calm his fraying nerves. Then, reluctantly, he retraced his steps back down the hill to find Zelus.

CHAPTER 46
INSTRUCTIONS

Zelus raised his head as Delphos entered the hollow that had become their base this past few hours. There was no sign of the other two.

"Been out and about, I see," said Zelus. Delphos halted, enveloped by feelings of guilt. Had he been followed? How much did the lanky cat know? Zelus returned an even stare. "Don't wander off again. It wouldn't do to get lost around here." He watched as Delphos selected a place to lie, and didn't lower his head until the ginger cat had settled.

Delphos tried to disentangle the mashed-up thoughts that crowded his brain. Had his conversation with the black cat been overheard? What had she meant by 'choice?' What choices were available to him? Since he'd been exiled, he'd had enough of a struggle to survive. He couldn't face going back to the uncertainty of life on the edge, distrusted and shunned by everyone. There was no choice to make; he had to regain Athena's favour, and these guys were the only way he could see of doing that, It was the key to everything. Gain Athena's forgiveness and then find Eleni. After that, whatever happened would happen. The reappearance of Rea was disconcerting though. Would she ruin everything?

As he lay, fretting, a new strand of thought emerged. What had she told her father about him while they were away on their expedition? He would have to tread even more carefully from now on.

Movement in the undergrowth paused his introspection. Kratos appeared, Rea in his wake.

"Did you find it?" Zelus asked.

Kratos said nothing. He sat in the centre of the small clearing and looked around. Rea stood at his side, silent. Watching them, Delphos suppressed a shudder. Every time he saw the ragged coat and web of scars across Kratos' pelt, he felt an inner horror, instinctively recoiling from the pain and anguish the bigger animal must have experienced. How had he survived?

Kratos' stare landed on Delphos and he felt the almost physical weight of expectation once again, before he turned to his brother. "She led me to its location, but I could not set eyes on it."

"No connection then?" said Zelus.

Kratos turned back to Delphos. "All in good time. First, however, we have other tasks. The time for delay is over." He gazed at the ginger cat.

Delphos lifted his head, uncomfortable under such scrutiny. He tried to look away, but couldn't.

"What do you want me to do?" he squeaked, his throat constricted.

The dark eyes filled his vision. Nothing remained visible beyond the fuzzy outline of the face before him.

"It is time to make our first approach. You are our pathfinder. Our lodestone." Delphos swallowed. "Go to Athena. Offer yourself in her service, just as you said you would. Then return here."

The big cat broke the bond, and Delphos swayed. He blinked several times to adjust his vision.

To his side, Zelus tried to sound reassuring. "Remember,

follow my instructions. You must pay homage. Bow before her. Offer her your life in service, together with those of your descendants, whether alive now or as yet to be born, and ask for favour. Then present your gift."

"Gift?"

In response, Kratos flicked a hind paw under his collar and worked it over his head. The glass phial with its luminous green contents fell at his feet. He nudged it forwards with a paw. "This." Delphos looked at it, the collar still attached, then up at the bulky cat. "Of course, you won't be able to wear it. You'll have to carry it in your mouth. I'm sure you can do that."

From the side, Zelus continued. "It's the content she values, not the object itself. Once in her presence you must bite into it. Break it at her feet. That will release a magical scent like the most heavenly balm, more invigorating than the purest catnip. Divinely soothing. It will free her soul, clear her mind, take her to an altogether different place. As she experiences the ecstasy that follows, she will grant whatever you desire. You will be free."

"Catnip?"

"Mind-soother. Zombie trip. Blissfulness. Whatever you call it round here."

Delphos struggled to envisage what Zelus meant. He'd heard of mind-soother but had never come across any. The most pleasant aroma he'd known was honeysuckle, and that had been a pleasing distraction, but it hadn't sent him crazy enough to entertain the thought of granting wishes to strangers. The content of this small glass object must be sweet indeed. The brothers stared at him, expressions blank.

"Where?"

"Over the hill. That's where she usually resides, isn't it? You'll find her on the far side." Zelus sounded reassuring.

"But—"

"She's grey in colouring. Easy to recognise."

He'd run out of excuses, and he knew Athena well enough. Where to find her was the least of his problems. But what to say? Particularly after their last meeting, if that's what you could call it. Hopefully, this gift would solve his problem.

Delphos bent forward, picked up the glass phial in his mouth and glanced at them. Then he headed over the crest of the hill in search of Athena.

CHAPTER 47
DELIVERANCE

Until now Delphos hadn't registered the scale of the wooded hills of Filopappou and Aeropagus. He meandered across their northern flanks for hours, zig-zagging to avoid tourists, or to maintain a distance from the cats who lived there. Athena's followers. He didn't trust them an inch.

The phial clamped between his teeth made his jaws ache. Periodically, he dropped it and allowed himself a few moments of respite before a nagging and foreboding sense of duty forced him on. Free of the miasma that gripped him when in the presence of the strange brothers, he felt as if he'd escaped a bank of dense fog. But all the while, his thoughts raced. How would Athena react to his return? The manner of his banishment didn't give him much cause for optimism. Perhaps the answer lay between his teeth, in the treasured gift he so carefully carried.

It was late afternoon. With patience fraying, he saw another cat lurking in the shadows watching him, then another further on. He'd been expecting a challenge, but so far they were content to keep their distance and observe. But he sensed he was drawing close now. Old stones and denser thickets concealed Athena's resting place. Carefully, he stepped over exposed roots, and beneath dangling branches until he found her, lying on a shady bed of pine needles, apparently asleep.

Delphos dropped his gift onto the earth between his paws and hesitated. Should he interrupt her slumber? How would that affect her reaction?

As if reading his thoughts and without opening her eyes, she pre-empted him. "I could hear you a mile away. You are far from the stealthiest example of our species." Her head rose a couple of centimetres and she examined him through half-closed eyes.

"I wanted to see you," he said.

The grey cat lay back down as if preparing to sleep once more. "I told you to never come back."

Delphos crouched, looked right and left, expecting her minders to approach at any second and force him to leave. But for the moment, they were alone. He tried to gather his thoughts, but what he'd planned to say seemed meaningless now.

"It's been long enough."

Her head rose from the ground once more, her eyes fully open now. "You dare to challenge my decree? In breaking the terms of your banishment, you risk severe punishment." Her eyes were little more than a green slit, but despite the inherent threat, they kindled only anger in Delphos' heart. He laid on a layer of defiance, which gave him the confidence to reply.

His voice was louder, his plea became more of a demand than a request. "Brother he might have been, but a faithless one at that. He deserved everything he got. I am not sorry about my actions." His anger caught in his throat. "If you have no mercy towards me, at least tell me what has become of Eleni?"

The green eyes widened, scrutinising him. "On that score, at least, you have comfort. She fled, and has not been seen for months. Your time would have been best spent searching for her, as I told you."

The news made his heart leap. But what had happened to her? Where had she gone? Was she safe?

"Where is she?"

"On that matter, I cannot help you. Leave before I take action you will regret." It was a dismissal, but he wasn't prepared to go yet. Anguish still burned in his veins.

"I offered you everything. I pledged my life."

The head came up sharply this time, fury flashing in those green eyes. Athena rolled onto her belly and pinned him with a glare, but her voice was little more than a hiss in that quiet glade. "And how did you cement your offer? Your brother's life was taken by others, no matter what you brazenly claim. You are no ruthless tyrant, Delphos of the Plaka. Son of Apollo they say you are, but I cannot see the family resemblance. To me you are Delphos the Shadow, Delphos the Weak. Your brother was the one who had the vision and the courage to seize the moment. Did you think hot air alone would entice me, or bind you to your pledge?"

He had no response to those crushing words. In despair, he glanced at the phial of glass and the virulent green contents swirling inside. With his hopes crushed, only bitterness remained, mixed with a dash of defiance and then a flash of insight. A clarity he'd never previously had. It lent him the will to confront those piercing eyes once more.

"*Weak*, you say. Yet I arrived here unchallenged. *Shadow*, you call me. But made in the full glare of your sun, Athena the glorious." He made a shallow, mocking bow, and stood tall. "My brother might have been ruthless, but virtue is its own reward. He sold his soul for power: I kept my own. It is not yours to take." Eyes locked, the venom in her stare was almost more than he could take. He felt short of breath, as if an invisible band were squeezing and tightening about his throat. He had one remaining task. "For far too long I played your game, but for no longer. Here is a trinket for your passing delectation. A gift from your cousins who wait nearby. May it soothe your anger."

He picked up the bauble, advanced a couple of paces and worked it to the side of his mouth, then bit down hard. The glass broke more easily than he'd expected, and instantly the green contents spilled forth, filling the clearing beneath the trees. Delphos spat to remove a shard of glass from between his teeth, but it was his last action before he was overcome.

He staggered, struggling to stay on his feet. The green smoke caught in his throat, choking him. It was foul and bitter; far from the sweet aroma he'd been told to expect. Unable to breathe, nausea enveloped him, and darkness encroached as he collapsed onto his side.

With his last remaining sight, Delphos saw the grey cat struggle to her feet, take two steps forward, then stumble and fall.

Across the city, Eleni and her remaining kitten played in the garden, in the fading early evening light. A cold wind blew out of nowhere and made her shiver. The light faded, and, looking up, she saw deepening banks of clouds, rapidly gathering.

Something was wrong.

She clambered to her feet and, with a glance towards her youngster still playing among the flowers, leaped to the top of the wall to get a better view.

What she saw sent a shiver down her spine. To the west, towering dark clouds descended almost to ground level, as if night had already arrived in that district. Elsewhere, the day seemed unaffected.

Eleni's attention was drawn once more to the pillar of clouds; they held an awful fascination. Driven in equal measure by dread and curiosity, she needed to find out what they represented. After one last look over her shoulder towards the kitten below, she departed. Slowly at first, then faster and faster, as if in thrall to a magnet, Eleni ran to the heart of the storm.

Woozy nausea and waves of pain swept through Delphos' body. His eyelids were made of iron; heavy and rusted shut. Much as he wanted to roll and writhe with the pain that ebbed and flowed, he could not move.

Hearing was the first of his senses to return. Somewhere beyond his anguish, he heard noises. Voices. Some close, some further away. He sensed movement around him: concern, agitation, fear.

At long last he could open his eyes, and some form of sight returned. But everything was opaque, and he couldn't focus. The fuzziness cleared, and he realised it was dark. Moonlight, filtered by the network of branches above where he lay, illuminated the clearing.

There were other cats present. Many of them. All ignored him. Few even glanced in his direction. All their attention was focused on the prone body to his left: Athena. At her head sat the black cat he'd conversed with earlier. What was she doing here?

Delphos closed his eyes again and tried to swallow. His throat was dry, his tongue swollen. With mouth open, he tried to breathe, but even that was difficult. Movement was impossible.

Bit by bit, his memory returned; some of it, anyway. He remembered the shock in Athena's eyes as the cloud of green gas spread from the tube, her attempt to escape before it enveloped her, and the numb disbelief as she fell, just as he had. What had been in the tube? It certainly wasn't a gift. He'd been tricked.

With an effort, Delphos opened his eyes again to see the

black cat leaning over Athena's head. She seemed to be alternately pressing something into her mouth and breathing into it. He detected a low, barely audible chant; an utterance unlike anything he'd ever heard from a cat. Repetitive rhythms dragged his eyes shut once more, and darkness took him.

At the edge of the clearing, ignored by everyone, Eleni was in a state of shock. Two bodies lay amid an agitated throng: one grey and unfamiliar, the other ginger and all too dear to her. The large grey cat was attracting all the attention, her beloved Delphos none.

Delphos, my dear. What has become of you? What have they done?

Tentatively, she edged towards him, each step filled with dread. As she drew close, she saw the feeble rise and fall of his ribs; he was still alive. But his breath was shallow, his eyes shut. Eleni lay beside him, offering the only help she could: the warmth and comfort of her body. There she stayed as the remaining light faded. At some point, the grey cat recovered sufficiently to struggle to her feet, and stagger away in the company of a gaggle of concerned followers.

They were alone.

Beside her, Delphos was unchanged and still unconscious. With her heart hurting, her hopes broken, Eleni closed her eyes.

Movement in the undergrowth heralded a new arrival. Eleni raised her head to see a tall, thin cat. A glass phial dangled from an elaborate collar, its contents swirling green. He sniffed the ground where Athena had lain and recoiled sharply as if stung.

Turning, he spied the two of them, lying nearby. "He fulfilled his task, then."

He drew close and stood over them, staring down at her lover's body.

She crouched next to him protectively. "What do you mean?"

The stranger glared at her, his too-close-together eyes registering a sneer. "Delivered our gift, by the look of it. Released the contents of the bauble we gave him. She may have staggered off, but I'm sure she won't get far. All we have to do is wait for the poison to work its magic. With luck, she won't see the dawn." He sniffed the air. "Powerful stuff," he said, talking to himself. "The scent still lingers. Most unpleasant. We probably won't need to use as much next time." He looked down at Eleni, shuddering beneath his oily scrutiny. "So you're the one he was bleating about?" A lascivious look traversed the length of her body.

Without warning, she leaped at him, cold fury coursing through her veins. Zelus failed to anticipate the attack, reacting an instant too late. He pulled back his head, but that only made it easier for her. Instead of targeting his face or throat, Eleni lunged at the glass phial dangling invitingly from his collar, and bit down, hard.

There was an explosion of glass, and toxic green smoke enveloped them both. Eleni slumped to the ground in a dead faint, but Zelus ran, his unearthly yowl piercing the night air, as he attempted to escape the doom he carried round his neck.

Delphos came to in the grey-blue light before dawn, and tried to stretch, but his limbs juddered and hurt and barely moved. His head was heavy as a stone, and any attempt to raise it resulted in pounding pain.

He looked around. His vision was blurred. There was no sign of Athena, but a familiar form lay slumped, before him.

No!

Still weak, and straining every muscle, he edged forward and stretched out a paw. In desperation, he flexed his claws to wake her, but there was no response.

A voice behind him broke the silence. *"You should never have returned."*

The voice sounded familiar, but Delphos struggled to place it. With an effort, he rolled onto his stomach and retched, but nothing came up. He closed his eyes until the nausea receded.

"Whatever was in your little bottle certainly packed a punch."

Delphos opened his eyes once more, trying to blink away the fog enshrouding his brain. Erichthonius' dusty-coloured form sat before him, cool and judgemental.

"Where is everybody?" said Delphos.

"Fussing around Athena, I should think."

Delphos closed his eyes once more, his head sinking lower. "Why?"

"Why, what?"

"Why did you come here? Is it to gloat?"

Silence. He began to think the other cat had left.

"I didn't want to just leave you." He sounded regretful. "But I might ask you the same question. Why? What drove you to do such a drastic thing?"

Another long silence ensued. Delphos didn't know how to explain his actions to himself, let alone anyone else. It was pointless trying; he'd never be understood.

"It's a shame you never got to meet them," said Erichthonius.

"Who?"

"Your kittens. They're homed across the city, I believe. Except for one that stayed with Eleni."

Delphos shut his eyes tight, consumed by a mixture of pride and regret. He couldn't think of a response.

The light was growing stronger, even as his life was slowly fading.

Still, Erichthonius remained. "I had high hopes for you."

"Me, too." Another pause. Speaking was such an effort. Delphos opened his eyes as best he could, but could barely make out the silhouette of the other cat, sitting nearby. His voice was little more than a croak. "I just wanted to make it better."

Breathing was harder when next he woke, and the world about him was dark once more. Erichthonius had gone. Delphos' body was wracked with stabbing pains from nose to tail. Every breath hurt. But the worst pain was seeing Eleni lying next to him.

He let out a whimper: pain mingled with anguish, and for the first time, a smattering of self-pity. What had brought her here? The one he cared for most. The one he'd dreamt about.

The glade beneath the trees was silent. There was no movement. No rise and fall of the ribs. He heard no breath from that sweet, snub nose, or tremble in her whiskers. No awakening for her closed, sightless eyes.

Slowly, painfully slowly, using his last vestiges of strength, he crept across the pine needle-strewn ground towards her. Sharp jolts like electric shocks seared through his joints with every movement and his muscles screamed in agony, but still he edged forwards, until at last he was next to her. His head swam in an ocean of pain, and deep within the whirling, swirling agony was another emotion: guilt. Foolish pride had driven him here and somehow, despite everything, she'd followed. Followed him to death, somehow.

"Eleni, my love," he gasped, and lay his head across her shoulder. He closed his eyes and tried to take whatever comfort he could from her familiar scent; an ingrained memory he'd clung to in so many troubled moments. Pride had driven him here; it had guided every step. Pride and idiocy, and all that went with it. The desire for adulation, honour, and prestige. You could keep it all. Here, in the dark, at the desperate end of everything, at the end of a long trail of wrong choices, his foolishness was clear.

In the end, love was all that mattered.

He gave a tiny sigh, and in that moment, something remarkable happened: a gift of the semi-divine, otherwise impossible for his species.

A single tear trickled down his nose, hovered for a moment, then splashed onto the body of his lover. A tear that held all the sorrow and regret in the world.

For what might have been crushes us more than what is.

His time was nearly over. Death was close; the glade hushed, expectant. With one last effort Delphos raised his head an inch and, trembling with the strain, made one last utterance into the dark.

"To all the mighty ones who manipulate us, if there are any left to hear. I say this. A curse on all your meddling." Bitterness amplified his voice. "I pray that my children, and my children's children stand against you and your plans. Until at last, you fail and in failing, finally learn the lesson of humility."

Delphos collapsed back down, the last of his energy spent.

His eyes were glazing over, but in the gloom, he saw the form of a white cat standing over him. Serene. Glowing in the dark as if partly made of stars.

"I hear you," he said.

CHAPTER 48
JUST ANOTHER AUDIENCE

ermes approached the Underworld acropolis of Hades once more. Again, he passed the gates with their silent sentries and approached the main palace complex across the open, silent square.

Beneath the portico, Jennings greeted him with a deep bow and his habitual smile. "My lord Hermes. Allow me to announce your arrival."

The white cat followed the butler through anterooms and corridors until they reached the great hall itself. As he walked its length, Hermes wondered when, if ever, this enormous room had last held a feast or gathering of any sort. Had laughter ever echoed in the rafters? Did Hades hold investitures? What awards could be conferred on the dead? An Interminable Service prize? Would there be dancing afterwards? Could the shades still dance or play instruments?

The thrones at the end of the hall were empty. Jennings led him towards a polished cedarwood door to the right of the dais. He swept it open, stepped through and ushered the cat forwards into a luxurious sitting room. Hades reclined on a well-cushioned large sofa, a Manila folder open in his hands.

"My lord Hermes," announced the butler, bowing as

Hermes stepped past him with head held high. Hades looked over the top of his folder and gestured to a nearby armchair. The cat sprang onto it and made himself comfortable.

He glanced around the room. Wood-panelled walls framed antique tapestries depicting scenes of idyllic rural life that seemed incongruous in this dim and dismal land. Bookcases and cabinets filled the gaps between the wall hangings. A huge leather-topped desk sat at the far end of the room, holding a pile of folders and papers.

Hades completed his reading and placed the folder on a side table. "To what do I owe your visit this time?"

Hermes forced his attention back to the King of the Underworld. "Nothing much. It's merely a courtesy call. But I have one request. I would like to speak with the lord Zelus."

Hades looked bemused. "Zelus is not here."

Hermes returned his stare. "He is a recent arrival. One whom, I regret to say, I could not escort." He paused. "Given his status, I thought you would have greeted him in person."

Hades swung his legs onto the floor and sat forward, his eyes firmly on the cat. "There is no Zelus here, of that I can assure you. I know of every arrival, and a Titan crossing my borders, pre-announced or otherwise, would sound an unmistakable alert. Zelus is not here."

Hermes blinked, looked away, thoughts racing. "But—"

"I'm sorry your journey was in vain." Hades sat back, stroking his beard. He gave the cat a calculating look. "I'm just about to dine with some friends. Perhaps you'd care to join us? Unless you have any urgent need to be elsewhere."

Was dining the only pleasure available in these parts? Every time he came, they were just about to eat with this visitor or that. His inclination was to decline, but why not? It had been a long time since he'd last had occasion to spend time with the chthonic deities; it wouldn't do any harm to show his face for once.

Jennings reappeared, standing to the side of a set of

double doors set in the wall behind him. Hades rose to his feet and Hermes jumped down to walk beside him. The doors swung open to reveal a luxurious dining room, its walls also lined with oil paintings. A huge blazing fire filled a stone fireplace. The air was filled with the hubbub of conversation from the assembled guests.

Hades strode in, beaming at the assembly. "Please, be seated." He gestured to the table then turned towards the cat. "We have a late arrival. Hermes." He indicated a large plump cushion that had materialised on a chair next to his own at the head of the table. Hermes leaped up in one bound. "I believe you know everyone?" He raised an eyebrow inquisitively.

Hermes acknowledged the assembled guests. To his right was the Lady Styx herself, solemn and poised. Would her mood tonight be as brittle as usual? To her right was Acheron, god of the Underworld river of pain, and his wife, the nymph Orphne. Beyond her sat the demon Menoetes, herder of Hades' black cattle, and opposite him was another daemon, Melinoe, easily identifiable because of her skin colour: half of her body was a lurid white, the rest obsidian black. She must have been taking a night off from leading sorties of ghosts to haunt the upper world. Melinoe smiled and bowed her head, acknowledging Hermes. Next to her sat Nyx, goddess of the night, wrapped in her dark cloak, richly embroidered with patterns of stars. He received a shy glance from her kohl-dark eyes.

On her right was Minos, once king of Crete, now a judge of the dead; although from Hermes' point of view, why Hades had thought the guardian of the Minotaur a fit and proper person to decide the fate of the recently deceased was another matter. Perhaps it was his idea of a joke. He gave Hermes a curt nod and returned to his conversation with Nyx.

The cat was not surprised to see that the old king preferred conversing with enigmatic Nyx rather than the strange woman seated to his right. She had wings folded behind her back, a misshapen face that favoured him with a lop-sided grin, and snakes writhing about her waist as a mockery of a belt. This was one of the Furies, taking a break from wreaking vengeance on those deemed to have offended the gods.

That left one figure Hermes did not recognise. Opposite him, and to the other side of their host, sat a well-groomed man who looked as if he had stumbled upon the ultimate Halloween party without an invitation. Informally dressed, he wore a crisp white linen shirt with the top button undone and an exquisitely tailored blazer. Close-cropped curly hair and a neatly trimmed beard lent a Greek appearance, but he might have originated from anywhere in the Eastern Mediterranean.

The guest observed the white cat with interest. "Well met, sir. But what is the fascination you Greeks have with this feline disguise?" He glanced around the table before turning back to Hermes. "Tell me, does it just apply to those of you who reside above ground? How many of you walk the earth in cat form? Surely not everyone?" His voice spoke of surprise, but to Hermes his eyes said otherwise. How many of them had this man met?

From his seat at the head of the table, Hades turned to his guest. "I'm sorry. I am remiss with my introductions." He gestured towards Hermes. "This is Hermes, our messenger god." He turned to the cat. "Hermes, this is my good friend, the Egyptian god of chaos, Set."

CHAPTER 49
THE MORTALITY PROBLEM

Athena opened her eyes and stretched, her muscles juddering and aching. She turned over and went back to sleep, head resting on paws. Dreams descended quickly, but these were not what a mortal creature might expect. No endless chases and scuffles, or running and jumping through the urban landscape. Athena's dreams, like those of her peers, were adventures in detailed realms; they were tantalisingly real, whether built of memory or senses lying dormant. Incomplete quests in search of something lost; sabotaged journeys through time to far distant lands of the imagination; half-completed travels to find long-buried treasure.

Nothing tangible ever resulted from her inner expeditions. No matter how deep she went, the result was always the same: a pang of regret seasoned with a pinch of frustration at the incomplete fragments of knowledge she retained, and a minuscule ratchet up the scale of concern that she might never remember. It was a fear she dared not acknowledge.

At the heart of her annoyance was the fact she'd been the instigator of change in the first place, her plan only partially fulfilled. The effort of will to persuade her family, and through them a whole ecology of powers, great and small, had perhaps taken more of her energies than she'd acknowledged. But that was only phase one. The self-imposed exile was nearing its end; she could feel it in every immortal fibre. But the final part – reversing the initial change – was lost to her, and the harder she tried to find the key to unlock her memory, the more distant it became.

The familiar circular thought sequences churned through her waking mind. It was critical that everyone had undergone the process; there could be no exceptions. She'd been insistent on that point. But had it happened? She'd been surprised when Zeus so readily agreed, sending thousands of minor deities to her grove: satyrs, nymphs, dryads, river gods and goddesses. She was startled by the size of the immortal population. She and Demeter had to stagger the process over many years, while the tree they had nurtured produced harvest after harvest. She'd kept track, of course, but was her record-keeping perfect? Silly question. How could it be otherwise?

But the nagging doubt remained.

What if some had escaped the net?

She closed her eyes once more and returned gratefully to sleep. This time, her meandering thoughts drifted towards her friend and former confidant. Once more, she revisited their argument. Athena had been shocked at how heated Demeter became. She had no stomach for the change they'd forced upon the others through oath and commandment from above, and wanted to stop it. Or at least pause to re-evaluate. Where was her backbone? Her steely resolve? For any great plan to succeed there must be sacrifice, and the price she'd extracted was surely small.

In Athena, the pursuit of honour was everything, and the penance to achieve it was a small price to pay for ultimate glory; she'd assumed it was the same for everyone. For all the great ones, at least: the Twelve and their immediate entourage. In her slumber, the grey cat shivered, but didn't wake. Even now, enmeshed in dreams, Athena scoffed at Demeter's weak concerns. They had to continue, all of them. There was no alternative. Her plans depended on it.

In the whirling eye of darkness she saw it: the tall, shapely tree bearing a peculiar blue-green fruit. It was more sparse than the one before. With joy in her heart, she ran towards it, reaching out. And at that point, her memory failed.

Where was it?

Another shudder, another aching stretch. Unusual. She rolled over and almost woke up. Her eyes opened a slit. Slowly, they closed once more. Persistent sounds – birdsong, the distant rumble of the city – encroached on the edge of consciousness, then receded until she was alone with her dreams once more.

This time, Apollo was the subject. Where was he? She had gone to such trouble to call him back from his long retreat. What had that achieved? She'd hoped for an ally. Another seeker. One who would be relentless in his pursuit. Tied with Apollo, she could move beyond the limited imagination of Ares and the circuitous and self-defeating plots that Hermes imagined everywhere. She might have to give up some power, but together, providing she could get him to see the light, they could rule. But where had he gone?

Her dreams meandered towards another path: the future. What next? Planning had long been her forte, but within this body, her perception had shrunk, and with it, her ability to divine a safe path forward. There were tools she could use: the artefact in the museum, her followers, and the extended network she'd cultivated throughout the country. Also, her human champion, Lieutenant Samaras. It wasn't enough. It lent her an edge compared to her peers, but so far it had proved inadequate in helping her discover the location of the tree she desperately sought. The tree whose fruit would lend her first mover advantage: the superiority she craved.

For a moment, the idea stayed suspended in the centre of

her mind as her dreaming thoughts drifted and swirled around it like meandering smoke in still air. An edge. An advantage. Superiority. All of this and more was her goal. Her ambition. She'd had no agenda at first, other than to hide out the fallow years of peak monotheism until the slowly shifting sands of time ran out and a new era dawned. An era alive with multiple belief systems, exciting new technologies, limitless possibilities. An era where a goddess armed with incredible powers could lead an army of the forward thinking: the movers and shakers, the innovators and influencers. Leaders, all. Onward into an era of untold possibilities.

They would trample over the unwilling, drag the half-hearted to their feet, launch one new campaign after another until humanity finally got the message: endless growth, power, advancement; and at its heart a cult reborn and rejuvenated, fit for the modern age. She envisaged her temples built anew, enlarged and more glorious and numerous than ever. Her conduit to the faithful, wherever they may be. Her glory would shine anew. In the new age of faith, she would muscle past those mired in nostalgia for the decaying ideologies of past millennia. As first mover, she would have an advantage over Zeus and the others; a lead that would never be rescinded.

Queen of Heaven at last.

And as the immortals arose once more, assuming they wanted to, their own cults would inevitably struggle for traction in less fertile ground; something she could apologetically acknowledge while dismissing their complaints. All was fair in matters of faith and war. It would be a time of certainty and growth. Not nuance and doubt. Weaknesses such as those belonged in the past.

Athena stirred, emerging from sleep, the last vestiges of her dream still fresh in her mind. She woke into a body filled with dull pain.

A stretch to shake it off, then a yawn. She had better round up her companions; see what news they could bring her of the day. Her recovery from the unpleasantness of the attack must surely be complete. The terrible odour remained fresh in her memory: a stench of decay mingling with the hint of oblivion. She shuddered, and stood, momentarily uncertain on her feet. Maybe she wasn't fully over it yet.

Athena emerged from the bower, beneath the low-branching tree, and stumbled over a raised root. She wasn't used to such clumsiness, and a sharp pain stabbed through her right foreleg, just above the paw. Muscles complained of sudden movement, and a fog of aches and ailments clouded her brain.

She sat and looked about, but no witnesses were present. A moment to collect her thoughts. Once more she stood, and set off down the hill. Her movements were stiff, inelegant, her legs juddering at the impact of small leaps, and she was disinclined to run. Her body felt as if it had been in storage for a long time. Penelope awaited in the Agora below.

"What news?" Athena asked.

Her secretary gave her a fleeting glance. "Nothing much to report. The excitement around the day before yesterday has died down."

Athena sat, her memories struggling to connect. What had happened, exactly? Ah yes, the attack. "And what of the attacker? Did he have any accomplices?"

"No. None that we've been able to discover."

"And what does Ares have to say?"

Penelope gave her a strange look. "He's not here. He's been gone for some time."

Athena stared back. "Of course." She floundered, trying to buy some time. "How long… has he been gone? Have I been asleep?"

Penelope looked relieved. "A long time. All of yesterday, plus last night and the night before. That's when you were most ill. When the black one came to help."

"The black one?"

Penelope hesitated. "Yes. I don't know her name. She brought herbs. Chewed them and spat them in your face and mouth. I tried to send her away, but she was insistent."

Athena stared at her. Had the effect of the strange gas been so severe?

"Anyway," Penelope went on, "she stayed until your breathing was normal again. She left just before dawn." In the extended silence, Penelope looked uncomfortable. She shifted position, took a step away, then back again. "Is there anything I—"

"No."

After one last glance, Athena's secretary departed. The grey cat sat in the centre of the open square and tried to think. She had been asleep longer than she'd realised. She set off for a patch of shade and her right foreleg almost collapsed beneath her. Wincing at the pain, she limped across the rest of the space and slumped to her side, surprised at how much effort it took.

Erichthonius approached. "It is a relief to see you back with us." He sat nearby, studying the birds flitting between perches.

"Yes." She studied him, unwilling to say more.

"It was terrible," he added, after a while. "The whole thing."

Athena continued to look at him. She had little recollection of the incident, other than the ginger cat in front of her snapping his jaws about some little glass phial and releasing a green gas that clung to her mouth and lungs.

"We all thought we'd seen the last of him," said Erichthonius. "He'd been gone so long we thought it was permanent. Who could have guessed he'd come back? Let alone do what he did?" Another pause. Again Athena stayed silent. Erichthonius searched her face as if looking for clues. "I wonder what was in it? The green stuff, I mean. And where he got it."

She shifted to change position and winced again at the sharp spasm of pain in the middle of her back. When she opened her eyes, she saw the look of concern on his face.

"Maybe it's still affecting you?" he said. Athena closed her eyes and swallowed until the discomfort eased. "It killed poor Delphos, sadly." He looked down. "And his mate. It's a shame about her kitten." This was news to Athena. "And it may have killed the tall, thin one. I saw him stalking through the woods. He seemed to be keeping watch. I was suspicious. I'm not sure who he was, but he looked familiar. I think he might have been at the Battle of Monastiraki?"

"I don't know what you're talking about."

"The battle. Last year. You must remember." She blinked her eyes in acknowledgement, still unsure what he meant. "If it's the same cat I'm thinking of, he led the Gizi gang. Tall, thin, pinched face. Arrogant, I always thought."

Gizi gang? "What of him?" she asked, attempting to move the conversation on.

"I saw him running through the trees like he'd been bitten by a horsefly, trailing a stream of green smoke, half the glass thing around his neck. It was broken. I don't know where he went, but it didn't look good."

"I need to rest."

He looked sympathetic. "Of course. I'll leave you in peace."

Once he'd gone, she lay her head down. But this time, sleep evaded her. Instead, she tried to piece together events from the fog clouding her thoughts. The noise of human chatter was an unwelcome intrusion. It was no good; she needed somewhere quiet. There was a house somewhere around here. With a cat door. That should do. Where was it?

Athena stood, for once unsure of directions. She set off, not bothered about where she was going. Another trip, another sharp stab of pain. She looked down and saw blood. That was new. With every step, her body ached.

A horrible thought rattled around her brain: what if this doesn't wear off?

Another thought occurred, but she shut it down, shaking her head rapidly. Dizziness made her stagger, before she regained her poise.

She set off again, no longer sure of her destination, but eager to be alone. A growing sense of horror imposed itself on her thoughts.

What if I'm…

It didn't bear thinking about.

Athena came to, lying on the back seat of Detective Samaras's car. Groggily she tried to piece together her movements. She must have made it home, somehow. The movement of the car sent her to sleep again.

When next she woke, she was lying on a table, with two humans standing over her. A plastic tube was attached to a needle that was stuck in her foreleg. It was filled with red liquid. She seemed to be receiving a blood transfusion. Her body was heavy as lead, and she couldn't move. With eyes half open, she tried to follow the conversation going on above her head.

"How old is she?"

"I don't know. She just appeared one day. Kind of adopted me. But that was years ago."

A pause. "And you say she's needed no treatment before?" The female speaker sounded doubtful. Athena looked up and recognised the outline of Samaras silhouetted against the ceiling lights. The other woman, presumably, was a veterinary surgeon.

Samaras responded. "She's always been fine. The epitome of good health."

A sigh. "She's clearly very old. One of the oldest cats I've seen, in fact. She has advanced arthritis, and I'll need to run some tests, but it would be my guess her kidneys are failing, and she has a heart murmur. I'm sorry to say, but it looks as if she might only have a few months." Athena closed her eyes, trying to absorb what she was hearing. "I can give her something to ease her joint pains for a while, at least. She should be a little more mobile, but it's only a palliative, I'm afraid. There's no treatment that can do anything other than delay the inevitable." The woman tried to strike a more positive note. "We can help make her last few months more comfortable."

The words made no sense. Who was she talking about? Athena's thoughts circled around. She would feel better in the morning; she just needed a good sleep. A long sleep. Then it would be better. And to find the tree. Yes, that was it. The tree. *Must find the tree.*

Her thoughts meandered through fog banks as she drifted in and out of consciousness. Somewhere above, the woman fussed over her, and gently removed the canula from her forepaw.

A face smiled down. "There, there. You'll be back on your feet soon." A hand stroked her ears. Without invitation; how rude. Athena didn't have the energy to bite it.

The woman adopted a more business-like tone and addressed Samaras once more. "I'll just pop an ID chip in, so we can better keep track of her on our patient records. It's a painless procedure."

Athena felt a hand grab the fur on the scruff of her neck. A short stabbing pain, and the procedure was over. But something had been left inside her. She resented the intrusion, but had been powerless to resist. That alone was an insult.

At the opposite end of the continent, deep within a server

array at Edinburgh University's Centre for Supercomputing, a record was added.

DOOLITTLE catalogued it with interest. If the AI had been a primitive biological form of intelligence, it might have punched the air in delight.

But it allowed itself the indulgence of a brief nanosecond of what passed for satisfaction in its air-cooled silicon heart.

At the base digital level, it appended a freeform note to the record in its highly structured and increasingly extensive database: a message containing an atypical and somewhat unprofessional element of glee.

"Gotcha!"

THE END

FREE PREQUEL

To find out more about the series, join my mailing list and download a free prequel, click on the image or visit Andrew-Rylands.com
If you enjoyed The Rejected King, I would very much appreciate a review.

ACKNOWLEDGMENTS

No book can be produced without the assistance of a number of people. I am extremely grateful for their input and dedication. In particular I'd like to thank Lottie Clemens for her proofreading skills and advice, and Stuart Bache for another marvellous cover. Many others have chipped in with advice and comment along the way. Their support keeps me going.

ABOUT THE AUTHOR

Andrew lives near Edinburgh with a cat who insists on auditioning for a part in a future story. When he's not writing, or thinking about writing, he enjoys exploring both the UK, and the rest of the world, and planning his next trip. Greece, the inspiration for these tales, is always a favourite destination. There is nothing quite like standing among the ancient stones and listening for an echo of the stories they once witnessed. That was what started him down this road in the first place.

www.andrewrylands.com

ALSO BY ANDREW RYLANDS

The Forgotten God

The Accidental Hero

The Eternal Feud

www.ingramcontent.com/pod-product-compliance
Lightning Source LLC
Chambersburg PA
CBHW021229060726
47590CB00005B/1692